Suddenly, from the shadows, a hand grabbed her arm.

Viviana found herself jerked into an unlit alcove. She looked up into Quin's angry eyes and lifted her chin.

"Madam, you have a great deal of nerve," he said icily. "How dare you try to ruin this."

Viviana tried to jerk her arm from his grasp. "Don't be a fool, Quinten," she said coolly. "Release my arm this instant."

Instead, he pulled her closer, his nostrils flaring with rage.

"Quin, *basta!*" She tore from his grasp. "The others are leaving us."

"I know how to find the goddamned dining room, Viviana," he rasped. "It's my bloody house."

"*Si, caro mio,* and I suspect you never let anyone forget it."

He leaned into her. "I shan't let you forget it, that's bloody certain."

"Oh, trust me, Quinten," she whispered. "That is one thing I have never forgotten. Your rank. Your wealth. Your unassailable British *privilege*. I did, however, make the mistake of forgetting your title, and now I see I'm to pay for it."

His face contorted unpleasantly. "You liar! You never forgot a damned thing you thought you could use to your advantage."

Suddenly, his meaning dawned on her. "Oh, *Dio!*" she said. "You are disgusting, and you are delusional. I could buy and sell you twice over, Quin Hewitt. Trust me, you have *nothing* I want."

True anger flared in his eyes then. "What I want, my lady, is to see you in private," he growled. "Tomorrow morning. In my study."

Also by Liz Carlyle from Pocket Books

One Little Sin

The Devil to Pay

A Deal With the Devil

The Devil You Know

No True Gentleman

Tea for Two

A Woman of Virtue

Beauty Like the Night

A Woman Scorned

My False Heart

Two Little Lies

Liz Carlyle

POCKET STAR BOOKS

New York   London   Toronto   Sydney

An *Original* Publication of POCKET BOOKS

A Pocket Star Book published by
POCKET BOOKS, a division of Simon & Schuster Inc.
1230 Avenue of the Americas, New York, NY 10020

ISBN 0-7394-6021-8

Designed by Melissa Isriprashad
Cover art by Alan Ayers; Hand Lettering by Ron Zinn

Manufactured in the United States of America

Two Little Lies

Prologue

In which a Proposal of marriage is Received.
Spring, 1821

Signorina Alessandri was ill. Again. With one hand re-straining the flowing folds of her fine silk night-clothes, she lurched over the closestool in her Covent Garden flat and prayed, in fluent and fervid Italian, for death to take her.

"Oh, please, miss, *do* speak English!" begged her maid, who had caught her heavy black hair, and drawn it back, too. "I can't make out a word. But I do think we'd best fetch a doctor."

"Nonsense," said the signorina, clenching the back of the closestool in a white-knuckled fist. "It was the fish Lord Chesley served last night."

The maid pursed her lips. "Aye, and what was it yes-terday, miss?" she asked. "Not fish, I'll wager."

With the other hand set at the small of her back, Vi-viana closed her eyes and somehow straightened up. "*Silenzio,* Lucy," she said softly. "We talk of it no further. The worst is over now."

"Oh, I doubt that," said the maid.

Viviana ignored her and went instead to the washbasin. "Where is the morning's post, *per favore?*" she asked, awkwardly slopping the bowl full of water.

With a sigh, Lucy went into the parlor and returned with a salver which held one letter covered in Viviana's father's infamous scrawl, and a folded note which bore no address. "Mr. Hewitt's footman brought it," she said offhandedly.

With hands that shook, Viviana finished her ablutions, then patted a towel across her damp face as her maid looked on in consternation. The girl had been both loyal and kind these many months. "Thank you, Lucy," she said. "Why do you not go have a cup of tea? I shall read my letter now."

Lucy hesitated. "But do you not wish your bathwater brought, miss?" she pressed. " 'Tis already past noon. Mr. Hewitt will be here soon, won't he?"

Quin. Lucy was right, of course. Viviana laid aside the towel and took the note. Quin usually came to her in the early afternoon. Yes, just as he meant to do today. And oh, how she longed for it—yet dreaded it in the same breath.

She tossed the note into the fire. She had not missed the furious looks he'd hurled her way in the theater's reception room after last night's performance. Viviana had sung gloriously, hitting every high note in her last aria with a chilling, crystal-clear resonance, before collapsing into her lover's arms in a magnificent swoon. The theater had been full, the applause thunderous.

But all Quin had seemed to notice was what had come afterward. The compliments and congratulations of her admirers. The champagne toasts. The subtle, sexual invitations tossed her way by the lift of a brow or a tilt of the head—and refused just as subtly in turn. It had not been refusal enough for Quin. One could hardly have ignored his cocky stance and sulky sneer as he paced the worn green carpet, a glass of brandy clutched in his hand. His uncle, Lord Chesley, had even had the effrontery to tease him about it.

Quin had not taken that well. Nor had he been especially pleased to see Viviana leaving on Chesley's arm, as she so often did. And today, God help them, he would undoubtedly wish to quarrel over it. Viviana was not at all sure she was capable of mounting a spirited defense. But it almost didn't matter anymore.

"Miss?" said the maid. "Your bathwater?"

Nausea roiled in her stomach again, and Viviana moved gingerly to a chair. "In ten minutes, Lucy," she answered. "I shall read *Papà*'s letter whilst my stomach settles. If I am late, I shall receive Mr. Hewitt here."

Lucy pursed her lips again. "Aye, then," she finally answered. "But I'd be telling him straightaway, miss, about that bad fish if I was you."

Finally, Viviana laughed.

The fleeting humor did not sustain her as she opened her father's letter. Even the scent of his letter paper tugged at her heartstrings. She knew the very drawer of his desk from which it had been taken; the same desk in which he kept his tobacco. Then there was the penmanship itself. The broad, slashing strokes always recalled to her his indefatigable strength, the tight loops and curls, his wisdom and precision, and the lyrical words, his artistry. He was one of Europe's most renowned composers, and not without reason.

She drew in the scent once more, then spread the letter

across her lap. She read it through once, disbelievingly, then again, very carefully. Chesley, it seemed, had kept his old friend well-informed. Already *Papà* knew that tonight was to be her last performance in *Die Entführung,* and that all of London's West End lay appreciatively at her feet. As *Konstanze,* at long last, she had triumphed.

And now *Papà* was writing to tell her she might return home. Viviana closed her eyes and thought of it. Dear God, what a strange confluence of fate and timing this was! It seemed an eternity since she had fled Venice with nothing but her panic, her violin, and her music folio to bear her company. And now, to return! Oh, it was what she had lived for and longed for almost every moment since, save for those spent in Quin's arms. He had been, in truth, her salvation.

But now she could go home. It was a bit of a devil's bargain, what was being offered her. Certainly it was not what she wanted. Nonetheless, as *Papà* pointed out, there were advantages to such an arrangement. Great advantages. It would also make his life a vast deal easier, though her father would sooner die than tell her so.

And so the decision was to be hers. *Nothing would be forced upon her.* Ha! Those were not her father's words, she'd wager. Apparently, Conte Bergonzi had changed his tactics. Moreover, Viviana could tell by his careful phrasing that *Papà* fully expected her to refuse Bergonzi's offer, and would forgive her if she did so. Viviana set her hand on her belly. She was not at all sure she would have the luxury of refusing.

The water was wonderfully hot when it came, and remarkably restorative. Feeling perhaps a little more at peace, Viviana was still luxuriating in it when Quin came stalking into the room. He looked at once angry and yet almost boyishly uncertain.

He stared down at her naked body and gave her a tight, feral smile. "Washing away the evidence, Vivie?"

It was a cynical remark, even for him.

For a moment, she let her black eyes burn into him. "*Silenzio,* Quinten," she returned. "I had quite enough of your jealous sulking last night. Be civil, or go away."

He knelt by the tub, and rested one arm along its edge. His eyes were bleak today, the lines about his mouth almost shockingly deep for one so young. He smelled of brandy and smoke and the scents of a long, hard-spent night. "Is that what you want, Viviana?" he whispered. "Are you trying to drive me away?"

She dropped her soap into the water. "How, Quin?" she demanded, throwing up her hands in frustration. "*Mio dio,* how am I doing this driving? I am not, and that is the truth of it, *si?*"

He cast his eyes away, as if he did not believe her. "They say Lord Lauton has promised you a house in Mayfair, and more money than I could ever dream of," he answered. "Not until I come into my title, at any rate. Is it true, Vivie?"

She shook her head. "Quin, what would it matter if it were?" she returned. "I am no longer for sale—perhaps not even to you. Why must you be so jealous?"

"How can I help but be, Viviana?" he rasped, brushing one finger beneath her left nipple. It peaked and hardened, begging for his touch. "Men's eyes feast upon you everywhere you go. But at least you still desire me."

Viviana glowered at him, but she did not push his hand away. "My body desires you, *si,*" she admitted. "But sometimes, *amore mio,* my mind does not."

He plucked the nipple teasingly between his thumb and forefinger. "And what of your heart, Viviana?" he whispered, looking up at her from beneath a sweep of inky lashes. "I have your body ensconced, ever so circumspectly, in this flat which I have paid for. Have I your heart as well?"

"I have no heart!" she snapped. "That is what you told me when we quarreled last week, if you will recall. And you need not remind me, Quin, of who has put this roof over my head. I have become mindful of it with every breath I draw."

As if to torment her, he let his lashes fall shut, then leaned forward to crook his head so that he might suckle her. Viviana sat perfectly still, allowing him to draw her nipple into his mouth, and then between his teeth. At that, she gasped, and cursed the old, familiar pull of lust which went twisting traitorously through her body. It curled deep in her belly and left her breathless.

He lifted his head with a satisfied smile. "Where did you go last night, my love?" he asked.

She looked at him defiantly. "To Chesley's town house," she said. "We dined with Lord and Lady Rothers, and some acquaintances they had brought from Paris."

"Ah, patrons of the arts, all of them, I've no doubt," said Quin almost mockingly. "My uncle's little coterie!"

"Why must you so often think ill of him? He is kind to me, no more."

"My uncle is a fine man," Quin returned. "It is his friends I do not trust. By the way, my sweet, what is this here, just below your jaw? A bruise? Or something else?"

Her glower darkened as he brushed the side of her neck with the back of one finger. "It is absolutely nothing," she snapped, having no need to look. He was trying to elicit some sort of guilty reaction. "It is nothing, as it has always been nothing, Quin," she went on. "Chesley is my father's friend. My mentor here in London. He thinks of me as his *ward,* for God's sake! How many times must we suffer this foolish argument?"

He broke his gaze, and looked away. "I cannot help it, Viviana." He choked out the words. "You—you drive me insane. Chesley runs with a fast crowd. I cannot bear how those other men look at you."

"And how, pray, am I to stop it?" she asked him. "What would you have me do, Quin? Give up my career? Enter a convent? I am a singer, for God's sake, and for that, one needs an audience." She seized her towel from the floor with a snap and pushed him away.

"I—I could pay you," he said. "A little now, and a great deal more—eventually. Then you would not have to sing at all."

She looked at him incredulously. "Sometimes, Quin, I do not think you understand me," she whispered. "I *must* sing. It has nothing to do with money."

He watched her almost warily as she stood to towel the water from her body. Viviana made no effort to hide her nakedness from his heated gaze as it drifted over her. She was, after all, his. He had bought and paid for her. She had let him do it, too—though she had fought it at first like a tigress.

"Lie down on the bed, Viviana," he said when she was dry. "Open your legs. I want you."

For a moment, she considered refusing. But God help her, she still desired him. Even though it had come to this. She had wounds and scars to last a lifetime, as, no doubt, did he. Petty jealousies and bitterness had eaten into their hearts. He was too young. Too inexperienced. And she— well, she was simply too lonely. They were just using one another now. Surely he understood that?

Certainly, she did. Yet she craved the pleasure and the peace his virile young body could give her. She craved *him*. And she remembered a time, not so long ago, when it had been enough to sustain her; a time when they had worshipped one another, and experienced together all the sweet delights of a first love.

"Lie down on the bed," he said again, more firmly. "You are my mistress, Viviana. I have the right."

And that, too, was perfectly true. Viviana tossed aside the towel, drew back the sheets, and did as he asked.

As the early-afternoon light spilt over his shoulder, Quin stripped off his clothes with the practiced ease of a man who was used to having his needs and whims accommodated. He was already hard and fully erect. As usual.

When his snug, buff trousers had been shucked and tossed aside, he crawled across the bed in an almost predatory fashion and mounted her without preamble. Viviana gasped at the invasion, her whole body arching upward.

"You are mine, Viviana," he whispered, thrusting the full length of his erection inside her. "Do not ever forget that."

She was not his, but she did not argue. Instead, she set her feet flat against the bed, and tilted up her hips to better take the deepening strokes.

In response, he clasped her hands in his, palm to palm, and pushed them high over her head and onto the bed pillows, holding them there as he rode her. They had become like cats in heat, she and Quin, hissing and squabbling even as they burnt for one another. She could already feel the quickening in his body—and in hers, too, despite the hurt he had done her. What manner of woman was she, to crave and cling to this?

It was as if Quin read her very thoughts. "You are mine, Viviana," he growled, bending over her and staring into her eyes, still pressing her hands high above her head. "You are mine, damn it, and no one else's. *Say* it."

Viviana turned her head away. It was not worth the fight. "I am yours," she whispered.

"Look at me, Viviana," he insisted, quickening his thrusts. "Look at me when I do this to you. Sometimes, I swear, I think you mean to break my heart. Say it again. You are mine, and no one else's!"

She returned her gaze to his, defiant. "I am *mine,* Quin," she said, her voice low and tremulous. "I am *my own person.* But I have chosen to be with you. There is a difference."

But Quin seemed not to hear her words. He had closed his own eyes now, and the flesh was taut across the hard bones of his face as he rode her more furiously. She felt her pelvis arch to his against her will, urgent and greedy. Oh, God, he had such a gift for this! She wanted to lose herself in this pure, physical act. Wanted to feel nothing but the joining of their bodies.

He sensed it, and the urgency drove him. In this one way, at least, he understood her. *"Si, caro mio,"* she crooned. "Ah, yes. Like that."

Sweat had beaded on his temples. His face was etched with strain, stark and beautiful. "God, Vivie!" he groaned. "Oh, God, I worship you!"

She jerked her hands from beneath his, and clutched at him, gasping for breath. He thrust again and again, harder still, then one last sweet, perfect stroke. Viviana cried out, her whole body trembling. The pleasure washed over her, engulfed her, drowning out common sense.

He fell across her body, his chest heaving, the weight of him bearing her down into the softness of the bed. She stroked one hand down his taut, well-muscled back and felt tears spring to her eyes. "Oh, *amore mio,*" she murmured. "Oh, *ti amo,* Quin. *Ti amo.*"

And in that moment, she did love him. She loved him with all her heart, though she had never once allowed herself to say the words—not in any language he could comprehend. Soothed and spent, she simply listened to the sound of his breathing for a time. It was the simplest of pleasures, she had discovered, to lie in the arms of a beautiful man—no, *this* man—sated and happy, and simply listen.

But the peace, of course, did not last. Soon they were quarreling again about the events of last night. Quin had apparently taken note of every man who had so much as kissed her hand or fetched her a glass of champagne. It was foolish, almost sophomoric behavior which had worsened with her ascending fame, and Viviana gave no quarter. She had reached her wit's end, and she told him so.

Quin reacted badly. "God, how I hate the way we must live!" he finally shouted. "I have the right to protect you. I have the right, Viviana, to show the world that you are mine."

"Quin, *amore mio,* we have been through this a thousand times," she whispered. "Such news would kill my father. He did not sacrifice everything to send me to England so that I might become a rich man's mistress."

Indeed, her father had sent her for precisely the opposite reason. But there was no point in saying as much to Quin. It would only serve to make him angrier.

"Signor Alessandri does not worry about this fast theater crowd his daughter runs with?" he retorted. "He does not care whose eyes are undressing you? And Lord Rothers! Good God, Vivie! His patronage comes at a price. He has bedded half the actresses in the West End."

"Well, he hasn't bedded *me,*" she returned. "Nor will he. Nor does he wish to. My God, Quin, he was with his *wife.* What do you think happened? A ménage à trois on Chesley's dining room table?"

His mouth thinned, and he moved as if to turn his back on her. "Yes, go ahead. Make a jest of it, Viviana. Make a jest of *me.*"

She laid a hand against his chest. "Oh, *caro mio,* you are so young!"

He turned back to her at once. "Damn it, Vivie, I hate when you say that!" he swore. "Stop acting as if I'm some ignorant pup. I'm almost one-and-twenty now."

"Yes, and we agreed, Quin, at the start of this—"

"I know, dash it!" he interjected, laying his hand over hers and squeezing it almost violently. "I know. I shall keep my word, Viviana. But I bloody well don't like it."

A heavy silence fell across Viviana's bedchamber for a time, broken only by the distant clamor of Covent Garden beyond their windows. Eventually, however, she rolled onto her stomach and propped up on her elbows to study him, as she had done so often at the start of their tumultuous relationship.

Dear heaven, but he was beautiful, this half man, half boy she had come to love with such a breathless intensity. And she realized, quite suddenly, that despite it all, she could not bear to lose him. Even after all the harsh words—plenty of them, on both sides—she could not imagine a life without Quin. But was there any hope? She prayed there was, and not just for herself.

"Quin, *caro mio,*" she said impulsively. "Tell me something. Where is life going to take you?"

He lifted his head from the pillow, and looked up at her strangely. "What do you mean, Vivie?"

Viviana shrugged lamely. "I am not perfectly sure," she said. "Have you ever considered . . . oh, going away, perhaps? Abroad, I mean?"

"Abroad?" he said bemusedly. "Good God! To where?"

"To the Continent?" Viviana lifted her brows. "To Venice or Rome, perhaps?"

He laughed. "Why on earth would anyone leave England?"

Viviana felt a prick of anger. "Perhaps because it is a stifling, moralizing place?"

"Vivie, it is my home," he said, stroking a hand down her hair. "Let's have no more talk of anyone going anywhere, all right?"

"But what of your future, Quin?" she persisted. "What do you mean to do with your life?"

"Live it, I daresay," he returned. "What else is one to do?"

"But have you ever thought that we might—" She stopped and swallowed hard. "Have you ever thought, Quin, of . . . of marriage?"

His eyes widened. "Good God," he said. "To you?"

She tore her gaze away. "To . . . to someone that you worship," she managed to answer. "To—yes, to me."

His expression gentled. "Oh, Vivie," he whispered. "Oh, if only life were so simple."

She pressed on, fully conscious of the hurt her pride would endure. "Perhaps it *is* that simple, Quin," she answered. "You say you cannot live without me. That you wish to claim me as yours. I ask you, how badly do you wish for this?"

He cut her a sidelong glance. "Is that what all this hesitance is about?" he asked. "Are you holding out for marriage? Oh, Viviana! You knew I couldn't marry you when we started this. *Didn't* you?"

Viviana shook her head. "I am not holding out, Quin," she answered. "It is not like that."

But Quin was still looking at her incredulously. "For God's sake, Viviana, I'm heir to an earldom," he continued. "Have you no idea what an obligation that is? When I must finally wed—which will be at least a decade hence, I pray—Mamma will marry me off to some pale, flaxen-haired English miss with a slew of titles hanging off her papa's name and fifty thousand pounds in the three-percents, and I shall have little say in the matter."

Viviana's eyes narrowed. "Oh! So I am too old and too foreign and too bourgeois for the grand Hewitt dynasty? Is that it?"

"Now, Vivie," he chided, sitting up fully. "I never said that."

"I think you hardly need to!" Viviana curled one fist into the bedsheet, grappling with the nausea again. Why in God's name had she raised such a topic? He was right. She had known all along this would not last. But she had asked, and there was no backing away from it now.

"In a few weeks, Quin, you will be one-and-twenty," she said, her insides trembling with rage. "Then, whom you choose to marry will be up to you. Do not dare pretend otherwise. You insult my intelligence."

"Aww, Vivie!" He screwed up his face like the impatient young man he was. "We have our whole lives before us! I am not marrying anyone anytime soon. Why spoil what we have now?"

She gave him a mordant smile. "*Si,* it is a tedious business, this future, is it not?"

Quin did not catch the sarcasm. "That's my girl," he said, kissing her again. "Look, Vivie, I brought you something. Something which will cheer you up." He climbed from the bed and rummaged through his coat pockets, returning with a small box. "Open it," he commanded.

Viviana lifted the lid and gasped. The box held a ring; a wide, ornately carved band set with one large, square-cut ruby. It was a truly magnificent piece of jewelry. Viviana started to hand it back. Why did he insist on showering her with gifts? What she wanted was something his money could not buy—and this ring had undoubtedly cost Quin far more dearly than even he could afford.

Quin pushed the box back at her. "Put it on, Vivie," he insisted. "Put it on, but just promise me one thing."

Reluctantly, Viviana slid the ring onto her right hand. "I . . . yes, I shall try."

"Promise me you will keep this one," he said. "Promise me you will never sell it, and that you will wear it once in a while, and think of me."

Viviana was still staring at the ring, and blinking back

tears of grief and rage and love and about a hundred other conflicting emotions. "I never stop thinking of you, Quin," she whispered.

"As I never stop thinking of you, Vivie." But there was mild skepticism in his eyes. "Now, what time are you due at the theater?"

"Six," she said hollowly.

"Yes, and I must go soon," he went on. "We are wasting precious time when we could be enjoying one another. I could be telling you, Viviana, that you are the most beautiful creature on this earth. That your eyes make my breath seize, and that your breasts nearly make my heart stop. Lie down, my dear, and let me make love to you again."

So it was *lovemaking* now. Not his earlier, more vulgar phrase.

She should have refused him. She should have told him to leave her bed that very moment. But the memory of a sweeter, happier time had drawn painfully near, and the future stretched out bleakly before her. So Viviana turned onto her back and let him join his strong, vigorous body to hers one last time.

Quin rose from her bed some hours later, his mood improved, but his gaze still wary. She watched him dress, drinking in his lithe, slender beauty, and wondering, not for the first time, what he would look like in the full splendor of manhood. Already, his shoulders were wide, and his face shadowed with a stubble which matched his heavy, dark hair.

He dragged his shirt on over his head, and she marveled again at the perfection which was his face. That patrician forehead, the thin blade of a nose, lean, high-boned cheeks, and the most stunning feature of all, eyes the color of the Aegean at dusk. Oh, it was no wonder he had caught her eye. But how had she been such a fool as to let him steal her heart?

She tried to watch dispassionately as he drew on his stockings and hitched up his trousers. It was not anger she felt toward him, no. It was more of a resigned acceptance. Nor did she blame him. It was her own passionate, romantic nature which had got her into this. Ah, but one could not sing without passion. And one could not truly live without romance. Viviana accepted the fact that, on this earth, one took the bad with the good, and lived a full life in return.

He pulled on his coat, then leaned across the bed, setting both hands on the mattress. He held her gaze for a time, his eyes so intense, she felt, fleetingly, as though he could look into her soul. "Tell me something, my dear," he said quietly. "Do you love me?"

It surprised her a little, for it was a question he had never asked. And she knew what was in her heart, just as surely as she knew what her answer must be. She had at least a little pride left. "No, Quin," she answered. "I do not love you. And you do not love me."

He looked at her with the eyes of an old man. "No. I suppose I do not."

She shrugged. "It is best, is it not?"

He straightened abruptly. "Well, Viviana," he said. "At least you are honest."

But she was not honest. She had just told him a blatant lie. And as she watched him stride toward the door, she wondered, fleetingly, if perhaps he just done the same.

No. No, it was not possible.

The door slammed behind him. Viviana exhaled the breath which she had been holding, then closed her eyes, willing herself not to cry. She listened to the heavy tread of his footsteps as he left her. One warm tear rolled awkwardly down her nose, then landed on her pillow with a soft *plop!*

Abruptly, she sat up in bed. No, by God, she would not cry. Not for him. Not for anyone. Not even for herself. One tear was too many—and if another followed, there might well be no end to it.

Lucy came back into the room just as Viviana was drawing on her dressing gown. "Shall I tidy up now, miss?" she asked.

"*Grazie.*" Viviana went to the small writing desk beneath the window. "Tonight is my last performance as *Konstanze,* Lucy," she said, unlocking the little drawer which held her meager savings.

"I know, miss," said the maid as she began to neaten the bed. "It's been a grand run, hasn't it? What will you do next, I wonder? Pr'haps you ought to go down to Brighton for a rest. Perhaps Mr. Hewitt would take you? 'Tis beautiful there, I've heard."

Viviana was already relocking the drawer. "Actually, Lucy, I'm to go home tomorrow," she said, handing a pitifully small roll of banknotes to the maid. "Here. I wish you to have this. Lord Chesley need know nothing of it."

The girl looked at her incredulously and pushed Viviana's hand away. "Why, I can't take your money, miss!" she said. "Besides, it ain't like you've got it to spare—which heaven knows it's not my place to say, but there. I've said it."

"Lucy!" she chided.

"What?" said the girl. "Do you think I don't know, miss, that you've been sending every spare penny home—and selling your jewelry and eating day-old bread, too? Besides that, Lord Chesley pays me well enough to look after you, which I've been glad to do."

With a wistful smile, Viviana put the money in the maid's hand and forcibly curled her fingers around it. *"Take* it," she insisted. "Where I am to go, neither *Papà* nor I shall need it. And I wish *you* to go back to Lord Chesley's estate and marry that handsome footman of yours. This money is my wedding gift. You must buy a cradle, a very beautiful cradle, for your firstborn, and think of me when you use it, *si?"*

Lucy uncurled her hand and stared at the banknotes. "But how can you just up and leave England, miss?" she asked. "What's to become of you, so far away, and in such a foreign place?"

Inwardly, Viviana's smile deepened. The poor girl was so naively provincial—just like Quin. "It is my home," she said quietly. "It is time I returned to it. Now, you must wish me happy, Lucy. I have just learnt that I, too, am about to be married."

The girl's face broke into an impossibly wide smile. "Oh, lawks, miss!" she cried, throwing up both hands. "I just knew it! I just knew Mr. Hewitt would do the right thing, soon you told him! I just knew it would all come aright somehow."

Viviana felt a hot, urgent pressure well behind her eyes, and turned at once back to her desk. "I think, Lucy, that you misunderstand," she said, pretending to neaten her pens and papers. "I am returning home to marry someone who used to . . . well, someone I used to know."

"Oh, no, miss!" She felt Lucy touch her lightly on the arm. "But . . . but what about Mr. Hewitt?"

Viviana regained her composure, and turned around again. Opera required one to be not just a good singer, but a competent actress as well. "Oh, I think we have come to an understanding, he and I," she said, forcing a smile.

"Well, I can't see what it could be!" said the girl.

"Hush, Lucy." Viviana set her hands on the maid's shoulders, and swiftly kissed both her cheeks. "I am leaving England, my faithful friend. Do not grieve for me. All good things must come to an end, *si?*"

One

In which Lord Chesley plans a Grand Aventure.

Autumn, 1830

A h, well, all good things must come to an end," murmured the Marquis of Devellyn as he peered into the bay window of Piccadilly's most exclusive jeweler. "Try to look upon marriage, my friend, as the beginning of a new life; one which is rich with possibilities."

"Yes, and a bloody awful lot of impossibilities, too," said the Earl of Wynwood.

Devellyn grinned slyly. "Such as?"

"Such as my setting up Ilsa Karlsson in a quiet little house in Soho, which has long been a notion of mine."

Devellyn nodded. "A tragedy," he agreed. "Though Ilsa is a touch above your usual fare, old boy. In any case, we are here to buy a wedding gift for your bride-to-be, are we not?"

Wynwood pointed at a bracelet set with large red cabochons. "Well, what of that one?" he asked. "I rather like the color. Rubies, are they?"

"Merely garnets, I fear," said Devellyn. "So do not even

think of it; neither the garnets *nor* the talented Miss Karlsson. The cheaper stones your new bride may not notice, but that dragon of an aunt of hers most assuredly will. And Ilsa, well, *she* never goes unnoticed. For you, Quin, it must be real rubies and true fidelity, I am afraid."

Lord Wynwood made a pained expression, and seized hold of the door handle. "Well, come along, then," he said. "We might as well go in and get something."

A little bell jangled high overhead as they entered. A fulsome young woman was polishing away at the expanse of glass which topped the wooden cases, and the tang of vinegar was sharp in the air. "Why, good afternoon, my lord," she said, flashing Devellyn a knowing smile. "And Mr. Hewitt, is it not? I trust you both are well?"

"Fine as a five pence, ma'am," said the marquis cheerfully. "But Mr. Hewitt is Lord Wynwood now. Accordingly, you may charge him extra."

The woman laughed throatily. "My lord, how you do jest!" she said. "I fear my husband is out on an errand. May I help you until he returns?"

Wynwood looked up from a diamond bracelet he had been looking at, but not really seeing. "I wish, I suppose, to see some jewelry," he managed. "Diamonds, perhaps? Or—or emeralds?"

"You must pardon his uncertainty, Mrs. Bradford," interjected Devellyn, winking at the jeweler's wife. "My friend is looking for a gift for a very special sort of occasion."

Mrs. Bradford lifted her finely arched brows. "Why, we at Bradford and Burnet make it a point to specialize in special occasions," she said smoothly. "Do I perhaps hear wedding bells?"

"The death knell, more like, by the look of him!" said Devellyn, laughing. " 'Tis a gristly tale, ma'am, of yet another fine and lusty lad about to be torn from his happy bachelorhood and hoisted high in the noose of holy matrimony."

"Oh, well, a hoisting definitely calls for fine jewelry," said Mrs. Bradford with a straight face. "Are you looking for a wedding ring, my lord?"

"No!" Lord Wynwood's head jerked up like a startled stag's. "I mean . . . not quite yet."

"Just a betrothal gift," added Devellyn. "There is to be an engagement party, and he wishes to make the occasion very special for her." He paused to gently elbow his friend. "Is that not right, Quin?"

Again, Wynwood looked up. "Quite so," he muttered. "I want something, er, you know. *Special.*"

Mrs. Bradford smiled brightly and inched farther down the counter along with Wynwood. "And you were thinking of diamonds?" she echoed. "But not a ring. Perhaps a bracelet? Or a brooch?"

"A necklace, I think," said Wynwood.

"Yes, a very fine one," added Devellyn. "She is quite a special young lady."

Ever the cynic, Wynwood was beginning to wonder how many more times they could all manage to use the word *special* before this taxing business was done with. He had a deep and abiding hatred of jewelry stores. And Dev was being damned pushy about this marriage, too, almost as if daring him to go through with it. Just now, Dev was urging him farther and farther down the showcase; pushing him, it seemed, toward the inevitable permanence of the wedded state.

Oh, bloody hell. Best pick something, then. Something special, of course. But it all looked the same to him. "That one," he said, pointing at a heavy collar of beaten gold set with a fat, multifaceted chunk of some blue-green stone. "It is not a diamond, but it looks very . . . grand."

Devellyn leaned nearer. "Er—I don't think so, Quin," said the marquis.

Mrs. Bradford was frowning vaguely. "Is she a very young lady, my lord?" she asked. "And what color, pray, are her eyes?"

"Her eyes?" Wynwood pondered it. "Well, her eyes are . . . well, they are sort of . . ." The devil! What color *were* Miss Hamilton's eyes? "They are hard to describe, but—"

"Green," Devellyn interjected. "She is very small, and very young, and her eyes are cool mossy green with some little flecks of gold. That collar would weigh her down like chain mail and clash with her eyes most abominably. Really, Quin, I begin to wonder if your brain is fully engaged."

Wynwood scowled. "You are forgetting, Dev, that I have not lived a life which revolved around slavishly indulging a string of expensive, overly emotional opera dancers."

"Oh, no indeed!" agreed the marquis in a low undertone. "The class of women you usually consort with prefers a cash transaction."

Mrs. Bradford let an indelicate little snort of laughter escape, then turned away, her face flaming.

Devellyn cleared his throat. "Well, I should like to see some earbobs, Mrs. Bradford," he said, as if nothing untoward had occurred. "I've a mind, Quin, to buy Sidonie some sapphire earbobs to go with that gown she wore to Mamma's dinner party the other week. What do you think?"

"I think you ought to buy her a pair every week," his friend returned. "Otherwise, she might come to her senses and begin to wonder why she married you."

Devellyn grinned, and proceeded to have Mrs. Bradford pull out three or four velvet trays, which he inspected with meticulous devotion. He was very keen indeed, Wynwood had noticed, on pleasing his own wife.

Wynwood, however, had just about lost interest in his task. Oh, he wished to please Miss Hamilton. He truly did. But the truth was, he did not know Esmée as well as a gentleman might wish to know his fiancée. He knew, of course, that she was beautiful. She was also refreshingly pragmatic and straightforward. He could not have borne a silly, simpering London miss, or one who would rather manipulate a man than tell him the truth straight out. God knew he'd had enough of that to last a lifetime.

Esmée, of course, did not love him. That was just one of the many pragmatic, straightforward truths she'd told him. But love was not necessary, or even gratifying, to Quin. He and Esmée would learn to rub along tolerably well. Of that, he had no doubt. Esmée was easy to get along with, and easy on the eyes, too. He looked very much forward to having her in his bed, and even more forward to giving her his child—preferably the son which his mother so desperately needed.

His father's death had been premature, unexpected, and most untimely. And at the age of not quite thirty, Quin had had no wish to give up his carefree bachelorhood in order to save the Hewitt dynasty from collapse.

His mother, however, was in a state of near panic now, though her good breeding and well-honed restraint hid it from all save those who knew her well. If Quin died without an heir, all would go to the dreaded Cousin Enoch, who would—and his mother did not exaggerate this—promptly toss her into the street. His mother would be left a dependent of her younger brother, Lord Chesley, or packed off to Oxfordshire to live with Quin's sister, Alice. And his mother would sooner die than do either.

So the dynasty it must be. He and Esmée were going to retire to Buckinghamshire and have three or four children, and a reasonably happy life. To that end, Quin told himself, he was prepared to make whatever sacrifices were necessary, his fantasies of Ilsa and his flagrantly wicked ways—well, *most* of them—included. It was worth it to have Esmée. For if not her, then it would be some girl solely of his mother's choosing.

"I shall take these," he heard Devellyn say.

Mrs. Bradford named a price that would have bought one a piece of freehold real estate in Chelsea. Devellyn agreed without a second thought, then turned to Wynwood. "What of you, Quin?" he asked. "What have you chosen for your pretty Scottish lass?"

"I am undecided," he admitted. "I think I had best talk to Lady Tatton first. She will know what her niece's preferences are, will she not?"

"Or Alasdair?" suggested Devellyn, as Mrs. Bradford disappeared into the depths of the shop to wrap his purchase. "You ought to just ask Alasdair what he thinks Esmée would like. He is very fond of her, and knows her better than anyone. I am sure he could best advise you."

Wynwood felt his temper flare. Sir Alasdair MacLachlan was one of their most disreputable and amusing companions. Or at least, he had been. Nowadays, however, Alasdair was behaving very oddly. Like Esmée, Alasdair was a Scot. And due to a convoluted misadventure involving a New Year's masquerade, and far too much whisky, it appeared that Alasdair was also the father of Esmée's infant sister, though almost no one knew it. Wynwood *did* know it, and he was getting damned tired of Devellyn bringing both of them up in the same breath. What the devil was the man getting at?

Just then, a clock could be heard striking somewhere in the depths of the shop.

"Devil take me!" said Devellyn. "Is that the time? I'm late for a tea in Grosvenor Square. Mamma will have my head on her best Minton platter. Mrs. Bradford? *Mrs. Bradford!* I must have that package, if you please."

The jeweler's wife bustled back into the shop and presented a sheet of foolscap requiring the marquis's signature. After scrawling something illegible across it, Devellyn tucked the box in his pocket and patted Wynwood solicitously on the shoulder. "Buck up, old chap!" he said, before bolting out the door.

Mrs. Bradford was setting down Devellyn's purchase in a green baize ledger. "May I show you anything else, my lord?" she enquired, flicking a neutral glance up at him.

"No, I think not, thank you," he said, slapping his hat back on his head. "I will make enquiries as to the lady's preferences and return another time."

Quin went back out into Burlington Arcade and strode toward the pressing rush of Piccadilly. All along the street, dead leaves were swirling, some of them so bold as to blow back into the entrance of the elegant arcade itself. The autumn day was surprisingly clear, though the air was sharp, portending winter's swift approach.

Pausing on the pavement, he narrowed his eyes against the brightness, feeling vaguely disoriented. Lord, he'd felt a fool inside the small, overheated jeweler's shop. Devellyn was right; he did not consort with the sort of women for whom one bought fine jewels. Not any longer. And even when he had done so, it had been rubies, and nothing less.

That was why the garnets had caught his eye. He had seen them, and for a moment, he had thought of . . . well, of Viviana Alessandri. He had realized his misjudgment at once. Garnets had never been good enough for her; he'd known that much without asking. The rich, bloodred ruby had always personified Viviana, and her delicate, faintly olive skin had made them shimmer with life. So he had chosen each bracelet, brooch, and necklace with the utmost care, just as Devellyn had chosen the sapphire earbobs for his beloved Sidonie.

But for all the care he had put into each, Viviana had turned around and sold it, quite heartlessly and calculatingly—to pay off her dressmaker, or settle her gaming debts, he supposed. Which was, of course, her prerogative as a kept woman. Or more accurately, as a whore. And at the end of that awful, heart-wrenching affair, he had told himself that never again would he expend his emotional energy in choosing a gift—even the slightest bauble—for any woman. For the last nine years, he had not so much as darkened the door of a jewelry store. Until today.

Quin set off down the street in the direction of Green Park, but just a few yards along, he paused opposite the

Bath Hotel. A fine coach and four had drawn up near the corner, where a gentleman and a lady were engaged in an animated quarrel, hands moving almost as fast as their words. He realized at once that they were wealthy, and that they were foreign. Their fine attire made plain the first. As to the latter, members of the English *ton* would sooner die than be seen squabbling in the street like fish-mongers.

The lady's face he could not see, but he had the strangest notion she would be stunningly beautiful. The gentleman was elderly, stooped, and somewhat frail in appearance. He was, however, holding his own. Quin caught snatches of the language, too. Italian, or something similar. As if he were the veriest rustic, Quin stopped to gawk, though he could not have said why.

Amidst all the waving and scolding, the crux of the argument was easy to discern. The lady wished the gentleman to get into the carriage. The gentleman wished to walk. The argument continued for a few more sharp words, then the elderly gentleman moved as if to leave her.

At last, the woman threw up her hands, signaling her surrender. The elderly gentleman hesitated. In an almost maternal gesture, the lady's fingers went to his muffler, pulling it snug around his neck and tucking the ends into his greatcoat. The gentleman bracketed her face in his hands, and kissed her once on each cheek, then set off in the direction of Mayfair.

And then she turned around.

Quin felt the breath suddenly slammed from his body.

As a boy, he'd once rushed a fence he'd no business jumping. His horse had had better sense. Quin had been tossed off to one side, where he'd landed ignominiously in the grass, his heart in his throat and gasping for air for what seemed an eternity.

This time, the boyish ignominy lasted only a moment. It was replaced by a burning, righteous fury. Yet the proud lady spared him not a glance before mounting the steps into her carriage and lifting a gloved hand to signal that they should depart.

Later, when he considered it, he realized that he had, in fact, seen very little. There had been a flash of color as the woman turned, skirts of deep burgundy, jewel-like against the black velvet of her swirling cloak. A black hat set almost flirtatiously to one side, and bountiful black ribbons tied at the chin, lifting lightly in the breeze. That unmistakably proud set of her shoulders. Those slashing black eyebrows. The way she carried herself, like the haughtiest queen, stepping up into the carriage as if she owned the world.

Her face, though—yes, there was something different about her face. She did not look the same. The nose . . . it was not quite right. And yet, he would have known her anywhere, even had a thousand years passed. It was Viviana Alessandri. Oh, yes. And still his breath would not come, and his heart would not leave his throat.

By the late afternoon, the mantel clock in Lord Chesley's Belgravia town house was running ten minutes slow, the pendulum's doleful *tock-tock-tock* echoing hollowly, as if it might tick its last at any moment. The atmosphere inside the parlor was oddly subdued, too. With a neatening rattle, Chesley laid aside his newspaper and studied his lone companion.

"I think I shall go upstairs, Vivie, and have a nap before dinner," he said, rising. "One never adequately anticipates the wear and tear of travel, does one?"

Viviana looked up from her sheaf of roughly sketched notes and music, and smiled at her host. "*Si,* it is trying, my lord," she agreed. "Even little Nicolo was exhausted yesterday. A remarkable thing indeed."

Chesley strolled toward the windows which overlooked the arboreal glory of Hans Place. "What do you wish to do tonight, Vivie?" he asked musingly. "Shall we look up Digleby, and go watch the rehearsals for *Fidelio*? Or—wait, I know the very thing! We could take the children to Astley's Amphitheatre!"

Her eyes lit for a moment. "But Nicolo is too small, *no?*"

"Nonsense," said Chesley. "He'll have a lovely time."

Viviana pushed away her cold cup of tea. She had promised herself she would not go about in London any more than was absolutely necessary. One never knew who one might run into. But at Astley's? No, surely not. Still, it had been a long trip from Venice to London.

"How kind you are, Chesley, to think of my children," she answered, coming to her feet. "But perhaps we ought simply to have a quiet evening here? I fear *Papà* may have overtaxed himself with the walk from St. James. And now he is upstairs romping with Nicolo."

"But of course, my dear," said the earl. "I sometimes forget just how old Umberto is now."

"*Si,* as does he," Viviana returned.

Chesley closed the distance between them, and took her hands in his. "Vivie, my dear, are you perfectly all right?" he asked. "You have not seemed yourself these last two days. Was it the travel? Have I asked too much of you, in pleading for this visit to England?"

She smiled, and squeezed his hands. "I *wished* to come," she said, lying unabashedly. "I wished to be away from Venice for a while."

Chesley laughed, and lifted her hands in his, as if he might dance her round the room. "Oh, indeed! Why stay in Venice when one can winter in England!" he said. "I'm sure it must be all the rage. No, admit it, Vivie. You wished to leave your French marquis cooling his heels, did you not? Poor devil! What was this one's name?"

"Gaspard."

"Yes, alas, poor Gaspard!" said Chesley.

Viviana grinned. "Gaspard had become tiresome," she admitted. "I shall not miss him."

Chesley's expression sobered. "But spring is far away, my dear," he said. "And Buckinghamshire will be very cold come January. I am feeling a little guilty for having asked so much of you and Signor Alessandri."

"You must know, Chesley, that I cannot bear to let *Papà* from my sight," said Viviana. "And in truth, the notion of collaborating on this opera has rejuvenated him. I think he was not so happy in his retirement."

Chesley looked down at the sheaf of paper strewn across the tea table. "Well, what do you think, my dear, of young Digleby's libretto? Will it challenge your father?"

Viviana lifted one shoulder, an almost Gallic gesture. "*Sì,* I believe so," she said. "Just enough. But already, I have a concern."

"What is it, my dear?" said the earl. "I value your opinion."

"Well, this piece—*Nel Pomeriggio*—I like it," she said

slowly. "The title is suggestive. *In the Afternoon.* It makes one wonder what the characters will get up to, does it not?"

"Yes, yes, go on."

Viviana was nodding slowly to herself. "And admittedly, it has elements which are delightfully witty," she went on. "So I believe we would be better served by opening something like this in Paris, at the Opéra-Comique, perhaps? But not La Scala, which Lord Digleby seems to have set his heart on."

"He wishes far more to open as a success," said Chesley dryly. "Your point is well made, my dear. I will explain to him how the world of bel canto opera works. He also wishes the character of Maria to have five arias. Is it too much, do you think?"

Viviana shook her head. "*Papà* will make it work," she said confidently. "But you will need a strong soprano for the role."

Lord Chesley tweaked her on the chin as if she were a mere child. "Yes, I know that, dear Vivie," he admitted. "You did not think you were invited simply for your looks, did you?"

Viviana felt a moment of panic. "Oh, no, I cannot!" she said, sitting back down again. "Oh, Chesley, I cannot do this for you. Nicolo is yet too young, and—I—I—"

"Nicolo is four years old now," Chesley interjected. "And you have sung with only two productions in all that time."

"Yes, but at home in Venice," she retorted. "Not Paris, nor even Milan."

"And nothing at all in the last two years."

Viviana looked away, her eyes staring into the depths of

the room. She had not the heart to tell Chesley the truth—
or her fears. "I had to mourn my husband," she said quietly. "I owed him that much, did I not?"

The earl shook his head. "Don't let your pipes rust, my
girl," he warned. "Besides, this production is months
away."

Viviana tossed a longing look at the untidy libretto.
"Well, we shall see what *Papà* comes up with," she said.
"But I daresay it will be something very clever and very
irresistible, and I shall wish very desperately to neglect my
children, and forget poor Gaspard altogether."

"If you ask me, Gaspard's fate is already sealed," said
Chesley dryly. "But you, neglecting your children? Not in
a thousand years."

Just then, a terrible clamor arose in the direction of the
entrance hall. The children came thundering down the
steps, their high-pitched shrieks echoing in the stairwell.
Two little girls burst into the parlor in a gale of pastel and
ruffles, followed by Signor Alessandri, who carried a
small boy perched upon his stooped shoulders.

"*Papà!*" Viviana started from her chair. "*Essere attento!*"

"Oh, he is fine, Viviana," said the old man.

"I am quite sure *he* is!" she returned. "What of you?"

"Go! Go!" cried the boy, spurring his grandfather with
his heels. "Go, *Nonno!*"

Go was his newest English word. Viviana tried to
scowl, but failed. "*Vieni qui,* Nicolo!" she said, lifting the
boy down.

The girls were giggling at one another. "Mamma, Lord
Chesley has a big swine!" said the smaller of the two.

"A *pig,* Felise," corrected her sister. "A big, hairy one—
but it is . . . it is *deceased.*"

"Ah, *dead* pig, is it?" Viviana set Nicolo on her hip, and lifted one brow. "And this creature is upstairs? I wondered what was causing all the noise."

"No, no!" Signor Alessandri laughed. "It is a—how you say—a taxidermy. A wild boar."

Chesley looked almost embarrassed. "A sporting trophy from my youth," he confessed. "I went out to Africa with a group of chaps to shoot at things. This one was old, I daresay, and simply died of shock upon seeing such a pack of silly fribbles. But I had him stuffed. I was quite proud of it for a time."

"We rode it, Mamma," said the eldest girl.

"Cerelia!"

"*She* did," said Felise. "I was afraid. It has big yellow teeth."

"Tusks, Felise," said her sister, with an air of superiority. "They are not teeth."

Nicolo was squirming now. Viviana was straining to keep a safe grip on the boy.

Lord Chesley caught her gaze, and grinned. "All fagged out, is he, Vivie?"

Viviana put the boy down and looked at the earl with chagrin in her eyes. "I am so sorry," she said. "The children are not used to being kept to the schoolroom. They will do better, I promise, when we reach Hill Court."

"Nonsense!" said Chesley. "Let them have the run of the house, I say."

Viviana threw up a staying hand. "Oh, *Dio,* I beg you!" she said. "My nerves will not bear it. You will have not so much as a decent bonbon dish remaining if you let Nicolo loose."

Chesley looked on at the children indulgently. "Well,

another few days of business here in town, then we'll be on our way," he said. "We can all run loose in the country."

A noise drew Viviana's eyes to the tea table. Nicolo had seen her cold tea and snatched up the fine Sèvres cup as if to drink it. "No!" she cried, prying it from his still-plump fingers. "Nicolo, no!"

The boy screwed up his face and began wailing. At once, Lord Chesley went down on one knee. "Nicolo, do you like horses?" he asked. "Felise, Cerelia, what of you?"

Nicolo closed his mouth. *"Hor-zees,"* he echoed, clearly not comprehending.

"I like horses," said Felise. "I'm to have a pony soon."

"Yes," said her mother. *"If* you are good."

"I already know how to ride on a horse," said Cerelia proudly.

Lord Chesley made a face of amazement. "Yes, but can you ride standing up, Cerelia?" he asked. "With no saddle?"

The girls' eyes were wide now.

From his position on the floor, Chesley flicked a glance up at Viviana. "My dear, I think I have finalized our plans for the evening," he said apologetically. "Will you indulge me?"

Viviana managed a smile. "Yes, of course."

Chesley pinched Nicolo's nose. "Come here, young man," he said in very bad Italian. "I have a little treat for you. Have you ever heard of a place called Astley's Amphitheatre?

Two

In which Lord Wynwood makes a new Friend.

Quin dressed for his evening's engagement with a measure of reluctance. His new life as a soon-to-be-reformed rake was not without its challenges, he thought, lifting his arms so that his valet might put on his shirt. He did not care for this business of being at the beck and call of a pack of females; specifically, his mother, and his fiancée's aunt.

As to his fiancée herself, Esmée seemed unaffected by all the uproar related to their engagement. Indeed, she did not seem to mind whether they sat quietly at home playing piquet or dressed up in their finest and trotted off to dine with the Queen. It was all the same to her, so far as he could tell.

But his mother was in rapture over the whole affair and insisting on all manner of things which seemed unreasonable. Indeed, it was all he could do to restrain her from haring off to Lady Tatton's to plan the wedding breakfast, as if the ceremony were to take place next week instead of next spring, as he and Esmée had agreed.

In the past, he had simply ignored his mother's imprecations to turn from his wicked ways and settle down. Indeed, he had seen very little of his mother at all. But after his father's death, he had been compelled to see a vast deal of her, much of the time spent with her clinging to his arm and wailing over her unexpected widowhood.

Perhaps it was indicative of a hidden weakness in his character, but his mother's tears Quin could not bear. So, in keeping with the duties of a belatedly good son and a newly betrothed gentleman, tonight he was to take Esmée and Lady Tatton out for yet another evening of facile entertainment.

Already he'd been wined, dined, theater'ed, and soirée'ed to within an inch of his life. And he had the strangest impression that Esmée was as almost as indifferent to all of it as he was. Still, as his mother was ever fond of saying, appearances mattered. A gentleman engaged to be married was expected to squire his bride-to-be out and about at every opportunity.

Suddenly, he would have given his right arm to stay at home alone tonight. "That will do, Blevins," he said to his valet impatiently.

"What of your neckcloth, sir? And your waistcoat?"

Quin waved a hand. "I shall finish," he returned. "Thank you. You are excused until this evening."

Blevins gave a subservient nod and made himself scarce. The poor devil knew enough to comprehend when his master was in a vile mood, something which did not, thank God, occur often.

Quin prided himself on being an even-tempered sort. Still, given his dissolute habits, there was the occasional unpleasant morning after, which made a chap feel snappish. And there had been rare instances over the years when his mother had actually managed to run him to ground so that she might subject him to a long and querulous harangue about wasting his life. Certainly that did nothing to improve upon one's mood. Other than that, he had long ago decided there was little on this earth worth getting riled over.

So why was he feeling so apprehensive of late? He was to be married, and to a young woman whom he liked very much. He was fortunate to have found someone both beautiful and sensible. Someone who possessed a remarkable strength of character. Someone who could make him laugh. But Quin was not fool enough to think he was in love, or that Esmée Hamilton was the only woman in the world for him.

No, Quin had learnt the hard way that there was always another woman to be had. His life had long been awash in them. Women, it seemed, found him attractive. At least, that was what they often told him, right before making him an offer they thought he could not refuse.

As an awkward young man, he had not fully appreciated the power which his looks, wealth, and rank bestowed upon him. As a man grown, he understood it all too well. And he had long ago decided that it was far better simply to pay for his pleasure, as any man might. He preferred that no one harbor any illusions about the relationship—and *no one* included himself.

Oh, Devellyn might joke about it, but there was much to be said for the simplicity of a clean cash transaction. That way, there was no misunderstanding. No expectation. And no delusive hope. That, too, was something he had long believed he could live without. Until, that was,

he'd met Esmée. He had liked her the moment he set eyes
on the little Scottish spitfire. Perhaps that was the very
problem? Perhaps he liked his affianced bride just a little
too well. Perhaps he was beginning to hope again. That
was most unwise. Because this afternoon . . . oh, Christ
Jesus. He would not think of it.

Almost without realizing it, Quin went to the small
writing desk between his windows and began to dig
through the bottom drawer for his old gilt snuffbox. He
had not seen it in an age. He found it wedged between a
pair of old inkpots, underneath a pile of truly bad poetry.
He really did need to pitch that drivel heap into the next
good fire, he mused as he shuffled through it, before
someone read it and got a good laugh at his expense.

Instead, he tossed the pile of paper back, seized the
snuffbox, and thumbed it open. Inside was not just a lock
of hair, but an entire ringlet; a silky black spiral several
inches long. Gently, Quin wrapped it round his index
finger as he had done perhaps two or three times a day in
the beginning. But not so often of late. And not at all,
surprisingly, since meeting Esmée. Was that, perhaps,
the definition of hope?

Impassively, he studied it in the lamplight. He realized
with a measure of relief that it stirred nothing in his heart
now. The beautiful ringlet was . . . just a lock of hair. A tri-
fling bit of sentiment, like his cache of bad poetry. A reminder of what a fool a man could be, were he not careful.
But Quin had become very, very careful. Ah, yes. Despite
the shock he had received in Piccadilly, his heart had
come, it seemed, full circle.

Once, however, this hidden treasure had meant the
world to him. But he had been so young then; barely past

his teens, in fact, when he had fallen so helplessly in love, and with a woman who had not the time to spare him so much as a passing glance. But he had worn her down, more fool he. And he had stolen the silken ringlet from the floor of her dressing room on a night which was forever fixed in his memory. Yes, he had taken it as a sign of hope.

Dimly, he became aware of the longcase clock in the downstairs hall mournfully sounding the hour. A very late hour. Swiftly, he replaced the lock of hair, and shoved the drawer shut. It was time to fetch Esmée. Time to think only of the future. He drew on his freshly starched neckcloth and began meticulously to tie it.

The theater, when they arrived, was rapidly filling. He escorted the ladies to their seats, which were situated in one of the much-coveted boxes on the lowest level of the ring, so that they would have an excellent view. But before the program had even started, Lady Tatton began to draw her shawl a little closer and tug at her gloves, her teeth almost chattering as she did so.

Twice Quin offered his coat, and twice her ladyship refused it, looking more miserable by the minute. Esmée tried to maintain a cheerful attitude. "I wonder if they will have clowns tonight?" she remarked. "I have never seen a real one, you know. I shall likely be all agog and embarrass you both quite thoroughly."

Wynwood reached out and gratefully squeezed her hand. He began to talk of the various bits of entertainment they were to see, much to Esmée's delight. But no line of conversation would dissuade her ladyship from her discomfort.

"I wonder, Wynwood," she finally said, "if we mightn't be warmer up a little higher? And perhaps safer, too. I have heard the horses' hooves often throw sawdust in one's face, and the clowns perhaps throw worse."

Quin came at once to his feet. "I shall find someone, ma'am, and enquire as to whether we might be moved."

But finding someone was no simple affair. Astley's Amphitheatre was not precisely a luxurious entertainment. Instead, it was a place where the *ton* actually deigned to rub elbows with lesser mortals for the sake of an hour or two of shamelessly unrefined amusement. But Esmée had very much wished to come. And during the whole of their betrothal, it was the only thing Esmée had actually asked him for.

Lady Tatton, however, was clearly having second thoughts about rubbing her elbows against anyone below the rank of baronet. She would have to be reseated, or they would know no peace. Quin went out and made his way along the rear of the circle of stalls, seeing no one official in the surging crowd. Farther around the circle, however, were narrow corridors leading to stage doors and dressing chambers. Surely they were attended by someone?

He was debating returning to the main entrance when he spied a lovely little acrobat dawdling near one of the corridors ahead. Though her back was turned to him, her costume of feathers, pink satin, and frothy netting revealed a wealth of feminine curves, and Quin decided she was the perfect person to speak to. Perhaps she would even know how to go about getting reseated.

But when he touched her lightly on the shoulder, and she half turned toward him, he was shocked to see that the gentleman she was speaking with was Lord Chesley. His uncle was standing just inside the corridor, and oddly, he had a child by the hand.

"Well, Quin, my boy!" said Chesley in a tone of amiable surprise. "You, here? At *Astley's?*"

Quin managed a faint smile. "It is a long story."

"Hmm," said his uncle. "I have been too long on the Continent, I see." Hastily, his uncle introduced the pretty acrobat as Nadia, who had a surname which was unpronounceable.

Alas, Nadia spoke little English fluently, save for that which was said with her eyes, now firmly fixed on Quin. When he did not return her gaze, she turned to touch the little girl affectionately on the tip of her nose, muttering something he could not understand, then began to saunter away. Still, one could scarcely miss the inviting glance which she tossed over her shoulder as she departed.

"Ah, another conquest, my boy!" said Chesley good-humoredly. "But have a care with the riding master. I am afraid he is her husband."

Quin was still observing Nadia's snug little arse as she sauntered off and wondering if it would be worth the risk. Then he remembered Esmée. "No," he said almost to himself. "I fancy not."

"A wise choice," said his uncle.

It was then that Quin remembered the child. Vaguely embarrassed, he turned back to his uncle. "And who have we here?" he asked, bending down to feign polite interest. "You have not introduced me."

"This is my friend Lady Cerelia," said his uncle. "She has traveled all the way from the Continent, and granted me the honor of squiring her to all the fashionable sights about town. Cerelia, my nephew, Quinten Hewitt, Lord Wynwood."

"Hello," said the girl. Her voice was shy but her curtsy was perfect.

"Charmed, Lady Cerelia," said Quin, clicking his heels like some Continental dandy. He had long ago grown accustomed to his uncle's habit of bringing home the strays and orphans of the artistic world, much as other men brought home lost dogs. Little Cerelia doubtless belonged to one of them.

Then the girl looked up at him again, truly *looked* at him, her dark blue eyes remarkably insightful for a child of so few years. There was a certain sadness, too, though her youthful features hid it well. And as he watched her, for a moment, it was as if time held suspended. Quin found his mind grappling for something he could not name. A question. A familiarity. Then Cerelia bubbled with laughter at a passing clown in bright orange trousers.

The strange moment was broken.

"Cerelia wished to meet one of the acrobats," said his uncle. "She wishes to learn to ride on horseback whilst standing."

"How very brave of you," said Quin. "Did Nadia share her secrets?"

The girl nodded. *"Resina,"* she said, glancing up at Chesley as if for assistance. And for the first time, Quin realized that English was not her first language. "Nadia puts the—the—how do you say it, my lord?" she went on. "The tree juice which goes on the feet?"

"Resin," said Lord Chesley. "I gather they rub the soles of their feet in something like pine tar."

The girl wrinkled her nose, then giggled. Quin, too, found himself laughing. The child really was a taking thing, though she was just a slight slip of a girl. Quin was no judge in such matters, but he gathered she must be seven or eight years old. Her heavy, straight hair was not quite blond and not quite brown, like a shimmering shade of bronze, and she was dressed with an elegance which made it plain she was no ordinary English miss.

But the child was no business of his, and he was neglecting his duties. "Well, I must bid you good evening," he said, nodded to them both in turn. "I am on a mission for an important lady."

"I daresay," said his uncle mordantly. "But I cannot imagine who."

Quin gave a tight smile. "No, you cannot."

"Ah, well! Enjoy the show, my boy!" said Chesley over his shoulder. He had taken the little girl by the hand again and was leading her away.

Quin lifted his hand, but said no more. He was still inexplicably fascinated by the child. Then, at the last possible instant, the girl turned round again.

"*Piacere,* my Lord Wynwood," she said, lifting one hand in good-bye. "*Addio!*"

Piacere. He wracked his brain. *A pleasure.*

And suddenly, he knew.

Good God! He felt, for a moment, like a fool. How could he not have guessed? Damn his uncle to hell. That child was no ordinary girl. She was the daughter of Conte Gianpiero Bergonzi di Vicenza. *She was Viviana's.*

Quin watched them wade into the thinning crowd. For an instant, he was required to suppress the urge to call her back. To let him have a second look, in case he was mistaken. Oh, but it was all there, he thought, in the slant of the girl's eyes and the angle of her cheekbones. The piercing way she had looked at him, with her head held at a slight tilt. And in the promise of beauty to come, already apparent in her face.

In the distance, she looked up at Chesley and smiled. Yes, it was the look of Viviana. More pale. More neutral. And so young. But Viviana nonetheless. He was quite certain it was Viviana he'd seen in Piccadilly. With her famous father, Signor Alessandri, no doubt. Why else would she have returned? She had taken what she wanted from England long ago, and Chesley worshiped Alessandri as only a patron of the arts can worship the creator of that which he lives for. Wholeheartedly. Without reservation. To Chesley, Alessandri had never written a wrong note. And Viviana had never sung one.

She had been a nobody when Chesley brought her to London. He had done it, he told Quin, as a favor to her father. Stellar sopranos were two a penny in Italy that year. Viviana had been sent to London to shine, and Chesley had made it happen. For well over a year, she had sung at His Majesty's Theatre, graduating to the lead roles in a matter of months. The more senior members of the company had been astonished at her talent. Some, even envious. The *ton* had thrown roses at her feet.

But Quin had met her even before the envy or the roses. Yes, before she was anybody special, she had been his, at least in his mind. Of course, she had also been the daughter of the famous Alessandri, it was true. And she had been beautiful beyond words. But no one, least of all Quin, had realized the adulation she would shortly find.

Nonetheless, when Viviana was finished with London—and finished with him—she had turned her back on all of it, leaving as unexpectedly as she had come. She had abandoned him without so much as a fare-thee-well, returning to Italy to a newly adoring public, and to a brilliant marriage which had lent her the respectability that an opera singer, even the most famous amongst them, did not easily achieve.

The child and his uncle had melted away. Vaguely, Quin was aware that he was standing in the middle of Astley's walkway, staring like a gudgeon into a crowd which was rapidly thinning. But he could think only of Viviana. Viviana, who had wanted only two things. She had wanted fame, and she had wanted a wellborn husband.

Her father, it seemed, had arranged both. In May, she had been in Quin's bed, and by June, in the powerful Conte Bergonzi's. Soon it was being whispered by her fellow sopranos that her reason for leaving Italy to begin with was simply to persuade Bergonzi to the altar. The rich and powerful *conte* had been her father's patron for many years.

Viviana must have known him well. Perhaps she had long been enamored with him. Perhaps they had been lovers. Perhaps every time she had cried out in Quin's embrace, she had been thinking of Bergonzi. For a time, the uncertainty of it had wracked him. It no longer did so. He dropped his gaze, and turned away.

He did not care how respectable Viviana was now. And he certainly did not care how pretty or how sad or how charming her daughter was. Indeed, what he *ought* to care about was just where the devil Lady Tatton could be happily seated. Already, the music inside the theater could be heard swelling to a cheerful, spirited overture. Quin shoved every thought of Viviana Alessandri out of his head, and went on about the business of being a dutiful fiancé.

Three

In which Lady Alice is the Voice of reason.

The entourage which departed for the Earl of Chesley's Buckinghamshire estate a few days later was truly impressive. Chesley and his latest candidate for symphonic sainthood, Lord Digleby Beresford, rode in the first carriage. Beresford was a composer of no small merit, but neither was he especially well known beyond London and Paris. And his roughly drafted libretto, just as Chesley had claimed, showed promise, too.

Viviana and her father followed in the second coach, whilst the children, their nurse, and the governess rode in the third. A fourth held the gentlemen's valets and Viviana's maid. Lastly came two baggage carts, one of them carrying Chesley's wild boar, which the children had begged for. This was followed by a well-padded van containing Viviana's harp and violin, as well as her father's piano and his collection of stringed instruments. Her father would sooner leave Venice without his stockings and drawers than leave his musical instruments behind.

The trip was not long, but the weather had turned sharp. Pulling her black velvet cloak a little closer, Viviana looked beyond the carriage window at the bare trees and dormant pastures of an England she barely remembered, and wondered if she had made a mistake in returning. She really did not need this emotional upheaval. Not now. No, not ever.

But what choice had she in the matter? Allow her father travel so far alone? Lord Chesley had been a good friend to both of them. He had asked a favor, a very *small* favor, which her father had seized upon with an enthusiasm Viviana had not seen in some years. The great Signor Alessandri now possessed a newfound sense of purpose. Lord Digleby Beresford.

Chesley had singled Beresford out as yet another artist worthy of his benefaction. And when Beresford had confessed a desire to write an opera, Chesley asked Viviana's father to help. Unfortunately, Beresford had two strikes against him. He had little experience with classic opera. And he was English. But Alessandri knew Beresford's work and believed the project worth his while. Viviana believed it might keep him alive. And so she had packed up her trunks and her children and her life, such as it was, and traveled far to this place she'd no wish to think about, let alone visit.

By late afternoon, Viviana began to see the signposts for the little village of Arlington Green. Her father had fallen asleep some miles back, his wizened frame rocking gently against the upholstery as the carriage rumbled on. Viviana relaxed against the banquette and felt herself begin to unwind for the first time since disembarking at Southampton. She was relieved to have London behind her. She had been afraid of . . . well, running into *him*.

Yes, she who had learnt to fear nothing had feared seeing Quin Hewitt again. But she had not seen him. Indeed, she had barely left Chesley's house. As to Quin, for all she knew, he had long ago removed to the country. Or died. Or married. Or some combination of all three.

No. Had he died, she would have known it on her next breath. There was a connection between them, she feared, which would reach beyond the grave. But almost certainly he had married his pale, flaxen-haired English miss by now. Well. She wished him happy. Certainly she did not wish him ill. And there was very little, in truth, that she blamed him for. For all his reckless ways and quick temper, Quin had never once lied to her. Instead, he had been painfully honest. And oh, how she had loved him.

She had met him, of course, through Lord Chesley. During her first fortnight in London, Quin had accompanied his uncle to a reception in honor of some French conductor whose name Viviana had long since forgotten. Chesley was trying to lend the boy a little polish, he quietly explained, since Quin had been isolated in the English countryside for much of his life, at the insistence of an overbearing father. Quin was enjoying the splendors—and the excesses—of London for the very first time. He had been but nineteen years old.

Viviana had been too busy trying to survive the splendor and excess of London to pay any great heed to Chesley's nephew, beautiful though he was to look at. Life alone in London was daunting, and it was the first time she had traveled beyond Venice without her father's protection. She had been trying very hard to play the suave Continental and to devote every spare moment to her work.

But Quin had dogged her steps for weeks on end. Viviana had been three years older and at least a decade more worldly-wise than he. At first, she had thought it vaguely amusing to be courted by one so young and so callow. But he had persisted in his attentions, pressing her with a near ruthlessness that belied both his age and his inexperience. And she could not say she had not wanted him. Oh, no. She had wanted him with an intensity which frightened her.

Only the thought of dishonoring her father and the sacrifices he had made for her had kept Viviana from giving in. But in the end, it had not mattered. In the end, Quin Hewitt had got what he wanted. And perhaps she had, too. She did not know. After all these years, she still did not know. Perhaps it had been worth it. Perhaps a few moments of unadulterated joy were all one could hope for on this earth.

On a sharp sigh, Viviana let her gaze drift to the window again, and resolved to think of something else. Something that mattered. Quin Hewitt did not. Whatever she had once felt for him had faded in the intervening years. She was not that woman any longer. Nothing about her was the same. She had had an astonishingly successful career. She had married and borne three children. She had been shaken to her very core, and survived it to come out stronger, inexorably altered in ways which no one else could possibly understand.

No, she would not think of that, either. She would think only of the things which mattered now. Her children. Her father. Her music.

At last they were entering the quaint little village of Arlington Green. The shops and houses were beautifully made of a mellow old stone, and set very close to the road. In the center of the village was a squat, steepled church, and opposite, an old stone market cross. Farther down the lane, Viviana could see a set of wide, magnificent gateposts made of marble, with a large gatehouse adjacent, but the carriages did not slow as she expected. Instead, the lead coachman whipped up his horses and went on another quarter mile beyond the village proper.

So Lord Chesley was not the only rich nobleman in these parts. Upon considering it, Viviana was not surprised. Hill Court was not Chesley's seat, but rather, a winter retreat which his family had long favored over their stately pile far to the north. As it happened, this house was not far from the road, and within minutes, the coaches and carts were circling around the carriage drive. Servants swarmed from the small manor house to begin the process of unloading, herded along by a black-garbed butler, a very stately personage who looked to be at least a hundred and five. A tall, thin woman in housekeeper's garb looked down from the top step.

The butler was introduced as Basham, the housekeeper as Mrs. Douglass. Dinner was to be served at half past seven, Basham announced once they were all inside. Lord Chesley and Mrs. Douglass lapsed into a conversation about the particulars of their stay. Viviana gave her father's valet a look which meant he was to take the elderly man upstairs at once and insist he rest. The look was well understood. Her father was whisked away.

Miss Hevner, the governess, asked to be shown at once to the old schoolroom upstairs. Viviana soon followed her up. But she was just halfway up the steps with the children and Signora Rossi, their elderly nurse, when Chesley called out to her again. She set her hand on the banister and turned back.

"Basham says my sister's giving a dinner party day after tomorrow," said the earl dolefully. "Family and neighbors. A dashed dull business, I'm sure. Will you and Alessandri go, Vivie? It isn't far, and my sister would be thrilled."

Viviana gave him a hesitant smile. "*Si,* Chesley, if you wish it."

"It would make it more bearable," he admitted.

"Then it would be our great pleasure to accompany you."

Chesley beamed up at her. "Well, we shan't stay long, Vivie," he said. "I promise."

A few days after his strange trip to Astley's Amphitheatre, Quin was in his study at Arlington Park going over some very dull accounts which Henry Herndon, his estate agent, had laid out for him. He had little enthusiasm for the task. Quin much preferred London to his country seat, though he did come and do his duty. And if he had to be in Buckinghamshire, he would rather spend his time up in Aylesbury, where he was not especially well known.

Last night he had passed a pleasant evening there at the Queen's Head, where the cards were honest and the serving girls were not. The view from the taproom had been excellent—creamy cleavage and swaying hips as far as a fellow could see—and Quin was of a mind to go back again that night. He was not yet a married man. There were a few months of freedom still left to him. Perhaps he should enjoy it. And yet, at Arlington, he could not quite do so.

The trouble was, he thought, looking about his wood-paneled study, Arlington still felt as if it belonged to his father. As a young man, Quin had longed to see the world beyond Buckinghamshire, or at least go away to school. Instead, his father had given him a prosy curate for a tutor and an occasional week of shopping in London with his mother and Alice. Until Chesley had rescued him, Quin had felt almost imprisoned at Arlington. Now he simply felt like a usurper to the throne.

At least Henry Herndon was still in charge. Herndon had been the family's agent for some fifteen years. Under his stewardship, the estate was more or less minting money, and the village and its environs had prospered as well. Quin was jotting out a reminder to give the agent a substantial raise come the new year when a soft knock sounded at his door.

"Come!" he cried.

His sister Alice stuck her head inside the door. She was wearing a deep blue habit which matched her eyes, and her color was high, as if she'd rouged her cheeks. "I am going to take a ride toward the village," she said. "I wish to see Mr. Herndon's new gristmill. Will you come?"

Quin had been meaning to have a look at the new mill. With a smile, he rose and came from behind the desk. "A fine notion, Alice," he said, after kissing her lightly on the cheek. "Besides, I'll gladly seize any excuse which gets me out of this study."

Alice looked at him mischievously. "Mrs. Prater is in the poultry yard wringing the necks of some unlucky chickens," she said. "I believe they will be attending your betrothal dinner tomorrow. You could always go and help with that, I daresay, if you are desperate?"

Quin grimaced. "Good God, I ought to knot your braids for that!"

Quin's fear of chickens was a standing joke at Arlington Park, and Alice never let him forget it. As a small and overly curious little boy, he'd once sneaked into the poultry yard alone, only to get himself thoroughly flogged by a bad-tempered buff cockerel who took umbrage at Quin's curiosity. Quin, being much doted upon by Mrs. Prater, ran squalling to the cook, who went promptly out into the yard, wrung the old devil's neck, then served him up for supper.

Alice had laughter in her eyes as they left the study together. "I haven't had braids, Quin, in a dozen years," she said. "You will have to think of a better punishment."

Quin linked his arm through hers and helped Alice up the small flight of stairs that led in the direction of the main corridor. "You are looking lovely today, Allie," he said quietly. "You have put on weight, have you not?"

"No, it is just that I have put off my black," she said. "Widow's weeds make one look so gaunt, do they not?"

Lady Alice Melville was but two months out of mourning. After nine years of marriage, her husband had died suddenly, leaving Alice alone with three children, a heavy heart, and a large fortune. Theirs had been an arranged marriage, one which Alice had not wished for, but one which she had nonetheless made the most of. Quin did not think that Alice had loved her husband in any romantic sense, but she had respected him. Certainly she had grieved for him.

In the great hall, Quin left Alice just long enough to change into boots and breeches. They said little until their horses were saddled and they were well away from the house.

They took the scenic route to the village, along the main carriage drive. From time to time, they would leave the canopy of bare-branched trees, and a vista of muted green hills would appear, dotted with sheep or deer. It was still hard for Quin to believe that the responsibility for all of this now rested with him.

The sun was bright, but the air was cool, and the wind was already whipping strands of hair from Alice's tidy arrangement. She was remarkably quiet. "You did not come home last night, Quin," she finally remarked.

Quin shot her a sidelong glance. "No, I didn't," he answered. "What of it?"

Alice shrugged. "Mamma remarked on it, that is all," she said. For a few moments, she said no more.

"Oh, God!" he finally said. "Go on, Allie. What?"

Alice seemed to falter. "Well, I just wonder . . . sometimes, Quin, I just wonder if you are ready to be married."

He looked at her in mild exasperation. "No, I'm not," he said. "And I am *not* married, am I? I hope I do not have to remind Mamma of that fact. It is a bit much to ask a man to be accountable to both a wife and a mother, when he is no longer a child and not yet a husband."

Alice looked suitably chastised. They rode on in silence for perhaps half a mile. "I do like your Miss Hamilton, Quin," she finally said. "She is beautiful, and wise, too, I believe."

Quin wondered what his sister was getting at. "Yes, you met her in London, did you not?" he said. "I had forgotten you were in town."

"Briefly, yes." Alice reined her horse around a large puddle from last night's storm. "I had business with John's solicitors. Of course, Mother thought it the perfect opportunity to introduce me to Miss Hamilton. I collect she regards the young lady as something of a *coup.*"

Quin laughed loud enough to make his horse to toss his head in protest. "A triumph of hope over reason," he said. "But yes, Miss Hamilton is a very nice young lady."

His sister gave him a long, sidling look which lingered. "But do you love her, Quin?" she finally asked.

Quin smiled. "I am fond of her, Allie," he said. "I truly am. And we get on well."

Alice surprised him by drawing her mount to a halt, and reining nearer. "Oh, Quin, do not let mother persuade you wrongly," she said, covering his hand with her own. "You must not marry if you are not ready. And you certainly must not marry where you do not love. Oh, I beg you, my dear, to listen to me. In this, at least, I have more experience than you."

Quin must have looked astonished, for his sister blushed immediately. "Mamma is not bullying me into this, Alice, if that is what you fear," he answered. "With Father gone, I need to marry. I know that. I do not need Mamma to urge me on."

Alice pressed her lips together, as if something pained her. "But why now?" she asked. "Why Miss Hamilton, if you do not love her? Why can you not take a few months and look about you? Perhaps you *will* fall in love, Quin."

Quin studied her for a moment, then nudged his horse on. "I want what you had, Alice," he said. "I want a marriage with someone who is compatible. With someone I can respect."

"You are persuaded, then," she said sadly. "There is nothing I can say?"

Quin shook his head and wondered what on earth his

sister was thinking. His mother had hinted that Miss Hamilton would make him a worthy wife, yes. But he had been the one who had seized upon the notion. The announcement had already been printed in half the kingdom's newspapers, and the ensuing ribald remarks in all of its scandal rags. Some forty friends, relations, and neighbors were coming to dinner tomorrow night in honor of his betrothal. There was no backing out of it now.

To his relief, his sister changed the subject. "Great-aunt Charlotte has moved up from the gatehouse for a few days," she said with false brightness. "Mamma thought it would be more enjoyable for her to be in the midst of all the excitement."

Quin was feeling a little like a bug beneath someone's quizzing glass. "And so it will be, I'm sure," he said. His great-aunt Charlotte was his grandfather's sister, a prying, prodding, somewhat impertinent old lady whom he nonetheless admired, if for nothing more than her tenacious grip on life.

"Mamma is fretting over Aunt Charlotte again," Alice went on. "She seems to regard her as some sort of living link to Papa. I do hope she lives a good, long life."

"My God, Alice, she is ninety years old!" said Quin. "She has already lived a good, long life—two or three, by some counts."

They were approaching the gatehouse now. Alice tossed him a speaking glance. "You know what I mean, Quinten," she said. "Mamma could not bear another loss just now. But yes, you are right. Aunt Charlotte isn't getting any younger. Her heart is weak, you know."

"Charlotte shall likely outlive us all," he muttered. Then, more loudly, "Look, Alice, at the size of that thing!"

He pointed across the village road to the soaring roofline of the new mill, which sat behind the village, along the river.

Alice gave him a bemused smile. "Did you not notice it when you arrived?"

He had not. His mind, apparently, had been elsewhere.

Soon they were dismounting along the edge of the pond, which Herndon had dammed for his vast operation. The waterwheel was turning at a brisk pace, making a rhythmic *shush, shush, shush* sound, whilst the deep vibrations of the grist wheels seemed to make the very earth tremble. The great mill had been designed to serve not just the estate, but the village—which also belonged to the earldom of Wynwood—as well as anyone in the surrounding countryside who wished to use it. For a small fee, of course. Thus the mill, Herndon had calculated, would pay for itself in five short years.

Herndon was observing the carpenters as they made some finishing adjustments to the hinges of the double doors—doors wide enough to permit a cart to be backed fully inside the mill. Upon seeing Quin, however, Herndon touched his hat brim and came up the slope toward him. When he noticed Alice, however, his demeanor changed. He snatched off his hat and softened his normally businesslike expression.

"Lady Alice. Wynwood." He nodded to them in turn. "Come for a tour of the new mill?"

"We have indeed," said Quin.

They went down the hill and entered the shadowy depths of the mill. Inside, the air was thick with dust, the floorboards were covered with grit, and the very soles of Quin's boots seemed to vibrate as the stones ground effortlessly.

The tour did not last long; the ancient process of the water-driven shafts and stones was a simple one. When they came back out into the daylight, Alice looked down at the skirt of her habit and gave a cry of dismay. "Oh, look! Lud, what a mess I've made!"

To Quin's surprise, Herndon snatched a starched white handkerchief from his coat pocket, and knelt to brush the mill dust from her hems. Herndon, it occurred to him, was a fine-looking man, if a little steely-eyed and sober-minded. He had also been extraordinarily fond of Alice during her girlhood, though he would have seen little of her after her marriage.

Quin hadn't seen much of her either, save for the occasional holiday. John, her husband, had not approved of London society, and he had distinctly disapproved of Quin's. Still, it had occurred to Quin from time to time that he ought at least to write his sister. Instead, he had told himself that there was little in his life a lady would wish to be privy to. It was a choice he now regretted. He had the feeling that perhaps his sister had been lonely in her marriage.

Herndon was on his feet by then, and tucking away his handkerchief. Quin had wondered before why a man of Herndon's background had not married. He had a fine house not far from the village. He was a third or fourth or perhaps even fifth son of an Oxfordshire baronet. He had attended university. He was well established in his career. But he must be all of forty now, and if ever he'd looked at a woman, Quin knew nothing of it.

Herndon and his sister were making small talk. "Will you be long at Arlington, Lady Alice?" the estate manager was asking.

Alice cut a shy look at Quin. "We are thinking—the children and I, I mean—of staying on through the New Year," she confessed. "Though I have not yet been invited to do so."

"Don't be silly, Alice," said Quin. "Arlington is your home, and always will be. If you mean to hang out after an invitation, you'll likely die of old age."

"And a pity that would be," said Herndon. It was the closest the man had ever come to humor.

One of Herndon's carpenters was leading their horses up the slope now. "Morning, m'lord," he said, passing over Quin's reins. "Happen a fine traveling coach just turned up th' park."

"Ah!" said Alice with a smile. "Thank you, Edwards. That will be Miss Hamilton and her aunt. Hurry, Quin. We will ride fast and take the shortcut through the woods."

Herndon had cupped his hands to take Alice's boot. "My congratulations on your upcoming marriage, Wynwood," he said. "I should have said so earlier."

"Thank you, Herndon." Quin was whacking his crop thoughtfully across his boot top. "You will be attending tomorrow evening's festivities, will you not?"

The estate agent seemed to hesitate. "Well, I had thought . . . the mill is not quite—"

"It will be dark, Herndon," said Quin impatiently. "And I shall feel mightily hurt if you cannot trouble yourself to attend my betrothal dinner."

Herndon's eyes seemed a bit more steely now. "I would not miss it for all the world, then, my lord."

"Excellent!" said Quin, smoothly remounting. "Sirs, I give you both good day."

Four

Sir Alasdair to the Rescue.

L ord Chesley and his houseguests were the first to arrive for his sister's dinner party the following evening.
They were so early, in fact, that Chesley's sister had not
yet come down. They were greeted at the door instead by
a beautiful young lady who kissed Chesley with great affection.

She introduced herself to Viviana and Signor Alessandri as Lady Alice Melville, Chesley's niece. Lady Alice was
a trim, tall brunet who appeared to be just past thirty. Her
eyes, however, looked far older. Viviana sensed that this
was a woman who had known both joy and grief, and felt
an immediate affinity for her.

After a few pleasantries, Chesley and Lord Digleby
drifted off to visit the cook, Mrs. Prater, to make sure she
was serving her famous curried crab.

"How kind of you to come to our little family affair,"
Lady Alice said. She took Viviana by the arm as if they
were the best of friends, then smiled at Viviana's father.
"Have the two of you been in England long?"

"We arrive just—ah, what is the word?—*si,* a se'night hence," said Signor Alessandri.

"Past, Papà," said Viviana gently.

"Si, a se'night past," he agreed. "We come, my daughter and I, with her . . . her *bambini,* to the *porto* of Southampton. It is my first time, Lady Alice, to see your beautiful country."

She had led them into a glittering, elegantly appointed drawing room which had been thrown open to the two small parlors on either side. Everywhere Viviana looked, polished silver and fine crystal gleamed, reflected in the candlelight by the floor-to-ceiling mirrors tucked between each exquisitely draped window. It was all rather grand, she mused, for a simple neighborly gathering.

Apprehensively, she took the glass of wine which Lady Alice pressed into her hand. "I understand you know my uncle well," Lady Alice was remarking to Viviana's father. "And I know he admires your work, *signore.*"

"Ah, Lord Chesley and I go back very long years," he said in his heavily accented English. "He is a great man, your uncle. All of Europe knows this."

Lady Alice's smile deepened. "And what of you, Contessa Bergonzi?" she asked. "Are you enjoying your visit to England?"

Viviana was beginning to feel a little ill. Everything looked so formal, so elegant. She had a sudden premonition of having made a grave misjudgment. Indeed, she had suspected it almost as soon as she accepted the invitation. *Chesley's sister!* Was she mad? But Chesley had many sisters, she had consoled herself. Six or seven, it was said. What were the chances that—

"Contessa?" Lady Alice Melville's voice came as if from far away. "Are you perfectly all right?"

"*Scusi?*" Viviana's head whipped around. "Oh, how rude of me! But this fresco around the drawing room, and the gilding on the ceiling—I think it quite the most elegant design I have ever seen."

Lady Alice beamed with pleasure. "Then you are in luck," she answered. "The architect who designed it is a friend of my brother's. Merrick MacLachlan. He will be here tonight, and you may tell him so yourself."

"A friend?" echoed Viviana. "Of your brother?"

Lady Alice snatched another glass of wine for herself from a passing waiter. "Yes, but Mr. MacLachlan is frightfully moody, as most people in the arts can be, of cour—" Then, as if realizing what she had just said, she flushed. "Oh, I do beg your pardon!"

Viviana managed to smile. "Ah, but a mere architect cannot hold a candle, I do assure you, to a *prima donna* in a black rage," she admitted.

Just then, Lord Chesley returned from the rear of the house, followed by four men in dark coats, all of them carrying stringed instruments. "Gwen has hired a quartet!" he said to no one in particular. "Look, Alessandri! We must help them set up."

Viviana's father looked relieved to have something to do which did not require a command of the English language. The three gentlemen were well occupied in their task in the back of the room when a small but sprightly old lady entered, hastening toward them. Out in the great hall, Viviana could here more guests arriving, and cheerful voices ringing down the grand staircase. Her anxiety began to ratchet sharply upward.

"Alice, my dear," said the old lady, regally presenting her cheek for a kiss. "How glad I am to see you out of those dreary blacks and back into a proper gown. You look lovely."

"Thank you, Aunt Charlotte," she said. Quickly, the introductions were made. Viviana exchanged a few pleasant words with the old lady, who then espied Lord Chesley and the gentlemen in the rear of the room and went haring off in that direction.

"I beg your pardon, Lady Alice," said Viviana when her aunt had gone. "May I collect that you are recently widowed?"

Lady Alice looked instantly pained. "I—yes, just over a year ago," she said. "It was sudden."

"My sympathies," said Viviana. "I know the difficulties you must suffer. I, too, am widowed, though not so recently."

Lady Alice gave a watery smile. "One hates it for one's children's sake," she said. "Mine are so very young. They do not quite understand why their dear papa has been taken from them."

Viviana could have made the argument that her children were no worse off—certainly, Cerelia was not—but she said nothing of the sort. Instead, she set one hand lightly on Lady Alice's arm. "But children are very resilient," she said. "I know this firsthand. I have three, and all are well."

"I have three also!" said Lady Alice. "How old are your children, Contessa?"

"My daughters are eight and six," she said. "And my son is four going on ten. Perhaps you know what I mean?"

Lady Alice nodded with alacrity. "They are almost the same ages as mine," she said. "We really must visit."

"I should like that," said Viviana truthfully.

"My children will be pleased to find new playmates so near at hand."

"Yes, it is but a short drive," said Viviana. "Will you be staying here long?"

"Six or eight weeks, I daresay," said Alice. "And it is a short drive, but a far shorter walk if one comes through the wood in between. There is a well-marked bridle path which we all use to go back and forth to Hill Court. I am told my parents wore it to a rut when they were courting."

The quartet was tuning up, and black-clad footmen were everywhere. Some two dozen guests were drifting through the drawing room now, greeting one another with handshakes, and even kisses. There were no strangers here. Viviana was feeling very much out of place, and even more uneasy when she saw Chesley approach.

"My dear, you really must come with me," he said, setting a hand on her arm. "The cellist is playing a Guadagnini!"

"Is he indeed?"

"Yes, can you believe it? Here, in a backwater like Buckinghamshire!"

Viviana flashed her new acquaintance a parting smile. "*Piacere,* Lady Alice!" she said. "You must call on us at Hill Court."

Alice brightened. "Tomorrow, then?" she suggested. "Would that be too soon?"

Viviana looked at Chesley expectantly.

"My home is yours, Alice," said her uncle impatiently. "You may move in if you wish."

Alice laughed. "But you are taking away the most interesting person in the room, uncle!" she protested.

Chesley's gaze, however, had turned toward the entrance to the withdrawing room. "Oh, I think not tonight, my dear," he said quietly. "I believe our guest of honor has arrived."

"The guest of honor?" said Viviana. She had not realized there was one.

Chesley was staring at a young lady in a silver-gray silk gown who had just stepped hesitantly into the room. She was slender, and almost diminutive, but elegant in her simplicity. Her light brown hair was twisted into an artful arrangement, and entwined with a strand of pearls. A second strand encircled her throat. She looked lovely. She looked, in fact, like the perfect English miss.

"Behold Mamma's long-sought prize," Alice whispered. "Miss Esmée Hamilton, Quin's bride-to-be."

"She is an heiress, too, is she not?" murmured Chesley.

"Yes, Lady Tatton's niece."

The words were sinking slowly into Viviana's brain. *Quin. Bride. Heiress.* Oh, dear God. Viviana's knees almost buckled.

"Well, she's pretty enough, I'll warrant," Chesley grumbled. "But she looks nothing at all like his usual type."

Alice laughed. "Oh, come now, Uncle Ches!" she said. "You are a man of the world, are you not? Men may keep company with one sort of woman, but they wed a different sort altogether."

Viviana felt herself begin to tremble with inner rage, but it was not Alice with whom she was angry.

"Oh, I daresay," said Chesley. "By the way, Vivie, you

do remember Quin, do you not? My nephew Quin Hewitt? He once had quite a tender for you, as I recall."

"Quin Hewitt?" Viviana managed. "Why, I . . . yes, I remember him well."

Alice shot her a sharp, curious look. "Is it true?" she asked. "Was Quin in love with you?"

Chesley, damn him, barked with laughter. "Oh, *he* thought so!" said the earl. "For a time, I feared I'd be obliged to pack the puppy up and send him back home to his papa. But Vivie here kept spurning him, and Quin eventually sought an introduction to the many pleasures of Town."

"Yes, and they became closely acquainted, too!" said Alice dryly.

"Indeed." Chesley gave a weak grin. "Always a reliable distraction for bored young blades, eh?" He winked at Alice, but she did not spare him a glance. Instead, she was studying Viviana, her expression unreadable.

"You and my rakehell brother!" she said musingly. "How romantic and intriguing this sounds, Contessa."

"It was neither," Viviana returned. "It was silly. I was an opera singer, Lady Alice. Do you understand what that means?"

"Why, I daresay it means you sing well," said Alice with a muted smile. Then, casually, she lifted one shoulder. "In any case, Quin is Lord Wynwood now, and Mamma is keen for him to marry. I collect it was she who chose Miss Hamilton."

"Well, of course she did!" said Chesley impatiently.

"Quin swears she did not."

"Oh, Quin wouldn't come within a mile of a parson if he hadn't a pistol to his back, the title bedamned," said the earl. "Now, come along, Vivie, do. You really *must* see this cello. Now, it is by *Lorenzo* mind. Not the son. But Umberto says he has never heard the like."

She went, because she had little choice. And because it was better to be in the rear of the room than in the front; better to put as much space between her and Quin's pale, pretty fiancée as was possible. Viviana was shocked and appalled. Shocked by her own stupidity in coming here, and by her physical, very visceral reaction to the news. And appalled by the awful, ugly feeling of jealousy surging in her chest. She could have yanked the pearls from Miss Hamilton's mouse brown hair, and cheerfully strangled her with them. It was irrational, and it was unfair. But there it was; petty envy, the ugliest human vice, laid bare. And after nine long years! How mortifying.

Mechanically, she offered her hand to the cellist, who seemed overawed to meet her. They exchanged a few words, which she barely heard, then Chesley intervened with a question about strings or tension or some damned thing. Still quaking inside, Viviana turned to set her wineglass on a small side table, before she dropped it altogether. In that instant, however, from the corner of her eye, she saw him.

Quin. Oh, *dio!* She should have turned away, but she could not. Her heart had begun to trip. The air in the room seemed to vanish. She felt as though the entire crowd watched her. But she, fool that she was, could watch no one but Quin.

He was no longer the beautiful boy she remembered. Oh, no. He was larger and harder and harsher and every other masculine superlative she could think of, in either

English or Italian. His heavy dark hair was just a little too long, and his face was hard and unsmiling.

But he smiled when he joined the young lady—his fiancée—at the entrance to the room. Of course, he towered over the girl. She looked up at him gratefully and took the arm he offered. In response, he laid one hand protectively over hers—a gallant, artless gesture.

He was fond of her. Even a fool could see that. Viviana swallowed hard, and felt something hot and horrifying well up behind her eyes. *Men may keep company with one sort of woman,* Lady Alice had said. *But they wed a different sort altogether.*

Oh, this girl was a different sort, to be sure. She and Viviana could not have been more dissimilar.

They were making their way around the crowd. Quin was introducing her to his friends and family, smiling and nodding to each person in turn as he did so. Dear God. It was just a matter of time.

Viviana felt for an instant as if she might faint. Then, on her next breath, she cursed herself for her cowardice. Good God, he was nothing to her now! He was just another arrogant, insufferable Englishman. In the years since her ill-conceived relationship with Quin had ended, she had molded herself into a different person. She was rich, successful, and—so she was told—still very beautiful. She was but thirty-three years old. The best of life might yet lie ahead of her.

Somewhat fortified by those recollections, Viviana steeled her expression and pushed her shoulders very rigidly and very stubbornly backward until her chest was open and her chin was up. She looked every inch a diva now, a pose she reserved for only the hardest of roles. Well, they came no harder than this. She would be damned before she let Quin Hewitt see her falter.

She realized the instant he saw her. His eyes flashed, dark and hard. Oddly, he did not look twice, as one might have expected. Indeed, he barely looked surprised. Her chin still lifted, she shot him a calm, vaguely condescending look.

Quin did not look calm. He hesitated but a moment, then set his hand over his fiancée's. After speaking a few low words near her ear, he returned her to the attractive, middle-aged woman with whom she had arrived, then turned on his heel and walked out. Viviana exhaled the deep breath she had not realized she was holding.

Viviana spent the next quarter hour going through the motions of meeting Chesley's friends and neighbors and endeavoring to say something witty and charming to each. It was not difficult. She had become adept at the mundane these last few years and able to veil her true emotions with a practiced ease.

Just then, Chesley touched her lightly on the elbow. She turned, and was introduced to a tall, slender woman of uncertain years. She knew at once it was Quin's mother. She had the same dark blue eyes, and looked very like Lady Alice in the face.

Lady Wynwood. Yes, Wynwood was the name of the title Quin was to inherit. She remembered it now. Viviana gave a slight curtsy, though by rights and by rank, she need not have done so. Lady Wynwood was warm, if a little distant. She quickly turned her full attention to Chesley, fussing over him if she were his mother instead of his elder sister.

To Viviana's horror, however, she had no sooner departed than Alice's elderly aunt, Lady Charlotte, approached with Quin's fiancée in tow. After speaking a few teasing words to the young woman, Chesley slid a hand beneath her elbow and steered her in Viviana's direction. Viviana held her breath again.

"My dear, may I introduce my nephew's intended bride, Miss Hamilton?" he said. "Miss Hamilton, the Contessa Viviana Bergonzi di Vicenza."

The young woman curtsied very prettily. "It is an honor, ma'am."

Viviana refused to let herself falter. "My felicitations on your betrothal, Miss Hamilton," she said. "I wish you many years of happiness in your marriage."

The young woman looked at a spot somewhere near Viviana's hems. "Thank you, my lady."

"You must forgive us for intruding on what was obviously meant to be a family celebration," Viviana continued. "Chesley did not perfectly explain the occasion."

Miss Hamilton lifted her gaze, eyes widening. "Oh, don't rake me over the coals, Vivie," said the earl. "I can't keep up. What difference does it make?"

Viviana looked at Chesley. "Why, none at all, I'm sure," she said coolly. "Miss Hamilton seems all that is amiable."

Just then, they were called to dinner.

"Thank God!" said Aunt Charlotte. "I'm famished. Come along, girl. You can acquaint yourself with the others after dinner. Oh, I do hope Mrs. Prater has made her curried crab tonight."

Knees still wobbly, Viviana brought up the rear, following Chesley and the other guests into the corridor. Everyone was chattering gaily as they made their way toward the dining room. Suddenly, from the shadows, a hand grabbed her arm. Viviana found herself jerked into an unlit alcove. She looked up into Quin's angry eyes and lifted her chin.

"Madam, you have a great deal of nerve," he said icily. "How dare you try to ruin this?"

Viviana tried to jerk her arm from his grasp. "Don't be a fool, Quinten," she said coolly. "Release my arm this instant."

Instead, he pulled her closer, his nostrils flaring with rage.

"Quin, *basta!*" She tore from his grasp. "The others are leaving us."

"I know how to find the goddamned dining room, Viviana," he rasped. "It's my bloody house."

"*Si, caro mio,* and I suspect you never let anyone forget it."

He set his hand on the opposite wall and leaned into her. "I shan't let you forget it, that's bloody certain."

"Oh, trust me, Quinten," she whispered darkly. "That is one thing I have never forgotten. Your rank. Your wealth. Your unassailable British *privilege*. I did, however, make the mistake of forgetting your title, and now I see I'm to pay for it."

His face contorted unpleasantly. "You liar! You never forgot a damned thing you thought you could use to your advantage."

Suddenly, his meaning dawned on her. "Oh, *Dio!* You aren't simply mad!" she said. "You are disgusting, and you are delusional. I could buy and sell you twice over, Quin Hewitt. Trust me, you have *nothing* I want."

True anger flared in his eyes then. "What I want, my lady, is to see you in private," he growled. "Tomorrow morning. In my study."

Viviana lifted both brows, and stared at him in haughty disdain. *"Veramente,* Quin?" Her voice was coolly disdainful. "I think you forget I am no longer yours to command."

"Eight o'clock," he growled. "Or I shall come to you, Viviana. Will your precious *Papá* wonder why?"

Viviana's eyes flared wide. *"You bastard,"* she whispered. "Are you threatening me?"

"My study is on the ground floor," he said, moving as if to leave her. "In the back, sixth window from the left. Use it, Viviana. Else I shall be knocking on the door of Hill Court and rousing every bloody one of you dilettantes from your beds, the venerable Alessandri included."

Just then, a shadow fell across the corridor. "Quin, old chap," said a dry, masculine voice. "Have you forgotten that your dinner guests are being seated?"

Viviana looked up into the eyes of an extraordinarily handsome blond-haired gentleman. He tilted his head in her direction. "Contessa Bergonzi, I believe?" he said quietly. "Sir Alasdair MacLachlan at your service. I think you'd best take my arm, don't you?"

Five

In which Mr. MacLachlan gives Good Advice.

Sir Alasdair MacLachlan was waiting, both barrels loaded, in the dining room after dinner. After sending Esmée upstairs with her aunt, Quin joined him there. There was, after all, no avoiding it.

Alasdair's brother, Merrick, poured all three of them a brandy, then sat back on one of the worn leather sofas as if anticipating a great entertainment. Alasdair was pacing back and forth before the fire, his face dark as storm clouds. In the room, anger smoldered like green kindling. Quin could not claim to be surprised. Alasdair had looked daggers at him all throughout the meal. And if Alasdair was looking for a quarrel tonight, Quin was of half a mind to oblige him.

But Scots were sly, and Alasdair especially adept. "A fine meal, Quin," he began. "And your Mamma's toast! So touching. I think Lady Tatton actually shed a tear."

Quin sat down opposite Merrick and exchanged glances with him. "Yes, Mamma is quite in alt," he replied, wondering what Alasdair was getting at. "It is a relief, to be sure. She has not been happy in a very long time."

Alasdair turned on one heel and went to the window. The servants had not yet drawn the drapes against the evening's chill, and, for a long moment, he simply stared out into the night and sipped at his brandy. "Correct me if I am wrong, Quin," he finally said. "But was that not Viviana Alessandri you had cornered in the alcove near the library?"

"Contessa Bergonzi, yes."

"Your mistress." The words were flat.

Quin hesitated. "She once was."

"Well, if the look in your eyes was any indication, old friend, you very much wish she still was." Alasdair dropped his voice to a whisper. "And I'll tell you here and now, Quin, I won't have it."

"*You* won't have it?" Quin's voice was incredulous. "I should like to know what business it is of yours if I have a dozen mistresses?"

Quin watched Alasdair's form quake with rage. God damn it, it wanted only this! He had an overwrought, meddling mother, a perfect fiancée who seemed suddenly not so perfect, and a coldhearted mistress who had picked the world's most inopportune moment to stroll back into his life. Wasn't his existence complicated enough without his best friend throwing more thorns in the thicket? And what the devil was wrong with Alasdair, anyway?

Finally, Alasdair turned around. "So help me God, Quin," he said, "if you take up with that Italian Jezebel again whilst you and Esmée are affianced—or worse, *married*—then you and I will be meeting at Chalk Farm one cold dawn. Do you understand me?"

"What I understand, Alasdair, is that my marriage is none of your goddamned business," he returned. "But I wouldn't have that spiteful bitch if she crawled to me on her hands and knees—and she was far from doing that, I do assure you."

Alasdair turned nasty then, setting his glass aside with an awkward *thunk*. "I *heard* you, you lying bastard," he answered, stalking toward him. "First, you all but ignore Esmée. Then I hear you arranging to meet Contessa Bergonzi in secret."

"I want to talk to her, yes," Quin responded. "We've things to sort out, she and I. But again, that is none of your bloody business, is it?"

Alasdair grabbed him by the coat collar. "You are betrothed to a good and gentle girl," he growled, dragging Quin to his feet. "And tonight you could barely spare her a glance. Humiliate her, hurt her, or even just mildly *annoy* her again, and so help me God, I will kill you."

"Oh, sod off, Alasdair! This is beyond the pale."

From the sofa, Merrick made a sound of disgust. "Need I remind you two addlepates that this house is full of guests and servants?"

Quin didn't give a damn about his guests and servants. Instead, he wished Alasdair would just take a swing at him. Why wait for Chalk Farm? He wanted desperately to pound the living hell out of something, and he was growing increasingly indiscriminate about who or what that something might be. Roughly, Quin shoved back.

Alasdair planted five fingertips in Quin's chest. "Name your second, old chap."

Merrick was on his feet now, wedging an arm between them. "Oh, for God's sake!" he said. "Alasdair, you are acting like a loutish schoolboy."

"Aye, that I am," said Alasdair, giving Quin a hearty push with both hands. "And perhaps I'll just black his eye now to make him mindful of my shortcoming, eh?"

Quin's every nerve was on edge. He shoved Alasdair back. "Have at it, then, you thickheaded Scot!" he growled. "If you wanted Esmée Hamilton, why the hell didn't *you* marry her?"

At that, something in Alasdair seemed to snap. He thrust Merrick aside and had Quin by the throat before he knew it. Somehow, Quin shoved him away, got an arm back, and swung. The blow caught Alasdair beneath the chin, snapping his head back.

"Oh, for God's sake, you fools!" Merrick was still trying to push them apart.

Bloodlust surged through Quin then, hot and compelling. He drew back again, swinging for all he was worth. It was a solid uppercut to the left jaw, which sent Alasdair reeling. He hitched up against one of the high-backed chairs, arms wheeling. Deftly, Merrick snatched a vase of tulips from his path. Alasdair righted himself and came at Quin again.

Another exchange of blows, and somehow, Alasdair got his arms round Quin's waist, hauling him into the floor. The fistfight was reduced to schoolboy wrestling, including a great deal of grunting, flailing, and kicking. Over and over they tumbled, like bad-tempered curs after a bread scrap.

Somehow, Quin got Alasdair by his cravat and tried to bloody his nose by pounding his head on the carpet. Alasdair responded with a ruthless jerk of his knee, nearly rendering the debate over Quin's marriage moot. Quin yelped with pain, and Alasdair scrabbled to his feet.

"You son of a bitch!" Quin caught him by the ankle and managed to pull off one of Alasdair's shoes. Alasdair was hopping about for balance when Merrick burst into laughter and fell back onto the sofa, still holding the tulips.

Quin leapt up, hurled the shoe toward the fire, and went after Alasdair. He backed him up against the dictionary stand, sending it crashing. Merrick, who was getting up from the sofa, tripped over the book. Alasdair tried to seize the moment, and let fly a lame left hook, boxing Quin's ear.

"Ouch, damn you!" he said, just before Alasdair came after him again, both fists swinging.

Finally, Merrick got an arm round his elder brother's waist and dragged him away. "Enough, gentlemen!" he ordered. "This is pathetic. Quin, go up to bed."

"No."

Merrick's eyes flashed. "If the two of you wish to beat one another to a bloody pulp, Quin, do it tomorrow," he ordered. "And for God's sake, do it where your servants won't be listening."

"I think we ought to finish it here and now!" Alasdair growled.

"Oh, aye, and you profess such concern for Miss Hamilton's welfare!" said Merrick sarcastically. "How typical of you, Alasdair! This ugly little set-to will stir more gossip and do her more harm than anything Quin has done tonight."

Alasdair's face flooded with color at that. The fight

went out of Quin. Merrick let his brother go. Alasdair jerked at his lapels as if to neaten his coat, but he looked beaten.

"The two of you are squabbling like children over nothing but pride," said Merrick accusingly. "Never in my life have I seen such a sorry excuse of a fight between ostensibly grown men. And it leaves me to wonder if either of you give a damn about Miss Hamilton."

Quin felt suddenly ashamed. The awful truth was, he wasn't fighting over Miss Hamilton. Indeed, he was not at all sure *what* he was so angry about. Ill luck? Ill timing? Certainly, it had little to do with Alasdair.

"You are quite right, Merrick," he quietly admitted. "Alasdair, you have been a complete ass tonight, but I daresay I have topped you, and for that, I apologize."

"Apology accepted," Alasdair gritted. "And go bugger yourself."

Quin bowed stiffly. Good God, his jaw hurt. "Gentlemen, I shall say good night," he managed. "Please make yourselves at home."

Merrick had replaced the tulips, righted the dictionary, and found his abandoned brandy, which he now polished off in one toss. "I believe I will join you, old chap," he said, setting the empty glass on the sideboard. "Alasdair, I'd suggest you do the same. Neither of you are fit company for civilized society tonight."

"I want another drink," his brother snapped.

Merrick just shook his head. They went quietly up the stairs, Quin and Merrick, neither speaking. There seemed nothing left to say. It had been the second-worst day of Quin's life, and he would be glad to see the end of it. With a curt good night to Merrick, he entered his bedchamber, stripped off his clothes, and hurled them across a chair. Blevins could deal with them tomorrow.

But the elegant, half-tester bed looked very large and very empty when he drew back the covers. He sat down on the edge of the mattress and tried to envision Esmée beside him, naked and waiting. Tried to imagine what it would be like to make love to her, this young woman who was to be his wife. But tonight, it seemed an oddly bizarre notion, like trying to have sex with a dainty china doll. Mere days ago, he had been almost eager to bed the girl. Tonight, he had barely been able to look her in the eyes. What had changed?

It was Viviana. The bad taste her reappearance had left in his mouth. She had come back, and at a most inopportune time.

Well, it was a free country, he supposed. Perhaps he had overreacted. Nine long years had passed, and he was well beyond the bitterness. Why had he demanded to see her again? What could they possibly have to discuss after all this time? He had meant it when he had said he wouldn't have her if she crawled back on her knees.

But Viviana had looked disinclined to go anywhere on her knees. She had looked as prideful and as spiteful as ever. Certainly she did not look like the kind of woman who would ever beg anyone for anything. Indeed, the one thing she had most wanted—a wealthy, titled husband— she had never begged for. Oh, she had asked him to marry her. Once. He had said no, and that had been the end of it. Viviana had promptly exercised her prerogative to move on to greener pastures. And her Italian count had been very verdant indeed.

Quin had been angry at first, yes. And terribly hurt,

more than he had ever admitted to anyone. It had taken him a long while to admit that Viviana's decision had been for the best. It had been time, really, for their relationship to end. He had been growing increasingly discontent with his secret mistress. And the word *mistress* was perhaps an overstatement. The truth was, he had paid Viviana's rent—after he'd badgered her out of her respectable, but not very private, ladies' lodging house—and he had given her gifts of jewelry, which she had never asked for and had promptly sold.

He now understood that that was not quite the same thing as employing a practiced courtesan, a far more costly affair. But then he had been young and foolish.

Yes, perhaps tonight he had simply overreacted. Seeing her again, in her sumptuous red silk gown, with that black cashmere shawl which kept sliding to the crooks of her elbows almost invitingly—yes, all of it had hurled him back nine years in a mere instant.

It was astonishing how little she had changed. She had even worn those ever-present rubies dangling from her ears. Strikingly tall and stunningly voluptuous, Viviana had worn her raven hair drawn back in its usual sleek, unfashionably formal arrangement, and carried herself, as always, with a queenly grace. But her face—something about it had changed somehow. It had seemed to possess just a shade less elegance, but a great deal more strength.

In the past, Viviana had always put him in mind of some Renaissance madonna, come to life from an artist's altarpiece. Vibrantly hued, yet pure and sacrosanct. Above his, or anyone else's, touch. But all that had been an illusion. Anyone with enough money could touch Viviana. If her *affaire* with Quin did not prove that much, her marriage to Conte Gianpiero Bergonzi di Vicenza certainly did. Bergonzi was a man known for his wealth and his power and his worship of beautiful things—but never had he been known for his benevolence. Perhaps he and Viviana had deserved one another.

Or perhaps she had regretted her choice.

For a moment, he considered it. Had Viviana loved her husband? Had he enticed her back to Venice to be with him? Or had Quin simply driven her away? Well. He would never know, would he? Certainly he was not going to ask her, no matter how much the question ate at him. Feeling suddenly weighed down by it all, Quin bowed his head, closed his eyes, and quietly cursed beneath his breath.

The carriage ride back to Lord Chesley's country house was uneventful. The gentlemen amused themselves by rattling on about the Guadagnini cello. Musically, Viviana did not favor the cello, so she sat quietly in her corner, peering out into the moonlit gloom of the countryside and considering the thing which Quin Hewitt had demanded. She could have refused him, of course. She was not afraid of him. Not really. The trouble was, simple curiosity was overcoming her better judgment.

"Chesley," she said when the conversation lulled, "I should like to go riding tomorrow."

"By all means, my dear," said her host.

Lord Digleby brightened. "I shall accompany you, Contessa," he said. "I adore a brisk autumn ride."

Viviana tried to look grateful. "*Grazie,* Lord Digleby, but I mean to go very early," she said. "I wish to see the sunrise and should not want to disturb you."

Lord Digleby did not look like the sort of fellow who rose before dawn. "Another time, then?" he suggested, covering a yawn. "I shall need my rest, I am sure. Your father and I mean to begin work on *Nel Pomeriggio* in earnest tomorrow."

"And you must put the opera first, by all means," said Viviana, turning to her host. "Chesley, I believe I should like to ride in that little wood to the east of the house. Do I understand you have a bridle path there?"

"How will you see the sunrise through all the trees, Contessa?" asked Digleby innocently.

Viviana smiled tightly. "First I shall watch the sunrise. Then I shall ride in the wood."

"There are bridle paths everywhere, my dear," said Chesley with a vague wave of his hand. "Just avoid the one that branches due north, or you'll be halfway to Wendover before you see another living soul. Ask one of the grooms to direct you."

Once inside the house, Viviana kissed her father, then left the gentlemen in the drawing room with a bottle of *porto* and a fistful of fine cheroots. Her father looked content and comfortable. That was reassuring.

Upstairs, Viviana checked on the children, all of whom slept soundly. As usual, Cerelia had pushed all her bedcovers onto the floor and lay curled in a tight ball. She was cold now, of course. After creeping quietly round the bed, Viviana shook out the covers and gently replaced them. As she bent over to tuck the counterpane round the child's neck, she noticed the faint glint of metal. With a rueful smile, she gently lifted the gold chain away. Cerelia did not stir. Viviana dropped the weight of it into her pocket, then set the backs of her fingers to the girl's check.

She marveled at the warmth and the softness. Cerelia was such a lovely child, inside and out. But Cerelia was not her favorite. No, not exactly that. Viviana loved all her children with an equal ferocity. And yet Cerelia was special to her in a way she could not quite explain, even to herself.

She wondered if she had made a mistake in bringing the children to England. The choice had torn at her heart. Stay with her children in Venice and leave her father to travel alone? Or surrender them to the care of servants whilst she followed him to England? Neither alternative had been acceptable. And so Viviana had compromised, just as she had been doing all of her life.

She wondered how long it would be before the children became bored with the cold English countryside. At present, the gardens and the surrounding woodlands were new and exhilarating. But soon they would wish for the familiar, and for playmates, too, no doubt. Lady Alice Melville and her brood would not likely be calling now. Quin would surely put a stop to that. He probably did not consider the children of an Italian opera singer fit companions for his fine English family.

Impulsively, Viviana went round the room, kissing each child on the cheek. Nicolo had his thumb in his mouth again. Gently she pulled it out. The boy slept on. Felise stirred faintly, but did not awaken. They were beautiful, her children. And she dared anyone to suggest otherwise within her hearing.

"*Buona notte,* my darlings," she whispered, pulling the door shut.

Once inside her own bedchamber, Viviana did not ring for her maid. Instead, after tucking Cerelia's necklace safely away, she stirred up the fire and lit the branch of candles atop the mantel. Then slowly she undressed before the gilt cheval glass, dropping her clothes into puddles of black and red across the floor and studying her body as it was revealed. It had been a long time since she had studied her figure naked. It had not seemed to matter very much. She was not perfectly sure why she bothered to look now.

At last, the final undergarment fell away, leaving Viviana in nothing but her black silk stockings. She let her gaze run slowly up her body. No man had seen her thus since Gianpiero's death. And for the last six years of their marriage, they had more or less lived emotionally apart; separate people living separate lives beneath one roof. But no matter how she begged, Gianpiero had refused to let her leave him. He had demanded his son. *His heir.* She had owed him that, she supposed. And so she had suffered his coming to her bed in the dark, and forcibly joining his body to hers. She had suffered other things, too. Things she would sooner not remember. Perhaps it was what she deserved. Perhaps it was the price one paid for marrying a man one did not—and could not—love.

Calmly, almost detached, Viviana slid her hands beneath her breasts and lifted them as she watched herself in the mirror. Assuredly, the years had changed her. But she was still a beautiful woman. Wasn't she? Countless men had told her so. But when one was wealthy, one could never be sure of sincerity. Since Gianpiero's death, she had received more proposals, both honorable and otherwise, than she could count. Some of them had even seemed heartfelt. Gaspard had merely been the most recent.

But naked in the candlelight, the truth was plain to Viviana. She was thirty-three years old. She had borne three children. And it showed. Yes, she was still a beautiful woman. But she would never again be the woman she had been nine years ago. Viviana turned from the mirror, picked up her nightdress from the chair, and swiftly drew it on. She did not like looking at the imperfections time had wrought.

She went to the dressing table and poured herself half a glass of Barolo from the decanter she kept at hand. Then she reconsidered and filled it to the brim. Slowly, she sipped it, and recalled the evening's events. It had been almost cathartic to see Quin Hewitt tonight, once the initial shock was over. She had rather enjoyed their little spat, loath though she was to admit it. They had always quarreled passionately—and made love passionately, too. But he was in her past. Tonight had served as a harsh reminder of that. And really, what did she care? She was no longer that rash, romantic young woman.

In the years since leaving him, her whole existence had changed. Viviana had married into the pinnacle of Venetian aristocracy. She had borne three beautiful children. She had brought half of Europe's royalty to tears with her voice and her passion; that same passion with which she had once loved. And she had learnt too well that opera was a better and far safer outlet for that sort of unrestrained emotion.

And now the mighty Lord Wynwood wished to speak with her. Well, she would go to his study at eight o'clock tomorrow, just as he had demanded. Not because she was afraid of him. She was not. She was just inordinately curious. She really did not believe Quin would tell her father any of the ugly truths he had threatened her with. He would realize soon enough that Viviana meant him no ill. Indeed, he would soon forget she was nearby, for she would take great pains to stay out of his way—after she satisfied her curiosity in this one thing.

Viviana slid between the cool bedsheets, her wine in hand, and considered again Quin's ugly accusation. He believed she had planned their meeting tonight. He was wrong—but perhaps not entirely so. It galled her to admit the truth. But intuitively, she must have been hoping to see him, or at least to hear news of him. There was no other answer, if she were honest with herself. She had had one whole day in which to ask Chesley which of his sisters they would be visiting. And yet, she had not done so. Chesley would have easily released her from her obligation. Or she could have pleaded a headache at the last moment.

Instead she had learnt something she would as soon not have known. That her old love—her only love—was newly betrothed, and to a girl who was at least a dozen years younger than Viviana. A lovely young thing, fresh from the country, just as he had always said. An heiress who wore pearls in her hair. A pale, pretty child-bride whose breasts were still small and high, and whose belly did not yet bear the marks of childbearing.

It was too much to think about. Viviana drained her wine, set the glass on the night table, and tried not to cry. It really was quite lowering to have such horrid, horrid emotions. She really had expected more grace and more pride from herself. Why? And, *per amor di Dio,* why now? Never once had Viviana mourned her lost youth. And yet now she wanted to weep for it.

Six

In which Contessa Bergonzi lashes out.

Quin made his way to the breakfast parlor just after dawn, in desperate hope of finding a cup of coffee and avoiding the rest of the household in the process. The latter was to be denied him. Aunt Charlotte had beaten him there and was flitting about like a frail bird, inspecting each chafing dish as the servants carried it in.

"Good morning, Quin," she sang from one of the massive sideboards. "The eggs are prepared just as you like them. Will you join me?"

Quin had already gone to the coffeepot. "No, ma'am, I thank you," he said. "I have work to do in my study. I shall just take a cup of coffee with me."

Aunt Charlotte's small, dark eyes twinkled. "Yes, you will wish to spend the day with your Miss Hamilton, will you not?" she responded. "She is a lovely girl, my boy. Your mamma is quite overjoyed. Of course, I have reassured Gwendolyn many times over the years that you would do the right thing, Quin, when the time came."

Quin set his cup on a saucer and tried to smile. "I am

glad I did not disappoint you, ma'am," he said. "After all, I have been disappointing my mother with appalling regularity for at least two decades. Now, if you will excuse me, duty calls."

It was a long walk to the oldest wing of the house, where his study was located. Quin pushed the door open on silent hinges, put his coffee on the desk, and went to the French windows, which opened onto the back gardens. The servants had not yet come into this room to build up a fire or open the draperies. They had been told by his mother, he suspected, that everyone would wish to remain abed late into the morning. A pity he had not been able to do so. But he had known from the moment he set eyes on Viviana last night that sleep would elude him. And if he was to suffer, by God, *she* could suffer. In the past, she had been unaccustomed to rising much before noon, and he rather doubted that had changed.

With a sweep of his arm, he pushed back the pleats of fabric to reveal the dawning day. The gardens were taking shape now; he could see his mother's prized rose garden, brown and dormant, and beyond it, the Tudor knot garden, which had faded to a dull shade of green. The sky was turning purple, the horizon blushing a bright pink beneath. The half-moon which had been visible upon his arising had vanished, and beyond the gardens the west wood loomed, still steeped in shadows.

He stood at the window, cradling the warm coffee in one palm as the wintry air radiated off the glass, cold and bracing on his face. He drew the air deep into his lungs, hoping it would clear his mind as well. This was a fool's errand. He knew it now. He half hoped Viviana would not come.

But she would. Not because she feared him, but because she was proud and stubborn and sometimes even foolish. And she would come, he supposed, from the direction of the trees. Someone, surely, would direct her to the short-cut? At this hour, the wood would be gloomy but penetrable. The path was clearly marked. The walk would take less than half an hour. But Chesley kept a good stable. Perhaps Viviana would ride. *Did* Viviana ride?

It struck him as odd that he did not know. There had been a time when he had believed he knew everything one could know about Viviana. But his had been a young man's confidence, born of arrogance and naïveté. In truth, he had known nothing of her, save for the beauty of her body and the taste of her mouth beneath his.

Just then, he saw her. She had tied her horse just inside the wood, he guessed. She was sauntering across the grass, a riding crop in her gloved hand, and a square-crowned, almost masculine hat set slightly to one side, as she always preferred. Her riding habit, too, was plain to the point of mannishness; a skirt and jacket, cut snugly to her figure and absent the almost comically full sleeves currently in vogue with English ladies. She did not bother to pick up her skirts in one hand, but instead let them trail across the dry, stubbled grass.

She did not knock, either. Instead, she simply opened the door and stepped inside. *"Buon giorno,* Quinten," she said in her rich, throaty voice. "I have come. What do you want of me?"

Suddenly, the anger rushed at him again, propelled by her dark beauty and haughty disdain. "I want to know the truth, Viviana." His voice was cool. "I want to know why you are here."

She cocked one slashing black brow, and looked at him as if he were a simpleton. "I am *here* because you bade me come," she responded. "I am in England because Lord Chesley wishes it. And I am in this village because I had no notion your estates were adjacent. You may believe that or not, as you please."

"Why?" he demanded. "What does Chesley want?"

Viviana pursed her lips for a moment. "I do not think, Quinten, that I need tell you more," she answered. "But for old times' sake, I tell you that Chesley has commissioned an opera, a very grand bel canto opera, and he has asked my father's help."

"Ah, yes!" said Quin. "The great composer, Umberto Alessandri, and his Cyprian daughter. You have a lot of nerve coming back to England, Viviana."

Her backhanded slap caught him squarely across the cheek but Quin did not so much as flinch. "Tell me, Viviana," he growled. "Does your beloved *Papà* know about us? Does he know what you were to me?"

Finally, he saw raw anger sketch across her face. *"Bastardo!"* she rasped. "My *Papà* knows what he needs to know. And if you take it upon yourself, Quinten, to tell him one word more, I swear to God, I will kill you with my bare hands!"

On that, she turned and yanked open the window as if to leave.

Quin grabbed her and almost dragged her back to the desk. "You still haven't explained why you are here, Viviana," he growled. "You are a singer, my dear. Not a composer. Do you think me too stupid to know the difference?"

"I came because my father needs me," she returned.

"Your uncle asked a favor of us, and we were glad to do it. God knows I owe him that much."

He set both hands roughly on her shoulders and held her eyes. "And my betrothal had nothing to do with it?" he demanded, giving her a little shake. "Tell me the truth, Viviana! I have a right to know."

She looked at him contemptuously. *"Per amor di Dio,* Quinten, what did I know of this betrothal?" she snapped. "What can it possibly mean to me? I fear you think too well of yourself if you imagine I have spared you a thought these last many years."

The derision in her voice was too much. He felt a powder keg of old emotions explode in his head. And then, somehow, his mouth was crushing hers. Viviana tried to shove at his shoulders, but reality had spun away, and there was only his frustration, raw and visceral. He drew in her scent, exotic and still too familiar, and urged her back against the desk.

Viviana moved as if to kick him, but he let his weight bear her down onto the desktop, and caught her wrists. It was as if a driving madness possessed him, compelling him to kiss her, possessively and openmouthed.

Beneath him, she shuddered and it felt, fleetingly, as if she relaxed. Quin plunged inside her mouth again, and felt lust go spiraling through him, stealing his breath and sending blood rushing. He felt as if he were drowning in her. Desperate for her. Every sense came alive, as if too long dormant. But beneath him, Viviana stiffened, and bit down on his lip. Pain snapped him back to reality.

With one last desperate jerk, she tore her face from his. *"Fa schifo!"* she spit, jerking up her knee as if to do him serious injury. *"Sporco!* Get off me, you bastard English pig!"

On a quiet curse, Quin shifted his weight away. Too late. Viviana had drawn back her hand and lashed her riding crop hard across his face.

Suddenly, there was a terrible *thud*. A short, sharp scream. Quin turned to see Aunt Charlotte lying across his threshold, her eyes rolled back in her head. Esmée stood in the corridor, her hand over her mouth. Two housemaids pressed in behind her, eyes agog.

Everything happened in a blur. Viviana shoved him away. She bolted across the carpet to Charlotte, the hems of her habit almost sending her sprawling. Esmée fell to her knees, the blood drained from her face.

He started toward them, but Viviana cried out, forestalling him. "Quin, you fool!" she said, stroking the hair from Charlotte's face. *"Basta! Basta!* Now you have killed your aunt!"

Esmée had her fingertips on the old woman's throat. "Her pulse is fluttering," she said. "But she is not dead."

Quin stood, frozen in horror. *Good God, what had he done now?*

Esmée looked over her shoulder at the gaping housemaids. "Shut the window," she snapped. "Wynwood, send someone to fetch a doctor. For God's sake, hurry!"

Quin was halfway to the door when Aunt Charlotte emitted a pitiful groan. "No . . . no doctor," she managed.

"Oh, *poveretta!*" Viviana murmured, rhythmically stroking the old lady's face. "Oh, *non ci credo!*"

Viviana looked stricken. Quin plunged into action, pushing his way past the housemaids and bolting for the great hall at a run. Dear God. His life was over. His servants had likely seen everything. Esmée would hate

him. Viviana already did. And now he had killed Aunt
Charlotte.

Quin lived much of the next half hour in turmoil, pacing
the floor in his mother's private sitting room as he waited
for the worst to happen. The footmen had carried his
great-aunt to his mother's suite, the nearest to hand, and
the immediate family had slowly gathered there, one by
one, their words whispered, their expressions stricken.
The aura of death seemed to surround them all, and Quin
knew it was his fault.

But Aunt Charlotte, as it happened, was made of
sterner stuff.

"Nothing is broken," pronounced Dr. Gould when at
last he came out of the bedchamber. "But her pulse is still
erratic, as it has often been this last decade or better. I wish
her to have a day's bed rest, and her usual heart tonic.
Tomorrow she'll be her old self, I hope."

Quin sagged with relief. "Oh, thank God!" said his
mother, clutching a crumpled handkerchief to her breast.
"Oh, I feared the worst!"

Quin's elderly aunts and uncles commenced a recita-
tion of Charlotte's many ailments, including her lifelong
propensity to faint at the slightest sight of blood—and
blood there had been, drawn quickly and viciously by
the lash of Viviana's whip. Reflexively, Quin ran his finger along the wound on his cheek. It was then that he
noticed his sister Alice, scowling darkly at him from her
corner of the room and twisting her own handkerchief
into knots.

"Remember, Helen, how Charlotte fainted and fell out

of the dogcart that time we ran over a squirrel?" one of his uncles rattled on.

"Oh, heavens yes!" said Great-aunt Helen. "She needed six stitches for that one!"

Suddenly, Esmée cleared her throat. "This was a terrible accident, too," she remarked in a clear, carrying voice. "Really, Wynwood, you ought not creep up on people like that. The contessa jerked instinctively, just as anyone would do."

The room fell deadly silent. Quin's mother was watching Esmée very oddly over her handkerchief. "Yes, a dreadful accident!" his mother finally echoed. "We are lucky Aunt Charlotte did not break a hip, Quin. Do have a care next time!"

"I'm sorry," he said for about the tenth time. "I'm just so bloody sorry."

The doctor scrubbed his hands together. "Well, I'd best be off then," he said. "I'll look in on Lady Charlotte tomorrow, just in case. She isn't getting any younger, you know."

Quin barely noticed when his family began to trickle from the room. His mother was still watching him warily, an unasked question in her eyes and a wounded expression on her face. The rumors were already out, then. The housemaids had assuredly seen something—and that which they'd not seen, their imaginations had likely supplied. His mother meant to rake him over the coals for it, too.

Well, she could hardly do worse than that which he wished to do to himself.

But he was to be spared his mother's ire, at least for the moment. Alice, God bless her, propelled her from the room after the others, murmuring something about seeing the children before breakfast.

He turned to stare through the window, looking out across the knot garden toward the trees, the same view he had held so intently this morning as he awaited Viviana's arrival. *Viviana.* Good God, what had he done? What had he been thinking? The damned woman still drove him insane!

But she had not come to England to torment him. Indeed, she really could not have cared less, and Quin did not know which notion angered him more.

She had vanished from his study this morning as soon as he had returned with the two footmen, giving Aunt Charlotte one last pitying look over her shoulder as she departed. She had not spared Quin so much as a glance.

Suddenly, a hand touched his shoulder, recalling him to the present. Quin's head whipped round, and he saw Esmée standing by his side. Good Lord, he had not realized that she had remained behind after the others left. No doubt that was why Alice had dragged his mother away. It was not her sympathy for Quin; it was her sympathy for the woman he had so publicly humiliated. The tittle-tattle was likely halfway to the village by now.

But Esmée looked surprisingly composed. "I fear there will be gossip, my lord," she said as if reading his thoughts. "But perhaps we can counter it. We must continue to assert that silly accident story."

He returned his gaze to the window, unable to look her in the eyes. "Esmée, I can explain."

"No, don't," she said hastily. "I would really rather not discuss it."

"I don't blame you," he whispered. "I am such a fool—

and worse, I've humiliated you. Can you ever forgive me?"

" 'Tis not a matter of my forgiveness," she said, her Highland accent soft.

"If you think that, my dear, then you are a fool, too."

Esmée drew a deep breath. "I ought to explain, Wynwood, that I came looking for you this morning to tell you . . . to tell you that I cannot marry you," she went on. "I made a grievous error in accepting your offer. I apologize."

At that, he laughed bitterly. "I am not surprised you'd wish to cry off now," he answered. "What an embarrassment this will be! And I believe it is I who owes the apology."

"You are not listening, my lord," she said firmly. "I was coming to tell you I wished to cry off the betrothal. I am sorry I interrupted you in . . . in whatever it was you were doing—"

"Ruining my life," he interjected. "That's what I was doing."

Esmée shrugged. "In any case, it had nothing to do with my decision. I mean to tell your mother so as well. I would not have her think you responsible for my choice."

It seemed Esmée had indeed noticed his inattentiveness last night. Damn it, Alasdair had not been wrong, had he? He had not meant to wound the girl so. "I will send a notice to the *Times* this afternoon," he said, dragging a hand through his hair. "No one will be surprised. My dear, I am sorry this has ended so badly."

"Don't be so sorry," she whispered. "Trust me, I never should have said yes. Something . . . something happened last night to convince me of that."

Yes, *he had ignored her.* That was what had happened. The sight of Viviana had disordered his mind. Quin was barely aware that he had begun to pace the room again.

"I thought it a good match, Esmée," he said, his tone almost mystified. "I persuaded myself we could make a go of it, you and I. I was a fool to imagine I could—or would ever—oh, damn it, why didn't I just listen to Alasdair?"

"To Alasdair—?"

"He told me from the very first I was not good enough for you," Quin admitted. "And I knew, even then, that he was right. I thought perhaps you might make a better man of me. But it isn't working, is it? Even Alasdair can see it. Last night, he read me the riot act, then threatened to thrash me into a bloody pulp."

"Alasdair? But . . . but why?"

"He thought I wasn't paying enough attention to you," Quin admitted. "He thought you looked unhappy. He wanted me to call off our wedding, but I refused, of course. How could I? A gentleman may not do such a thing." He flashed her a crooked, bittersweet smile. "But now you have done it for me."

Esmée refused to look at him. "Aye, and I think it best," she said. "We do not perfectly suit after all."

For a time, he simply watched her without speaking. "Are you a secret romantic at heart, Esmée?" he found himself asking. "Do you believe there is but one perfect partner for all of us?"

"I—yes, I begin to believe that might be so," Esmée admitted.

He turned again to the window and braced his hands wide on its frame. He stared into the distance, wondering how to make his point without further hurting her. "I do not know, Esmée, what there is between you and Alasdair," he finally said. "Certainly it is none of my business now."

She began to interrupt, but turned, and threw up a staying hand. "Please, just let me speak."

Esmée nodded. "Yes. Of course."

He lowered his hand and looked her in the eyes. "All I am saying is that if there is even a scrap of sincere regard between the two of you, I urge you not to let it go," he whispered. "Not until you are sure nothing more can be made of it. For once you let it go of that tiny scrap—by accident or by design—it is sometimes gone forever."

Esmée was staring at the floor again. "That is good advice, I am sure," she answered. "Now, if you will excuse me, I must go and tell my aunt what we have decided."

"I shouldn't wish her to be angry with you," he said hastily. "Tell her the truth, by all means."

"The truth is that we do not suit," she repeated. "We never did. We are meant for other things, you and I. We were fools ever to think otherwise."

He looked at her wistfully and wished to God he wanted her. It would have been so easy. But he didn't want her, not really. His actions this morning, and the embarrassment he had caused her, could not have made the truth more plain. She was wise, very wise, to be rid of him now, before he got her to the altar and doomed them both to a life of bitter dissatisfaction.

"Little Esmée," he murmured. "Always the wise one. Why is it that we cannot love one another? It would make life so much easier, would it not?"

She returned the smile ruefully. "Aye, but I begin to think we do not get to choose whom we love," she answered. "And that life was not meant to be easy." Then she stood on her tiptoes and lightly kissed his cheek.

Her father was already at the piano in the parlor with Lord Digleby when Viviana returned in a headlong rush from the stables. The men were bent over a piece of music scrawled across a scrap of paper, experimentally plinking out notes.

"Buon giorno, Papà. Lord Digleby." She kissed her father on the cheek and hastened out again, barely noticed. The great Alessandri was once again absorbed in his work, and for that Viviana was grateful.

She was not grateful—at least, not initially—when she ran straight into Lord Chesley exiting his library. "Vivie, my dear!" he said, catching her by both shoulders. "You are about to bowl me over—and not with your charm and beauty."

Viviana felt her cheeks heat. *"Scusi,* my lord," she murmured, moving as if to pass. "I was not attending."

Chesley was looking at her in concern. "No, my girl, you were not," he agreed. "Come into the library, won't you? Basham has just brought coffee."

Viviana pulled the pin from her riding hat, and lifted it off. *"Grazie,* Chesley, but I should change first."

Chesley waved his hand in obviation. "Nonsense! Now come in, sit down, and tell me what is wrong. Did you not enjoy your grand adventure this morning?"

Grand adventure was not quite the word for it. For an instant, she weighed not telling him, but that would not have done. Better Chesley should hear it from her lips. "I—I rode over to Arlington Park," she answered, unable to hold his gaze. "I went to see Lord Wynwood."

Chesley's brows went up, and he pushed open the library door, motioning her in with a tilt of his head. "To see Quin, eh?" he said when she was seated and he had poured her a cup of strong black brew. "Was he expecting you, Vivie?"

She nodded, and took a fortifying sip of the coffee. "He—he asked me to come," she said. "Well, ordered me, really. I thought merely to humor him, you see. But . . . but there was an accident."

"An accident?" the earl echoed. "Of what sort?"

Viviana shook her head, not entirely sure she could explain. "We quarreled," she began. "And he—he took certain liberties which I did not appreciate. I was very angry, Chesley, and I struck him. With my crop."

"Gad!" the earl interjected.

"Indeed," said Viviana witheringly. "We did not realize Lady Charlotte had come into the room with Miss Hamilton. Oh, Chesley! It was an ugly scene. I drew his blood."

"As well you should have done, devil take him!"

"Oh, no, I should *not* have!" Viviana cried, leaping from her chair. "Lady Charlotte swooned, and Miss Hamilton—well, I think she saw everything. I am not perfectly sure. And there were servants."

Chesley groaned and shook his head. Viviana was roaming restlessly about the room now, sliding her hands up and down her arms. She was cold, she realized, despite the fact she still wore a wool habit. It was her nerves, she supposed. She really had suffered something of a shock. She had gone to spar a bit with Quin, and to put him in his place. And now innocent people were left to suffer the consequences of her temper. Would she never learn?

"Damn Quin for a fool!" Chesley finally muttered. "Gwendolyn will likely give herself an apoplexy over this. I'd best get over there and find out which way the wind blows."

"Oh, it blows very ill," said Viviana. "Lady Charlotte looked most unwell. The doctor was being sent for when I left."

"Hmph," said the earl. "Never mind Charlotte; she's tough as an old hide. What, precisely, did the servants see?"

Viviana sat down again, careless of her skirts. "I cannot say," she admitted. "I was in one of my *diva* rages."

"Yes, yes!" said Chesley. "One can only guess."

"Still, I think they cannot quite have seen *everything,*" Viviana continued. "But I am not at all sure they needed to. *Dio,* I feel so sorry for that poor girl. And I can only imagine what she thinks of me."

"Miss Hamilton?" asked the earl. "Yes, there will be gossip. Ah, well! The child did not look resolute enough to keep Quin on a leash anyway. Still, we must endeavor to keep the servants quiet."

Viviana set down her cup, and pushed it a little away. "I am sorry, Chesley," she whispered, dropping her face into her hands. "I am your guest here. This reflects very badly on you, I fear."

"The deuce!" said the earl again. "It reflects badly on my rogue of a nephew, and that is all. He has come to believe every fetching female under the age of forty is his for the taking. I should like to take *my* crop to the handsome devil."

"Miss Hamilton may beat you to it," said Viviana mordantly. "I do not believe she is as meek, Chesley, as you seem to believe. And afterward, I expect she will jilt him."

"And so she ought," said the earl, rising. "You must pardon me, my girl. I shouldn't waste any more time. Let me go over to Arlington and unruffle Gwen's feathers and see how Charlotte goes on. Then I'll call upon Mrs. Prater, and discover what tittle-tattle the housemaids are passing and what can be done to stop it."

"Oh, Chesley!" said Viviana, coming swiftly to her feet. Impulsively, she kissed him on the cheek.

He looked at her with a hint chagrin in his eyes. "I only wonder," he finally said, "what Quin was thinking, Vivie. You did discourage him quite thoroughly all those years ago, didn't you, my girl?"

Viviana swallowed hard, and hesitated. "Perhaps, Chesley, I ought not answer that," she finally answered. "I have the right to avoid self-incrimination, have I not? That is the English law, I believe?"

"Hmph," said the earl for the third time. "It is the letter of the law, yes, if not the spirit. Keep your secrets, my dear, if you must. But I sometimes begin to wonder if you haven't kept just one or two too many."

By the early afternoon, Lord Chesley still had not returned to Hill Court. Mrs. Douglass sent plates of cold meat and cheese to the parlor in some hope, Viviana supposed, that her father and Lord Digleby would actually stop working long enough to eat. It had fallen to Viviana to smooth the housekeeper's feathers when they did not.

Viviana dined in the schoolroom with Miss Hevner and the children. The governess, who was looking rather frazzled, expressed a need to do some shopping in the village. Nurse Rossi could no longer handle all three at once. Viviana offered to take the children to play in the gardens for the rest of the afternoon. Better that, she decided, than simply sitting and stewing whilst she awaited Chesley's return.

But it was not Lord Chesley who eventually appeared on the path which led from Hill Court to Arlington. The children were playing hide-and-seek in Chesley's maze when Viviana heard distant laughter. She lifted her hand to shield the low, slanting sun from her eyes. Below the stables, she could see a lady and three children emerging from the trees.

Lady Alice. Viviana was sure of it. The smallest child Lady Alice carried on her hip. Behind her, the two older children appeared to be wrestling good-naturedly over something. Lady Alice turned around and whacked the smaller of the two soundly across the bottom. Swathed in coats and cloaks as they all were, Viviana doubted the swat had much effect, nor had it been meant to.

Suddenly, something struck her. *Allie.* Alice was Allie—Quin's elder sister. She had recalled vaguely that Quin had had a sister. But she could not recall his ever having called her Alice. There was yet another small mystery resolved, she supposed. A pity she had not tried to solve them all a little sooner.

When the three saw Viviana by the maze, they hastened toward her, giving every impression of being well-mannered children on their best behavior. "I hoped to find you here," said Lady Alice brightly as she set her smallest child down. "The day has turned quite clear, has it not?"

"Yes, it is lovely," agreed Viviana.

"I thought the children might play together," Lady Alice suggested. "Do your children like battledore?"

By then, Nicolo was tugging at Viviana's skirts, and the girls were peeping from the maze. "I do not think we know this game," Viviana admitted, lifting Nicolo to her hip. "My Felise does not speak English perfectly—and this little one, not at all."

Lady Alice's children were carrying several wooden paddles, rather like small tennis rackets, but solid and stringless. "This is the battledore," said the boy, thrusting one of his paddles toward the maze to Cerelia.

"And this is the shuttlecock," said the girl, balancing a befeathered object in the palm of her hand. Viviana recognized it as the object the children had been squabbling over. "We hit it back and forth with the battledore and try to keep it in the air."

Lady Alice laughed, and plucked the feathered object from the girl's hand. "Do not be deceived, Contessa," she said. "This is really just an old cork stuck full of feathers. Mr. Herndon, Arlington's steward, made it for my children." Hastily, she introduced them.

The eldest was Charlotte, so named for her great-great-aunt, a fact which made Viviana inwardly cringe. "But we call her Lottie to avoid the confusion," Lady Alice went on. "And this is Christopher, who is seven, and Diana, who is four."

Cerelia had taken the wooden paddle from Christopher's outstretched hand and was studying it. Hastily, Viviana translated the introductions and presented her own children in turn.

Lady Alice did not appear to need further encouragement. She drew a long piece of red yard from her pocket, went out onto a square patch of lawn, and stretched it out across the grass. Nicolo squirmed his way down and dashed off to investigate it.

"This is the boundary line," said Lady Alice, pointing authoritatively. "Cerelia, you shall play with Christopher on that side of the line. And Felise, you will play with Lottie. You must not let the cork touch the ground, or the other side will score a point. Does everyone follow me?"

"*Si, Signora,*" said Cerelia, nodding.

"*Yes, my lady,*" prompted Viviana from the sidelines.

Cerelia laughed. "Yes, my lady," she agreed. "We will be sure to send your feathers flying."

The elder girl had given one of her paddles to Felise and was showing her how to use it. Lady Alice gave the last two paddles to the youngest, and moved them into place behind the elder children. Little Diana was hopping up and down excitedly, but she looked just as confused as Nicolo.

"I shall keep score," cried Lady Alice over her shoulder as she left them. "Contessa, I fear my feet hurt and I wish to sit on that bench just there. Will you indulge me?"

She left Viviana little choice, other than to appear inhospitable. "Yes, of course," she said, falling into step. "But the little ones, they cannot play this batting game, can they?"

"Oh, heavens, no!" Lady Alice agreed. "In two minutes' time, they will have thrown down their battledores and wandered off to chase one of Uncle Ches's cats or poke about in the shrubbery. But if we do not give them any, they will whine and cry until we wish we had."

Viviana could not argue with her strategy. "You are

very kind to visit," she said quietly. "My children were growing bored with hide-and-seek in the maze."

"It isn't even much of a maze, is it?" Lady Alice admitted, her gaze running over it. "More like hide-and-*peek*, I should say. The thing looks on the verge of death."

Viviana found herself laughing. "Your uncle says there was a blight last year," she answered. "Much of it had to be cut back."

"One all!" cried Lady Alice suddenly. "Lottie, watch Felise's toes!"

In her next breath, she returned to their discussion of the shrubs. Then she turned the topic to the coming holidays, and after that, to the unseasonable temperatures. But all the while, Viviana knew Lady Alice had had another purpose in coming to Hill Court.

Finally, Viviana had had enough of the suspense. "Lady Alice," she said quietly. "Why have you come here? Not, I think, to talk of the weather?"

Smiling benignly, Alice turned on the bench to face her. "To let the children play," she repeated. "And also to invite you to join Mamma and me for luncheon tomorrow at Arlington Park."

"Ah, to luncheon!" said Viviana. "But I think you must know, Lady Alice, of the incident which occurred this morning in your brother's study."

Lady Alice clasped her hands in her lap for a moment. "I apologize, Contessa, on my brother's behalf."

"Do you indeed?" said Viviana a little mordantly. "Are you quite sure?"

Alice's brows knotted. "Quite sure that I apologize?"

"On your brother's behalf."

The smile did not fade. "By the time Mamma has had

done with him, yes, I am sure he will be quite penitent indeed."

"Oh, dear." Viviana bit her lip. "She must be frightfully angry."

Alice shrugged. "Three-two, Chris!" she called across the lawn. "Do *not* elbow your sister!" At once, she returned her attention to Viviana. "Mamma has been reduced to mere mortification now, I think. Her bosom bow, Lady Tatton, has gone haring back to London with her oh-so-eligible niece in tow, whilst Quin has already penned the announcement ending their betrothal, and sent it on a fast horse ahead of them. By tomorrow, it will be in the London papers."

"Oh, Dio!" whispered Viviana, pinching hard at the bridge of her nose.

"Contessa?" Alice asked. "Are you quite all right?"

No, she was not all right. She had a terrible headache coming on. And what she utterly could not fathom was the sense of relief which was surging through her just now. Quin's betrothal was ended. An innocent young woman had been humiliated, perhaps even devastated. It was hardly a thing to feel good about.

"Miss Hamilton has jilted him, then?" she managed to whisper.

"Oh, yes!" said Alice. "Though she insisted to Mamma that she had meant to do it anyway. Indeed, she claims that was her very reason for asking Aunt Charlotte to show her the way to his study."

"I cannot believe that."

Lady Alice smiled tightly. "Well, in any case, Quin seems almost relieved, though he will never admit it. Of course, this is all for the best, if you ask me."

"Oh, Lady Alice, you cannot mean it!" said Viviana. "Consider the embarrassment to your family, and to that poor girl!"

Again, the shrug. "Miss Hamilton would have been incapable of making Quin toe the mark," she said. "And that is what he needs; someone whom he cannot bully or wheedle. A man cannot be cowed by a woman he does not love. Besides, what of the embarrassment to *you*, Contessa Bergonzi?"

"Viviana," she said without looking at Alice. "Please, call me Viviana. And yes, I was embarrassed. Both by your brother's behavior, and by my reaction. It was . . . excessive. I lost my temper. And those servants! I fear they saw everything."

"Oh, they saw enough to encourage some idle speculation," Alice agreed. "Without a doubt they saw Aunt Charlotte on the floor. But can they say with utter confidence what had caused her to swoon? No, that they did not see."

"Grazie a Dio!" whispered Viviana. "But that won't stop the rumors."

"No, it won't," agreed Lady Alice. "Which is why you must come to luncheon tomorrow."

"I—I don't understand."

Alice reached for her hand and gave it a swift, reassuring squeeze. "Viviana, tomorrow the announcement of Quin's ended betrothal will be in the papers," she said again. "It will not do for it to be put about that the fault was yours. And it *was not*. I believe that."

Viviana studied her for a moment. "You seem to place a vast deal of faith in one whom you do not know well."

"Oh, but I know my brother."

"Whatever do you mean?"

Alice's face colored faintly. "My brother has been unhappy, Contessa, for a very long time," she answered. "He has lived a hedonistic, careless life, and this notion of marriage has perhaps made matters worse. I wonder if he isn't regretting . . . oh, something! I know not what—but I know he is not thinking clearly. I tried to warn him, but he ignored me. He said . . . he said he just wished for a marriage like mine."

Viviana lifted one brow. "And what sort was that, pray?"

Alice lifted one shoulder lamely, and looked away. "A marriage made for family and duty," she said. "A more or less emotionless marriage."

"I see," said Viviana. It sounded little better than her own marriage.

Alice turned on the bench to fully face her. "Oh, do say that you will come tomorrow, Viviana!" she implored. "Do give us Hewitts a chance to prove we are not all jaded boors. And I do think that your coming will ensure that there will be less gossip about this morning's little altercation."

Viviana shrugged. "I cannot think it matters," she said. "No one in England knows me now."

Alice's brows shot up. "Oh, you are a fool if you believe that," she responded. "The greatest soprano of our time? London's own fair *Konstanze*? Yes, my dear, even here in this backwater of Buckinghamshire, we keep up with the world of opera."

Viviana considered it. It was despicable of Quin to have put her in such a position. But Alice was right. Her name was not unknown. And in a few months, if all went as planned, her father's name, along with Lord Digleby's, would be on everyone's tongue. And there were always her children to consider.

"We must all appear on good terms, Viviana," Quin's sister continued. "From now on, my brother will be on his most gentlemanly behavior, or he will be on his way back to London. Because he will take Mamma's tongue-lashing only so long before he stalks out."

"I see," said Viviana quietly. "But your mother . . . these circumstances cannot but pain her. And I cannot imagine she wishes to befriend me."

Alice was silent a moment. A stiff breeze sent leaves skirling around their skirt hems, and across the makeshift battledore court. The shuttlecock lifted, and went spinning off-course, making the children shriek with laughter.

Alice watched it all with a muted smile. "I won't deny that Mamma can be a high stickler," she answered. "But I've already told her that at this point, she'd be better served by accounting you a dear friend."

Viviana stiffened her spine. "I did nothing to invite your brother's attentions, Lady Alice," she said. "And I shan't be foisted upon anyone socially. I have my own pride. And much as it may surprise you, in my country, we, too, have high standards of deportment."

Swiftly, Alice laid a hand on Viviane's arm. "I am sorry," she said at once. "I did not mean to insult you. Please, can you not at least consider being my friend? I think it perfectly natural, myself. We are going to be living very near one another for a few weeks, and we have a great deal in common."

Tightly, Viviana nodded. "Yes, all right," she finally said. "I thank you, Alice, for your offer of friendship. Yes,

I shall join you and Lady Wynwood tomorrow. May I ride over? Or is that thought dreadfully unfashionable?"

"Not at all." Lady Alice leaned nearer, her eyes dancing. "Now, as your new friend, I claim the right to ask you a prying question."

Viviana turned to face her. "You may ask, by all means."

A slow, lazy smile curved her mouth. "How well did you know my brother, Viviana, when last you were in London?"

Viviana held her gaze quite steadily for a moment, and considered her question. "I think, Lady Alice," she finally said, "that perhaps I did not know him at all."

Seven

In which Lord Wynwood's refuge is Discovered.

At half past eleven the following morning, the Earl of
Wynwood put on his boots and breeches and stalked
off toward his stables. It was, he had decided, a good day
to begin the visits to some of his larger tenant farms. He
had no real wish to do so; it still felt as if he were usurping
his father's role. But there was another, more overriding
reason than duty which prompted his burning desire to
escape.

Today Viviana—Contessa Bergonzi—was to take
luncheon with his mother and his sister. It was Alice's
crackbrained notion. But his mother had fallen in with it,
albeit witheringly, after hearing Alice's reasoning. A part
of him knew Alice was right, and he was grateful that his
mother and sister were trying to mitigate the damage his
temper had caused. Nonetheless, it made him feel like a
fool.

When he reached the stables, Quin saddled his own
horse with quick, impatient motions, and rode off in a

cloud of dust. He expected to make a long day of it. In his saddlebag, he carried a slice of bread, a hunk of cheddar, and a flask full of Alasdair's best whisky, the latter having been accidentally left behind by his hastily departing houseguest. Alasdair's loss might as well be his gain, Quin had decided, since he had a strong suspicion that wind was blowing the other way where marriage was concerned.

Yes, Quin had every notion that, as soon as decency permitted it, Alasdair would be placing his betrothal announcement in the *Times*. Well, he wished him happy. Quin had not wanted to marry anyway. He was far better off with Alasdair's whisky than Alasdair's woman, if that's what it really was coming to. He worried, though, about Esmée. Would Alasdair be good to her? He hoped so. He prayed so. He had no choice but to trust that Esmée knew what she was doing.

Quin had enough trouble managing the women he was not wedded to; his mother, his sister, and Viviana Alessandri. As to his mother, Quin had decided a heart-to-heart talk was in order. He had decided that marriage—or at least a rushed marriage—was not for him. She would not take the news well, and he dreaded it. She really did not deserve to be hurt. But this disaster with Esmée had made him realize that he needed more time to sort out his own mind. And he simply could not think straight when Viviana Alessandri was in the same country, let alone the same *village,* as he.

Ah, Viviana. Now, there was a woman he had once considered wedding. Another lifetime and another world ago. She had stunned him when she had first proposed marriage. Yet once the shock had passed, and he had lain sated and happy in her arms, the wheels of his mind had begun to turn.

She had wished to marry him. And he had known, even then, that to live without her would have been an unbearable hell. But he had been so young, his mind had known little beyond that nebulous truth. He'd had no notion how one even went about getting married.

Stripling that he was, he'd always assumed his parents would find him some pretty, dutiful girl of good breeding, hammer out the details, and present him with a fait accompli. To him, it was rather like buying a broodmare at Tattersall's—and he didn't even have to do the haggling. And by then, he'd seen enough of Town ways to know that that was how his new London friends saw it, too.

Viviana's proposal had thrown him badly off-balance. Although it had been a little frightening, the question had sent a world of possibilities whirling through his imagination. He could have Viviana forever. In a way which would bind her to him for all eternity. But he had wanted more than her name on a license and her head on his pillow. He had wanted the one thing Viviana had never given him. He had wanted her heart. So he had asked her the question which had been eating him alive.

Do you love me, Viviana?

She had admitted that she did not. In the space of that quiet, husky whisper, all the fragile, half-formed notions flying about in his head had crashed back down to earth again, shattering and splintering like so much spun glass. He had known it, of course. Viviana had resisted his overtures for months. And when he had finally managed to bed her—an inane euphemism if ever there was one, for there had been no bed involved—still, she had resisted.

After that maddening taste of her, Quin had had to lay siege to Viviana's stage door for another two weeks. And then he had been permitted to take her to supper. Another two weeks, and finally she had agreed to move out of that convent of a boardinghouse in which she had been living. No, she had never loved him. She had tolerated him. Been amused and sexually satisfied by him. But never, ever had she given herself to him.

He wondered what his life would have been like had he never had that first perfect taste of her. Of course, he had relived that fateful evening a thousand times, sometimes wishing to God it had never happened. And sometimes clinging to every shred of remembrance as a dying man might cling to life.

It had been the opening night of *Fidelio,* and the soprano who was to sing the role of Marzelline had fallen suddenly ill. Viviana was the understudy. Viviana's dresser had been unable to cover her heavy tresses with the elaborate wig which the role required. Quin had sat quietly in one corner, watching their futile efforts, for at the time, a visit to her dressing room was the only intimacy Viviana would permit him.

But Quin had been as determined to have Viviana as her dresser had been determined to have Viviana's hair stuffed under that bloody wig. Both had seemed a hopeless case. He had been following her like some besotted pup for almost a month. And the dresser was having even less luck, for the wig had been made for a woman with something less than Viviana's long, heavy tresses.

In a fit of frustration, the dresser snatched up the scissors, and, at Viviana's acquiescent nod, chopped off a good ten inches. The hair fell in a puddle about Viviana's chair.

The wig was fitted. And when no one was looking, Quin had stolen the ringlet of Viviana's hair and folded it carefully into his handkerchief. By the next morning, Viviana was the toast of London. And, so far as Quin was concerned, his mistress.

Before her dresser's act of desperation, Viviana's hair had been an inky cascade of curls reaching to her waist. Afterward, it had looked like a hacked-up mess. Quin had not minded. They could have shaved Viviana bald, and he likely would not have cared, so long as he could still gaze into her eyes. He had believed himself capable of seeing into her soul.

Oh, what a foolish, foolish boy he had been. So green. So gullible. Viviana had no soul. Her feigned reluctance, her ingenuous demeanor, that utterly guileless way she had of looking at him; yes, all of it had been one grand illusion. She had toyed with Quin as a cat might a mouse—an especially stupid mouse. And in the end, she had ripped out his guts with her claws, just as cats were wont to do.

Ah, but he was wasting him time again, just thinking of her. The first cottage was coming into view now. He could see a stout, maternal-looking woman standing by the tidy front fence, stretching freshly laundered linens across it. Dear old Mrs. Chandler. He lifted his hand and waved. Her face broke out into a smile.

Quin felt his heart warm. Thank God. At least someone was glad to see him.

Perhaps this tenant business was not so bad after all. He looked beyond the large, tidy cottage to the barns and outbuildings beyond. The old granary appeared to be crumbling a bit.

Mrs. Chandler pinned up the last of her laundry and hastened through the garden gate toward him. "Now young Mr. Quin," she chided, hands on her hips. "In the village all of a se'night, and no time to visit me?"

He gave her a diffident smile, and took the plump, callused hand she extended. "Mrs. Chandler!" he said warmly. "I hope I find you well?"

"Aye, well enough," she said. "But Philip's inside with a sprained ankle and a sore temper. Will ye come in and sit with him a bit?"

"To be sure," said Quin, tying his reins to the fence.

Mrs. Chandler pulled open the gate and motioned him through.

"Your granary, Mrs. Chandler," he mused as they went up the garden path. "It looks like the witchert wall is falling in at the southerly corner."

"Oh, aye, 'tis in a sorry state," she agreed, cutting a swift, sidelong glance at him. "D'ye mean to fix it this year?"

He stopped on the path and appraised her. "Well, yes," he said. "What choice have we?"

She gave a small, sour smile. "Aye, well, ye can put it off another year, I daresay," she replied. "But Philip's been after getting it fixed these last two—and this year we lost a good deal o' the harvest to the heavy rain. No one has any use for moldy corn, eh?"

Quin was surprised. He had always believed his father a perfectionist. Why had Chandler's granary been let go? It certainly was not a matter of money; the estate was extremely profitable. Perhaps too profitable?

Quin thought back to the long list of repairs Herndon had pressed upon him almost as soon as he had arrived.

Perhaps it was time to actually *read* it. Suddenly the needs of the estate and its tenants seemed not just nebulous annoyances, but very real—and reasonable—concerns. He set one hand on Mrs. Chandler's shoulder.

"I shall have Herndon out here tomorrow," he said.

Mrs. Chandler beamed and pulled open the door.

Viviana was near a state of nervous agitation by the time she left her luncheon at Arlington Park, though she had schooled herself carefully to hide it. This time, she had arrived at the front door of Wynwood's grand estate in the company of Lord Chesley's favorite groom. After thanking Lady Alice for her thoughtfulness, Viviana remounted with the groom's assistance, then reined her horse around to face him.

"Thank you," she said to the young man. "You may return to the stables now. I mean to ride on a good deal further, and take the air."

The groom furrowed his brow. "Are you sure, my lady?" he asked. "I was told I was to wait."

"And so you have," said Viviana over one shoulder. She had already started toward the bridle path. "But I would feel guilty keeping you longer from you duties."

With one last look of reluctance, the young man touched his hat brim and urged his horse on past her. Viviana watched him go, slowly exhaling. For the first time since leaving the stables that morning, she felt as if she could breathe again. Inside, she felt as tight as a clock coil, as if someone had stuck a key into her brain and wound her almost to the breaking point. She wanted to ride fast and hard away from Arlington—and away from Hill Court, too.

Luncheon had seemed interminable. Lady Wynwood had been stiff and exceedingly formal, her expression perpetually dyspeptic. Viviana had responded by behaving with chilly civility, until she realized how desperately Lady Alice was struggling to maintain the illusion of harmony in front of the servants. Viviana had forced herself to warm toward Quin's mother. The lady herself had not followed suit. Or perhaps it was her usual demeanor. With the English, one could never be sure.

In any case, Viviana now had no wish to return to the confines of the house. What she needed, she decided, was a thundering ride with the cold air in her face. No one had need of her at Hill Court. The children were at their lessons today. Lord Chesley was meeting his steward. And *Papà,* well, he was in another world altogether: the world of music, the only place in which he was ever truly happy. Viviana had no wish to disturb him. She remembered too well his misery when, for a year and a half, he had had no work at all, a deprivation which was due to her stubbornness—and to Gianpiero's cruelty.

But she would not think of Gianpiero, and add that trouble to those which already weighed on her mind. She trailed slowly after the groom, who had all but vanished into the trees. After a quarter mile, she reached the path which split to the north. This path, Chesley had warned, was isolated. She would have to ride many miles before reaching a farm or village. Perfect, then. Isolation was just what she longed for.

The path, when she turned onto it, narrowed almost immediately. Here, the branches hung lower, and the tree trunks edged nearer, giving one the impression of being embraced, almost sheltered from the temporal world beyond the forest. Drawing the cold air deep into her lungs, Viviana set her mount, a spirited bay gelding, at a brisk pace and plunged into the shadowy depths. Here, the air was still, the ethereal silence broken by nothing save the muffled beats of the gelding's hooves, allowing Viviana to clear her head of all but the horse's graceful movements.

But the forest's embrace did not last. Some three miles later, her humor much improved, Viviana felt the sun dapple her face and looked up to see the trees thinning. She could see that the path curved slightly, then melted into a narrow farm lane but a few feet ahead. The gelding, tired of trotting sedately through the trees, danced sideways into the wintry sunshine and tossed his head with an impatient snort.

Narrowing her eyes against sudden brilliance, Viviana looked down an undulating stretch of road which was as close to straight as one was apt to find in this part of England. To either side lay open pasture, dotted by an occasional copse of trees. Far in the distance, the dilapidated roof of an old barn or cow byre peeked over the horizon.

Again, the horse tossed his head. Viviana could see his point. It really was a very empty road. And in the end, the temptation was too much. Viviana checked her grip on the reins, then touched him lightly with her crop.

The gelding sprang like a shot, leaping from a dead stop to a thundering gallop so fast Viviana lost her breath. Along the gelding's powerful thigh, her skirts billowed and whipped. Vaguely, she knew it was folly to give such a horse his head, but prudence seemed to have escaped her. The intensity of the horse's raw physical power felt liberating. The rush of cold air cleared her head and tore at her hair.

Viviana leaned low over his withers, urging him forward. On and on they went, the gelding flying over the rolling hillocks, his powerful legs eating up the distance. Viviana felt the cashmere scarf around her neck loosen, then tear away. Her hat lifted buoyantly, but held fast, caught by its pin. In the wintry air, the tang of horse sweat was sharp, the chimera of escape exhilarating.

But alas, they soon reached the last stretch. The fantasy was over. The old byre was nearing, and beyond it a bend which even Viviana dared not risk. Gently, she reined the gelding back on the downhill grade. He began to slow in obedience, but in that instant, Viviana caught a flash of movement to her left.

It was as if lightning struck. She was jerked violently right, the horse shying wildly, nearly pitching her from the saddle. But Viviana was an experienced rider. She regained her seat neatly and reined the gelding in, crooning soothingly at him. His sidestepping ended in a cloud of dust and a clatter of stones. The horse stood shuddering beneath her, his head tossing, his nostrils flared wide.

After slicking a hand down his neck, Viviana turned him in the roadbed and trotted back to see what the devil had set him off. She wished at once that she had not.

Lord Wynwood stood at the corner of the dilapidated building, reclining lazily against it, one boot propped back on the stone foundation. He was dressed for the country, in snug, buff-colored breeches, a coat of dark brown, and riding boots just a shade darker. She could still make out the weal across his cheek, though it looked like little more than a scratch now. Behind the barn, a big black horse tugged halfheartedly at the colorless grass.

Wynood held a yellow apple in one hand, half of it

eaten. He appeared to be still chewing as his dark gaze shrewdly appraised her. Finally, he swallowed. "Well, Viviana," he said dryly. "Fancy meeting you here."

Viviana's heart was still pounding. "Why, how dare you!" she cried. "You—you did that deliberately!"

He tossed what was left of the apple to the black horse, and pushed away from the barn. "Did what deliberately?" he asked, approaching. "Made you go haring off like some bedlamite down a narrow country road? No, you imbue me with powers I do not possess, my dear."

Viviana slid off her sidesaddle, and caught her reins in one hand. "Good God, Quinten, this is not funny," she answered. "You spooked my horse! I could have been killed. Is that what you wish? Is that what would it would take to make you happy?"

He shot her a chiding look. "Viviana, you flushed a covey of grouse," he returned. "Don't ride so damned fast when you don't know the terrain."

Viviana felt her face heat.

"What, you didn't see it?" he asked incredulously. "You don't believe me?"

"I do not know," she admitted. "What . . . what is that, a flush of grouse?"

He eyed her riding crop warily. "You frightened some birds in the weeds beyond the cottage," he answered. "They burst into the air. Your horse saw them, Viviana, even if you did not."

He was telling the truth, she realized. Her attention had been focused on the blind curve ahead and on getting her horse to slow. But she had seen something—a very indistinct something—from one corner of her eye as she passed.

Quin stepped closer, and lifted his hand.

Instinctively, she drew back. *"Non mi tocchi!"*

The gelding took offense, nearly jerking the reins from her hand as he tossed his head and wheeled his hindquarters restlessly about.

"Put away the crop, Viviana," said Quin, reaching again, more slowly. "I've learnt my lesson. What is this? A new Continental fashion?"

She was a tall woman, but Quin was far taller. She felt him tug on her hatpin, and lift the hat from her head. She felt surprisingly lighter, and turned in some embarrassment to see that her lost scarf dangled like a banner from her hatpin.

"You looked a sight, Vivie, with this flying out behind you." Quin did not look up at her as he deftly disentangled the mess, but she could see the faint, familiar grin curving his mouth as he struggled. She could smell him, too; warm wool, perhaps a hint of whisky, and the clean tang of soap—bergamot, she was sure. It was her favorite scent in all the world, and she was a little shaken to realize he still wore it.

"There," he said just as her knees began to weaken. "The pin is freed. You may put your muffler and hat back on."

But when he lifted his gaze, he faltered. "Your hair," he said. "It is . . . it is coming down."

"Non importo," she answered, snatching her hat and slapping it back on. "I fix it later. *Grazie,* Lord Wynwood. I must be away."

He caught her gently by the shoulder. "Viviana, I—" He stopped, and shook his head. "Contessa Bergonzi, I owe you an apology. Uncle Ches told me everything—

why you are here, I mean. That it was all his doing. I was . . . I am just . . . well, I apologize."

She surveyed him coldly. "*Si,* my lord, as well you should," she returned. "And me, I should not have been there. That was my mistake."

He dropped his hand, and smiled sourly. "I left you little choice."

Viviana did not drop her gaze. "You are ten times a fool, my lord, if you believe that."

He glanced at her oddly. "So my threat meant nothing to you?" he murmured. "Then why, pray, were you there?"

Still holding the gelding's reins, Viviana stepped back a pace, then lifted one shoulder. "Perverse curiosity, perhaps."

He held her gaze steadily, as if waiting to see if she would falter. Instead, she looked boldly back at him, and pretended she did not see the pain in his eyes. Yes, let him mourn for a lifetime the loss of his pretty fiancée. Viviana did not give a damn. She had not lived almost ten years of emptiness without learning how to harden her heart.

"You know that Esmée has jilted me?" he said. "Yes, I daresay my sister will have told you everything."

Viviana had led the gelding to an old gatepost, now half-rotted away. "It is none of my concern, Wynwood," she said. "I am not responsible for it. But I am sure your mother can yet find you a blue-blooded, flaxen-haired English miss."

"I don't know what you are talking about," he said. "Miss Hamilton is Scottish, and her hair is decidedly brown."

"The bride of your dreams." Viviana gave a muted smile. "Do you not remember? You once told me what she would be like."

"You don't know anything about my dreams, my dear, and you never did," he said. But there was little anger in his tone.

Viviana stepped gingerly onto what was left of the post, and mounted unaided. Lord Wynwood did not offer to help. Instead, he looked up at her a little bleakly. She wished he would not do that. She wished he would come out and fight the fair fight over whatever it was that so angered him. She could see it, not just the bleakness, but the rage, too. How easily one recognized one's own shortcomings in another. And, oh, how she wished to scream at him! How she longed for the merest excuse. But he said nothing.

Viviana spurred the gelding halfway around. *"Buona sera,* Lord Wynwood," she answered. "I must be off."

"Viviana, wait!"

She turned back. *"Si?"*

"You took luncheon with my mother today, did you not? I hope . . . I hope that she was kind to you?"

"She was polite," said Viviana. "Exceedingly polite."

"Ah, I think I see." His face softened slightly. "Viviana, how long do you mean to be here?"

She bristled. "Until Chesley no longer needs my father. Why?"

He shrugged, and dragged a hand through his hair, a young man's gesture. Her heart lurched. Ah, she remembered it well.

"It behooves us, Viviana, to get along," he finally said.

"You have been talking to your sister," she remarked. "Fine, then. We will get along—if we see one another, which is not likely, is it?"

He did not answer. Instead, he offered up his hand.

"Then let there be peace between us, Viviana," he said. "We are too old now to make fools of ourselves."

Viviana leaned down and shook it. His hand felt warm and strong, even through her glove. "Pax, Wynwood."

Their hands slid apart. The touch was broken. Viviana straightened in her saddle and started to nudge her mount around. Suddenly, she noticed for the first time that the stone building was actually a small house—a cottage, he had called it. The gardens were overgrown, but the place must have looked charming at one time. The house had a cowshed attached to one side, and it was that which was collapsing.

But Quin was still looking at her, as if he had something more to say. "Viviana, you look . . . different."

"It has been almost ten years, Quinten," she said quietly. "Time alters us."

"No, not like that," he said. "Your nose, it—it isn't quite the same. Is it?"

Instinctively, she touched the slight hump with her gloved forefinger. "This, you are asking?" she answered. "No, I fell down the steps. I broke it."

"When?"

Again, she shrugged. "Two years past, perhaps," she said vaguely. "Awkward of me, was it not? But now my face has—what does your uncle call it?—yes, *gravitas*. You English value that, I find. But as to me, well, I would much rather have my nose back."

And then she touched the brim of her hat with her crop, spun her mount around, and cantered back up the country lane.

*   *   *

Quin watched her go until she had vanished in the distance; watched until even her dust had disappeared. Then he returned to the little cottage and shoved the door open with one shoulder. Inside, he sloshed a little water into the kitchen basin and meticulously washed the apple juice from his hands. A pity he could not wash away the memories of Viviana so easily.

Bracing his arms wide on the sink base, he looked through the small window at the dull green pasture beyond. Viviana seemed wholly unaffected by him, almost as if their months together had never been. For well over a year he had courted her and pursued her and made love to her, never entirely sure that she was his. Now he was certain. No matter how desperately he had wished to possess her, he had never even come close.

Viviana had been owned by the opera, and by the admirers and patrons who worshiped her. Men like his uncle. And many men less benign than his uncle. Quin had tried to warn her about them, believing, he supposed, that she did not fully comprehend the dangers.

He had been envious of her talent, it was true. Well, envious of the attention it attracted, and of the suggestive looks and offers it brought her way. He had loved her. He had wished only to protect her. And yes, to have her entirely to himself—because he had been so desperately afraid, so almost laughably insecure. He was half-ashamed to admit that now.

He wished to God he'd been just a little older, just a little more experienced when he'd met her. He wished, too, that she had not been so much older than he. Oh, perhaps it was nothing now; a few years, no more. But then, it had seemed insurmountable. It had felt to Quin as if Viviana already knew the secrets of life. As if she were watching him with veiled amusement as he struggled to come to terms with his manhood.

Gianpiero Bergonzi, it seemed, had been fully confident of his manhood. And he had wanted Viviana, too, had wanted her badly enough to make an honest woman of her. Perhaps Bergonzi had simply had the backbone to do what Quin should have done. Perhaps Quin should have married her. Perhaps Viviana would have come to love him in time. And perhaps he could have been the father of her children.

She had *three* children, he had discovered. Not just the pretty little girl he'd seen at Astley's but another daughter, and a son, too. It boggled the mind when he considered it. Her body was so little changed. Oh, she was more voluptuous. And yes, there were a few tiny lines about her eyes, and when she frowned, about her mouth. But she had *three children.* And another man had given them to her.

Another man had done what he had not the guts to do. Another man had enjoyed the beauty and the pleasure of living with Viviana every day, for the whole of his life. Because Quin had given up the chance. That was the awful truth.

The aching sense of loss nearly swallowed him up then. The yawning emptiness of the last decade reached out for him. And this time, there weren't enough whores in all of Christendom, or enough virgins in all of Scotland, to push away the truth. His arms still braced wide on the sink, Quin squeezed his eyes shut and willed himself not to cry.

Eight

In which Lady Charlotte becomes Shockingly forgetful.

December settled over Buckinghamshire like a mantle of gray wool, each day shorter than the last. Then came two days of wind and rain. At Hill Court, Viviana was seized with a restlessness which no one else seemed to share. The children had fallen into a happy routine of study and play, and were well entertained by Lady Alice's children, whose governess brought them over almost every afternoon.

Lord Chesley was a devoted host, but he preferred to spend his time with the gentlemen in the music room, observing "the miracle of creation," as he called it. Viviana spent an hour each morning seeing to the running of the household with Mrs. Douglass, a duty Chesley had charmingly foisted off on her. The rest of the forenoon was devoted to her harp or her violin.

Nowadays, however, even her music no longer soothed her as it had done during some of her darkest and loneliest days in Venice. When it failed her now, she would

simply leave the house to walk or to ride if it was not rain-
ing—and sometimes even the ill weather did not deter
her. Rarely did anyone wish to accompany her. The chilly
English air, Viviana found, had its advantages.

It was just such an afternoon when she was stopped by
the gentlemen in the music room. "Why, there she is
now," she heard Chesley cry out. "Most fortuitous!"

Her father had turned round on his stool near the pianoforte. *"Vieni qui,* Vivie," he said, eagerly motioning her
inside. "Sit, sit!"

"Sicuro, Papà." She went in, still carrying her cloak and
gloves, and took the chair he had offered.

Lord Digleby had risen from the pianoforte's bench.
"Have a look, Contessa," he said eagerly as he passed a
sheet of roughly marked music to her. "This is Maria's last
aria, when she discovers Orlando making love to her
maid. What do you think?"

A little nervously, Viviana scanned it, mentally hum-
ming. The lyrics she had already seen, but the music was
new to her.

"Here is the opening," said Digleby, sending his fingers crashing down in a dramatic fashion. But the passage
soon turned dark and heart-wrenching, and Viviana
could see that the beauty of the lyrics was intended to
take over. Her father's eyes followed Digleby's hands on
the keyboard as a father might watch a much-loved child.
Indeed, his music was much his progeny as was Viviana
herself.

The music came to a halt. Viviana tried to hand the
sheet back. "It is lovely, Lord Digleby. Utterly haunting."

Digleby smiled a little tightly. "How kind you are,
Contessa," he said. "Your father and I wrote it together.

But can you sing it, please, and give us your suggestions?"

"My suggestions?"

"Here, for example," said her father, pointing to a particular passage as he spoke in rapid Italian. "I think it may be too funereal, when it needs instead to soar. I must hear you sing it to be sure."

Viviana stood, and laid the sheet on the pianoforte. "Oh, you cannot possibly need my help," she insisted. "It is quite perfect as it is."

Her father gestured at the music. *"Dio mio, Vivie!"* he said impatiently. "Sing! Sing!"

"Oh, give it a try, old girl," said Lord Chesley from the sofa. "I must admit, I am eager to hear it first from a master."

"Va bene," she agreed.

There was nothing else to be done. She had known, eventually, it would come to this. And so she stood, her knees shaking a little, and snatched the sheet from the pianoforte. Digleby smiled, and played the opening chords again. The haunting feel of the melody began to emerge, then to dominate. Viviana filled her lungs and began to sing.

The lyrics began simply enough. The betrayed Maria was plotting revenge against her faithless lover, and the words and music reflected it. Viviana tried to do the piece justice, but several times she faltered, and had to look to the gentlemen for direction. Once her father stopped her, snatched the sheet, and altered the notes slightly. He passed the sheet back.

"Continue, *cara mia,*" he said, lifting his hand.

Viviana stumbled on. Of course, no one expected her to sing well on a rough first pass. The music was yet half-formed, the gentlemen themselves still unsure of just how they wished it to sound.

Apparently, she did not bungle it too badly. When she finished, Lord Chesley stood, applauding enthusiastically. "Brava, brava, my girl!" he said. "You still have the voice of an angel."

Viviana was not at all sure that was the case. She glanced at her father to gauge his response. But he and Lord Digleby had turned back to the pianoforte, already haggling over what changes needed to be made.

Chesley caught her hand as she passed. "You look pale, my dear," he murmured.

She shook her head. "I am well enough, Chesley, thank you."

"You are bored," he said, frowning. "This damned weather has cooped you up. You are used to a life of glamour, and two or three handsome men fawning over you at every turn."

"That is hardly the case," she murmured.

Chesley laughed. "It is *always* the case when I see you, my dear girl," he said. "Now, what to do for this rustic ennui? I know! We shall have a dinner party!"

Viviana smiled wanly. "That would be lovely."

With one last squeeze to her hand, Chesley let her go and returned his attention to the music. In the passageway, Viviana tossed her cloak across her shoulders and drew on her gloves, then made her escape into the cold winter's day.

She would walk, she decided, into the village. She had seen a dressmaker's shop there, and she needed a few warmer, more serviceable things to see her through the English winter. Surely neither Quin nor his mother would frequent the village shops?

The walk was less than a mile, and she saw no one until she entered the village outskirts. Her trip was cut short, however, as soon as she passed by Arlington Park's massive gates. A gig was parked by the gatehouse, attended by a servant. A handsome young man was coming out of the front door carrying a brown leather satchel. In the doorway, Lady Charlotte leaned upon a brass-knobbed stick, eyeing him a little nastily, as if to reassure herself that the gentleman was indeed departing. Her keen eyes did not miss Viviana.

"Good afternoon, Contessa!" she called in her quavery voice. "Do come in. I'm just ridding myself of this plague, as you see, and have no one else to amuse me."

The young man paused by the gig and offered his hand. "I am the plague," he said, bowing neatly over her hand. "Dr. Gould, at your service."

"I hope I shan't require them," said Viviana with a smile. "But I am glad indeed to meet you. I am Contessa Bergonzi."

He smiled warmly. "I guessed as much," he said. "We get few such celebrated visitors here."

But Lady Charlotte was looking impatient now. Viviana could see no polite way of refusing her, though she could not imagine why Quin's elderly aunt would wish to see her, particularly given the circumstances of their last meeting. But it was for those very reasons Viviana could not refuse her. To do so would have looked . . . well, guilty.

"You must be frozen through," said Lady Charlotte when they were comfortably situated in her front parlor. "I must find Mrs. Steeple, and tell her to send tea."

Viviana raised her hand. "Please do not put yourself to any trouble on my account."

"Nonsense," she said.

Lady Charlotte was gone but a moment. She settled back into her chair with a gleam in her eye. "How lovely of you to visit me, Contessa," she purred. "The elderly live such quiet existences, we must look to the young for our window on the world."

Viviana looked at her appraisingly. "My window has narrowed considerably, I fear," she said. "May I ask, ma'am, after your health?"

"I'm quite well, thank you." Lady Charlotte looked puzzled.

"You have recovered, then, from—from your fall at Arlington Park?"

"Oh, that silly business!" said the old lady. "Yes, yes, they do say I fainted. I've no memory of it."

Viviana wasn't sure she believed her. Perhaps Lady Charlotte was simply being polite. Still, it was time to change the subject.

Lady Charlotte beat her to it. "I do admire your wardrobe, my dear," she remarked, eyeing Viviana's bottle green walking dress. "Such vivid colors. Such instinctive élan. You must feel like a hothouse orchid amongst a field of common daisies here in our little English village."

"My hair is jet-black, and my skin is too pale," Viviana murmured. "I have always felt I needed color."

"I agree," said the old lady. "We English ladies have such insipid taste."

Viviana turned the subject again. "You spoke of a window on the world, ma'am," she said. "Have you seen much of it?"

"Oh, by no means!" said the old lady, leaning intently forward. "You have visited places I can only dream of.

Tell me, Contessa, what is Vienna like? I have always wished to go there."

Viviana hesitated. "Well, from the little I saw, it was very grand," she said. "I sang in two productions at the Kärnthnerthor, but we had little time for pleasure."

"In my day, we scarcely knew what opera was," said Lady Charlotte wistfully. "Nowadays it is said to be the great new thing. Can you imagine?"

Viviana smiled. "I was simply born to it," she said. "I never thought of it as new or fashionable."

"Ah, yes!" she said. "And you were born in Venice?"

"No, in Rome," she said. "We moved nearer to Venice when my father acquired a patron there. We lived in a villa on his estate."

"Well, when I was your age, plays were the thing," said the old lady. "I actually saw Voltaire's *Irène,* when it opened in Paris. The great man himself was there. It was my only real trip abroad—if one considers France to be so."

"You chose well. Paris is very lovely."

"You've sung there, too, I daresay?"

"Many times," Viviana agreed.

The old lady went on to ask a number of mundane questions about the capitals she had visited and the important people for whom she had performed, until even Viviana began to feel bored. What on earth could Lady Charlotte find so interesting in the career of a has-been soprano? Just then, a young woman came in pushing a trolley which seemed overladen with delicacies.

"Heavens, what a lot of food for only two," murmured Viviana.

But the servant was lingering uncertainly. "Hello, miss," she finally said. "You don't remember me, do you?"

Viviana looked up and sprang at once to her feet. "Lucy—?" she cried, lifting one of the woman's hands in her own. "Oh, Lucy! What a surprise! Oh, *cara mia,* how could I forget you?"

"Have you met our Lucy, Contessa?" Lady Charlotte looked surprised.

"But yes, she looked after me for a time," exclaimed Viviana. "She was sent to me by Lord Chesley when first I came to London. And I have not been so well cared for since."

Lucy blushed. "You always were kind, miss."

"Lucy comes in on Wednesdays to help Mrs. Steeple," Lady Charlotte explained. "But she has four children now who take up most of her time."

"Lucy, let me look at you." Viviana caught her other hand. "Four children!"

"And all healthy, miss," said Lucy.

"This is such a pleasant surprise," said Viviana breathlessly. "And your family? They are well?"

"My sister keeps house for Squire Lawson now," she said. "And Aunt Effie is still at Hill Court."

"Why, I had quite forgotten Mrs. Douglass was your aunt." Viviana smiled. "I did hear, of course, that you'd married your handsome footman, but I got the impression you'd moved away."

"Oh, just to the next village," said Lucy. "Joe came into a little money, miss. He bought the Queen's Arms near Lower Hampden."

"How happy I am for you," said Viviana, dropping Lucy's hands. "I must call on you one afternoon."

"I wish you would, miss," said Lucy shyly. "I've something I'd like to show you."

Viviana lifted her shoulders. "Well, I've nothing to do this afternoon," she said. "What time do you start home?"

"I'll be another hour, thereabouts," said Lucy, looking a bit embarrassed. "But it's a far piece, miss, if you've no carriage. Do you mind the walk?"

"Indeed, I should be glad for it."

"All right, then." Lucy bobbed a little curtsy and started to go, but just then, the sound of a carriage drawing up distracted her. "That'll be his lordship and Lady Alice," said Lucy. "Shall I let them in, ma'am?"

Lady Charlotte looked suddenly confused. "Who?"

"Lord Wynwood and Lady Alice," said Lucy, looking at Lady Charlotte oddly. "They're to take tea with you, ma'am. Had you forgotten?"

"Oh, dear!" said Lady Charlotte. "Have I got myself mixed up again? It cannot be Wednesday already, can it?"

Viviana looked at her suspiciously. "You must be patient with the elderly, my dear," murmured Lady Charlotte, as Lucy left. "When you are old, you will marvel at what one can accidentally forget."

Viviana did not believe this was an accident. But she had little time in which to consider it, for Lucy had thrown open the parlor door, and Alice was sweeping across the room to greet them, her arms wide.

"What a delightful surprise, Viviana!" she said. "Aunt Charlotte did not mention she'd invited you."

Lady Charlotte was looking very small and frail now. "I must have got my days mixed up, my dear," she said, offering her cheek to be kissed. "And Quinten! Come here, my boy. You know Contessa Bergonzi, of course."

Quin bowed stiffly in Viviana's direction. He did not

look pleased to see her. "Good afternoon, ma'am," he murmured. "I trust I find you well?"

Viviana forced a polite smile. "Quite, I thank you."

She did not, however, feel especially well. She said little as Quin and Alice settled in and took a cup of tea from their aunt. Viviana had the sensation of having just walked into a room in which she was not wanted—even resented, perhaps. The vow of peace she had shared with Quin seemed to have been declared null and void on his part. No doubt he resented her presumption in calling upon his aunt. But what choice had she had in the matter?

She realized Lady Charlotte was urging a plate of sandwiches in her direction.

"Thank you, no," she murmured.

"I was fortunate to catch the contessa on her way to the village this afternoon," said Lady Charlotte, setting the plate away. "I had to beg her quite shamelessly to visit me."

"Viviana does love her long walks," said Lady Alice. "And her long rides, too."

"Alice tells me you have three children," said Lady Charlotte. "How lovely that they have traveled to England with you."

"I do not like to be away from them," Viviana admitted. She could feel the heat of Quin's stare burning into her.

"I do so love little ones," said the old woman. "What are their names and ages, pray?"

Viviana hesitated. "Cerelia is my eldest," she said. "Felise is in the middle, and my son, Nicolo, is little more than a toddler."

"Nicolo is Conte Bergonzi di Vicenza now," added Alice. "I collect he looks very like his father?"

"Yes, a little," she admitted. *Liar,* Viviana thought. He looks exactly like his father—which was a very good thing, she supposed, for a boy who was to inherit such a title, and the wealth and power which came with it.

"And how long were you married, my dear?" asked the old lady. "Was it a love match? Or did your families arrange it?"

Viviana was taken aback. "Why, about seven years," she answered. "It was a marriage arranged by my father whilst I was living in London."

Lady Charlotte clucked sympathetically. "So you did not know him, then? That must have been difficult."

"No," said Viviana swiftly. "I mean, yes. I did know him. Bergonzi was my father's patron. As I said, I grew up in a villa on his estate."

"Ah!" said Lady Charlotte. "That made it easier, I daresay.

Easier than what? Viviana wondered. *Easier than bearing a child out of wedlock?* But she was not at all sure of that now. She was not at all sure that, had she the chance to do it all over again, she would not have chosen to live her life as a scandalous, fallen woman.

"And how is your brood, my dear?" said Lady Charlotte to her niece. "Has Christopher got rid of that cough?"

Alice grinned. "It lasted just as long as Lucy's homemade horehound drops," she admitted. "And then we had a miraculous recovery. Where is Lucy, by the way?"

"In the kitchen." Lady Charlotte brightened. "Did you know Lucy used to work for Contessa Bergonzi? They met again this very afternoon."

Alice looked at her in some surprise.

"Yes, when I first came to London," said Viviana quietly.

"Why, I remember!" said Alice. "Uncle Ches sent Lucy to London to look after for one of his protégés. Was that you, Viviana? Oh, how I wish I had met you then!"

Viviana felt herself blush. Quin had twisted in his chair and was studying a landscape hanging above the mantel with grave intensity. Suddenly, Alice's eyes lit with mischief.

"Quin," she said sharply, "you knew Viviana when she lived in London, did you not?"

Quin returned his gaze to the ladies and cleared his throat. "I—yes—I believe we did meet." His brow furrowed. "Did we not, Contessa?"

"*Si,* Lord Chesley introduced us," Viviana murmured.

Lady Charlotte clapped her hands with delight. "How fascinating!" she said. "Did you never run into one another afterward?"

Viviana opened her mouth, then closed it again. Alice played a dangerous game, for she'd already had part of the story from Lord Chesley himself. As to Quin, his posture had gone rigid, his face pale. He was ashamed of what she had been to him. Well, damn him. She was not proud of it, either.

"I think we met again, once or twice," she answered. "I am not perfectly sure."

Quin was eyeing her over his teacup, his eyes hard and dark. "We met again," he said tightly. "Once or twice."

"Oh, come now, Quin!" said Alice teasingly. "Uncle Ches told me you were madly in love with her!"

"In those days, I fell madly in love with a frightening ease," he coolly returned. "Young fools tend to do that."

Alice looked as if her fun had been spoilt. Abruptly, she took another tea cake and nibbled at it.

Lady Charlotte smiled benignly at her grandnephew. "And how long do you intend to rusticate, my boy?" she asked. "London is not calling you yet?"

Alice winked at her aunt. "London has suddenly become a very small town, I'm afraid," she said. "It is not quite large enough to hold Sir Alasdair MacLachlan *and* Quin just now."

Lady Charlotte blinked owlishly. "Oh, dear! I hope, Quin, that the two of you have not quarreled? I like Alasdair, even if he is an unabashed scoundrel."

"Well, his days as a scoundrel are over," said Alice. "Depend upon it."

Her brother rolled his eyes. "Oh, for God's sake, Alice!"

"Well, we might as well all behave sportingly about it." Alice paused to brush a crumb from her skirt. "Sir Alasdair will be announcing his betrothal to Miss Esmée Hamilton shortly," she went on. "Mamma had it from Lady Tatton herself."

"Good Lord!" said Lady Charlotte. "Is Lady Tatton pleased?"

"Not especially, no," said Alice, pausing to pluck a biscuit from the tea table. "Ooh, is that a macaroon? I must have one. No, Lady Tatton isn't thrilled, but she acknowledges, I daresay, the delicacy of the situation. They are to be married in the spring, and as soon as the weather clears, they are going to Castle Kerr for a very long visit."

A dead silence fell across the table. Quin looked as if he'd like to strangle his sister. "Castle Kerr?" said Lady Charlotte lightly. "Where is that?"

"In Argyllshire," said Alice. "It is Sir Alasdair's seat."

"Ah, I did not know," said Lady Charlotte.

"They are to spend much of the spring and summer

there," Alice went on. "It will be very dull in town this season, I daresay, without Sir Alasdair to stir up any scandals."

Viviana imagined his marriage would be scandal enough for two or three seasons. Unfortunately, she was more than a little complicit in that unfortunate mess. Suddenly, Viviana could bear it no longer. She jerked abruptly to her feet. "I am sorry," she stammered. "I had best go finish my errands. Thank you, Lady Charlotte, for your hospitality."

"Oh, but you mustn't, my dear!" said the old lady. "We are all amongst friends here. Besides, you're to wait on Lucy."

"I shall return for her later."

"Well," said Alice, "if Viviana is leaving, I believe I shall have that last macaroon."

Quin, too, came to his feet. "Pray do not get up, Aunt," he said. "I shall see the contessa out."

Alice's eyes flickered with interest, then cut a swift glance up at Viviana. "It was lovely to run into you, my dear," she said. "Shall I see you tomorrow for battledore?"

"Yes, as you wish," said Viviana. "Thank you, and good afternoon."

Wordlessly, Viviana retraced her steps, pausing only long enough to retrieve her cloak. She did not look at Quin, whose tread was heavy behind hers. She went down the stairs, her mind in turmoil.

Good Lord, this was adding insult to injury for Quin! Sir Alasdair MacLachlan was one of his dearest friends. No wonder he looked like a storm cloud. And what had Alice been thinking, to bring it up in such circumstances? Their accidental meeting had turned into a fiasco. She was angry; angry with all of them, herself included—but most of all, she was angry with Quin. His cynical remark about falling in love had cut her, and deeply.

She put her hand on the doorknob just as Quin grasped one of her shoulders from behind. His grip was firm. Heat radiated from his body, warming her spine. "Viviana, wait."

She whirled about to face him. "Why?" she snapped. "And why must you follow me, Quinten? We have nothing further to say to one another. What must your aunt and sister think?"

His eyes glittered darkly. "They think something's afoot," he gritted.

"Oh, I have no doubt of it!" she agreed. "So why are we standing here together?"

His jaw had hardened to match his eyes. "Damn it, Viviana, did it never occur to you that perhaps we ought to get our stories straight? These questions shan't stop, you know. Not until one of us leaves this village."

"Yes, and whose fault is that?" she asked bitterly. "But by all means, Quinten, let us get it over with. I am tired of this subtle inquisition. What was that place yesterday? A cottage, you called it?"

"A cottage, yes."

Viviana narrowed her eyes. "Be there tomorrow at one, then," she challenged. "Be there, and let us settle this once and for all. And while we are there, perhaps we can think of some way to avoid running into one another again."

He stepped back with a soft oath. Viviana jerked open the door. She rushed down the steps, still carrying her cloak across her arm, heedless of the cold. She hastened into the little lane which led through the village, but instead of turning left toward the High Street and its shops, she turned right and retraced her steps but a few yards, pausing near the corner of the gatehouse's side garden.

She stood there for a moment, grappling for strength and reliving the feel of Quin's fingers digging into her flesh. Damn it, he was right, loath though she was to admit it. The Spanish Inquisition was nothing compared to Lady Alice's probing and Lady Charlotte's sly meddling. But what sort of fool was she, to arrange to meet Quin in secret?

He wished them to get their stories straight. And there had been a raw frustration in his voice and some other nameless emotion with it. Perhaps he wished for something else altogether. Would she agree to that, too?

Suddenly, she did not know. *Dio!* She did not know, and it terrified her.

For nine long years, she had hated him. Hated him for making her love him. Hated him for making her doubt herself and what she had done to survive. And now she had arranged for them to meet. Alone. At that run-down little house in the middle of nowhere. And he had agreed quite readily.

Perhaps he was in need of another mistress, now that his pretty bride had run into the arms of his best friend. Suddenly, guilt assailed her anew. She should never have gone to his study that day. Just as she now had no business going back to that cottage.

A door slammed in the distance, recalling her to the present. Viviana looked about and saw Lucy coming around the corner of the house with what looked like a mop bucket. She tossed the contents unceremoniously into the shrubbery.

"Lucy!" Viviana hissed.

Lucy peered into the shadows toward the lane. "Is that you out there, miss?" she asked. "Are you ready to go, then?"

Viviana hastened toward her. "When you are ready," she answered. "You mustn't hurry on my account."

But Lucy was drying her hands on her apron and looking at Viviana strangely. "Just let me fetch my cloak, miss," she said. "And if I were you, I'd be wearing that one, and not carrying slung over my arm like this was May Day."

The walk to Lower Hampden was not so long after all. By the time they reached Lucy's house, a pretty white-washed cottage which sat some distance from the actual village, Viviana had managed to relax and put Quinten Hewitt from her mind. It was wonderful to laugh with Lucy about old times. During their early days in London, Viviana's imperfect English, combined with Lucy's rustic expressions, had made for some humorous misunderstandings.

Looking back on it, Viviana realized just how much they had shared. Both of them had been homesick and a little frightened of London. Viviana was sorry they had not kept in touch, but Lucy did not read or write. Nonetheless, Viviana had managed to hear bits and pieces from Chesley, enough to learn of Lucy's marriage and her first child. Then Lucy had moved away—or so Viviana had understood.

Lucy pushed open the heavy wooden door, and the delicious aroma of ginger and the tang of dried apples wafted on the air. Inside, the house was dark and still. The older children, Lucy explained, were still at the village school, whilst the youngest, a little boy, was under the care of her husband's mother, who lived next door to the Queen's Arms.

"Joe don't really care for me working," said Lucy as she bustled about the kitchen. "He says it's not proper for a tavern keeper's wife. But once in a blue moon, Aunt Effie needs me up at Hill Court. As to Lady Charlotte, 'tis but once a week. And I remind Joe that she's old and set in her ways. I know how she likes things done. And she won't always be around, will she?"

"None of us will," murmured Viviana.

"Besides," Lucy went on, "there's no money changes hands since the old earl died."

"What do you mean?"

Lucy set two mugs and a heavy earthenware pitcher on the table. "If I do for Lady Charlotte when I'm needed, Mr. Herndon said, then Lord Wynwood agreed we could stay here rent-free," she said. "And frankly, miss, I don't want my young ones hanging about tavern folk all the livelong day—and especially not at night."

Lucy poured what looked like cold, delicious cider and settled down in a chair near Viviana. After a few sips and a little more idle chatter, she leapt up, and motioned Viviana into one of the side rooms, a small bedchamber.

The bed inside was draped with a blue woolen counterpane, and beside it sat a cradle carved of solid oak.

"It's a beauty, miss, ain't it?" said Lucy, giving it a little nudge with one finger so that it gently rocked.

Viviana understood at once. This, then, was her gift to Lucy. She had bought it, just as Viviana had asked all those years ago. "Lucy, it is the prettiest cradle I've ever seen."

"I've laid me four babies in that cradle now, miss, and thought of your kindness every time," said Lucy. "And—oh!" She turned to a small deal chest, and drew open the top drawer. "Here is the little gown you sent when Hannah was born. I wish you could have seen her, miss, I really do. Pretty as a proper little lady, she was."

But Viviana was still staring at the empty cradle and fighting down an unexpected wave of maternal yearning. "Our children are our most precious possession, are they not?" she said quietly. "The joy, and sometimes the sorrow, which they bring us cannot be understood by one who has not raised them."

The room fell silent for a moment. Quietly, Lucy shut the chest drawer, and slowly turned to face her. "Miss, forgive me for asking, but . . . but *why* did you do it?"

Viviana turned and drifted back toward the tidy kitchen. "Do what, Lucy?" But she was afraid she knew what Lucy was asking.

"You know," she answered. "To just up and leave London like that. To marry someone else. It's not my place to say, miss, but it don't seem right, somehow."

"Right for whom, Lucy?" asked Viviana quietly. "For my child? Would it have been better for her to be born a bastard?"

"I'm not saying that." Lucy drew out a chair at the table for Viviana, then picked up the earthenware pitcher of cider again. "But perhaps . . . perhaps you didn't give Mr. Hewitt a chance."

"I gave him a chance," said Viviana, dropping her gaze. "He did not wish to marry. Not to me. I was not surprised, of course. So I kept my pride—and I kept my troubles to myself."

Lucy sat down abruptly. "Lord Gawd, miss!" she whispered. "You didn't tell him?"

Viviana stared into her cider and shook her head.

Lucy's opinion was plain in her tone. "You ought to have done, miss," she warned. "Really, you still ought. It don't seem wise to keep such a thing from a man."

Viviana's head jerked up. "Tell him now?" she echoed incredulously. *"Dio mio,* Lucy! What good would that do my daughter? She is the only person who matters now. Her father made his choice."

"Well, it's not my place say," Lucy repeated. "But I was the one, miss, left to explain your haring off like that to Mr. Hewitt. You weren't there. You didn't see him."

"My leaving spoiled his fun, *si?*"

Lucy looked at her chidingly. "Oh, miss, it weren't like that," she said. "Devastated, he was—and not quite right since, if you ask me."

"Oh, Lucy!" she said. "You are having romantic imaginings."

Lucy frowned. "Well, I do live here, miss, not a mile from Arlington's back gates," she said. "Pr'haps I don't see the family regular, but I know a thing or two about what goes on up there. And he's not happy. Any fool with eyes can see that."

Viviana almost wished Lucy spoke the truth. How pathetic that was!

"Well," said Lucy after a moment had passed, "do as you think best, miss. I believe you're wrong, but you can depend on me to keep my mouth shut. And your husband's dead now, so I reckon that part's laid to rest."

Lightly, Viviana touched Lucy's arm. "Lucy, I did not lie to Gianpiero, if that is what you think," she said. "He wished desperately to marry me. I—I told him I carried a child."

Lucy's eyes widened. "And he married you anyway, miss?" she answered. "Many a man would not have been so kind."

Viviana's mouth twisted. "It was not a kindness," she said.

"What, then?" Lucy looked at her blankly.

Viviana hesitated. "It was a matter of possession," she finally said. "Gianpiero wished to make certain I did not slip from beneath his thumb and vanish again. Not unless he wished it."

"And so you struck a bargain, miss? Is that it?"

"A devil's bargain," Viviana whispered. "My body for his name."

Lucy's expression soured. "It is often the way of men, isn't it, miss?"

"It is the way of most men, I sometimes think."

Lucy lifted one shoulder. "Well, my Joe's been a good man to me," she said. "I guess that Gianpiero must have wanted you something frightful."

Frightful. Yes, that was one word for it. "He said that he did," Viviana whispered. "And he married me, Lucy, with his eyes open, knowing that I did not love him. But I was a good wife. I did not wish him dead. I swear, I did not."

Lucy leaned forward, and patted her hand where it lay upon the table. "Well, just put it from your mind, miss," she said soothingly. "It's water under the bridge now."

At Viviana's quizzical look, Lucy smiled. "It means that what's done is done, and no point mourning over it," she clarified, pushing away the mug. "Now, I suppose I'd best hasten up to the Arms and get little Teddy. Will you come along with me, miss? I know it's just a tavern, but it's a respectable enough place."

Viviana smiled, and pushed her chair back. "I should be pleased, Lucy, to go. Very pleased indeed."

The feeble afternoon sun had finally emerged by the time Lord Wynwood and his sister departed their great-aunt's house. They left Lady Charlotte in good spirits, intent upon paying an afternoon call to the vicar, which was yet another duty Quin had neglected.

Suddenly, he decided to neglect it just a little longer. Squinting his eyes against the low sun, Quin helped Alice up the steps into his carriage. "You go on without me, Allie," he said when she had settled in. "I cannot bear another call today."

Alice frowned down on him. "We shan't be over half an hour," she said. "Really, Quin! What has got into you? And how will you get home?"

"I shall walk," he answered. "The fresh air will do me good."

He did not wait to hear his sister's further protests and set off in the direction of the footpath, a shortcut through the woods. He had no taste for the endless round of social calls which life in the country now required of him. Instead, he found himself surprisingly eager to return to Arlington. He wished to summon Herndon to his office so that they could discuss the planned repairs to Chandler's granary.

After his day spent touring tenant farms, Quin realized it was also time to review Herndon's list of projects, to see what other urgent needs had been left hanging.

And in doing all of this, Quin had begun to feel the faintest stirring of usefulness. That feeling had been bolstered by Herndon, who had seemed grateful, and eager to begin the work. They had parted quite amicably. And yet, Quin had been avoiding his estate manager ever since.

Quin looked up to see that the rolling grounds of the gatehouse had given way to the dense patch of forest which encircled Arlington Park. Within, it was darker, and a little colder, too. Quin realized he had not fastened his greatcoat, and did so at once. He thought again of Herndon, and wondered what, if anything, he ought to say to the man. There was something which had been weighing on his mind.

That same evening he had given Herndon his list, Quin had escaped the house after dinner in a strange state of mind. Still disconcerted by his little contretemps with Viviana at the cottage, Quin had decided to walk alone in the Tudor garden. At least, he had believed himself alone—until he had seen Herndon with Alice.

Quin still could not quite put his finger on what it was that had so disturbed him. Perhaps it was the way they had walked, like the very dearest of friends, their heads so close together they almost touched. Or perhaps it was his sister's light, lilting laugh; the one he had not heard since well before her marriage. But most likely, it had been the expression of unadulterated joy which he had caught on Herndon's face.

Quin had always thought of his estate manager as being stern, almost emotionless. He certainly had not looked emotionless with Alice. And Quin had felt—well, not anger. He had not even felt that Herndon was being presumptuous. He had felt ... *envy*. Yes, that was it. Envy that someone—two people, actually—whom he admired so thoroughly could find such joy in one another's company.

Quin wondered if he would ever know that kind of joy. Oh, he had known pleasure and comfort aplenty—perhaps too much of the former. He had had the good life handed to him on a crystal platter, and fed to him with a silver spoon. He knew it, and was not ungrateful. But where joy should have been there seemed only a restive emptiness.

Of course he had once loved Viviana—or thought he had—and he had experienced a great many emotions in her company. A rushing, crashing riptide of emotions. Angst. Pleasure. Jealousy. Desire. But joy? No, that he could not recall.

Yes, he envied Alice and Herndon. He wished them both very happy, though he deeply doubted they would find happiness together. His mother would put a stop to that. And he could not manage Allie's problems for her. He could barely manage his own.

Just then, something hard struck the top of his beaver hat, bounced off, and landed on the path. Quin stopped and picked it up. A conker—round, brown, and perfect. And enormous. For a moment, he studied it, boyhood bloodlust surging in his heart. He weighed the nut in his hand. Yes, a sixer, for sure. He would not even need to wheedle Mrs. Prater into baking this one. It could probably take out a pane of glass at a hundred paces. Feeling silly, and strangely sentimental, Quin slipped his prize into his pocket.

But no sooner had he set off again than another struck

him, a little harder this time. And this time he did not miss the spate of soft giggles which followed. He turned all the way around on the footpath, the hems of his great-coat swirling out around his boots. Nothing. And then he looked up, as he should have done at the outset.

From amongst the bare branches, a soft, perfect oval of a face looked back at him. *Viviana.* But not Viviana, either.

"I saw you," said the child in the tree.

Quin picked up the horse chestnut. "I noticed," he said, tossing it up at her.

She tried to catch it and failed miserably. "No, I meant I saw you at the amphitheater," she said, scrabbling down one branch as if to better study him. "Nadia was flirting with you. I think she wanted you to kiss her."

Ah, the fetching little acrobat! He had quite forgotten. But he had not forgotten the child. "You'd best come down, Cerelia," he ordered. "You are up too high—unless you have become an acrobat since last we met."

"I can climb," she said disdainfully. Then, clever as an organ-grinder's monkey, the girl swung down another branch, her petticoats flouncing about her dainty boots as she did so.

Quin tried to scowl at her. "The truly professional tree climbers don't go it alone, you know," he remarked after a few moments had passed. "Who would send for help if you fell?"

The girl was halfway down. Her heavy, bronze-colored hair was sliding from its braid on one side, and he could see that she'd rent a seam under the arm of her coat. "I shan't fall," she said in her faintly accented English. "I never do. Besides, I'm not alone."

"Oh?" he asked. "Who is with you?"

She clutched tight to a branch and grinned down at him over her shoulder. *"You* are, *signore,"* she said.

Quin could not help but grin back at her. "Ah, but I am a most unreliable sort of chap," he answered. "Never around when I'm needed. Ask anyone who knows me."

The girl kept winding her way down, carefully placing her hands and feet. Somehow, he knew better than to offer his help. "Actually, I came with my friends," she said, as she caught the last branch. "Lottie and Christopher. Do you know them?"

Her feet touched the ground, light as a thistle blossom. Quin swept off his hat, for it somehow seemed the right thing to do. "I do indeed," he said. "But I certainly don't see them here, and I am fairly sure I would recognize them. I am their uncle, you see."

Her face brightened a little at that. "Are you?" she asked, looking up at him. "Your name is Lord Wynwood, is it not? Do you know the little brook just at the bottom of this hill?"

"Yes, yes, and—er, yes. I do know the little brook."

She gestured toward the coombe below. "Well, they went down there to look for salamanders."

Quin crooked one brow. "Isn't it a little cold for that?"

Looking mildly embarrassed, she shrugged. "I don't know what it is, this salamander," she confessed, as a cascade of bronze hair slithered over her shoulder.

Quin searched his mind. He had briefly studied Italian, back when he had harbored the foolish notion of rushing off to the Continent and dragging Viviana back to England. "A salamander is a creature," he said. "And rather like *un . . . un alamaro."*

"A frog?" she said sharply.

He shook his head. "No, not a frog," he responded, trying to dredge up the right word. "I meant to say *una lucertola*. I think."

The girl was trying not to laugh. "A lizard, do you mean?"

He gave up, and nodded. "Yes, like a lizard."

Her face broke into a smile that was like a ray of sunshine. "You are very kind to try to speak Italian to me."

"Grazie," he said. "I fear I do not know any Venetian. It is much the same, is it not?"

She laughed. "Somewhat, yes," she said. "But at home, Mamma and I speak Italian or English."

Lord, she was going to be a beauty, he thought. Her face looked so much like her mother's it was breathtaking. A pity her father was dead. In a few years, it was going to require six or seven resolute parents to keep the young men at bay. At that thought, something swift and protective surged through him. Followed by a sense of grave unease.

Quin remembered himself as a young man, recalled with horror the lascivious thoughts and wicked imaginings which had utterly possessed his mind. God preserve her from that! But she was not his responsibility, was she?

Well, no. But she was a child. A child who was standing in the freezing cold in the middle of his wood. There was a certain moral obligation in that, wasn't there? He looked up through the bare, clattering branches, and saw something—snow, or perhaps just ash—come swirling down.

"You had best go fetch the others, Cerelia," he said. "We shall walk you home first, then I will take Chris and Lottie back to Arlington Park."

The girl stuck out her lip. "I wanted to climb another tree."

"This isn't negotiable," he said firmly. "I think we might be in for a little snow."

The child's face lit up. *"Snow—?"*

Just then, a crashing arose in the tangle of rhododendron which meandered up from the stream's edge. The two wanderers burst from the greenery. "Uncle Quin! Uncle Quin!" Lottie rushed up the hill to greet him. "Have you come to find us? We are not lost, you know."

"Are you not?" Quin caught her around the waist, lifted her off her feet, and spun her round on the footpath. "Perhaps I am lost, Lottie. Perhaps you have found me. Did you ever think of that?"

"Oh, poo!" said Lottie. "Mamma says you are a vagabond. They are never lost."

She was laughing when he set her back down on her feet again, and she clung to him dizzily, her arms wrapped round his neck. It was then that he noticed the expression on Cerelia's face. She looked . . . not envious, but almost painfully alone. She literally stood apart from them, on the opposite side of the footpath, which might as well have been a gaping chasm.

Lottie and Chris, however, did not notice their little friend. "Look, Uncle Quin," said Chris, ramming his hand deep in his coat pocket. "We've got conkers! Great, hard ones!"

"Oh ho!" Never one to be outdone on such an important point as the size of his conker, Quin dug into his own pocket, and produced the one Cerelia had bounced off his hat.

"Lud!" said Lottie.

Quin smiled. "Now this, Christopher, is a *conker,*" he said. "Go ahead and string yours up if you've a mind to take a thrashing. But it shan't stand a chance against this behemoth."

"Crikes!" said the boy. "That's the biggest ever! Where'd you find it, Uncle Quin?"

Quin restored the nut to his pocket. "Actually, it belongs to Cerelia," he said, turning to wink at her. "I am just keeping it for her."

"See, Lottie!" The little boy tossed a disdainful glance at his sister. "I told you there wouldn't be any salamanders down there. Perhaps I could have found that one."

"They're just big acorns," said Cerelia. "I cannot see what all the fuss is about."

"Actually, Cerelia, they are chestnuts," said Quin. "But not the kind you eat. Now, it is going to be dark soon. Let's be off, shall we? And on the way, we shall tell you all about conkers, and how we English like to string them up, and swing them at one another, usually until someone's nose gets bloodied."

Cerelia cut a strange glance up at him. "That sounds silly."

"It is silly," said Quin. "Frightfully silly—especially when grown men engage in it."

They set off for home with the girls on either side of him. Lottie, of course, slipped her gloved hand into Quin's. On impulse, he caught Cerelia's hand in the other. Chris darted on ahead, pausing now and again to shuffle through the dead leaves beneath the chestnut trees.

Cerelia's good humor was restored. She and Lottie chattered gaily as they wound their way back out of the wood and in the direction of Hill Court. But as the evening's chill deepened, the girls' teeth began to chatter. Quin opened his greatcoat, tucked them close to his sides, and folded it around them as best he could. Laughing, they waddled along together, looking, he imagined, rather like a drawing he had once seen of a great American grizzly bear.

It felt strangely pleasant to be walking with his arms and his coat wrapped about two small children. It also felt as though he'd seen more of his nieces and nephew these last few days than he had in the whole of their lives. And to his surprise, he had rather enjoyed it. They seemed genuinely fond of him, especially Alice's youngest, who had developed something of an obsession with his cravat pin.

Each time he visited them in the nursery, Diana would clamber onto his lap and pluck at it most determinedly. He had finally decided simply to remove it and give it to the child, but Alice had caught him and soundly scolded him. Four-year-olds, apparently, were prone to swallowing small, pretty objects.

Such a thing would never have occurred to him. Indeed, he knew nothing at all of children. Oh, he had always assumed he would have two or three; it was expected. It was necessary, especially for his mother's sake. But he had always imagined they would be like small adults, and that he would see little of them. They would be raised by nurses and governesses, he had supposed.

But why had he supposed it? He and Alice had not been reared in such a way. Their parents had been an ever-present force in their lives. Family outings had been frequent affairs. Their father, for all his reserve, had seen them two or three times a day. Their mother doted on them; never had she failed to kiss them good night and see them tucked safely into bed.

The truth was, he simply felt no connection to these preordained children he was meant to have. He had not

actually tried to imagine what it would be like to be a father since—well, since Viviana Alessandri. It was almost
an embarrassment to recall it now, how he would sometimes thrust himself so deep inside her, reveling in the
rush of his seed toward her womb, and hope.

In those rash, heedless moments, he had been unable to
stop the vision of what it would be like to see her soft,
smooth belly grow round with his child. He had wanted it
so very desperately, even as he had realized the hell they
both would pay should it ever actually happen. Good
God, his father would have disowned him. His mother
would have swooned and taken to her bed for a week.

But neither of those reactions seemed so horrific now.
He was almost ten years older. He had lived through some
dark days. To worry about his parents having fits and
swoons seemed almost laughable now.

They were not so laughable when one was but twenty
years old, and unsure of one's place in the world. And yet,
those had been the only children Quin had ever pictured
in his mind. The ones he had wanted to give Viviana
Alessandri. He was damned lucky he hadn't got his wish,
too.

Then, he had assumed Viviana understood concep-
tion—or rather, how a woman avoided it. She had seemed
so sophisticated, so urbane. But he now realized that, in all
likelihood, she had done nothing. Certainly she had taken
no steps which he, now older and wiser, would have recognized as contraception.

He looked down again at Cerelia, who looked so very
much like her mother it suddenly made his heart ache.
Gianpiero Bergonzi had got his wish, had he not? He had
made three children with the wife he had so boldly mar-

ried. Quin wondered if all three were this beautiful. If they looked anything like their mother, then the answer was a resounding *yes*.

Unexpectedly, Cerelia tugged on his hand. "I know the way from here, Lord Wynwood," she said softly. "You may let me go now."

They were nearing the end of the wood, and through the thinning trees, he could see the soft lights of his uncle's stables coming into view. He felt Cerelia's fingers loosen about his own. And suddenly, Quin became aware of an awful, choking knot in his throat. His hand tightened on the child's almost involuntarily.

He did not want to let her go, this beautiful piece of the woman he had once loved. He wanted to gaze upon her face and think upon the past. The awful, miserable past he had once sworn to forget. But something seemed to have changed.

Oh, he knew what had changed. Everything. His whole life. The past had returned to torment him, and his future seemed blighted and barren again.

Good God, Viviana Alessandri! After all these years. And this time, he was not at all sure he could survive it. This time, there was no easy way to deaden the pain of an old wound sliced open to bleed anew. And though he would never have admitted it to anyone, he was tired, so bloody weary of living a life devoid of hope and joy. A life where one could imagine, and even wish for, a future, and for the love and the family which came with it.

Yes, he was beginning to fear that he knew what had changed—or perhaps *not changed* was the more correct phrase.

"Lord Wynwood?" said the small voice again.

He gave her hand one last squeeze and let her go.

Cerelia slithered her way out of the folds of his coat. Cold air breezed in and wrapped around his heart. They watched her go in the swiftly approaching dusk, the hem of her heavy wool skirt brushing across the lawn as she dashed up the hill toward his uncle's house.

She had almost reached the back terrace when he saw an indistinct figure come sweeping round from the front of the house. A woman in a bottle green gown and cloaked in black, whose face he could not see. But he did not need to see it, for the proud set of her shoulders and the angle of her chin gave her away.

At the corner of the house, mother and daughter met. He saw Viviana embrace Cerelia ardently, then urge her up the terrace steps. Neither spared a glance toward the three who waited at the foot of the hill.

He waited until they had reached the back door. A shaft of glowing gold lamplight spilt out across the terrace as they opened it. Then they slipped inside, their happy laughter carrying down the hill on the cold winter's wind. The door closed, and the shaft of golden lamplight vanished. Quin felt, inexplicably, as if he had just been shut out. Viviana and the children were safe and snug together now. They were happy. They were a family, the four of them. And he was not a part of it. A sinking sense of emptiness weighed him down.

He had the strangest feeling that he had just made a terrible, irreparable mistake. But how could that be? Somehow, he turned to Chris and Lottie and forced himself to smile. "One down," he said. "And two to go."

Nine

In which the Contessa has An Assignation.

Viviana was chilled to the bone by the time she reached the old cottage the following afternoon. A freezing rain had fallen during the night, icing the trees and weighing down the hedgerows which lined the last of her route. The clothes which she had brought with her from Venice—the very warmest things she possessed—were woefully inadequate to the Buckinghamshire winter. She wished desperately for some thick stockings and a habit of good Scotch wool; indeed, she should have ordered them from the village seamstress yesterday.

Instead, she had let herself be distracted by Lady Charlotte. And this, apparently, was where her foolishness had taken her, she mused as she surveyed the scene beyond the rotted gateposts. The ramshackle cottage looked as abandoned and unkempt as ever. With grave unease, she slid off her saddle and somehow landed on both feet, which felt like torpid blocks of ice.

After leading her mount around to the back of the cot-

tage, she secured him in the rear of the shed—the half
which had not yet buckled under the weight of its roof—
and looked about. Obviously, the collapse was not recent.
The former Earl of Wynwood must have been a dreadful
old pinchpenny to let one of his properties come to this.

By the time she returned to the yard, the wind had
picked up afresh. She knocked, and, getting the response
she had expected—nothing—lifted the latch and pushed
on the door anyway. It was stuck, but not locked. Stubbornly, Viviana set her shoulder to the wide planks and
gave it a hearty shove. The hinges squalled, and the door
swung inward, the bottom edge dragging on the flagstone
floor.

Inside, the cottage had an air of forsakenness about it,
but was not without charm. There was a smell, a hint of
the mustiness one associated with old wood and a cold
hearth, but there was another, more familiar scent, too.
Viviana drifted about the place, wondering at it, and
pausing from time to time to blow warm air down her
gloves for heat. The cottage's plain, roughly plastered
walls reached up to a low ceiling which was supported by
three broad, age-blackened beams. The flagstone floor
had been swept clean, and the hearth was already laid
with kindling. Yes, the place was vacant—but not entirely abandoned.

The cottage appeared to consist of two rooms with a
kitchen across the back. There was a rickety little con-
traption which might charitably have been called a staircase, but was really just a ladder, ascending into a hole
between the beams. The front room was fitted with an old
chest, a deal corner cupboard, and a pair of sturdy armchairs. She tossed her hat onto one of the chairs, then

peeked into the tiny bedchamber adjacent. In the gloom, she could see a rough-hewn bed covered with an old wool counterpane.

Viviana drifted into the back room, which was more or less empty save for an old-fashioned kitchen basin lined with zinc, and an ancient Welsh dresser, still filled with blue-and-white dishware bearing the cracks and chips of age. A peck basket of apples and two pails of fresh water sat near the sink. How very odd.

Just then, she heard the door scraping open again. She whirled around to see Quin stooping low beneath the lintel. He carried something in on his shoulder and was stomping the slush from his boots as he came. Viviana cleared her throat. He looked up, his eyes widening in surprise.

"It was freezing," she said, her voice tart. "I had no wish to wait in the wind."

He smiled coolly and tossed down the bundle which had been balanced on one shoulder. "I'm late," he admitted. "Mr. Herndon, my steward, detained me. I apologize."

Viviana drifted back into the front room. "Whose house is this?"

"It was occupied until recently by the widow of an old tenant farmer," he answered, shucking his heavy coat and gloves. "But she has gone to live with her daughter in High Wycombe. Herndon cannot let it again until some repairs are made."

"Yes, the shed is falling in," she said crossly.

Quin's smile thinned. "It seems my late father did not believe in making any repairs unless they were urgent," he answered. "And the shed, I collect, was not used by the widow."

"I sheltered my horse there." She looked at him sharply. "Will he be safe?"

"Safe enough," he answered, kneeling by the hearth. "You are cold. Let me start a fire."

"Don't trouble yourself," she returned, her tone impatient. "I cannot stay." She chided herself at once. Good Lord, she was nervous as a cat. How did Quin get under her skin so easily?

He said nothing more but drew a dented old vesta box from his pocket and struck a match on the hearthstone. It flared to life, its unpleasant stench wafting through the room. He held the match to the kindling, which began to smolder, and finally, to burn.

"The new French matchsticks are not so malodorous," she complained. "The tobacconist in the Burlington Arcade sells them a ha'pence a dozen."

He did not answer, but instead stared into the incipient fire. "I am sorry, Viviana, that it is so cold out," he finally said. "And I'm sorry that my shed is about to collapse on your horse. And that I was detained by Herndon. And that my lucifers are stinking up the room. In fact, I'm beginning to be sorry I bothered to come here at all."

Viviana drew back an inch. "*Si,* I am being a—a—what is the English word?" She paused to glare at him. "*Una crudele strega.* A bitch? A witch? I forget how to say it."

"Either will do," he said dryly.

"Well, I shan't apologize," she answered. "I did not wish to come here. Not really."

"And I did not wish you cutting up my peace," he retorted.

"Cutting *your* peace?" she answered, not entirely sure

what he meant, but unwilling to give an inch. "What about my peace? Is it not cut, also?"

"The peace of this cottage," he clarified. "It felt like the only tranquil place in the county until five minutes ago." He was on his feet now, his glossy riding boots set stubbornly wide.

She put her hands on her hips and looked past him, to the bundle he had dropped in one of the wooden armchairs. It looked like blankets. "Someone has been living here," she said. "It is you, is it not?"

He lifted one brow, and said nothing.

"Your scent, it is in the room," she challenged.

"Perhaps it's just the stench of my matches," he said sardonically. "Perhaps you cannot tell the difference anymore, Vivie."

Viviana narrowed her gaze and wondered what to say next. Why was she trying to goad him? She did not know this implacable, steely-eyed man who looked as though ice water might run in his veins. In the old days, Quin had always been hot-tempered and eager for a fight— and eager to make up afterward, too. And she—well, she had been little better. *Like cats in heat,* she thought again. Emotional. Fiery. Passionate. Well, the passion was obviously gone now—thank God.

She resisted the urge to stamp her foot. "Well, let us get on with this, Quentin," she said. "Let us 'get our stories straight,' as you insist we ought."

He took a step toward her. "Firstly, I should like to know what you have told my sister."

"I?" she snapped. "What *I* have told? *Niente affatto!* Nothing! You dare suggest otherwise?"

He looked at her grimly. "I just think it behooves us,

Viviana, to say as little as possible about . . . about the past."

"Andare all'inferno!" she spit.

Oh, he knew how to interpret that one, thought Quin. *Go to hell.* Too bloody late for that. It felt as if he was already there. Somehow, he caught both her hands in his. "Oh, Viviana, for pity's sake," he said. "I only meant that—"

"I know what you meant," she snapped, jerking her hands from his. "Do you think, Quinten, that I am not ashamed of what I was to you? I did not choose it, no. But I gave in to you. And I am still ashamed. More than you will ever know."

"I am sorry to hear you say it," he answered quietly. "I was never ashamed of you, Viviana. I was always proud that you were my—"

"Silenzio!" Viviana's face had gone taut and pale. "I was never yours, Quinten. Never! Can you not comprehend? And you may thank your uncle Chesley, not me, for what little your sister does know."

"Uncle Ches?" Quin was bewildered. "What did he tell her?"

"That you once pursued me, no more," she answered. "What else would he say? He knows nothing."

That was probably true. Quin had taken great pains to hide the relationship from his uncle, in part because Viviana had begged him. But in part because . . . well, because he had feared Chesley's wrath. He had known, had he not, that his uncle would not approve? Chesley had treated Viviana almost as a niece or goddaughter. That very fact should have told Quin something.

But there was something else in Viviana's tone which

Quin did not like. He lifted his head, and pinned her with his gaze. "What did you mean, Viviana, when you said you 'did not choose it'?"

Viviana dropped her eyes. "I just meant that I did not—" She swallowed hard, then glanced back up at him almost accusingly. "That I did not wish to—"

He set both hands on her slender shoulders and gave her a little shake. "What are you saying?" he demanded. "That you did not wish to be my lover?"

She closed her eyes. "I did not wish it," she whispered. "I told you so, Quinten. I told you so a hundred times."

His hands tightened on her shoulders. "Oh, don't play the martyr with me, my dear," he said. "Perhaps I pursued you rather determinedly. But you wanted it, Viviana."

"Determinedly." Her gaze flicked up again. "*Si, caro,* that is one way of putting it."

"Are you saying, Vivie, that you didn't *want* me?" He looked at her incredulously. "That just won't wash, my dear."

She looked weary and a little ill now. "I am not trying to wash anything," she answered. "Please, Quinten, I must be going now. I think there is nothing for us to settle after all."

But a distinctly unpleasant suspicion was creeping over him. "Viviana, good God! Are you . . . are you claiming that I—that I *violated* you?"

The hurt in her eyes deepened. "No, not that." Her voice was so soft now he could barely hear. "I did not scream, did I? I did not kick or strike you, or—or . . ." The words fell away.

"Viviana." His voice was hollow, even to his own ears. "Viviana—that first time—I did *not* force you. Do not you dare try to claim that now, after all that you have put me through."

"Force?" Her eyes widened. "I never said it was that."

"What then? What the devil *are* you saying?"

She looked away. "I just did not wish it to be like that," she answered, sliding her hands up and down her arms. "Can you not understand, Quinten? Not the first time. Not on a divan in some tawdry backstage dressing room, with my skirts hiked up and the filth of the stage still on me. And I wished to be loved. To be *married.* Even the bourgeoisie, *caro mio,* have dreams and principles."

Dreams? Principles? Good God! He dropped his hands and turned away. The walls of the little cottage seemed to shift unsteadily.

He thought back on that night, his brain whirling, his palms beginning to sweat. He had been drinking, but no more than usual. He had been frustrated, yes. He had been growing increasingly desperate for Viviana and beginning to fear he would never win her. And halfway through her amazing performance, he had realized, just as everyone in the theater had, that Viviana Alessandri's life as a mere understudy was over. He had realized, too, that the admiring glances which had driven him to near madness were about to increase tenfold.

But underneath all the anxiety, he had been so very proud. He had known how hard she had slaved for her success. He had awaited her return to her dressing room with an awful mix of delight and nervousness, pacing the floor and waiting for her to make her way through the throng of admirers which always crowded behind the stage. She had arrived utterly aglow with the light of success. Giddy from the thunderous applause. She had thrown herself into his arms with wild abandon. And he had believed that it meant something, something more than it apparently had.

He turned and walked into the shabby kitchen, where he could brace his hands on the old sink and stare through the window as he fought to collect himself. He felt, rather than heard, her follow him in. "You never desired me, Viviana?" he whispered. "It was just me, pushing you into something . . . something you did not want?"

"I was inexperienced, Quinten," she whispered, lightly touching his arm. "How was I to know what I wanted? Did I desire you physically? Yes. You know that I did. But I let my . . . my exuberance get out of hand. I let things go too far."

"How far, Vivie?" he rasped. "How far was too far for you?"

She hesitated, as if measuring her response. "I was not sure, Quinten," she said. And then she answered the question he was afraid to ask. "I had lain with no man before you, *caro*. I did not know—did not even think about the fact that there was a point, emotionally and physically, at which one could not so easily turn back. Did you . . . did you not understand?"

He dragged a hand through his hair, and said nothing.

"I thought it was obvious," she went on. "Obvious, I mean, that I did not know what I was doing. I had always assumed that the first would be my husband."

Quin opened his mouth, then closed it again. "I . . . I never dreamt . . . ," he finally said.

She had circled around the narrow room and into his field of view. She looked deathly pale but almost frighteningly composed. "You never dreamt what, Quinten?"

she went on, no anger in her words now. "Did you simply believe that all singers were whores?"

Yes, he had believed it. It was what everyone said. But who was everyone? His new, ramshackle London friends? "I don't know, Viviana, what I thought," he lied. "I just . . . wanted you."

"And damn the cost?" she finished. "Well, it has cost us both, Quinten. I was a good Catholic girl, but I did not count on the terrible temptation you would present. My resistance lasted all of what—? Two months?"

"But you never said anything," he managed. "You seemed . . . to want me as I wanted you."

"One often wants what one oughtn't have," she answered softly. "You were as beautiful, *caro mio,* as the devil in angel's wings."

He had believed her reticence a game. He had believed that she teased and tormented him deliberately. Hadn't he? With her lush figure and dark, seductive beauty, Viviana had seemed so much older than he. So worldly and sophisticated. He had supposed that she knew what he did not. How to make love instead of just have sex.

Good God, it all seemed unfathomable to him now. Had they both been green as grass? He had been so nervous. So desperate to have her. And he had wondered afterward if she had laughed at him, at his inability to wait. Yes, he had taken her there on the shabby leather divan in her even shabbier dressing room. She had still worn her costume and that hideous wig.

Quin bowed his head and pinched the bridge of his nose until the pain calmed him. "I am sorry, Viviana," he said quietly. "I was nothing but a green boy just up from the country. It is no excuse, I'll warrant, but . . ."

She was looking at him with a worried expression now. *"Non importa,"* she said quietly. "It is just some water under a bridge, *si?"*

He laughed, a sharp, pathetic sound. "Yes, my dear, it is just some water under a bridge."

They remained thus for a time, her hand resting lightly on his arm, his gaze focused blindly through the window. Eventually, he drew in a ragged breath and straightened up. "Well, Viviana, I am sorry it has come to this," he said, without looking at her. "I am sorry for all the mistakes I made. But they were the mistakes of youth and inexperience, if that matters."

"I, too, made mistakes," she admitted.

He let his shoulders fall. "We just need to decide, you and I, what we are going to tell people when they go prying into our business—as my sister is wont to do. So . . . so tell me what it is you wish me to say, Vivie, and I shall say it."

"I did not come here to embarrass you, Quinten," said Viviana. "You have always been free to deny everything if that was your wish."

At last he turned and looked down at her. "I never imagined, Viviana, that you came to embarrass me," he answered. "You are a respectable widow. You have three children. I think you have far more to lose than I."

He meant it, too. What did he have to lose, truly? Esmée had already left him. And sadly, he had scarcely thought of her since. In Town, his reputation was already black as pitch and likely getting worse. He remembered those awful first days following Viviana's return as if they were some sort of dream. Indeed, he wondered if he'd been a little mad.

In the years since they had parted, the breath of scandal had not touched her, so far as he knew. Why would she wish to throw away her respectability? She did not want revenge. Indeed, she had not even wanted *him*. He would do well to remember that it had been she who had left, and not without reason. Her marriage to Bergonzi ate at him, but it was a pain best kept to himself.

He tried to smile at her but it was a rueful, half smile at best. "We will keep to the story we told at Aunt Charlotte's," he said. "We met once or twice, and I tried to court you. You spurned me, and that was the end of it."

Viviana's expression was still unreadable.

"It will work," he said reassuringly. "There is no one who can contradict us, save for Lucy Watson, and she can be trusted."

At last, she nodded. *"Si,* it will work," she echoed. *"Grazie,* Quinten. I should go now. It is a long ride back to Chesley's."

He stepped away and bowed his head. "Yes, of course."

She turned as if to go, sweeping the longer hem of her habit over the kitchen threshold. But at the last minute, she turned around, her eyes suddenly wide and sorrowful. "I have often wondered, Quinten," she said quietly. "After I left, did you . . . did you miss me? Even a little? Or was I just another whore to you?"

He crossed the little room in two strides and snared her hand in his. "Don't say that, Vivie," he growled. "Don't ever use that word again."

She blinked as if startled from a dream. "A Cyprian, you called me," she murmured. "Is that not a whore?"

He bowed his head, and carried her gloved hand to his lips. God help him, but he had said it—and not that long ago. And then he had kissed her, quite rapaciously and cruelly. He was fortunate his mother and his uncle had been able to hush up the worst of the damage.

"Forgive me, Viviana," he managed. "I did say it, but I was wrong. I was angry. You were never that to me."

"Why?" Her voice was plaintive now. "Why, Quinten, were you so angry?"

Inexplicably, he wanted to tell her. To unshackle himself from the awful truth. "Because, Viviana, when you left me, I did miss you," he answered. "Very much."

"In what way?" she asked. "How? I need to know. I need to know that that part of my life was not entirely wasted. That it meant . . . something. To someone."

He dropped her hand, his smile bitter. "It probably was wasted, Vivie," he said. "But it meant something to me, if that helps. I don't think I ever deserved you. And when you left, it was as if someone had stripped my very soul away."

She started to reply, but he set a finger to her lips. "You were never a whore, Vivie. Never a Cyprian. You were my light and my life."

Gently, she pushed his hand away. "Oh, Quinten, would it have been better for the both of us if we had never met at all?" she asked, her voice suddenly unsteady. "Would our lives have been easier? Our hearts less damaged?"

He shook his head. "You cannot look back, Vivie," he answered.

She surprised him then by lifting her hands to his face. "I know," she whispered. "I don't look back. I cannot let myself. I cannot bear to question the choices I have made. But today, I—I just don't know."

He closed his eyes and turned his face into the palm of her glove. He could feel her ever-comforting warmth beneath the supple leather. "Your touch is like a dream to me," he whispered, almost unaware he spoke the words aloud. "So many times I have awakened to this, only to find . . . that it was not this at all."

"Quin, I—" She stopped, and shook her head. "I never meant to hurt you. I never even knew that I had. I am sorry. I regret we could not part as friends."

"It would not have been possible then, Viviana." He set his hands on her shoulders and tried to resist the urge to pull her into his arms. "My feelings for you were not so simple."

"Is it too late now?" she asked. "Oh, Quin, I don't want to be like this. I don't want to die old and bitter. I want to remember my first lover with happiness and not regret. Is there any little scrap of fondness or friendship that we might salvage from this mess we've made?"

He felt a little piece of his heart crumble again. It was not fondness or friendship which he felt for her. It never would be.

Later, he could not have said if Viviana came against him of her own accord, or if he pulled her into his arms. But somehow, his hands were spread wide across her back, and his face was buried in her hair. "I don't know, Vivie," he whispered. "I don't know what is left of my heart. Nothing, I sometimes fear."

"You hurt me, Quinten," she whispered. "I will not pretend you did not. But I think I did not comprehend that I had hurt you."

He drew a deep, unsteady breath. "You spoke of happiness, Viviana, and not regret," he said. "Perhaps we parted on terms so bitter they poisoned us. Perhaps we will look back on this visit of yours and know that we tried to make peace."

"I would like to be rid of the bad memories." Viviana let her eyes drop shut and set her cheek against his chest. "A thousand times, Quinten, I have thought of this. Of what it would be like to have your arms round me again. To feel no anger, but instead, only peace."

He set his lips against the top of her head, and inhaled the soft scent of her hair. "I wish, Vivie, that I could live that time over again," he said. "I know we cannot turn back the clock. I know our ways have parted and will likely never merge again. But I cannot say I won't think of you often."

She looked up, and he felt her shiver in his embrace. Her eyes softened in that too-familiar way he had once loved. And suddenly, it seemed the most natural thing in the world to lower his lips to hers. This time, however, he was slow and patient. This time, he gave her every opportunity to refuse him. She did not. Instead, she lowered her sweep of long, black lashes, and sucked in her breath on a little gasp. Delicately, his lips brushed the swell of her bottom lip.

"Vivie, let me—" he rasped. "No, let *us,* Vivie—let us wipe away the bad memories with a memory of something sweet and good."

He felt her hands move uncertainly to his waist, then felt them settle there, pulling him incrementally nearer. His mouth molded fully over hers, and he kissed her deeply as he drew in the scent which had so long haunted him.

Good God, he had thought never to do this again! Perhaps he oughtn't be doing it now, but Viviana's mouth was softening beneath his, and her lips were parting in sweet invitation. After a moment's hesitation, he answered her, stroking his tongue along the seam of her lips, then sliding gently inside. For long moments he held her, thrusting slowly into her mouth, and reveling in the way her breath caught and the way her body came fully against his.

They came apart breathing rapidly, both of them thinking the same thing, he would have sworn. "Oh, we should not," she whispered, her eyes holding his quite unflinchingly. "Quin, you know where this is going. We never possessed an ounce of restraint between the two of us."

"No, not an ounce," he whispered, pulling her back, and tucking her head beneath his chin. "Is that so bad, Vivie?"

She set her lips against his throat. "Oh, Quin! Oh, God, is this . . . is this wise?"

He felt his own hands begin to shake. "Vivie, I don't know," he admitted. "But who will ever know? How can it be wrong if we agree to it? Just once more, and then perhaps we will . . . we will be able to part in peace. Perhaps we will be erasing the bad with the good—and bringing back the memories of a time that was so fleetingly sweet."

Viviana's mouth opened against his throat, then skimmed along his collar. He felt her whole body shudder against his. She knew what he was offering, then. What he wanted. And dear God, she was going to do it. Relief and joy and desire ran through him like a lightning strike. She returned her mouth to his and kissed him hungrily— the kiss of his dreams. His heart literally skipped a beat.

"Then do it, Quin," she said when she tore her mouth from his. "Leave me with a good memory and wipe away the bad."

His hands went to her shoulders, and he squeezed them gently. "Vivie, are you sure?" he choked. "Be sure. I have to know it is something you want."

She shook her head and pressed her eyes tighter still. "It is something I want," she whispered.

And then, somehow, Quin had her in his arms, her long skirts draped across his coat sleeve, and he was carrying her back through the little parlor. The fire was blazing there, radiating warmth into the room. He swept past and into the dark, narrow bedchamber. He laid her down and set one knee to the mattress, making the bed creak beneath his weight.

Viviana reached up, and lightly embraced his face with her hands. Her gloves, he realized, were gone. "We will not regret this, *amore mio?*"

"We won't let ourselves regret it," he answered. He shucked off both his coats, and let them slither to the floor. His boots followed, then he sat back down on the bed.

"Vivie, we will tell ourselves this is just for old times' sake," he said, sliding the backs of his fingers across the infinitesimal softness of her cheek. "That we left something undone all those years ago."

She reached up, and he felt her fingers run through his hair, gently stroking him from his temples, all the way back. It was one of his favorite touches, one which left him shivering with delight. This afternoon was no exception.

"Just for old times' sake, then," she whispered. "Just once more. To make good memories instead of bad."

Viviana's heavy cloak had fallen away and slithered

half-off the bed. His hands went to the throat of her habit, and slowly he began to undress her. Not once did she hesitate, or move to stop him. Every button, every hook, revealed something indescribably sweet. An inch of lace. A patch of creamy skin. A scent. A gasp. Like tiny drops of water in a drought, they quenched an emotional thirst, as though he were parched to his very soul.

She watched him through eyes half-closed as her body was unveiled. Her throat, so long and so perfect. The neat, round turn of each shoulder, and her still slender arms. Her heavy skirts. Her boots so small they fit across the length of his hand. Even her drawers, which she untied herself, almost bashfully. All of it fell away until she lay stretched out before him in her thin chemise of fine lawn and lace. So fine he could see her dusky aerolas, and her nipples already hard—though whether from the cold or from desire, he could not say.

Lightly, he brushed one finger over the peaked fabric. Viviana's eyes closed fully, and her head went back into the softness of the old feather bolster. "Quin." She paused to swallow hard. "Quin, don't . . . don't torture me. Not this time."

He smiled, and remembered how it used to be; how, after those first few weeks of uncontrolled lust had been sated, he had learned to go slow. So slow he could make Viviana writhe and beg. What a feeling of power that had been; a feeling he had not enjoyed—or even tried to enjoy—with any woman since. Then, there had been no mistaking Viviana's desire for him. He took comfort in that now and lowered his mouth to her breast.

Viviana gasped, her hips surging upward and he sucked the hard, perfect tip of her breast between his lips.

He listened in satisfaction as her breath ratcheted slowly upward. She shifted one leg restlessly, and Quin set his palm against the inside of her calf and began slowly to push the fine lawn chemise higher and higher, until he reached the tender flesh of her inner thigh. For long moments, he simply caressed her there, suckling her gently with his mouth as his palm circled and stroked.

When he sensed the restlessness growing in her again, Quin eased his hand higher still, stroking one finger deep into the softness which he found there, and eliciting a small, weak cry of pleasure. Forcing himself to be gentle, he touched her in the way he remembered. The way she liked, the tip of his finger gently grazing her sweet feminine nub.

Viviana began to tremble a little. Her hands, light and warm, settled on his shoulders. "Come into the bed now, *caro mio.*" Her voice was husky now. "Give me your warmth and the hardness of your body."

Quietly, he rose from the bed. He found it strange that he felt no need to rush. He had dreamt of this moment a thousand times. And always, it had been a dream which turned into a nightmare upon his awakening, for his bed was always empty. In the weak afternoon light which permeated the tiny room, he undressed. Viviana had never been shy, but this time, her eyes never left him. When at last his shirt had been dragged off over his head, and his hands went to the tie of his drawers, he saw her swallow hard. Quickly, he tore them away, half-fearing that the blatantly aroused state of his body might yet give her pause. Viviana's eyes widened, and she moved to throw back the old wool coverlet and the heavy bedcovers beneath.

He went to the bed, and reached for her. A little desperately, he stripped away her chemise. The fabric breezed up, baring her breasts and teasing her nipples. Quin made a little growling sound in his throat. "Oh, holy God," he whispered. "Oh, my God, Vivie."

"I—I am not the same, Quin," she answered. "I have aged."

He leaned over her, and set his right hand on the turn of her waist, then slid it slowly up and over her ribs, until her breast was cradled in his hand. "No, you have ripened," he whispered. "You are a lush, lovely woman, Vivie, instead of just a pretty girl." Gently, he ran his thumb around her nipple. But Viviana wanted more. She moved restlessly in the bed, silently pleading for him. Quin felt suddenly humbled by it all. He pushed back the bedcovers and slid in beside her.

Viviana felt the heat radiating from Quin's body and drew to it like a moth to flame. She wanted to lose herself in him, to be enfolded in his embrace until they were one—at least for a few sweet, perfect moments. She snuggled against him, pressing her body to his from chest to knees and trying not to question her own judgment.

She wanted, oh, how she wanted this man. Nothing had changed. He made her feel alive with her every fiber. He thought she was lush, and lovely. He was temptation in the flesh, and his touch sent a sweet, hot need spiraling through her, tugging her toward him. She yearned to be pressed down into the softness of bed by the weight of his body. She fought an urgent, wanton wish to be impaled by him. Her body craved the perfect pleasure which only Quin could arouse. Yes, long after leaving him, she had ached for this, until the need had been numbed by the years of bitterness. How quickly and how hotly it could spring to life again.

The old bed creaked more loudly as he pushed her onto her back and dragged his weight over hers. His heavy, dark hair fell forward to shadow his face as his mouth closed over her breast again. Her every tactile awareness came alive to him. His legs felt hard and rough splayed over hers. His beard softly abraded the tender flesh of her breast as he suckled her. The muscles of his arms and thighs weighed her down, held her tight, left her captive to his desire.

His tongue laved and circled her nipple, and the white-hot need twisted in her belly again. Viviana became dimly aware of his teeth closing over her nipple, biting and sucking until her desire was drawn taut. Impatient, she pushed him away. He lifted his head, smiled, and allowed her to push him onto his back.

Eagerly, she mounted him, then sat back on her knees to drink in the beauty of his body. Even before she had loved him, she had loved to look at him. And again, nothing had changed. Oh, he was bigger. Heavier. And broader, too. The light was beginning to fade ever so slightly, casting a beautiful warmth to his skin. Though she would not have believed it possible, he was more handsome as a man than a boy.

Gone were the dark, often accusing eyes. Instead they were warm, and slightly crinkled at the corners. There was no softness to his face now; it was all hard planes and angles. His arms were thicker, and taut with power. His chest was sculpted with muscle and dusted with dark hair—something else she did not remember. He really had been so very young, all those years ago.

She set her hands on his wide, hard chest, and leaned over him. "Ah, *caro mio,* you grow more beautiful with age."

He smiled up at her. For the first time, it struck her that she was naked and astraddle him, her every short-coming—well, save for that slight sag in her rear—fully exposed. It had not, however, lessened his interest. That was readily apparent. Impulsively, she took his erection in her hands, finding joy in the sleek, hard strength of him. His body pulsed with suppressed power and promised her pleasure well remembered.

She stroked both hands up the full length of him, and beneath her, Quin shuddered. "Oh, Vivie," he half groaned, half laughed. "You always get right to the point, don't you, love?"

She said nothing, but instead rose up on her knees, and slowly took him, inch by sweet, hot inch, until he was groaning in earnest. Then clenching her muscles tight, she rose onto her knees again. Twice. Three times. Over and over, until Quin set his hands on her hips, and urged her to move more slowly. She gentled her pace, but not the intensity.

"Oh, God!" he choked. "Minx. Wanton. *Stop.*" A little roughly, he literally lifted her up.

"Quin, no!"

"Come here," he growled, more serious now. He urged her forward until her knees clasped his upper rib cage. "Quin, *caro,* what—?"

With his hands still set at her waist, he plunged his tongue deep into her most sensitive place. Her eyes opened wide and her breath seized. Oh, for so long she had yearned for this. Quin's tongue touched and teased, sliding through her flesh until her breathing became audible. He stroked again, deeper, more intimately. Viviana gave a sharp cry of pleasure and reached out to grasp the rough wooden headboard.

He held her there, a prisoner to his ravening tongue, his hands firmly clasping her buttocks. It was wicked, almost embarrassing, to be touched so. But she had little time to consider it, for she was drowning in pleasure. She felt her climax teasing, inching nearer. Oh, too soon. Too fast.

Quin sensed it, and drew back a little, soothing her more gently until her breathing had calmed a little. Then, with a sound of impatience, he slid his hands around until his thumbs touched the folds of her flesh and urged them fully open. Then his tongue touched her again, a sweet, searching circle. With his strong hands, he urged her thighs apart until she was fully exposed to his mouth's ravishing demands. At last, she came apart, shattering into slivers of crystalline pleasure as she clung to the bed and trembled.

When she returned to her senses, Quin was kissing her; kissing her curls, her belly, then nuzzling higher. She moved as if to sit back, and he caught her breast in his mouth, suckling her yet again, like a desperate man.

"Vivie," he rasped. "I need you. On your back, love. The old-fashioned way."

Viviana smiled inwardly and did as he commanded. She loved the feel of Quin atop her. He followed her, dragging himself fully over her, and the years fell away. He was again her beautiful boy, thrusting himself home on one awkward, enthusiastic stroke.

"Ah, Vivie!" he managed, as he began to move inside her. "Oh, so good."

In response, Viviana tilted her hips to fully take him, and set her feet firmly against the mattress. It had been a long time, too long, since she had been taken with such joy, such raw, unbounded enthusiasm. She was oddly glad that Quin had not changed. Like a cat being stroked, she arched her back, lifting her hips to move with and against him.

It was just what he wanted. Indeed, she always knew what Quin wanted. In bed, they spoke without words. On a guttural sound, he thrust deeper. Viviana held herself perfectly against him, and he moved and thrust inside her.

"Ahhh, God almighty—!" she heard him moan, his mouth buried in her hair. "God. Viviana. Am I . . . hurting you?"

Softly, she laughed. It felt wonderful to be pinned beneath him, so thoroughly impaled by him. He lifted himself off ever so slightly, then his hand slid between them, down her belly, his fingers urgently seeking the swollen nub of her sex. It had been a long time, Viviana thought, since a lover had so concerned himself with her pleasure. Not since Quin. And nothing had changed.

With a practiced hand, he touched her, making her gasp. But she did not need his touch. Not that way. Already she was eager. She whispered in his ear, and told him so in very wicked words, a passionate mix of Italian and English, for she could no longer think straight.

He understood, and slid his hands around to cradle her hips, stilling her to his thrusts. His urgency was like a match strike, setting her afire, and soon she was sobbing and whimpering his name as she struggled for yet another release.

She could feel his chest, damp with perspiration. She could hear the raw hunger in each breath as the air bellowed in and out of his lungs. Suddenly, she cried out sharply. Quin buried his face in her neck and sank his teeth into the tender flesh of her throat, rocking and rocking his hips with that sweet, perfect rhythm until she was crying out his name and shaking beneath him.

For an instant, he drove harder and deeper. He fell against her, the warm heat of his seed pumping deep into her body as his erection pulsed again and again, then fell still.

"God, Viviana." His hands tightened on her buttocks. "Oh, dear God. It will never be so good again. Never again, not as long as I live."

She could find no words. She could only caress him, long, soothing strokes down the length of his back, now damp from exertion. After a long moment of silence, he lifted himself off her, his expression almost sheepish. She followed, rolling onto her side and tucking herself against him. Oh, *dio,* what a mistake this had been! A mistake to think she could ever forget him. And a mistake to think she could take mere comfort from his body.

It was more. So much more. She prayed it would be enough to sustain her through the lonely days to come. Weakly, she smiled. "Have I changed, Quinten?" she whispered. "Have I lost my touch?"

He made a sound, something between a laugh and a cry. "Honed it to a razor's edge, more like," he answered. "Lord, Vivie. There's no one like you."

She propped her head on one elbow. "Have we done it, then?" she asked. "Have we made a pleasant new memory? One good enough to push away some of the old and painful ones?"

He dragged one arm over his eyes, as if he meant to

drowse. "I don't remember any pain," he murmured. "I remember only this." And then, to her shock, he did indeed drift off to sleep.

Viviana knew it was unwise to linger, but she had neither the heart nor the will to wake him. Instead, she allowed him to doze for a time, and allowed herself the pure luxury of watching him do so.

He had missed her. It was a rather pathetic notion to cling to, after all the anguish she had suffered. And yet, it did help to know that she had not been the only one left miserable. He had thought of her at least a little bit over the years. Oh, tomorrow, she would doubtless regret what she had done today. But it was not yet tomorrow, and in this small, sweet moment, she regretted nothing.

On impulse, she reached out and stroked his cheek, a gesture from the past. "Oh, I have missed you Quinten," she whispered. "With all my heart."

After a few moments, he roused, looking up at her with heavy, half-open eyes. "Vivie," he whispered. "Come snuggle against me."

She set her hand on his chest. "I should be away," she said softly. "It is a long ride. The children—I am expected."

He circled an arm about her waist, and half pulled her down anyway. She conceded defeat by tucking herself against him. "You love them very much, don't you?" he murmured against her hair. "It was obvious when you spoke of them at Aunt Charlotte's yesterday."

"I love them very much," she agreed. "They are my life now."

"Cerelia is a beautiful girl," he said. "I like her, Vivie. She reminds me of you."

Viviana had stiffened in his arms. "Cerelia?"

Quin had set his lips to the turn of her shoulder. "I walked her home last night through the wood," he murmured. "Did she not tell you?"

"N-No, she did not." Viviana tried to still the sudden panic. "She should not have been there alone. I—I shall speak to her."

"She wasn't alone," he answered. "She was with Chris and Lottie. She was fine, Vivie."

"Yes, I am sure." Viviana paused to swallow hard. She had been afraid, very afraid, that he was going to say something else altogether. Indeed, she was sometimes afraid of what Cerelia herself might say. Gianpiero had too often been cruel to the girl, and Cerelia was old enough now to start asking hard questions.

"What do the others look like?"

"Scusa?" She turned to look at him.

He was smiling at her innocently. "The younger two," he clarified. "Cerelia looks like you—except for that unusual hair of hers. Whom do the other two resemble?"

"Oh." Viviana forced herself to relax. "Felise looks much like Cerelia, but darker. Like me. Nicolo . . . he looks like his father."

"I see." Quin rolled up onto one elbow, and began to toy with a strand of hair which had escaped its pin. "Vivie, may I . . . may I ask you something?"

"Si?" She looked up at him expectantly.

He would not quite return the gaze. "Your husband," he said. "Did you love him?"

She hesitated. "No. I did not."

"Not . . . not even at the first?"

"No." She spoke the word quietly. "Not even at the first. Now, you owe me a question, *caro.*"

He gave her a weak, bemused smile. "Turnabout is fair play, I suppose."

Her head was nestled deep in the pillow. Quin was still on his elbow, looking down at her a little apprehensively. "Why do you stay here, Quinten, in this little cottage?"

He lifted one shoulder. "I don't stay here."

"But you spend a good deal of time here."

"Sometimes I have a late night up in Aylesbury," he answered. "I dislike disturbing the servants at such an hour."

It was a weak excuse, thought Viviana. And Quin looked a little embarrassed, too, as if he knew how feeble it sounded.

"Sometimes, Vivie, I just want a little time to myself," he went on. "Buckinghamshire isn't like London. There, a chap can hold on to a little anonymity if he pleases. Here, I am the Earl of Wynwood, and everyone knows it. My mother, in particular, knows it."

Viviana lifted one brow. "Ah!" she said softly. "You are trying to make a point to her?"

"Yes, and I have made it," he answered. "Where I go and what I do is no one's business but mine. Besides, I like this little cottage in the middle of nowhere. No one else has need of it just now. If I wish to have peace and quiet, I can come here. Herndon knows where to find me if I am wanted."

The afternoon sun was slanting low through the narrow window now, casting a soft glow across Quin's shoulder. It reminded her again of how late the day was growing. She had no business lingering here. By the time she rode home, changed from her habit, and bathed, she was apt to miss the children's dinner.

Viviana smiled and rose onto her elbows. "I have to go,

Quin," she said. "I really must. This has been—I don't know—lovely, I daresay, is the word I want."

He sat up now, his elbow on one knee, the bedcovers pooling about his taut, still-slender waist. Viviana cut her eyes away. He still looked far too tempting, with his dark shadow of beard and rumpled hair. But when she looked back, his deep blue eyes were searching her face as if he sought an answer to some unasked question.

"How long, Vivie?" he finally said. "How long until you must return to Venice?"

She shrugged one shoulder. "The opera progresses quickly," she said. "Chesley wishes to cast it as soon as possible—probably in Paris. He is already negotiating with theaters."

Quin watched as Viviana rose from the bed and began to shake the wrinkles from her clothes. Dear God, he had not lied to her. The years had only ripened her beauty. And as he watched her pull on her drawers and rummage about for her chemise, he had the awful sense that something beautiful and precious was slipping from his grasp.

For a long moment, he watched her, realizing that had life turned out differently—had *he chosen differently*—he could have had the pleasure of watching her dress like this every day these past nine years. "They will open the new opera in Paris?" he finally said, his voice hollowly. "Not London?"

She looked up from the stocking she was rolling deftly up her leg, and flashed him a muted smile. "London has not quite the cachet of Paris, *caro,*" she reminded him. "Not in the vain world of opera."

He watched her intently. "And what of you, Vivie?" he

asked. "Am I to assume you will be going to Paris with them? Shall you sing the lead role?"

Swiftly, she shook her head. "I shan't be singing," she said. *"Papá* will wish me to attend the opening, no more."

There was a strange little catch in her voice, he noticed. "And after that?"

"After that, we go home." Her voice was firm. "To Venice."

"Yes, and you sound as if you mean never to leave again," he said teasingly.

"Perhaps not." Hastily, she dragged her riding coat on. "I am not certain."

"Surely, Viviana, you will soon be singing somewhere again?"

Her eyes softened, but not, he thought, from joy. "No," she said swiftly. "I think I will not sing again. My children—they need me. A long production is too demanding."

Quin turned to sit on the edge of the bed. "But there are other options, are there not?" he asked. "Full operas are not the only opportunities open to a soprano of your fame and talent, are they?"

"My children need me," she said again. Then she looked at him and smiled, but it was a smile brittle in its brilliance; beautiful, but easily cracked, he thought. "Quinten, this has been such a special afternoon to me, but I must go. And please do not spoil our sweet, new memory with talk of work. It is so very dull, is it not?"

How odd it seemed to hear her speak so. In the past, Viviana had not thought the world of opera dull. Instead, she had lived and breathed it. She had fought and worked and driven herself to a near collapse until she was the best.

He knew that. He had seen it firsthand. He did not for one moment believe she had given it up. Not willingly.

But she obviously thought it no business of his. And it wasn't, was it? Reluctantly, Quin stood, and began to gather his clothes. He did not miss the heated gaze which slid down his length.

Well. Perhaps this had not been simply for old times' sake. He would try very hard to take comfort in that fact tonight, when he was tossing and turning alone in his massive bed at Arlington Park. He would look back on these moments of pleasure he had enjoyed in this shabby little cottage, in this old and rough-hewn bed, and think only of how glorious it had been. He would not allow himself to think of what might have been.

He watched her finish dressing, her movements neat and quick, and tried to think clearly, but it was hard when his head still swam with the scent of her.

Viviana was swiftly repinning her hair by the small, cracked mirror which hung on the wall opposite the bed. "There!" she said when finished. "Now, what have I done with my hat?"

Quin left the bed, twining the sheet about him as he rose, then retrieved the rather dashing little hat. "Will I see you, then, tomorrow evening, Vivie?" he asked, passing it to her.

She turned around, both brows aloft. "Tomorrow?" she said sharply. "Oh, Quin—no, I do not think we should . . . I mean, this was just for . . . "

He tilted his head to one side. "My uncle has invited the three of us to dine at Hill Court," he said quietly. "Mamma, Alice, and I. Did you not know?"

She looked as if she had not, then suddenly, her confused expression cleared. "A dinner party!" she said. "Yes, yes, he did mention such a thing. But I did not think . . ."

"Do you wish me to refuse the invitation, Vivie?" His voice was very soft. "I shall, of course, if you wish it."

She opened her mouth, then shut it again. "Do not be silly, Quinten," she finally answered. "Yes, I shall see you tomorrow night."

He felt suddenly like the young man he had once been. Callow. Angry. How could she be so distant? So dismissive? Moments earlier, she had been like fire in his arms. Well, by damn, he would not beg her for her companionship. For a moment, he considered ignoring his uncle's invitation. He had the feeling it was going to be painful indeed to see Viviana after all that had passed between them on this fateful afternoon.

They had meant to make a new memory to displace the bad, and they had succeeded well. Perhaps too well. He exhaled on a sigh and tossed the sheet onto the disheveled bed. Beyond the bedchamber's entrance, he heard Viviana open the front door and slam it shut behind her.

Ten

The Magic Ring.

At a quarter past five the following afternoon, Quin found himself standing at his sister's door and listening to the soft murmurings beyond. Inside, if he knew Alice, there was a beehive of feminine activity, with discarded dinner gowns flung into a heap upon her bed and a rainbow of shoes strewn across the carpet. But surely she was at least halfway dressed by now?

Softly, he rapped on the door with the back of his hand. Alice opened it herself, her hair still down and her feet still bare. "Quin!" she said brightly. "Oh, how handsome you look! I so rarely see you in dinner dress."

He smiled wryly as she motioned him in. "Don't be silly, Allie," he said. "You see me every night at dinner."

"Well, not looking like *that,*" said Alice, returning to the bench before her dressing table. "I do not think I've such crisply starched linen in my life—and is that a new frock coat?"

Quin did not answer. No one had ever accused him of

being even remotely foppish, but tonight he had exerted perhaps a little more effort in his toilette than was his custom. Yes, he had wished to look his best. He would just as soon not consider why. Behind him, Lily, Alice's maid, was plucking gowns from the pile on the bed, and shaking out the wrinkles as she returned them to the dressing room.

"Do sit down, Quin," said his sister, leaning nearer the mirror to dash a little powder on her forehead. "You make me nervous looming about. Has Mamma already come down? Am I late?"

"Not yet, no." Quin grinned, and took the dainty chair Alice offered. "It is just that I am early."

Alice looked up from her powder box and grinned. "Nervous?"

Quin did not find the question humorous. "Do not be ridiculous," he said. "Tell me, Allie, is Herndon coming tonight?"

Her chin came up a notch and was energetically dusted with powder. "Good Lord, Quin. How should I know?"

"I think you do," he said quietly.

Coyly, Alice smiled. "I know he was invited, along with every other gentleman and near gentleman in the village," she said, picking up a plate of cheese and sliced apples from her dressing table. "Uncle Ches is as much an egalitarian as Mamma is a snob. I sometimes wonder if they were really born into the same family. Here, will you have a little bite? It is Mrs. Chandler's best."

"Good Lord, Allie," he said, surveying the near-empty plate. "We're to dine at eight, and you've eaten a half pound of farmhouse cheese?"

Alice's expression turned defensive. "Only the tiniest

bit!" she said. "I was perishing of hunger. I hadn't any breakfast this morning."

"You are going to plump up on us, old thing, if you don't have a care," Quin chided. "That dress you are wearing could stand to be let out a notch or two as it is."

"Perhaps I have gained a half a stone. What of it?" Alice made a moue with her mouth and dotted it with something she scooped from a little pot on the dressing table.

"You are right," Quin admitted. "You look lovely—better than you have in years, actually."

Alice put the little pot back down. "Surely, Quin, you did not come in here just to quiz me about Mr. Herndon and watch me paint my face?"

Quin felt his mouth turn up in a slow, wide smile. "Actually, that is precisely why I came in," he said. "That, and to ensure your heap of discarded dinner gowns didn't slide off the bed in an avalanche and bury poor Lily alive."

Lily tried to suppress a snort of laugher, and snatched the last dress. "We've got to get that hair up, my lady," she said over her shoulder. "Best settle on which shoes."

"The rose satin, then," said Alice, shooting Quin an irritated look. Then, turning halfway around on her bench, she leaned over to pick up a pair of dainty pink slippers. Her hair slithered over one shoulder in a shimmering, golden brown curtain as she thrust the first foot into its shoe.

"I hope Mamma's mood is better than yours, Quin," said Alice, fastening the buckle. "Or it will be a miserable evening, and never mind Henry Herndon. The new curate and his sister are coming, and those two can make one wish to watch paint dry. And then there is—" Alice jerked up straight. "Was that a knock at the door?"

But Quin was still staring at his sister. Something about

the way the light caught her hair was oddly familiar. But he hadn't seen Alice's hair down in years. He shook off the strange notion and looked up to see that his mother had entered the room. He jerked at once to his feet.

"Mamma. Please, have my chair."

"Thank you, Quinten." His mother pressed the back of her hand to her forehead, and sank into it dramatically. "I declare, I am quite faintish from exhaustion!" she complained. "Whatever can my brother be thinking to serve dinner at eight? It is unheard of in the country."

Alice had returned to her mirror. "Uncle Ches keeps Continental hours, Mamma," she said. "But at least he has invited us to come at six for sherry. I think that very hospitable of him. Have some cheese."

Quin had drawn up a chair from the hearth and sat down again.

"It has nothing to do with the Continent," said Lady Wynwood, cutting a suspicious glance in his direction. "It is because of *that woman* and her foreign airs."

"Well, she is foreign," said Alice, dotting some sort of cream onto her cheekbones. "So that would explain the airs, I daresay."

Their mother pursed her lips. "Pray do not be impudent, Alice. It ill becomes you."

"Besides, the contessa's children dine at half past five," Alice went on, as if their mother had not spoken. "She never misses it."

"Actually," said Quin, "I was just remarking on how fine Allie looks. I believe the country air has put a blush on her cheeks and given her a decent appetite."

Alice grinned. "That blush just came out of a paint pot, Quin, in case you are blinded by my beauty."

"Well, I had an interesting letter today," said their mother, changing the subject, as usual, at her whim.

"Do tell, Mamma," said Alice good-humoredly. "Some gossip from town, may we hope?"

"A lack of it, more like." Lady Wynwood cut another quick glance at Quin. "It was from the Duchess of Gravenel," she went on. "She tells me there has been no betrothal announced between Sir Alasdair MacLachlan and Miss Hamilton."

"Well, I should hope not, Mamma," said Alice. "It is early days yet. Besides, they do not mean to marry until spring."

"They may not mean to marry at all," snapped Lady Wynwood. "Really, Alice! Perhaps Miss Hamilton is having second thoughts about her impetuosity. Perhaps Quinten can yet effect a reconciliation."

"Mamma, I thought your wish was to avoid any more scandal," he replied from behind a copy of *Ladies' Fashion Quarterly* which Lily had just uncovered on Alice's bed. "At this point, a reconciliation would but fan the flames. Good Lord, Alice! Are these wide, fluffy frocks coming back into fashion? Looks as though they've got parasols stuffed under their skirts."

Alice leaned over and wrinkled her nose. "Hideous, are they not?"

Lady Wynwood was frowning. "What are you saying, Quinten?"

"That these ball gowns do not become a lady's figure," he said dryly. "And that Miss Hamilton and I are through. She never loved me, and I never loved—

"Love!" interjected his mother. "What does love have to do with it?"

"Mamma!" Alice shot her a dark look. "Love has everything to do with it."

Lady Wynwood's lips thinned. "You did not love John, and look how well it turned out."

"Yes, look indeed!" said Alice a little bitterly. "I am a widow at two-and-thirty, with three fatherless children and few fond memories to look back on."

"Alice!"

"It's true, Mamma," she said, dropping her voice so that it would not carry into the dressing room. "I never wished to marry John. You know that."

"But he was a splendid catch!" said her mother. "You were intended for one another from the cradle. Your papa arranged it all."

"I know that, too," answered Alice. "And I did my duty as I was told I must. So do not now deny me the right to grieve over the loss of my romantic ideals."

"But you can marry again, Allie," said Quin. "You will marry again, and this time, you will marry for love."

"Quinten, don't be a fool," said his mother. "Who, besides a gazetted fortune hunter, would want a widow with three small children?"

The mood inside the room suddenly shifted. Quin flicked a quick glance at his sister. He could practically feel her unease ratcheting upward. "Someone will," he said quietly.

"You are speaking, I daresay, of that upstart Henry Herndon," said their mother impatiently. "He has always been far too familiar with Alice."

Quin felt his temper slip. "I do not think either of us is in a position to advise Alice with regard to whom she might marry."

His mother opened her mouth, but Quin cut her off. *"Neither* of us, Mamma." He laid the magazine aside, and stood. "Alice is of age, and possessed of a fortune which she earned in the hardest of ways—by sacrificing her heart on the altar of family duty," he went on. "She has earned the right to do as she pleases now."

His mother's lips had been pursed into a thin, tremulous line. And unless he missed his guess, Alice was blinking back tears. "I cannot countenance such a notion!" said his mother. "We are Hewitts, Quinten. We may not go about behaving as we wish."

Quin went to the door and laid his hand on the doorknob. "I suggest you grow accustomed to my views in this regard, Mamma," he advised, his back to the room. "As you are ever fond of reminding me, I am the head of this family now. It is my place to decide such things, and this is what I have decid—"

"But you don't even know whom she will choose!" interjected his mother. "What if he is unsuita—"

"I know Alice," Quin interjected, returning from the door. "I know she is not a fool. I trust her to do what's best for herself, and for her children. So that is the end of it, Mamma."

"You married for love, Mamma," Alice quietly reminded her. "It was a brilliant match, 'tis true. But a love match, nonetheless."

Lady Wynwood rose to her feet. "It was my duty to love my husband," she said. "And so I did."

Alice shook her head. "It was not like that, Mamma," she countered. "Uncle Ches remembers. You used to slip away to meet Papa."

Their mother flushed with color. "Perhaps I did do,

once or twice," she admitted. "Now if you will pardon me, I think I shall exchange this shawl for something more substantial. Quin, you may send round for the carriage."

And then, like the countess she was, Lady Wynwood swept past him and out of the room, her head held high. Quin looked at his sister and gave her a weak smile. They had won the battle, he thought. But the smoke had not yet cleared.

As soon as Alice's hair was up, she and Quin went downstairs to the great hall. "Where are the children?" he asked. "Are they not to go?"

"Miss Bright took them over in the dogcart at four," said Alice. "They were to have an early dinner in the schoolroom. They will return home long before we shall."

That made sense, Quin supposed. He had been a little surprised when Alice told him the children were to go. But playmates in the country were rare, and the children had begged. They would be kept in the nursery, Alice had explained, to play games and romp whilst the adult guests enjoyed themselves in more sedate pursuits.

Lady Wynwood was on her best behavior during the short carriage ride to Hill Court. Quin wondered if he had made his point, or if his mother was simply lying in wait for her next opportunity.

At the well-lit front entrance, they were greeted by Lord Chesley, who made a great fuss over his elder sister, relieving some of the tension. In the parlor adjacent, Quin could see Signor Alessandri and Lord Digleby Beresford relaxing at the piano with glasses of wine. Viviana was nowhere to be seen.

"The other guests will arrive at seven," Lord Chesley was explaining. "I am glad the family could gather beforehand."

Signor Alessandri was bowing low over Lady Wynwood's glove when a small herd of ponies—or something very like it—came tramping down the stairs.

"Uncle Quin! Uncle Quin!" said Christopher, bursting into the room. "Can you come upstairs with us?"

Quin cocked one brow in Alice's direction. "I daresay I can," he answered.

Diana was hopping up and down on both feet, her plump hands clasped before her. "There is a pig!" she said. "A pig! Felise is riding it. Come see."

"Felise must be very brave," said Quin, ruffling her hair. "Uncle Ches? Alice? Shall I shall go have a look?"

Chesley was already caught up in conversation with Quin's mother and Signor Alessandri. Alice waved him away. "An old shooting trophy," she explained. "The children like to play on the hideous thing."

Cerelia Bergonzi fell in beside him as the children rushed back up the stairs. "The pig is dead now," she said in a small voice. "But it still has tusks and looks very fierce."

Quin grinned down at the girl. "I'll bet Christopher likes that."

Cerelia smiled as if glad to share his joke. "He says he is going to Africa and shoot one for himself," she confided. "But for now, all he has is his slingshot."

"I hope he is not using that inside the house?"

Cerelia pressed her lips together, then a giggle escaped. "He did do, once," she admitted, as they turned onto the landing. "But Miss Bright smacked his hands."

Unfortunately, as the gaggle of youngsters reached the schoolroom door, a frightful wail sounded from within. They burst into the room to see Miss Bright brushing the

dust from a little girl's skirts—the bold Felise, unmistakably. Tears welled in the child's eyes.

Miss Bright flushed when she saw Quin. "Lady Felise
fell from the boar's back, my lord," she said, motioning
toward the hideous beast. "I turned away but an instant,
and she decided to stand up on it."

"I w-w-wanted to ride like an acrobat," the child
wailed.

Just then, another young woman burst into the room
carrying a tray filled with mugs and a large silver chocolate
pot, still steaming. "Oh, heavens!" she said. "Whatever has
happened?"

"Just a little fall, Miss Hevner," said Miss Bright. "This
is Lord Wynwood, the children's uncle."

The second woman flushed with color, and curtsied,
tray and all. "My lord," she said. "I am Miss Hevner, the
Contessa's governess."

Quin smiled warmly. "You have brought hot chocolate," he remarked. "That will set all to rights, I expect."

Miss Hevner introduced the slender, teary-eyed girl as
Felise, and the small, dark toddler as Nicolo—now the
Conte Bergonzi di Vicenza, he supposed. Quin withdrew
to one end of the schoolroom as the children—all save
Cerelia—began to clamor round the long schoolroom
table. Miss Hevner began to pass out the mugs as Miss
Bright scooted Diana and Nicolo up in a pair of high
chairs.

Nicolo did not spare the chocolate pot a glance and
began to stack a set of wooden blocks which had been left
upon the table. Cerelia went instead to an old pianoforte
against the wall where Quin stood and sat down backward on its bench, her feet barely touching the floor.

Quin sat down in an old wooden rocking chair, and studied the girl, who seemed far older than her years. "Do you play the pianoforte, Cerelia?" he asked.

She shook her head shyly. "The harp a little," she said. "But not very well."

He laughed. "In your family, 'not very well' is probably the equivalent of 'a near virtuoso' in mine."

Cerelia smiled, then dropped her gaze. "Miss Hevner says Felise has a gift for music," she remarked. "And she says that I play very prettily, too."

"Hmm," Quin responded. "What does your Mamma say?"

The girl's smile did not fade. "Oh, she says I could not carry a tune in—in *un secchio*."

"In a bucket?" Quin suggested.

"*Si,* yes, in a bucket."

Quin nodded solemnly. "You have my sympathies," he said. "I find that I cannot dance. My right foot gets tangled in my left, and next I know, I cannot tell them apart. I actually tripped over the dais once in Uncle Ches's ballroom."

It was not much of a fib, though he'd been half-sprung at the time. Worse, he was almost totally tone-deaf, too. Cerelia seemed to find it all funny. She was giggling behind her hands.

"Did your Mamma really say that of you, Cerelia?"

"Yes, but she said God has given me a gift for words and language." If her mother's honesty troubled her, Cerelia gave no indication. "Mamma told Felise that everyone has different gifts and all are precious, not just music."

"Words and language are very important," Quin agreed.

Cerelia's eyes lit. "I can speak four languages now—Venetian, regular Italian, French, and English," she said excitedly. "Next I'm to learn German. I learnt my English very fast, the fastest ever, Miss Hevner says. But Felise, she struggles."

Quin considered all that Cerelia had said. It would be very like Viviana, he thought, not to mince words with her children. And very like her, too, to help them find a balance in their lives. Felise looked to be a clever, handsome girl, but Cerelia's face held the promise of real beauty. And yet, Viviana had always seemed unaware, or unappreciative, of her own beauty, whereas she valued music above all things. He hoped it was not a disappointment to her that one of her daughters was musical whilst the other was not.

"You do speak English extraordinarily well," Quin told the child. "Better, even, than your mother."

"Miss Hevner does not let us speak anything but French and English," Cerelia remarked. "Do you know my Mamma?"

Quin hesitated. "Well, yes, I do know her."

"For a long time?"

He smiled down at her. What was the harm in it? "Yes, Cerelia, for a very long time."

"Did you know her when she lived in London?" asked the girl. "Were you especially *good* friends?"

What on earth was the child getting at? "Well, yes, I daresay we were," he answered.

Just then, Miss Hevner turned from the table. "Cerelia, do you not wish to have chocolate?"

"No, thank you," said the girl.

"Well, join us at the table, my dear, whilst the others

finish," she chided. "You must not detain his lordship."

Quin followed Cerelia to the table. "Cerelia is not detaining me," he said, as she sat down opposite Lottie. "She is charming me."

Miss Hevner smiled approvingly. "Cerelia charms everyone."

Later, Quin could never be quite certain what happened next. Nicolo, he thought, pushed over a teetering pile of blocks, upsetting Lottie's mug. The girl jumped, threw out an arm to catch the mug, and instead struck the chocolate pot, sending it over in a cascade of hot milk.

Shrieks and chaos ensued. Cerelia, standing at the table's edge, took the worst of it. Miss Hevner snatched a tea towel which she had carried in on the tray. Miss Bright grabbed two more from a cupboard. Quin seized one, and began to wipe furiously at Cerelia's frock.

"Ow, ow!" said the girl. "It burns!"

Quin pulled her toward the light. "Are you scalded?"

Cerelia had screwed up her face as if she might cry. "Nooo," she wailed. "I don't—I don't *know.*"

Carefully, Quin plucked the ruined fabric away from her skin. Her throat was indeed quite red. "Miss Hevner!" he said. "Leave that. Cerelia is burnt."

The governess flung the tea towel aside. "Quickly, into the nursery," she said, as Quin swept up the child in his arms. Leaving Miss Bright to console the others, he carried her in and set her on the sturdy oak table Miss Hevner indicated.

"There's a good girl," she said to Cerelia, swiftly loosening her smock. "Let's have this off, and then the buttons."

In short order, Cerelia's smock was tossed aside, and her

dress loosened from the back. The girl was choking back sobs. Around the neck of her ruined chemise, her skin was mildly pink. "I think it is not bad," said Miss Hevner.

Quin looked about for the bellpull. "All the same, I will ring for some cool water."

"Oh, child," he heard Miss Hevner say behind him. "This silly trinket of yours! Hot metal against the skin *will* burn."

"It wasn't hot until the chocolate spilt on it!" the girl complained. But she sounded as if she was already recovering.

When he turned from the bellpull, Miss Hevner was removing a gold chain from about the child's neck. Some sort of watch fob or large bauble dangled from it, glistening bloodred as it caught the lamplight. Cerelia's gaze followed it, her eyes a little sheepish. Miss Hevner frowned and laid it on the table behind her.

"She is not badly burned," the governess confirmed. "The skin beneath her chemise is pink, but not truly scalded."

Just then, a maid entered. Swiftly, Miss Hevner ordered that water and more towels be brought up. Quin laid his hand lightly on Cerelia's shoulder. "I should go now," he murmured, glancing back at the strange trinket the governess had removed. "Miss Hevner will wish you to change out of those clothes."

"All right," she whimpered.

Quin tried to look her in the eyes. "Do you wish me to send your Mamma to you?"

Cerelia stared down at her hands and shook her head.

Quin gave her shoulder a little squeeze. "All the same, I think I shall."

Another maid had come in carrying brass cans filled with water. In the schoolroom, he could hear the clank of a bucket being set down. Miss Hevner opened a wardrobe and began to pull out clean garments. With one last pat on the child's back, Quin left them.

In the parlor, the dinner crowd was growing. The dull curate and his equally dull sister had arrived, as had Henry Herndon. Basham was in the entryway, taking Dr. Gould's coat and hat. Quin slid past them all and went straight to Viviana, who stood by the windows alone, her long, elegant fingers wrapped round a glass of sherry.

He slid his hand beneath her elbow, startling her. Her head jerked round, making her long ruby earrings dance. The lamplight caught them, putting him in mind of Cerelia's bauble. He shook it off. "Perhaps you should go up to the schoolroom," he whispered. "Cerelia is fine, but—"

"Cerelia?" she said sharply. "What is wrong?"

"There was a little accident."

"An accident!" She almost tore from his grasp.

"Just some spilt chocolate," he whispered, giving her arm a reassuring squeeze. "She was not scalded, just frightened. She is in the nursery changing her clothes."

Viviana said no more, but set down her wineglass with an awkward clatter. He released her arm. She held his gaze searchingly for a moment, then rushed from the room.

"Ah, there you are, my boy!" Quin turned to see his uncle, who appeared to be held hostage by the new curate. "Mr. Fitch was just telling me that he is a bird-watcher. Frightfully exciting stuff!"

Viviana hastened through the hall and up the stairs at a frantic pace. Cerelia. Poor child. And more alarming still, what on earth had Quin Hewitt been doing in the nursery? She went straight there, to see that Cerelia sat perched on a table, stripped down to her stockings and drawers. Miss Hevner was offering her a fresh chemise to put on.

"She is not burnt?" asked Viviana, hastening across the room.

"No, my lady," said the governess. "Just startled. But her dress, I fear, is ruined."

Viviana slicked a hand down the child's hair and lightly kissed her temple. *"Mia cara bambina!"* she said. "Was it your yellow muslin?"

"Yes," said the child sorrowfully. "And it wasn't my fault! Nicolo pushed the pot over."

"It was no one's fault," said Miss Hevner. "It was an accident."

"Felice fell off the pig, too," said Cerelia, as the chemise was dragged over her head.

Miss Hevner looked at Viviana ruefully. "It has been an eventful evening, my lady."

"So I gather." At that moment, however, Viviana spied the gold chain lying on the table behind Cerelia. She picked it up and concealed it in her palm. Something like panic coursed through her. "What was Lord Wynwood doing here?" she demanded.

Miss Hevner looked suddenly worried. "I cannot say," she confessed. "I was belowstairs heating the chocolate. Ought he not have been allowed to come up?"

"I cannot think why he would wish to," said Viviana, too sharply.

"Lottie and Diana went down to get him when they heard his carriage," Cerelia interjected. "They begged him. I went, too. We wanted him to see the pig."

Dio, that damned stuffed boar again! Viviana closed her eyes and felt the weight of the golden chain and its makeshift pendant grow heavy in her hand. "Was his lordship here in the nursery, Miss Hevner?" she asked lightly.

"Why, he carried Cerelia in," said Miss Hevner. "Poor man. He went quite pale, as if he'd seen a ghost."

Viviana's eyes flared wide. "Pale?" she said. "What do you mean?"

Miss Hevner looked confused. *"Pallido,* pale, with no color in his face," she clarified. "I collect he was afraid the child had been burnt, until I reassured him she was not."

"Va bene." Somehow, Viviana forced a smile. "Miss Hevner, will you excuse us, please? I shall help Cerelia finish dressing."

The governess curtsied, lowered her gaze, and left.

Viviana opened her glove, and tried to keep her hand from shaking. "Cerelia," she said quietly. "I found this on the table behind you."

Cerelia looked chagrinned. "I thought it was burning my skin," she said. "The hot chocolate spilt on it."

"Did anyone see it?" she asked. "Miss Hevner? Lord Wynwood?"

"Miss Hevner took it off," said Cerelia into her lap. "What does it matter? She has seen it before."

Fleetingly, Viviana closed her eyes. *Dio!* "I have asked, Cerelia, that you keep this safe in my jewel box," she said, keeping her voice gentle but firm. "May I not trust you to do that? Must I ask Nurse and Miss Hevner to help me ensure that this happens?"

Cerelia gave two shuddering sobs. "B-But it-it is *mine,"* she whimpered.

Again, Viviana stroked her hair. "Cerelia, *bella,* I do not wish to be harsh," she said. "But this is not something to be lightly worn. It is very valuable."

This time, the child burst into tears in earnest. "But you said it was mine!" she cried. "And how can it be valuable? You let *him* ruin it! It is crushed! And you let him do it, Mamma! You did not even try to stop him."

Viviana went down on one knee. "Hush, Cerelia," she said, wiping at the child's tears. "You do not know what you speak of, *cara mia.*"

"I do know!" she cried. "You said I might have it. You did not even wish to have it repaired."

Viviana gathered the sobbing child into her arms. "Oh, *cara,* nothing is so simple as it seems," she said into Cerelia's hair. "I said it would be yours someday; and then I shall have it fixed. I just do not wish you to wear it yet."

Please, God, not yet. And not here. Of all places, not here.

But Cerelia was crying in earnest now, her frail, narrow shoulders shaking uncontrollably against Viviana. Viviana tightened her grip, patted the child's back, and felt her own heart breaking all over again. How unfair life had been to this child! And in great part, it was Viviana's fault. Her poor choices had been compounded by another's cruelty, and Cerelia had paid the price.

It seemed as if the world she had so carefully built was collapsing in on all of them. As if all her sacrifice and suffering might be for naught. At that thought, the anger and resentment swept over her anew, and Viviana was suddenly, and almost frighteningly, glad that her husband was dead. For were he not, she might have been tempted beyond reason to kill him.

Eleven

In which Lucy speaks Her Mind.

Quin found that dinner was a pleasant enough affair. Inexplicably, he was seated between Miss Fitch, the curate's spinster sister, and Viviana—the contrast being Chesley's idea of a joke, most likely. Viviana smiled politely as he helped her into her chair, but otherwise occupied herself with Henry Herndon, who sat on her other side.

Quin's mother had been placed near the head of the table adjacent to her brother, but next to Signor Alessandri, who seemed to have thoroughly charmed her. Quin had not missed the Continental kiss the dapper old gentleman had placed on his mother's glove upon their arrival, nor did he fail to notice how closely his mother attended to Alessandri's conversation during dinner. It had been a long time, he suspected, since a gentleman had attempted to flatter his mother so excessively.

After dinner, Chesley opened the double doors which connected the parlor to the larger withdrawing room, then ordered the furniture pushed back and the carpets rolled up so that they might have some impromptu dancing. Lord Digleby Beresford went at once to the pianoforte and began to play a lively tune as several of the younger people took up their positions for a country dance. Viviana's mind seemed elsewhere. Quin watched from the corner of his eye as she excused herself and headed for the stairs.

She was going up, he suspected, to put her children to bed. Alice had often remarked on Viviana's careful attention to such details. As for Alice, her brood had departed during dinner. Quin had heard Miss Bright bring them down in the middle of the soup course, where they had proceeded to make enough racket for eight or ten children as they pulled on their coats and mittens, and said their final good-byes.

Viviana was gone no more than five minutes before sweeping back down the stairs, through the entrance hall, and into the Lord Chesley's parlor, where the evening's refreshments had been laid out. She wore a gown of shimmering blue silk, the color so dark it almost matched her raven hair. The gown was set well off her shoulders, and left a vast deal of her creamy, faintly olive skin to be admired. And to his chagrin, Quin found his eye almost uncontrollably drawn—but to her eyes, rather than anything lower.

Tonight her lovely madonna's face appeared strained and wan. Faintly etched lines were plain about her eyes; not lines of age, he thought, but of something worse. Suffering, perhaps. How he hated that. Never would he have wished such a thing on her, not even in his darkest days. At least he hoped that he would not have done so. But then again, he had been so impetuous and insecure. Perhaps he had even wished worse on her. He was ashamed to think of it now.

Viviana seemed unaware of the music, or of the few people who yet lingered in the parlor. She went straight to the sideboard and poured herself another glass of wine, this time something as dark and red as the earrings she wore, and far less insipid-looking than the sherry they had sipped earlier.

Just then, her eyes caught his across the small room. "Barolo," she said, her gaze wary over the rim of her glass. "Will you take a little?"

He joined her there. "You look tired, Viviana," he said, filling a glass for himself. "Is anything wrong?"

She cut an uncertain look in his direction. Just then, Alice and Henry Herndon approached. They looked disconcertingly like a couple tonight, Quin thought, with Alice's hand lying lightly on Herndon's arm. And Herndon had that tight, faintly uncomfortable look about him, as if he were reluctantly obliging Alice and her wishes. Quin was glad, for Alice's sake, that his mother was well engaged with Signor Alessandri.

"There you are, Viviana," said Alice. "Are the children asleep?"

"Almost," she answered in her low, throaty voice. "Nicolo's nurse is reading a story, but it no longer holds his attention. The book is one he has seen a thousand times."

"I sympathize," said Alice. "Mine are forever clamoring after more books. I am thinking of giving in. After all, Christmas is almost upon us."

"Christmas!" said Viviana, her voice suddenly wistful.

"A wonderful time of year, is it not?" said Herndon.

"Yes, my favorite." Viviana smiled. "I have such memories of my childhood Christmases in Rome, when my mother was still alive."

"I am sorry," said his sister. "How old were you when she died?"

Viviana lifted her slender shoulders beneath the shimmering fabric of her gown. "About twelve," she answered. "Sometime later, *Papà's* work took us to Venice, then everything changed."

Alice looked at her in sympathy. "Do they celebrate Boxing Day in Venice?" she asked. Then, without waiting on an answer, she turned to Quin. "Oh, I know! We must send to Hatchard's for some new books for Christmas. Quin will help us."

"Hatchard's?" said Viviana.

"A bookstore in town," Alice clarified. "You will doubtless have someone going back and forth, Quin. You could arrange for a few packages to be brought from town, could you not?"

Quin inclined his head. "It would be my pleasure," he said. "You have only to make a list. Indeed, I shall fetch them myself."

Viviana seemed reluctant. "I—no, I could not impose."

"It would be no imposition," Quin assured her. And indeed, it would not. If Viviana wanted books, he would fetch books. If she wanted him to slice open a vein and bleed for her, he might well do that, too. Indeed, it had been slowly dawning on him since these last few days that very little had changed so far as his feelings for Viviana were concerned. He was still at her mercy. And still in love with her. Worse, he was beginning to comprehend just what he had given up all those years ago.

But his sister and Henry Herndon were still rattling on—something to do with holly and pine boughs. "It is something of a tradition in the village," Herndon was explaining. "The children hang greenery everywhere, even in the shops. We usually take a couple of Arlington's wagons."

Quin must have looked at them blankly. "The children are already clamoring to decorate the village and church for Christmas," Alice repeated. "And they have persuaded Mr. Herndon to take them out into the forest next week for the annual gathering of pine and holly. Have you any objection?"

"None whatsoever," said Quin. He had no objection to anything, save for the awful flip-floppy thing his heart seemed to be doing in his chest every time he looked at Viviana.

Alice gave him one last curious glance, then turned to Viviana. "Would your children care to go, my dear?" she asked. "All the village children are invited."

"I daresay they would," said Viviana. "I cannot thank you enough, Alice, for including them in so many lovely things."

Alice smiled. "We will make an afternoon of it, then," she said. "Perhaps my brother can be persuaded to accompany us?"

Quin watched a little of the color drain from Viviana's face. "I would not wish to burden him with the children's outings," she said. "And I cannot think he would enjoy it."

He considered her words for a moment. Perhaps she really had meant what she'd said that afternoon in the cottage. Perhaps she really did believe it best they not see one another again. The thought seemed suddenly to weigh him down.

"I would not wish to intrude," he said, more gruffly than he intended.

With a lift of one shoulder, Alice seemed to let the matter go. "Very well," she said. "Let us plan for Thursday if the weather holds."

"Ah, Herndon," cried a jovial voice. "There you are! I have been meaning to speak with you all evening about my damp meadow."

Quin turned to see one of the local landowners wading through the crowd.

Alice took her hand from Herndon's arm. "I see duty calls," she grumbled. "Mr. Lawson can never be put off, odious man. I wish his south meadow would turn into a peat bog. But I daresay I ought to go to Mamma now anyway."

With a murmured good-bye, Herndon slipped away. Alice, too, melted into the crowd. In the distance, Quin watched Lord Digleby pause for breath, then begin the next dance as a laughing crowd of young people drew away from the pianoforte and back onto the dance floor.

"Do you wish to dance?" said Viviana quietly.

He turned to look at her. "I beg your pardon?"

"I said, do you wish to dance?" She was still regarding him warily. "You were watching them a little longingly."

He shook his head. "You would soon regret it, my dear," he said. "I cannot dance at all."

"Oh." Her voice was soft. "I did not know that."

He looked down at her hand, which rested lightly on the sideboard. "No, you did not know that, did you?" he said. "In fact, there isn't very much about me that you do know, is there? Not really."

"Perhaps not," she agreed.

For a long moment, he was silent. "And does it ever bother you, Vivie," he finally said, "that we *don't* know those kinds of things about one another? Does it not trouble you that there are things we should have shared and did not?"

She surprised him by going suddenly pale. "P-Precisely what sorts of things?"

He shrugged both shoulders, feeling as if his jacket had grown suddenly too tight. "I cannot dance," he repeated, dropping his voice. "You love Christmas. Your mother died when you were a child. For well over a year, we lay together, you and I, knowing one another's bodies but neither of us ever learning the other's heart or habits or memories, or anything, I now think, that truly mattered."

He seemed to have stunned her into silence. Viviana looked up at him, her eyes wide and her mouth a little tremulous. He realized he had struck a nerve, and he was not at all sure that he had wished to. But it was too late.

"Why, Vivie?" he demanded, his voice an urgent whisper. "Why did we never share our hearts?"

"Oh, please do not start this," Viviana whispered. "Please do not do this to me, Quin. Not here, amongst all these people. For God's sake."

Quin lowered his voice even further. "When, then?" he rasped. He caught her hand between their bodies, turning his shoulders so that no one else might see. "When can I see you again? Vivie, there are things I need to ask you. Things I need to understand."

She shook her head and closed her eyes. "There is nothing left for us to discuss, Quin."

"I think there is," he said, a little roughly. "I think there might be. Viviana, come into the library with me."

"*Dio mio,* are you mad?" she whispered. "We agreed, Quin. Just once."

"God damn it, Viviana, did I ask you to *do* anything?" he asked. "Anything other than talk?"

She shook her head, her eyes hardening. "Not here," she said again. "I cannot. I must go."

She had half turned away when he caught her by the arm. "Tomorrow, then," he said. "Meet me at the cottage."

"No, Quin. I shan't do it."

His jaw clenched. "Then I shall call at Hill Court."

Viviana dropped her gaze. "And I cannot stop you, can I?"

"No, you cannot," he agreed. "Not this time. I have a few questions for you, Viviana. And by God, you are going to answer them."

But Viviana did not reply. She had already turned her back and walked away. Her spine was set in a straight, elegant line as she floated across the room toward Aunt Charlotte. Already, her smile had warmed, albeit a little tremulously, and her hands had extended in greeting. To anyone else's eyes, she had again become the serene madonna. Viviana, the consummate actress. And a trained diva to her very core. Or was he simply fooling himself? Perhaps they really did have nothing to talk about. Perhaps Viviana was just as hardened as she seemed.

Was this wise, he wondered, to press her to answer questions when he feared to hear the answers? He didn't even know what he wanted of her. More than her body. But something less, he thought, than her soul. He wanted, really, what he had once thrown away. He wanted a chance.

Was it too late? Was there anything left of Viviana's heart to hope for? Or his, come to that? Perhaps he was going to be sorely disappointed. Perhaps he was making a terrible mistake in forcing the issue. But like so many he had made in life, it was a mistake that he already knew he was going to make. And then, as he always did, he would simply have to live with the result.

Viviana managed to cross the room without stumbling or trembling. She even managed to greet Lady Charlotte and enquire after her health, with a measure of composure. But all the while she felt Quin Hewitt's eyes burning into her back.

After a moment with Lady Charlotte, Viviana was able to excuse herself. She went at once to the ladies' retiring room, hoping desperately for a moment alone in which to fully compose herself. Quin's questions had shaken her badly. She wished to God he had never gone into that schoolroom.

Her moment alone was not to be. Alice was there before her, bent over a basin of water, her face more bloodless than Viviana's doubtless was. Alarmed, Viviana touched her lightly on the elbow. "Alice, *cara,* what is wrong?"

Alice gave a nervous laugh. "What a question that is!" she said, snatching up a hand towel to wipe her brow. "But never mind. I'm well enough now."

Viviana's eyes searched her face. Alice was not well, and even a fool could see it. "Myself, *cara,* I was always prone to the—the *nausea mattutina,"* she said quietly. *"Si,* the morning sickness."

Alice's hand suddenly stopped. The towel fell to the floor. "Oh, Viviana!" she whispered. "Oh, God! What am I to do?"

Viviana settled one hand between Alice's shoulder blades. "Tell me, Alice, does Mr. Herndon know?"

"No," she whispered sorrowfully. "Until today, I was not certain. And now I am afraid, Vivie, to tell him."

"Alice, you must." Viviana rubbed her shoulders soothingly. "Trust me, I know of what I speak."

Alice looked at her beseechingly. "It was just the *one time,* Vivie!" she said. "I promised him it would be all right. And I thought it *would* be! Why, oh, why do I have to be so bloody fertile?"

"But Mr. Herndon will do the right thing, will he not?"

"Oh, yes," said Alice on a sniff. "He will. But he will be so angry with me."

Viviana was confused. "He does not . . . he does not care for you, *cara?*"

Alice began to cry in earnest. "He a-a-adores me," she admitted between sobs. "We have been in love for an age now—since long before I married. But Mamma will make his life a living hell, Vivie. She will say that I am marrying beneath the family."

"Does it matter so much what she thinks?" asked Viviana. "You love him. Your brother likes him, yes? And your children?"

"Yes, yes, and yes," sobbed Alice. "I just want Mamma to be happy, too. I just want her to approve. It—it's silly, isn't it?"

"Not silly, no," said Viviana. "But impossible, perhaps, at first. And you do not have time, Alice, to win her favor in this regard. Promise me, *bella,* that you will tell Mr.

Herndon tonight? A Christmas wedding would be lovely."

Alice's sobs were subsiding. "Yes, it would, wouldn't it?" she managed. "The children are going to decorate everything with greenery. It would be perfect—if we had time to call the banns."

"The banns?" Viviana did not know the word. "Is there no other way one can marry without this calling?"

Alice shrugged. "A special license would enable us to wed quickly and privately," she said. "Mamma would tolerate that more readily, perhaps? But I'm not sure Henry has the connections to obtain one."

Viviana cupped Alice's cheek in her hand. "But your brother would, would he not?" she asked. "You must ask him, *bella,* for his help in this. He will do it, I know."

"Yes, all right," said Alice. She was sounding more herself. "Yes, of course Quin will help me. And he might back Mamma down, too. He did so this afternoon, at any rate."

"Eccellente," said Viviana. "Now, you must go to Henry at once, then to your brother. Will you do it?"

Alice nodded. "I have no choice, have I? Yes, I will do it."

Viviana smiled. "Good, then announce the wedding tonight," she said. "Do not wait. Your uncle must propose a toast, and pretend it was the reason for this sudden dinner party. Everyone will think it desperately romantic."

Alice laughed. "They will, won't they?" she said. "Oh, Viviana, you are so daring."

Viviana shook her head. "I wish that were true."

Alice dashed a hand beneath her eyes. "How do I look?"

"Like a bride," said Viviana with a smile. "A beautiful bride. Now, go. I will follow you down."

Alice's news did little to dispel the sense of dread hanging over Viviana. After five minutes, she returned to the withdrawing room to see that Alice and Mr. Herndon were already deep in conversation. Viviana's attention was distracted, however, when Lucy appeared at the door of the butler's pantry.

Lucy had been summoned by her aunt to help with tonight's preparations, and with good reason, perhaps. She was now crooking her finger at Viviana a little frantically.

"What is wrong, Lucy?" asked Viviana. "Does Mrs. Douglass need me?"

"She says to tell you we're all out of orgeat syrup, miss," whispered Lucy. "Becky dropped the last bottle in the stillroom floor and it broke in ten thousand pieces! Nigh cut her finger off doing it, too."

"Oh, *dio!*" said Viviana. "Poor girl! Ought we to put out more wine instead?"

Lucy shook her head. "Lady Charlotte isn't allowed any by the doctors," she answered. "And Mrs. Lawson won't touch it, nor let her family, neither. From a stiff-rumped Methodist family, that one. And none of 'em look to be leaving anytime soon."

"Yes, I noticed," said Viviana dryly.

And once Alice's announcement was made—*if* it was made—another half hour of toasting and gossiping would likely follow. "What else, Lucy, can we serve?"

Lucy looked worried. "Aunt Effie says we've lemons, though they might have gone off already."

"We must have a look," said Viviana, grateful for a chance to escape.

When they arrived in the stillroom, a ruddy-cheeked kitchen maid was just finished mopping up the last of the orgeat syrup. Lucy pulled out one of the bins to reveal perhaps two dozen lemons in varying degrees of desiccation.

"*Disgustoso,*" muttered Viviana.

"Amen to that, miss," said Lucy.

Just then, Dr. Gould stuck his head into the stillroom. "I hear we have had some misfortune down here," he said. "How may I help?"

"Well, there's no help for these lemons," said Lucy. "The risen Christ himself couldn't bring 'em back. But Becky's in the servants' hall bleedin' like a stuck pig."

"She cut her finger," Viviana clarified. "Could you help Mrs. Douglass dress the wound?"

"Yes, I should be glad to."

With Dr. Gould dispatched, Viviana returned to the lemons. "Give me a knife, Lucy," she said. "You make the sugar water. There must surely be enough life in these lemons for a little lemonade."

Lucy looked dubious, but drew a knife from one of the drawers. "I reckon we can try, miss."

Ten minutes later, Viviana had hacked and quartered and dissected every lemon in the bin. Lucy managed to wring them dry, salvaging just enough juice for a gallon of strong, sweet lemonade. The ruddy-cheeked housemaid reappeared, and at Viviana's instruction, carried the tray up to the withdrawing room.

Viviana collapsed into a slatted chair at the small wooden worktable and propped her face in her hand. "*Dio,* what next?" she asked. "Lucy, have we any wine in here?"

"Just the cooking sort, miss," said Lucy. "And some of

Aunt Effie's dandelion. But oughtn't you get back up-stairs?"

"Yes," said Viviana. "I ought. But pour us something anyway."

Lucy frowned disapprovingly. "I'll have to fetch glasses from the—"

"A mug," Viviana interjected, holding up her hand. "A jam jar. Anything. Just don't open that door to the outside world for a few moments, and I shall be forever in your debt."

"That bad, is it, miss?" asked Lucy, taking down a pair of jars from the cupboard.

Viviana managed a smile. "My nerves are rubbed raw," she admitted. "But for the most part, I've no one to blame but myself."

Lucy set down a stout, brown jug and drew up a chair. "Lord Wynwood again, is it, miss?"

Viviana shrugged. "Oh, it is a little bit of everything, I daresay," she answered as Lucy poured. "But had I known he would be living here, in such proximity to Chesley . . . well, I hope I would have had sense enough not have come."

"You hope not, miss?" Lucy gently pressed. "But you're not sure?"

Viviana picked up her jar and pensively swirled the wine around in the bottom. "Lucy, I am not very sure of much anymore," she admitted. "But yes, I am sure I would never have come here."

"Well, you know what I think, miss," said Lucy warningly. "Besides, your husband's in the grave now, so there's no harming him."

Viviana felt her heart lurch. "I know what you are suggesting," she said quietly. "But I cannot risk making my daughter the subject of gossip. And what if . . . what if Wynwood won't forgive me? What if the things I assumed all those years ago were just wrong?"

Lucy patted her hand. "Mind you, miss, I'm not saying they *were* wrong," she answered. "I think you had the right of it back then. Mr. Hewitt was young, rich, and a little spoilt. He might not have done right by you. But to keep such a secret now? I don't know . . ."

For a moment, they sipped their wine in silence. "I saw your eldest in the village last week, miss," said Lucy when she spoke again. "I've got worries in that direction, too."

Viviana's eyes widened. "Worries? Of what sort?"

Lucy shrugged. "Well, she favors you in the face, miss," she said. "But that mess of coppery brown hair? It's not brown, and it's not red, and it's not quite blond, either. And from the back, miss, she looks the spit and image of Lady Alice when she was young. It mightn't be long, miss, before someone besides me notices, too, if you take my meaning."

Viviana froze. In her husband's family, where dark hair and eyes were so common, Cerelia's unusual shade of brown had been often remarked upon. And Lucy was right, now that Viviana considered it. Their coloring was shockingly similar.

When Viviana looked up from her wine, Lucy was studying her face rather intently. "Your nose has been broken, hasn't it, miss, since we last knew one another?" she remarked, as if determined to change the subject. "A nasty break, too, if I don't miss my guess."

Reflexively, Viviana touched it. "Yes, I broke it," she confessed. "Ugly, is it not?"

"Oh, no, miss!" said Lucy. "I think it gives you—"

"Do not say it!" Viviana's hand came up. "I beg you!"

"Say what, miss?"

"That it gives me *character*," said Viviana. *"Per amor di Dio!* I shall scream at the next English person who tells me that."

"All right, then." Lucy grinned. "I won't say it."

Viviana felt her mouth curl at one corner. "No, but you are thinking it."

Together, they laughed. It felt good, Viviana realized. Some of the strain fell away. She finished the last of her wine and made a face. "What is this, Lucy?" she asked. "It's perfectly dreadful, you know."

Lucy just grinned, and poured her more. "I told you it was Aunt Effie's dandelion wine."

"Dandelion? Like the—the little flowers? It has no fruit?"

Lucy shook her head. "Just the flower heads, with water, yeast, and sugar," she said. "Along with orange and lemon juice."

Viviana found it horrifying—and yet strangely funny. She gave the wine a little sniff, then pushed it away. *"Non più!* I cannot drink any more."

Lucy smiled. "Well, at least your nose still works, miss," she said. "No harm was done, right?"

"No," she said quietly. "No harm was done." But that, she knew, was a lie. Great harm had been done, and she was suffering for it.

Lucy was watching her face. "What happened to your nose, miss? Was it an accident?"

Viviana had perhaps had a little more of the bizarre dandelion wine than was wise. She was also growing weary of maintaining the façade of a happy marriage. "That depends on your definition of 'accident,' I daresay," she answered.

A knowing look flashed across Lucy's face. Viviana realized that she had said too much. She neither wanted nor deserved anyone's sympathy. Not even Lucy's.

"Was it your husband, miss?" she asked, her voice quiet. "Was it that Gianpiero? If it was, then, well, I reckon I'm glad he's dead."

Viviana did not answer that. Instead, she drew her chair a little closer to the table. "Lucy, there is something I wish to tell you about my husband," she said. "And then, I wish never to speak of it again."

"As you wish, miss," she answered. "I'm not one to be pushy, as I hope you know."

But Viviana had been wrong to leave this matter hanging unexplained for so many years. Lucy had been a good and trustworthy servant—and yes, a friend, too. If she was given to idle talk, she would have told all that she knew a long time ago. "Gianpiero was my father's patron, Lucy," she said. "Do you know what that means?"

Lucy shook her head.

"He provided financial backing for my father's artistic endeavors," Viviana said. "He had great influence in Venice and all over Europe, too. In the world of opera, Gianpiero could decide who ate and who starved, Lucy. Do you understand?"

"Like a steward or a butler?" asked Lucy. "He could hire you, or turn you off?"

"Something like that," Viviana responded. "We lived in a villa on the edge of his estate. Eventually, Gianpiero began to pay a marked attention to me. He—he made it plain he wished me to be his mistress. I was appalled, as was my father. It created a terrible rift between Gianpiero and my father."

"Ooh, he sounds like a bad egg, miss," said Lucy chidingly.

"A bad egg?" asked Viviana.

"It's an expression, miss," said Lucy. "He was a nasty sort of fellow."

"Nasty, yes," said Viviana. "He could be. Yet he could also charm the birds from the trees if he wished it. But my father was very protective of me. When Gianpiero began to press me to return his—his affections, my father sent me away and asked Lord Chesley to help me find a place in an English opera company."

Lucy nodded. "And that's when you came to me," she said. "I always knew, miss, that you carried a heavy weight."

"Yes, Gianpiero became very angry," she said. "As soon as he realized I was gone, he tried to break my father financially, but *Papà* would not relent. Finally, after many long months had passed, they had a reconciliation of sorts. Gianpiero offered marriage. *Papà* left the decision to me."

"Aye, and it seemed the best thing to do, did it, miss?"

"It ensured my father could return to the work he loved," said Viviana. "And so I went home, and I told Gianpiero that I carried a child. I thought that, one way or another, telling the truth would end it."

"But did you tell him about Lord Wynwood, miss?"

"I said only that he was a wealthy Englishman," Viviana answered quietly. "Gianpiero was enraged, to be sure. But he married me. And now he is dead, so I suppose there is no point in dwelling on the past, is there?"

"Still, I am sorry for your children, miss," said Lucy soberly. "My little ones do love their father."

"My daughters saw little of Gianpiero," she said a little hollowly. "He was not fond of children."

"But he took care of the child you carried," said Lucy. "He kept his bargain, in that way, at least."

Viviana hesitated. "In the end, yes."

Lucy lifted one brow. "What do you mean, miss, 'in the end'?"

She swallowed hard and looked about the tidy still-room, wondering in some surprise that she was actually speaking of it aloud. But Lucy was the only person who knew the truth, and Viviana was beginning to think she might well go mad from keeping it bottled inside.

"As soon as our vows were spoken, Lucy, he took me away," she answered. "To a villa in the south of France. And there he told me that if the child was a boy, he meant to forswear it and leave it with the nuns to raise."

"Oh, miss! No."

Viviana was staring into the depths of the kitchen. "He kept me there for the whole of my confinement," she whispered. "Because he could not bear the thought of another man's son inheriting his wealth and title. I had not thought of that, you see. I was so naive. My family was not noble. We did not have a dynasty to protect. And so I spent the last seven months of my pregnancy, Lucy, on my knees, praying for a daughter. I was lucky. God was very kind."

Lucy stared silently into her wine for a moment. "Aye, he was, wasn't he?" she answered. "The pure spite of people never ceases to surprise me, miss. I'm sorry for you. I truly am."

"You needn't be," she replied. "It is just as you used to say, Lucy. If one makes one's own bed, one must lie down, *si?*"

Lucy smiled. "Something like that, miss," she said.

Just then, the clopping of hooves and the reverberating grind of carriage wheels broke the stillness.

Lucy cast her eyes up at the narrow casement window which peeked out aboveground. "That'd be the first carriage coming up from the stables, miss," she said warningly. "Lady Charlotte's, belike. You'd best get on upstairs, or you'll be missed for certain now."

They both stood, each looking at the other uncertainly. "Oh, Lucy!" Viviana finally said. "I have made a shambles of my life, have I not? And now I have burdened you with it, and I don't even know why."

Lucy touched her hand lightly. "It's not a shambles, miss," she said. "You've had hard choices, that's all. Sometimes it's just a woman's lot in life, and—"

A light knock interrupted them. Dr. Gould stuck his head into the room. "Ah, you are still here, Contessa Bergonzi!" he said. "I've put three stitches in Becky's thumb, and all's well. And now I hear that our presence is requested in the withdrawing room. His lordship is about to make some sort of important announcement."

Viviana plastered the smile back on her face and swept across the stillroom toward him. "An important announcement?" she said brightly. "How exciting! I wonder what it could be?"

Twelve

In which Contessa Bergonzi tells yet Another lie.

The following day, Viviana went out in the early afternoon for her ride, slapping her crop a little impatiently against her thigh as she walked along the corridor to the back door of Hill Court. She had wasted her morning anxiously awaiting the sun which never broke, and the guest who never came. And so she had decided to go for a ride; a hard, thundering gallop, despite the dreary skies and the skiff of snow which tipped the grass with white.

She was but partway down the hill, however, when she saw Quin emerge from the shadows where the bridle path left the woods. He rode alone, mounted on a large bay horse which was still tossing his head with stable-fresh impatience. He had come straight from Arlington Park, then.

She watched as Quin quieted the horse with a stroke of his hand, then smoothly dismounted and passed the reins to one of Chesley's grooms. There was no leaving now, she realized. There wasn't even any point in going back into the relative safety of the house. Confined by walls and the civilizing influence of fine furniture, Quin would still seem just as large and just as ominous.

But somehow, she would handle Quin Hewitt and his questions. She could not afford to let him shake her again as he had done last night. So she stood her ground, and waited.

Quin saw Viviana in the distance as soon as he set off up the hill from the stables. She looked as beautiful and as fiery as ever in her plain wool habit and jaunty hat. With resolute steps, he ascended the path, still unsure of the wisdom of his decision yet perfectly certain of what he meant to do.

They had agreed on "just once." Well, once was not enough. He wanted Viviana, and he was determined to either have her, or to be rid of her. They could not go on as they had last night, making idle social chitchat, and pretending that there was nothing more between them. There *was* more. Much more. And if she persisted in saying otherwise, then she was a damned liar—or worse, a tease.

Quin did not think she was either. He was beginning to wonder if she was hiding something, but what? There was a coolness and a distance to Viviana which he neither liked nor recognized. Even his sister did not seem to know what was on Viviana's mind, and he had quizzed Alice quite thoroughly this morning.

Only in his arms did Viviana seem herself to him. And then, when the barriers went down between them, she was again the girl he'd loved. The solution, therefore, was to keep her in his arms. And in his bed. So he meant to do what he ought to have done a decade sooner. He was going to marry her. And he really did not care what price had to be paid in the doing of it, either. He did not care if Arlington Park fell down about his ears, or his mother had a damned apoplectic fit.

But even from a distance, he could see that Viviana was already tapping her crop impatiently against the skirts of her habit and looking at him with barely veiled suspicion. "You have an affinity for that damned thing, don't you?" he said, eyeing the crop as he topped the hill.

"One never knows, *cara,* when it will come in handy."

At that, he threw back his head and laughed. "You are a hard woman, Viviana Alessandri."

At those words, Viviana dropped her gaze, and turned away. "I am sorry," he said at once. "Did I say something wrong?"

"Alessandri," she murmured. "I have not been called that in a very long time. And if I am hard, Quinten, it is because life has made me so."

Quin offered her his arm. "Come," he said quietly. "Walk with me. There is something I wish to ask you, Vivie, and I don't wish to do it in the house."

Viviana looked at Quin's arm, so strong and unwavering, and knew that the conversation they were going to have was unavoidable. His resolute expression told her that much, though his eyes were not unkind. So she took his arm in one hand and caught up the skirts of her habit in the other, the crop swinging from her wrist. "Chesley's gardens are lovely in December," she said mordantly. "Shall we stroll there?"

His mouth twitched with humor, and they set off.

Chesley's house was but a small manor property, but his gardens were some of the most talked-about in Buckinghamshire. In the spring and summer, they were flooded with guests. His late mother, he had once said, had possessed a passion for formal French gardens, Italian statuary, and freshly cut flowers. He had honored her memory by maintaining all of them as she would have wished. Only the maze was less than perfect.

"Good Lord," said Quin when they reached it. "This looks moth-eaten."

Viviana smiled vaguely. "There was a blight," she said. "It had to be cut back by the gardeners."

It was a large maze, and they circled its outer edge slowly and without another word passing between them. He seemed strangely content just to walk with her hand on his arm. Viviana cut a swift, uneasy glance up at him. Quin's boyish charm was definitely gone, replaced by the implacability and strength of manhood.

He looked not so much beautiful today, but determined. His jaw was set in a hard line, and his dark blue eyes were cooler, absent the heat of emotion which she had seen in them last night. Indeed, he looked altogether a different man from the one who had gripped her hand and sworn to see her today.

She did not wish for this meeting. She feared too much what he might ask and what she might be tempted to say. And if he knew the truth, he would hate her.

Viviana was a little unsettled by how much the years had changed Quin. She had once believed she knew him; knew what he would want, how he would react. Not so long ago, she had told Quin that she could not bear to question the choices she had made. That answer was growing more honest with every passing day. What if she had been wrong all those years ago? What *if*?

It would mean that all of her sacrifices had been for

naught. Everything she was, and everything she had done, had been predicated on that decision. She could not afford to second-guess herself now. And so she steeled herself, as she had done so many times over the years, and drew a deep breath.

"You wished to see me," she prompted him. "What is it, Quinten, you wished to ask?"

He looked down at her with a muted smile. "Trust you, Vivie, to get right to the point," he responded. "What did I wish to say? I hardly know."

"Then you have come a long way for nothing," she said.

"Have I?" He stopped on the path, his eyes holding hers. "It does not feel like nothing, Viviana, walking with you like this. It feels . . . well, a little like old times."

"We never walked this way, Quinten," she coolly reminded him. "We fought. We had sex. And then we fought some more."

"Well, that is a cold, clear-eyed assessment of a relationship if ever I heard one," he admitted. "Is there nothing of the romantic left in you, my dear?"

"Very little," she answered. "Romance, *cara,* is for men. Women can ill afford it."

He lifted one brow and resumed his pace. "I suppose, in hindsight, that it was not much of a relationship anyway," he said. "And yet it has loomed large in my life, Vivie, all these years. Why do you think that is?"

"I cannot say."

"I think it is because we left unfinished business," he said pensively. "Did you ever feel that way, Vivie? Or did you just . . . never look back?"

Viviana focused her eyes hard into the distance, toward

the long row of outbuildings which rimmed the house's rear gardens. "I never looked back," she lied. "I could not. I had a life to live."

"A life without me," he said flatly.

"You made your choice, Quinten," she whispered. "Do not dare to try to make me feel guilty for it now."

"Ah, you are speaking, I daresay, of that marriage proposal you once made me," he said, his tone darkening. "I have found myself thinking about that a great deal lately. Why, Vivie, could you not simply tell me that it was all or nothing? Why could you not just be honest? Perhaps I . . . perhaps I would have answered you differently."

She snatched her hand from his arm. "How dare you?" she asked, her voice low. "How dare you come here now and accuse me of dishonesty after all that has passed. Was I to hold a gun to your head? A knife to my own throat? And if I did not, is it now all my fault? Well, damn you, Quin Hewitt. Damn you straight to hell. There. I have said what I have long wished to say to you—and in English, so that you may plainly understand it."

He held up one hand. "Viviana, wait," he said. "I never accused you of dishonestly."

"It is precisely what you said," she answered. "Have you no idea, Quinten, how it humbled me to have to ask you such a thing? Have you any notion how you hurt me with your eyes and your words? And now you claim to wish that I had *threatened* you into agreement?"

He lost a little of his color. "I just wish, Vivie, that you had been honest," he said. "I just wish you had told me precisely what was at stake."

"Oh, *si,* you wish that I had begged!" she hissed. "Is that it? And what kind of husband, Quinten, would that have won me? A husband who woke every morning seething with resentment? A husband who felt as if he had been trapped or cajoled into lowering himself, and disappointing his oh-so-fine English family? I should sooner die."

She moved to turn around, but he seized her by the arm. "Now, wait just a minute, Viviana."

"Andare all'inferno!" she hissed.

His grip quite ruthless, Quin hauled her back. "I'll be damned if I mean to stand out here in the garden where anyone can hear if we're to quarrel like a pair of fish-wives," he gritted, dragging her down the path. "What's that up ahead? The greenhouse?"

"How should I know?" she snapped. "Release my arm, you arrogant ass."

"Shut up, Vivie," he said. "I guess we are going to have this out once and for all, you and I. And I don't need an audience to witness my humiliation."

"Your humiliation!" Viviana had stopped struggling, because she looked like a fool, and he clearly did not mean to release her. "You do not know the meaning of the word."

Quin pulled open the heavy wooden door, and shoved her inside, into a world of muted light and cotton-wool warmth. She blinked and looked around. The smell of damp earth surrounded them. They had entered a large, low-ceilinged shed, but beyond it lay row upon row of wooden beds filled with lush, growing greenery under arching gables of glass.

"Thank God." He let her go, and stripped off his coat and gloves. "At least they have the fires kindled in here."

She set one hand on her hip, and glowered at him. But even in her agitated state, she could see that whilst the anger remained, much of the fight had gone out of him. As if disgusted, he flung his hat onto the table where he'd tossed his coat, then dragged a hand through his too-long hair. "Why is it, Vivie, that you can still get to me so?" he asked, his voice frustrated. "Why is it that after all these years, you can still tie me up in knots and make me feel like a goddamned green-as-grass boy again?"

She did not quite follow. "Well, I have no wish to tie you up or make you into grass," she said regally. "And I certainly have no wish to squabble, Quinten. I thought . . . I thought we had finished this business two days ago. At the cottage. I do not know what you want of me now. Be so obliging as to explain it, *per favore,* and let me go."

"I just want to know—" His words seemed to catch in his throat.

"What?"

"I want to know, Vivie, why you left me."

The boyish uncertainty had returned. Viviana looked at him, and let the question sink in, fighting the almost overpowering urge to go to him, and envelop him in her arms. "I left you, *caro mio,* because it was time," she finally answered, her voice a little sad. "I had a life which I had left behind, and it was time for me to return to it. I had a father whom I loved with all my heart. I would sooner have died than let him see what I had become. A rich man's mistress. I did not wish to leave you, Quin. I did not. But it was time to make a choice. And so I made it. Can you not understand?"

He closed his eyes and pinched hard at the bridge of his nose. "And if I had said yes, Vivie, would you really have married me?" he asked quietly. "Would you have braved my family's wrath? And what if my father had cut me off and left us to starve? Would you have seen that through with me, too?"

"I—I do not know," she lied. "All I know, *caro,* is that it is easier to marry a man whom you do not love than to marry a man who does not love you."

He dropped his hand and tried to smile. For a long time, he said nothing. "Well, it is all in the past," he finally responded. "I suppose there is no point debating it now."

She shook her head. "No. There is not."

He set both hands on his hips and paced back and forth across the flagstone floor of the workroom. Amidst the rough-hewn worktables and racks of gardening tools, he looked like a caged animal. She should have taken the opportunity to excuse herself and go, but, inexplicably, she did not.

"Was he good to you, Vivie?" he finally asked, his back turned to her. "Was he a good husband, Bergonzi? Were you happy?"

"It was a marriage, like any other," she said. "We managed."

He turned to look at her then, his eyes bleak. "But I think, Viviana, that most marriages are happy," he said. "Or at least, they should be. Am I the only person in the world who believes that? Am I just . . . pathetically naive?"

Viviana clasped her hands tightly in front of her. "I do not know about most marriages," she said. "I know only that I tried to make the best of mine."

"He must have loved you," said Quin. "He must have been very proud."

She shrugged ambivalently. "Perhaps."

Quin did not take his eyes from her face. "Why else would a man of his wealth and position allow his wife to keep singing publicly?" he asked. "It was because he wished to show you off. To show the world that he had won you."

Viviana suppressed a wince. Quin's words hit closer to the mark than she liked to think. "Gianpiero was obsessed with opera," she said. "To him, I was but another means to an end. And yes, he liked to show me off."

"And you have three children now," he said quietly. "Three beautiful children. I still cannot get over it, Viviana."

"Did you never think of me as a mother?" she asked. "Was I never anything more to you than just a woman to be bedded?"

He flashed a crooked smile. "I often thought of you as a mother," he admitted. "You had that look, Vivie. Like some sort of marble madonna come to life, so serene and lovely. Sometimes . . . sometimes, Vivie, when you would walk across the floor, so naked and beautiful, I would imagine . . . I would imagine that—" His words broke away. "But we were speaking of your children, were we not? They are lovely. You must be proud of them."

Somehow, she managed to smile. "*Si,* very much."

He had begun his pacing again, this time with one hand set against the back of his neck. She wished to God he would stop. There was a grave sense of uncertainty churning in her stomach. A doubt—no, a fear, clinging to her heart like some insidious cobweb. What if she had been wrong about him, all those years ago? And why, now, did she remain here with him? Clearly, Quin would not try to stop her from leaving. And yet, he held her mesmerized, enthralled by his almost cathartic questions.

"I remember now, Viviana, what I meant to ask you

last night," he said out of nowhere. "It was about that trinket Cerelia wears round her neck."

Viviana stiffened with fear. "I beg your pardon?"

She got her wish. He stopped pacing. "Do you remember that ring I once gave you?" he asked, turning to face her. "The large ruby?"

"I fear I have many ruby rings, Quinten," she answered. "I cannot remember one from the other."

His smile faded. "Yes, no doubt you are awash in them now," he said. "And how could it be the same one? After all, you sold every piece of jewelry I ever gave you."

She kept her face a mask of implacability. "They were mine do with as I wished, were they not?"

He shrugged. "But that misshapen chunk of gold with the red stone set into it," he went on. "The one which Cerelia wears about her neck. I just thought it looked a little bit like a ring I once gave you."

"Did it?" she asked, her voice surprisingly calm. "Which one?"

His mouth curved bitterly. "The one I gave you on our last afternoon together," he said. "As I said, it was a rather unusual stone—a square-cut ruby. They are mostly rectangular or oval, are they not?"

"I daresay," she answered. "I never thought about it."

"So it is not the same ring?" he pressed.

She shook her head. "Paste and pinchbeck, more likely," she said. "Something Cerelia found. I cannot think where. She has an unnatural attachment to it. Children are like that, you know."

He shrugged, and seemed to accept her answer. "Did you sell it, then?" he asked. "That last ring I gave you?"

Quin was not cruel enough to remind her that he had

made her promise never to sell it. And so Viviana lifted one shoulder and told another white lie. "I cannot recall," she said. "Do you wish it back? If so, you are welcome to pick through my jewel case and take it if you can find it."

He shook his head. "No, it is long gone, just like the others, I am sure."

She had no wish to hurt him. Not really. And yet she wanted—no, needed—him to understand. "No doubt you are right," she said quietly. "But you saw those gifts, Quinten, as payment to your mistress for services rendered. If I treated them as such, is it fair for you to cry foul over it now?"

"It was not like that," he said. "I never saw them that way, Vivie. They were gifts from the heart. And I am not crying foul."

She gentled her tone. "Then what are you doing, pray?"

"Viviana if you had duns or gaming debts, why did you not come to me?" he demanded. "I would have taken care of you. I would have paid them for you."

She turned her head and gazed out into the depths of the glass greenhouse beyond. "I had no wish, Quinten, to be further beholden to you," she said. "Besides, I did not have debts. I did not live beyond my means. I could not afford to."

"What, then?" he prodded. "Why can you not tell me? What difference does it make now?"

But it seemed to make a great deal of difference to him, she realized. Yes, after all these bitter years had passed, perhaps such simple, silly things still mattered.

Viviana exhaled, a slow, steadying breath. She already knew she was going to regret this. "I sent the money to

Papà," she finally answered. "Every month, I sent him what little I could spare. And pathetically little it was, too. Especially in the beginning."

"But Vivie, that makes no sense. What need had he of money? Your father was a renowned composer."

"Oh, *si,* a famous artist!" she said. "And like most of them, he served at the whim of his patron."

"Bergonzi, yes?" said Quin sharply. "Is that whom you mean?"

Viviana nodded tightly.

"But Bergonzi employed him for many years, did he not?"

"After I left Venice, they quarreled," she admitted. *"Papà* was told that there would be no further commissions for him. Not from the powerful Conte Bergonzi— and his displeasure meant, of course, no one else dared hire him."

"But they later reconciled," said Quin.

"Yes, later they reconciled," she answered.

"Christ Jesus," said Quin. "This is unbelievable."

"Unbelievable?" she echoed softly. "What part of it, Quinten, do you disbelieve? Why did you think I was singing my heart out night after night? Why did you think I was fighting and scrabbling for every part I could get? It was for the money, *caro.* To make something of myself."

Quin could not miss the ache in her words. "I believe you, Vivie," he answered. "And had you told me this nine years ago, I would have believed it then, too. I—I would have done something."

"Would you, Quin?" she whispered. "I wonder if that is so. I really do."

Quin did not answer that remark. She had reason, perhaps, for her doubts. As a young man, his foremost concern had been an almost petulant wish to have his own needs met and his own insecurities assuaged. He had loved Viviana, yes. But he had been unable to see very far past that fact. Perhaps he would have seen or felt no obligation beyond it, either.

"Why did they fall out, Vivie?" he challenged. "Was it something to do with you?"

She shot him a dark, sidelong look, and said nothing.

"Was it over you, Vivie?" he repeated, his voice more demanding.

She pushed a hand into her hair almost wearily, and leaned back against the rough wooden wall of the work shed. "I really do not wish to answer that," she said quietly. "And frankly, *caro,* it is none of your business."

He took a step toward her. "I'm not sure if I believe that any longer," he answered, his tone low and ominous. "I begin to think, Viviana, that there is much you are not telling me, and I mean to have the whole truth from you."

Viviana felt a stab of panic. "I do not have to answer your questions," she said, pushing away from the wall and heading for the door. "You are nothing to me. Nothing but a memory."

He was faster. He turned, refusing to let her push past him. "This is not finished, Viviana."

"Go to hell," she snapped.

Somehow, he snatched her crop from her wrist. "You are wearing that expression out, my dear, and in two different languages," he returned. "Why don't you just call me a pig again?"

Her eyes widened. "You *are* a pig," she said. "You are despicable."

"Oh, don't play the innocent with me, Viviana!" he said. "I understood a little more than you think I did that day in my study. And I understood something else, my dear. I understood your mouth was not entirely indifferent to my kiss, no matter what your riding crop said."

She moved to snatch it back, but he jerked it from her reach. "Oh, I waste my time with you!" she said. "There must be another door." On that, she turned and strode into the musky warmth of the greenhouse.

She strode down the straw-covered aisle between the elevated beds of lilies and asters. Farther along lay the tables of green, potted plants and rooting vegetables, and beyond that, almost hidden by a swath of lush palms, another exit. But she was nowhere near it when Quin caught her, snaring her by the elbow, and spinning her around to face him.

She brought up her hand to slap him, but he caught it and jerked her against him. His mouth came crushing down on hers, already hot and uncontrollable. He bound her to him, one arm about her waist, driving her head back as he tasted her. Viviana's battle ended as it began, quickly, in a flash of unrestrained emotion. She gave herself up to it, opening her mouth fully beneath his.

Quin surged inside, twining his tongue with hers until her knees literally went weak. She felt her hat go tumbling into the straw. His mouth moved to her cheek, then skimmed hotly along her jaw with a soft groan. Her head swam with the scent of warm, damp earth, flowers, and Quin.

"Let me," he whispered. "Let me, Vivie."

She tried to shake her head. "No."

His hand had slid beneath her riding coat, urgently

seeking. Through the layers of linen and silk, he weighed her breast in the warm cup of his hand. Her nipple hardened traitorously to his touch, and a small whimper escaped her mouth.

Quin slid his mouth down the length of her neck, and she shuddered. "Stop, Quin. Please. I—I cannot. Don't . . . don't make me."

Lightly, he thumbed her nipple through her shirt. "Do you like that, Vivie?" he whispered. "Tell me."

"You—you know I do," she answered. "Please. Not here."

"Where, then?" His voice was a tempting whisper.

"Tonight," she managed, trying to buy herself time—and sanity. "I shall . . . I shall come to you tonight . . . somewhere. Anywhere."

"Will you?" His hand was slipping loose the fastenings of her coat, then pushing it away. "Anywhere?"

"Anywhere," she whimpered, her resistance fast failing. "Anything."

"Anything," he returned. "I like that, Vivie."

His mouth settled over her breast, suckling her through the layers of shirt and chemise. He slid his broad palm over her buttocks, and made slow, lazy circles through her skirts, urging her closer. He drew her nipple into his mouth, sucking none too gently, and it was all too much. Viviana felt that old, familiar spiral of lust bottom out in her belly and tug at her very core. Her breathing ratcheted up. Too fast. Too shallow.

His hungry mouth left her breast, only to be replaced by his hand. "Must I, Viviana?" he whispered, his lips hot against her ear. "Must I wait?"

Viviana mumbled something inarticulate. Somehow,

he drew her away from the aisle and pulled her down into one the piles of straw which lay in mounds between each bed. She came down on top of him, straddling one of his thighs. Roughly, he pushed her coat from her shoulders. She let it slide off, eager to be free of it in the hot, musky air. *Madness. Oh, this was madness!*

But she let him pull her down to him, and kiss her again, slowly and sweetly, his tongue plunging almost lazily into her mouth now, as if he had all the time in the world. She returned his kiss, unable to resist the urge to ride down hard on the wide, solid muscle of his thigh. Oh, she wanted him! Wanted and wanted him. In all the years, the wanting had never seemed to end. She kissed him again, opening her mouth hotly over his, aware that this was foolish beyond words. Knowing she would regret it.

His fingers slid into her hair, stilling her movements so that he might kiss her more intently. Part of her hair fell down, and went slithering over her shoulder. Her hands found his shirt, and tore it from his breeches.

"Good God," he whispered when her palms slid up his belly, all the way to his chest, and over his strong, broad shoulders, bringing her body almost fully against his. "Good God, Vivie."

She felt his hand fumble between them, felt the pressure of his hand as he tore at the buttons. She sat back and watched as he struggled with the last. Never had she felt so wanton. So desperate to do something foolish. "Let me," she said, releasing it. She pushed down the fabric of his breeches and drawers. His throbbing erection sprang free from the crumpled clothing, and she took it in her hand. She drew her fingers down his length, amazed at the heat and hardness.

Quin made a sound in the back of his throat. Viviana closed her eyes and stroked him again. She was in too deep to stop. She was aware that they might be caught at any moment. That they lay in a pile of straw, with nothing but glass between them and the heavens. And still, she did not stop. Instead, she slid back, stroked one hand up Quin's chest again, and bowed her head to take him into her mouth.

He cried out, another choking, inarticulate sound. Already, sweat had beaded on his brow. The heat of the sun seemed to beat down on them, roiling up the damp from the moist beds of green. She held his throbbing heat in one hand and drew her tongue all the way along its length.

He had taught her this one lazy, rainy afternoon; how to make a man almost mad with her hands and her mouth. Apparently, it was a lesson she had not forgotten. Quin was almost shaking beneath her. "Christ Jesus, Vivie," he panted. "Stop. *Stop.*"

She did as he asked. His hands went to her skirts, dragging them up. He found her drawers, and slipped one finger into the slit. Viviana felt her desire flow forth, and moaned as she rode down on his hand.

"Get on me," he ordered, tormenting her with the ball of his thumb. "Now, Vivie."

She opened her eyes and looked down at him, half-mad with lust. "We could be seen," she whispered. "Quin, we could be caught."

"Good God, Vivie, I don't *care,*" he answered. "Let them watch. Let them envy us."

"I've gone mad now, I know it," she whispered, taking his cock in both hands. "But I burn for this. *Dio,* Quin!

We are like animals together. We have no business being near—"

"Later," he interjected. "We'll sort it all out later. Come, love. Take me deep."

Still in her boots and skirt, she pushed away her drawers and mounted him, taking him fully with one smooth stroke. "Oh, wicked, wicked girl," he said on a groan. "Oh, holy God."

She rose onto her knees and let the pace of his body take her. Never in her life had she felt so wanton. Never had she wanted anything so much. The rich, earthy scents of the greenhouse surrounded them, and grew hotter. She pushed the fabric of his shirt all the way up as she rode him, and watched the muscles of his abdomen flex and relax. Closing her eyes, she let the rhythm wash over her, until time seemed indefinable, and regret seemed so ephemeral.

Oh, this would not last. Not for either of them. It had come on too fast. Too hot. Another few strokes, and she cried out, feeling perfect ecstasy edge near. Beneath her, she felt Quin surge, felt him set his hands on either side of her hips, and thrust one last and perfect stroke. Viviana shattered as he trembled beneath her, her voice sobbing softly in the heat.

She came to her sense to find she had collapsed onto Quin, her face buried in the dampness of his neck. She drew a deep, unsteady breath, rich with the scent of sweat, soap, and bergamot. Quin. Always, always Quin.

"Oh, God, Vivie," he whispered, his voice soft with wonder. "You are a dangerous woman."

Viviana pulled herself from the sensual fog, and sat up a little. "It isn't me," she whispered. "It . . . it is *us,* I think. Together, we are like . . . like *polvere nera*. Like gunpowder."

"Yes," he agreed. "And may it always be so, Vivie. I should rather endure your temper and your horsewhip a thousand times over, just to have one moment like this with you."

She said nothing but simply pressed her lips to his forehead, praying he would say no more.

He crooked his head to look at her. "There could be many more days like this, Vivie," he whispered. "Did you ever think of that? Do you ever wonder whether . . . whether it really is too late for us?"

She had thought that nine years with Gianpiero had been payment enough for her sins. But she had had no idea what a just price truly was. For an instant, she considered telling him everything. On her next breath, she realized what an unforgivable mistake that would be. The truth would make him hate her. And so she said nothing. Instead, she lifted herself off him and turned away to right her clothing.

"Vivie?" His hand came up to cup her cheek. "Vivie, look at me. Is it? Is it too late?"

She turned and looked at him, just as he asked. "It is too late," she whispered. "Too late for anything more than this, Quin."

"Why?" he demanded, rolling up onto one elbow. His face had gone suddenly bloodless. "Why does it have to be that way?"

She could not hold his gaze. Blindly, she pulled on her jacket. "We have separate lives now, Quin," she answered. "Yours is . . . here. Mine is not."

"Vivie, you cannot deny what we have," he began.

"Chemistry," she interjected. "Pure, physical . . . magic, Quin. Yes. I know what we have. What we have always had. But life is not so simple as you make it out. Life is filled with hard choices."

"My choice is how and where to live my life, Vivie," he answered. "I'm tired of wasting it. I want to be with you."

"It is not possible."

"It *is,*" he countered, his voice firm. "I have never wanted anything else, Viviana. I know that now. I am willing to do what I must to have that. Do you understand me?"

She rose to her knees in the pile of straw, and slowly tidied her shirt and coat. "In a few weeks or months, Quin, I must return to Venice with my children," she said. "You will forget me then as you forgot me all those years ago. And I will forget you."

His eyes flashed with anger. "Will you, Vivie?"

"I will try, *si.*"

"And it's just that easy for you, is it?" he growled. "Well, by damn, it's not like that for me."

She looked at him with hurt in her eyes. "How many tears, Quin, have you shed for me these last nine years?" she asked.

"I won't dignify that with an answer," he said.

She touched him lightly on the cheek, and gentled her tone. "Quin, *caro,* your life is here," she said. "You are Lord Wynwood now. You have responsibilities."

"Nothing Herndon cannot manage," he returned. "In less than a week's time, he and Alice will be married. He will be a part of my family."

Viviana looked at him incredulously. "You would actually go away with me?" she whispered.

"I am willing to do whatever is necessary," he answered. "I said that, and I meant it. I want to put an end to this foolishness which has separated us all these years. Viviana, I . . . I want us to marry."

Viviana found herself blinking back tears and swiftly turned away. She had waited a long time to hear those words, and now they were bittersweet indeed. How could she wed Quin, knowing he would inevitably discover what she had hidden for so long? She dared not do it. Indeed, she would not.

She jerked awkwardly to her feet. "I am too old for you, *caro mio*. I have three children, and many responsibilities. Find someone your own age, and be happy."

He made a sharp, incredulous sound. "Too *old*? Oh, Vivie, that won't wash. And I adore your children. It cannot be easy for you, raising them alone."

She shook her head. "Think of your mother, *caro,*" she said. "A marriage between us would kill her. No, Quin, I won't do it. Stop asking me."

He rolled up onto both elbows and watched her as she mechanically picked the straw from her clothes. His shirt was still rucked up, exposing an expanse of lean, taut belly, and his hair was tousled almost boyishly. But his expression—oh, she knew it well.

Quin rose almost languidly to his feet. "What a liar you are, Viviana," he said, stabbing his shirttails back into his riding breeches. "Yes, I heard all about that little bucking-up you gave my sister last night. You told her, I believe, that Mamma's wishes could not come first. That there were more important things."

"Alice is with child," said Viviana.

"As you may well be, too," said Quin. "Did you ever think of that, Viviana? Did you?"

Viviana felt the blood flow from her face. The panic rose like bile in her throat.

Quin leaned into her. "What if you were, Viviana?" he rasped, seizing her arm. "What then?"

Viviana jerked away. "I would not marry where I did not love," she said. "I have already made that mistake once. I shan't make it again."

"Conceive *my* child, Viviana, and you *will* be making it again," He gripped her arm so hard she wondered he did not bruise it. "Besides, I don't believe for one moment, Vivie, that you don't love me. A woman cannot make love as you do and not feel love, too."

"Believe it, Quin," she answered, pushing his hand away. "What we have is pure lust. I do not love you, and you do not love me."

"There they are again, Viviana," he answered. "Those two little lies that ruined our lives. I wasn't confident enough to disbelieve them the first time. But I sure as hell don't believe them now."

"Then you are a very arrogant man," she said, scooping up her hat. "I am leaving now. And if you are any manner of gentleman at all, Quin Hewitt, you will not follow me. You will not press your suit where it is not wanted. You will stay away from me, my children, and Hill Court in general. Do I make myself plain?"

His eyes hardened to small, black slits. "Quite plain."

Stiffly, she inclined her head. "Then I bid you good day," she said. "I wish you well, Quin. I will leave you to find your own way out."

Thirteen

An Adventure in the Forest.

Quin Hewitt kept his word. During the days which
followed, Viviana saw him but once, riding through
the village on his big bay. At the Black Lion, he dismounted, handed his reins to a waiting servant, and vanished into the shadows of the tavern's entrance. If he saw
her, which he almost certainly had, he did not acknowl-
edge her presence by so much as a tip of his hat. Viviana
told herself she was relieved.

"What on earth have you done to my poor brother?"
asked Alice two days later.

They were sitting by the schoolroom hearth, Alice with
her needlepoint and Viviana with some hemming, waiting for the children to finish a board game Lottie had
brought from Arlington Park. "I have no notion," Viviana
murmured. "Why? What has he said?"

Alice's mouth curled into a knowing smile. "Very little,"
she said, drawing her stitch taut. "But he's cross as an old
mule, and we dare not speak your name in his hearing.
Mamma has grown suspicious."

Viviana winced inwardly. "I'm very sorry to hear that."

"Well, I am not," Alice declared. "It draws her attention from my little faux pas."

"Yes," said Viviana dryly. "Having to welcome Mr. Herndon into the bosom of her family is one thing. But having one's son entangled with an Italian opera singer would be quite beyond the pale, would it not?"

Alice froze in midstitch, and looked at her pointedly. *"Are* you entangled with my brother, Viviana?"

Viviana dropped her gaze. "I am not," she said firmly.

"Does he wish you to be?" Alice still did not resume her sewing.

Viviana shook her head. "It is just that your brother is stuck in the country and bored by it, I daresay," she answered. "I am sure he is accustomed to a much more exciting life."

Alice laughed. "Oh, Quin is infamous in town for his exciting life," she admitted. "But no, I do not think that is his problem. Indeed, he seems not to miss it at all. Henry says Quin seems finally to have found his place at Arlington Park."

Viviana smiled. "Speaking of your betrothed, how is he holding up?"

"Mamma has him taking all his meals with us now," Alice admitted. "And she won't take her eyes off the poor man."

"Why?"

"I think she is afraid he'll confuse his egg cup with his fish fork, or some such nonsense, and embarrass us all irrevocably," Alice admitted. "And it is all so unnecessary, Vivie. Henry is from a fine old Oxfordshire family. He is every inch a gentleman."

"His feelings must be quite hurt."

Alice bit off her thread. "Strangely, not a bit of it," she said. "He says that Mamma has a right to want only the best for me."

"But Mr. Herndon *is* what is best for you," said Viviana indignantly. "You love him."

"And I always have," Alice quietly admitted, tucking her needle away. "In three days' time, we will be wed, and it won't much matter what Mamma thinks. Which reminds me—I do hope the weather won't keep him from home again tonight. I heard Basham say his bad knee had gone stiff, and that it will be deathly cold to-morrow."

"To those of us with Mediterranean blood, it has been deathly cold for weeks now," said Viviana on a shiver. "Where has Mr. Herndon gone?"

"With Quin to London," said Alice. "To get the special license and to do some Christmas shopping at Hatchard's. By the way, I asked Quin to bring back some things for your children, too."

"You should not have done so, Alice," Viviana chided. "You are involving yourself in matters you do not under-stand."

Alice shoved her needlepoint back into her wicker bas-ket. "Oh, I think I've grasped the situation," she said. "But never mind that. What of our little escapade tomorrow? I hope you have some old clothes with you—warm ones, too, I might add."

"What escapade is this?"

"Our trip to cut the Christmas greenery, assuming Henry gets home," said Alice. "We will be tramping about in the forest with the village children half the afternoon. I only hope it does not rain. Christmas is but three days hence."

"It will be snow, more likely," said Viviana, shuddering at the thought. "Or sleet."

"Well, snow is tolerable, perhaps even pleasant," said Alice. "But rain is not. Unfortunately, it is already looking gray, and Basham's bad knee is never wrong."

But Viviana arose after yet another near-sleepless night to find that there was no snow the next morning, though the sky remained leaden, and a strange, expectant stillness lay heavy in the air. Inexplicably, she felt as if the Sword of Damocles was suspended above her head, just waiting to drop.

Matters worsened when, in the midst of breakfast, Alice sent word that the gentlemen had been detained in London for yet another day, and the children's outing was to be postponed. Viviana could barely hide her disappointment. She yearned for Alice's company, and, pathetically, almost any word of Quin. Instead, she was relegated to the music room, where she spent much of the day at her harp, plucking out the most melancholy tunes she knew.

Quin's bittersweet proposal haunted her waking moments, and many of her sleeping ones, too. Was this, then, to be her punishment? To awaken every night with her beloved's feverish words echoing in her brain? To know that, but for the fact she was a liar and a fraud, she might have had one last chance at happiness—and with Quin, the man she had never once stopped loving?

Viviana was relieved the following afternoon when she looked down from the schoolroom window to see Alice and Henry Herndon arriving at last. They brought with them the dogcart and two large wagons, one of them already filled with the village children. But Viviana's relief was short-lived when she saw the unexpected guest who accompanied them.

Lady Wynwood sat regally in the dogcart as if it were the finest landau. She was wrapped in what looked like a heavy wool blanket and was wearing a hat bedecked with ribbons more appropriate to an afternoon soiree.

In the schoolroom behind her, Nicolo and Felise were quarreling over a pair of red mittens, whilst Cerelia was tugging on her coat. Eventually, all three were dressed. Viviana took up her wool muffler and began to follow suit.

"Are you sure, my lady, that you do not wish me to go?" asked Miss Hevner.

Viviana shook her head. "There is no need for both of us to freeze to death," she answered, tugging on her gloves. "Besides, I wish to be with the children. Why do you not enjoy a few hours of solitude?"

Miss Hevner looked relieved.

Outside, the children rushed around the wagons, trying to decide with whom they would sit and on which side of the wagon. The older boys sat on the open end, their feet dangling. Cerelia looked at them longingly, then gingerly squeezed between them and went to join Lottie in the front.

"Will you join me, Contessa Bergonzi?" called Lady Wynwood from her dogcart.

There was no polite way of refusing. Alice already sat with Mr. Herndon, who was driving the first wagon. "I should be pleased to," Viviana answered, stepping up onto the rear gate, which had been let down. Lady Wynwood gave her a hand, and soon they were snugly ensconced on the rear-facing seat. The groom at the reins clicked to his horse and they set off, the second wagon bringing up the rear.

"What a pleasant surprise to see you, ma'am," said Viviana. "This must be quite an important village tradition."

Lady Wynwood made a dismissive noise in the back of her throat. "Oh, pish, I never go," she said. "But this year, my daughter has left me little choice."

A breeze was picking up now, lifting the brim of Lady Wynwood's hat. Viviana pulled her muffler tighter and tried to hide her incredulity. "You—you are here to lend propriety, then?"

"Oh, heavens no!" said Lady Wynwood, clamping one hand down on the crown of her hat. "Even I am not such a high stickler as all that. I am here to show my approval of this marriage. Society will be on guard for the slightest sign of family discord. I shan't give them the satisfaction."

Viviana managed to smile. "I am sure, ma'am, that you are doing the right thing."

Lady Wynwood somehow managed to look down her nose at Viviana. "I *always* do the right thing," she sniffed. "Whether I wish to or not."

Just then, as if her icy words had summoned it, the snow came whirling down. In the wagon up front, the children shouted with glee.

"Mamma! Mamma!" screeched Felise from the lead wagon. *"Neve umida!* Snow! Real snow!"

The snow was very real indeed, but heavy and wet. On the road, it was turning to slush, but by the time they had circled around behind Hill Court and Arlington Park, a distance of perhaps two miles, some of the snow was sticking in the hedgerows. Another mile farther, along the

Wendover road, they passed the Watsons' cottage to see Lucy dashing madly about in the side yard, jerking board-stiff pieces of laundry from her shrubs and fences. At the sight of the entourage, she waved a pair of frozen drawers and shouted greetings to the children.

Soon they reached the entrance to Arlington Park's great forest. Mr. Herndon slowed his wagon and turned sharply uphill, into the shadowy canopy of the trees. They went something less than a mile, for the road was little used and not very wide. Here, there were no bare, wintry branches clattering overhead. Instead, there was only a cold, tranquil silence punctuated by the soughing wind, and lush, dark evergreens as far as the eye could see.

"It's like an enchanted forest!" cried Cerelia, climbing down off the wagon. "Look at all the snow floating through the trees!"

"Do you not have snow in Venice?" asked Lottie.

"A little." Cerelia made a face. "But it always melts."

"*Si,* and this is lovely, is it not?" said Viviana, giving Cerelia a swift hug. "Now take hold of Nicolo's hand, *cara,* and do not let him from your sight."

The footmen and two of the oldest boys were given hacksaws, and instructed to do all the cutting. The younger children were to carry the greenery for loading onto the wagons. Soon they were all dashing excitedly into the trees, their happy cries shattering the forest's silence. Alice accompanied them, but Herndon stayed long enough to build a fire with dry kindling he had brought with him. Then he covered a low stump with a large, thick rug, and situated Lady Wynwood on it.

Soon the children began to return with armloads of pine boughs and baskets of holly. Each child was permitted to gather enough to decorate their own cottage or village shop, as well as the church, thus the need for two wagons. Viviana supervised the loading of the greenery onto them, taking care that the little ones did not slip and fall on the slick pine needles.

In short order, the bottoms of the wagons were covered. The snow was still falling, faster than before, and Viviana could feel the chill deepening. They were almost an hour in the forest before the breeze roughened, and the whirling snow turned to spates of sleet. The fire still burned brightly, but despite it, Lady Wynwood's teeth were soon chattering. By then, both wagons were heaped with pine boughs and holly. Leaving Alice and Viviana to count heads, Mr. Herndon and the servants shooed the children out of the pines and back to the wagons.

With pink cheeks and red noses, the children all seemed to wish to speak at once as they clambered back into the wagons. There was a great debate about who had found what, and which of them had worked the hardest. Lady Wynwood settled the dispute by regally declaring Ben, the fourteen-year-old baker's son, the victor.

"I want to sit on the end of the wagon," Lottie declared as the children clambered onto the first wagon. "Cerelia, Hannah, and I are the oldest. We should sit on the end of the last wagon so that the boughs don't slide off."

"Very well," said Mr. Herndon gruffly. "Boys on this wagon, girls on the last."

With screeches of glee, the girls and boys divided, the littlest girls climbing over the mounds of pine and holly to sit squarely in the middle of the wagon, like chicks in a nest of green. On the open end, Lottie looked very pleased with herself and let her dangling heels swing back and forth triumphantly.

Herndon knocked the fire down and kicked a little soil over it. Clearly, the weather would take care of the rest. Viviana turned around to see Christopher holding securely to Nicolo's hand as he climbed into the boys' wagon.

"Your grandson Christopher has the makings of a true gentleman," she said to Lady Wynwood as she helped her up into the dogcart.

Lady Wynwood acknowledged the compliment with a slight incline of her head. "Alice has raised her children well." Then, almost reluctantly, she added, "Your girls are very prettily behaved, too. But what of your youngest? Is he still a handful?"

Nicolo *was* a challenge, and Viviana did not mind admitting it. They spent much of the drive back commiserating on the difficulty of raising boys, and Lady Wynwood began to thaw ever so slightly.

At the foot of the hill, Herndon turned his wagon onto the main road. But when the groom driving their dogcart did the same, Viviana felt a sudden jerk as the wheel beneath her slipped in the slush. The wagon bringing up the rear slowed to a near halt. Viviana looked up to make sure it followed. After a moment had passed, the wagon edged carefully around the turn and back into Viviana's line of sight.

Beside her, Lady Wynwood shivered. Her cloak and heavy blanket were not enough to keep her warm. Viviana looked around for something more. "Oh, dear," she said quietly. "I believe we forgot that rug you were sitting on, ma'am."

Lady Wynwood seemed touched by her concern. "It

would have done nicely across our laps, would it not?" she remarked. "Will you share my blanket, Contessa?"

"Thank you, I am fine." But the return was perfectly miserable as the precipitation spattered down on them, half ice and half cold, freezing rain. Eventually, even the heaviest wool began to dampen. Ice began to form on the hedgerows and trees lining their journey, and Viviana began to wonder if the wagons would make it back up the high hill to Lord Chesley's house.

Relief surged through her when at last the wagons were pulled around the circular carriage drive. The eldest boys hopped off, and began piling part of the greenery by the front door. Herndon ordered one of the footmen to hold his horses' heads, then leapt down to lift Nicolo from the wagon.

"Why do you not come in, ma'am, and sit by the fire awhile," Viviana suggested to Lady Wynwood. "Chesley is out, but on his return, he can send you home in a proper carriage with a brick beneath your feet."

She looked longingly at the front door. "Oh, I suppose not," said her ladyship witheringly. "I should rather just get it over with."

Just then, Viviana's gaze fell upon Alice, hovering over Lottie, who had climbed down from the last wagon. Viviana hastened to Alice. "I think you should get back in the wagon," she advised. "Hurry home before the children catch their death."

Then her eyes fell on Lottie, who was holding her mother's hand and looking rather pale. Alice, too, looked worried.

Suddenly, it struck her. "Lottie," said Viviana sharply. "Where is Cerelia?"

Alice set a hand on Viviana's arm. "Oh, Vivie, she isn't sure!"

"What?" Panic gripped her. "What do you mean? What has happened?"

Alice's grip tightened. "Oh, Viviana, I don't think she came out of the woods!" she cried. "Henry! Henry! Come here at once."

Even Lady Wynwood had climbed down from her perch. "What has happened?" she asked, her tone shrill. "Who is missing?"

All the children were babbling now, most of them climbing down to see what all the fuss was about.

"Cerelia went back, Mamma," said Lottie plaintively. "She got on the wagon, but then she had to jump off."

Viviana knelt and grasped the girl's arms. "But why, Lottie?" she asked, struggling to keep her voice calm. "And where?"

She could feel Herndon now, hovering anxiously over them. Lottie sniffled pathetically. "It-It was a-at the foot of the hill," the child answered. "Before we turned onto the Wendover road. She said she had lost something."

"Dear God!" said Alice. "What?"

"I don't know!" wailed Lottie. "She said she just had to find it. That she had to go back and would catch up with us."

"Dio mio!" whispered Viviana.

"I—I thought she could do it," the child sobbed. "Cerelia runs so fast. B-But we traveled all of the Wendover road, and th-then the village road, and she never came, and I didn't know what to do!"

Lottie was sobbing in earnest now. Fighting down her own terror, Viviana gathered the child against her and gave her a swift hug. "It is not your fault," she said. Then she stood. "I need a fast horse." Her eyes fell on one of Chesley's servants, who stood holding an umbrella ineffectually over Lady Wynwood. "Wardell, go to the stables. Tell them to saddle Champion, and bring him up at once."

Wardell looked nervously at Lady Wynwood. Abruptly, she snatched the umbrella from him. "Well, good God, man!" said her ladyship. "Go! Go!"

Sans umbrella, Wardell bolted down the hill.

"I shall leave the children here," said Herndon hastily. "I must go back at once."

"A wagon is too slow," said Viviana. "Hurry everyone home, Mr. Herndon. All the children are wet and cold. I shall ride back and fetch her." She was trying hard not to panic, but even she could see that her gloved hands were shaking. "I shall just need a blanket, and—and a—"

"What if Cerelia is lost, Contessa?" Herndon interjected. "You do not know the lay of the land here."

"And what if one of the other children takes a chill?" Viviana said. "They need their wet clothes off and something warm to drink. Besides, a horse is faster. But follow me, Herndon, as soon as you can, *si?*"

Herndon nodded. "We must divide the children up," Alice insisted. "Henry, you take the village children."

"Where is Lord Chesley?" asked Herndon.

"Out for the afternoon," said Viviana. "They are not expected back until dinner."

But Alice had leapt into action, and was shooing the children back onto the wagons. "Get back in, everyone. Quickly! Quickly, now! We must go back to Arlington Park and fetch Quin."

Quin. Alice spoke the name as if it were a given. And

thank God. Quin really would know what to do. Viviana felt a wave of relief pass over her.

"Thank you, Alice," she said, looking over her shoulder as she pushed Felise toward the door. "Tell him . . . oh, please, tell him to hurry! I shall meet him on the Wendover road."

Alice nodded tightly. "Cerelia is like to catch her death in this."

Herndon whipped up his horses, and left.

By the time Viviana had changed into dry clothes and one of Chesley's old greatcoats, her mount had been brought round. The sleet had turned into a cold, driving rain, which swept across the carriage drive in sheets.

"It will be dark soon, my lady," said Wardell, shouting above the rain as he helped her mount.

Viviana nodded. "Watch for Lord Wynwood," she shouted. Then she reined her mount into a tight circle and rode off down the carriage drive.

Quin was in his study trying to make sense of some of his father's old account books, his mind almost numb from the rhythm of the rain, when Henry Herndon burst in through the French window, water streaming off his coat and hat.

"Bloody hell, man!" said Quin, springing from his chair. "What are you doing out in this?"

It took Herndon but a moment to explain. Alarm shot through Quin at once. "It will be pitch-dark in less than two hours," he said anxiously. "There is no time to waste. Ring for someone to have my horse brought round."

"I already left word at the stables," said Herndon. "Your horse and mine."

Quin shot him a quick, assessing gaze. "Change into dry clothes, then," he advised. "You go out by the back gate. I'll go round by the village road, then past the Watson cottage."

"A good plan," agreed Herndon. "Approaching from opposite directions, one of us is bound to see her."

Quin was already stripping off his frock coat as he headed for the door. "If you find her first, Herndon, take her to the nearest house," ordered Quin. "Here. Hill Court. The Watsons. Wherever hot water and a fire can be quickest had."

"Yes, sir."

Quin had his hand on the door and Herndon on his heels when the latter spoke again. "My lord, I should warn you that Contessa Bergonzi meant to go on ahead of us," he said quietly. "The gentlemen were all from home. She was calling for her horse when I left Hill Court."

Quin cursed audibly. "What the devil is she thinking?" he snapped. "A woman's got no business out in a storm like this! She doesn't even know these roads well."

"I tried to point that out, my lord," Herndon reported. "But she would not listen."

Quin was already striding down the narrow corridor in the direction of the stairs. "Damned stubborn woman," he muttered.

Herndon touched him on the shoulder just before he hit the first flight.

Quin spun around. "What?"

Herndon did not step back. "Have a care with Contessa Bergonzi, my lord," he said gently, his hand still on Quin's shoulder. "The little girl is, after all, her flesh and blood."

"And what of it?" snapped Quin. "Cerelia is still just as lost. Still in grave danger."

Herndon lifted one shoulder. "I have no children," he said quietly. "I cannot imagine the terror that poor woman feels just now. Can you?"

Quin grappled with his own panic for a moment. To him, it felt very like terror. Outside it was cold, wickedly damp, and soon it would be dark on top of all else. There was little shelter along the Wendover road, unless Cerelia made it back to Lucy Watson's, or circled six miles in the other direction and stumbled upon the vacant cottage. What were the chances of that? Already he was imagining the worst. Quinsy. Pleurisy. Lung fever. Were those fears more intense for Viviana? If they were, then God help her. "No, Herndon," he said on a sigh. "No, I suppose we cannot imagine."

The ride back to the Wendover road was but two miles on familiar ground. Sick with worry for Cerelia, Viviana spurred the big horse on, and he sprang willingly. They were going too fast for the weather, she knew. But Cerelia would be drenched to the skin by now, and likely terrified. Maternal instinct drove her deeper and faster into the driving rain. She only hoped Champion could see the road ahead a little better than she could.

A crossroads came upon them suddenly, the signposts unreadable through the torrent. Viviana turned right and pushed the horse hard uphill. But less than half a mile in, Viviana realized that her surroundings were not quite familiar. The hedgerows were higher and growing too near. The lane was too narrow. Panic shot through her heart. *The wrong turn?* Dear God, had she turned too soon? She had been this way but twice, once on foot with Lucy.

Abruptly, she pulled her mount up and reined him sharply around. Champion tried to obey, but it was futile. With the road awash, the shoulder was too soft. Amidst the wet leaves and loosened stones, the horse lost his footing and had to scrabble for purchase. Viviana hadn't a prayer of hanging on to the sidesaddle. She slid off and tumbled into the ditch, twisting one foot awkwardly beneath her, and wrenching the opposite wrist behind as she tried to catch her fall.

With a muttered curse, she tried to push herself up, but a blinding pain shot through her arm. For an instant, she simply lay there, stunned, dimly aware of the cold ditchwater which was soaking through Chesley's greatcoat and even her heavy wool habit.

Cerelia! Her poor baby! The child was out alone in this hard, unforgiving English weather—and it was all Viviana's fault. She dragged herself into a sitting position and clicked to Champion. The big horse obeyed, edging up to the side of the ditch, huffing anxiously through his nostrils. The stirrup dangled tantalizingly, just inches beyond Viviana's grasp.

But what would she do if she caught hold of it? She could not remount, she did not think. And her wrist was of little use. How could she carry Cerelia? Tears sprang hotly to her eyes. The foot—the one she most needed—was sprained, if not broken. She would have to stay on her good leg, bearing her weight onto Champion. And she would have to walk back to Hill Court; to tell them that she had failed and that someone else must go out and do what she had been too incompetent to accomplish.

And then she remembered Quin.

Relief coursed through her. Herndon had gone to fetch him. At that very moment, Quin was already riding hard toward Cerelia; of that she had no doubt. And he would be looking for Viviana, too. He would not, however, be looking on this godforsaken little pig path. But he would press on, and eventually, he would find Cerelia. He was relentless when he put his mind to something. Yes, somehow, Quin would find her. She had to believe in that.

Viviana's body was beginning to shake from the freezing cold water. *Dio,* she had to do something. What use would she be to Cerelia once Quin did bring her home, if she simply lay here and took ill with the cholera or whatever dread disease one got from lying in cold, nasty ditchwater.

Just then, Champion edged up another few inches. Viviana snared the stirrup, and somehow hauled herself up. The pain was remarkably bad. With Champion's reins in one hand, and bearing her weight on the stirrup with the other, she managed to hobble a few feet back along the road. She set a course for Hill Court and began quietly to pray.

Fourteen

In which Lucy almost Lets It Slip.

Quin was drenched by the time he reached Arlington Park's gatehouse. Through the gloom, he could already see the glow of lamplight through the tidy village windows, and in Aunt Charlotte's drawing room, too. Along the narrow lane to his left, shops and cottages lay still. The sign of the Black Lion swung wildly in its cast-iron bracket, the sound shrill and grating to his ears. Quin turned and nudged his horse in the opposite direction.

The rain did not let up and ran off his hat brim in tiny torrents. Along the main road, he saw no one, and reached the narrow country lane which led to Arlington's evergreen forest without incident. Here, he dismounted and began to walk, calling Cerelia's name into the hedgerows. It was possible, he supposed, that she had sheltered there.

A small part of him wondered why he was doing this. Surely he could have sent out all the servants to comb the hills and forests—and quite possibly he still would do, if the child was not easily found. But a larger part of him was truly worried. He had developed a deep fondness for the girl. It was rooted, in part, in his love for her mother. And yet it went beyond that, in a way he could not quite explain, even to himself.

He wondered how far ahead of him Viviana was. He prayed the drenching rain would drive her to Lucy Watson's, or perhaps even on to the cottage. There, a good fire was already laid in the hearth. He hoped she would think to light it.

He was heartsick over the bitterness with which he and Viviana had last parted. But what choice had she left him? Her emotional guard had been up, and for no real reason that he could see. He did not for one moment believe that Viviana was cowed by his mother. No, there was something else. Something far more painful than that, he thought. Perhaps it had something to do with her first marriage?

"All I know, caro," she had said to him, *"is that it is easier to marry a man whom you do not love than to marry a man who does not love you."*

Since that awful day, Quin had given her strange sentiment a great deal of thought and decided they were wise words indeed. It had been true even of him, had it not? Quin had been perfectly happy to marry Miss Hamilton, whom he had not loved. But if Viviana came to him now on her knees and begged him to have her, begged him to be a father to her children, and to protect her with his name and his honor for all of eternity—no, he would not do it. Not until she told him she loved him. He had not, however, given up in that regard. He had thought long and hard about Viviana during his trip to London with

Herndon. And now he had, as Alasdair was fond of saying, one card yet up his sleeve.

But all that must be set aside for the moment, he reminded himself. Cerelia was all that mattered. He continued on foot for another two miles, calling first for Cerelia, then for Viviana. At last, however, he topped a high hill and looked down upon the Watson cottage, tucked neatly behind its stone fence, its every window aglow like a beacon of hope.

This, he prayed, was where he would find Cerelia. Lucy was a sensible woman. She would put the child in a tub of warm water by the fire and fill her belly with hot porridge. Feeling strangely hopeful, he hurried down the hill.

His heavy knock was answered by Lucy herself. Her eyes widened as Quin shook the water from his hat and ducked beneath the lintel to enter.

"My lord," she said, bobbing a quick curtsy. "What on earth—?"

Through the wide kitchen door, he could see children seated at the table. Cerelia was not amongst them. He returned his gaze to Lucy, but his face must have fallen. "I've come about Cerelia," he said. "Lucy, what can you tell me? Anything?"

Lucy's expression faltered. "I—I beg your pardon, sir?"

"Surely you've seen Viviana by now?" he went on, panicked by Lucy's blank look. "Surely you've heard?"

The confusion in Lucy's expression cleared. "Ah, told you everything, has she?" Her voice went suddenly soft. "Well, thank God in heaven, my lord. It's been a heavy burden to me these many years."

For a moment, Quin simply stood there, dripping onto

Lucy's flagstone floor. "I'm sorry," he finally said. "We . . . we seem to be at cross-purposes here."

Lucy suddenly went white. "I—I beg your pardon," she said again. "I'm afraid . . . I'm afraid I mistook you. What is it you've come for, sir?"

Quin looked at her quizzically. "Cerelia got separated from the other children this afternoon," he said quietly. "Hasn't Viviana been by here looking for her?"

Still pale, Lucy shook her head. "There's been naught come by here, my lord, since Mr. Herndon brought the wagons out this afternoon," she whispered. "What can have happened to the poor child?"

"Yes, and what of Viviana?" he said grimly. "She should have been riding ahead of me. I hoped they would be here."

Lucy touched him lightly on the elbow. Her color was returning. "Do come in by the parlor fire, my lord. You'll catch your death in those clothes."

He shook his head. "I must find Cerelia," he said, slapping his hat back on his head. "And now Viviana, too. We'll be lucky if the child doesn't take a chill or worse."

Lucy nodded and opened the door. "I'll keep a lamp burning in the window, my lord," she promised. "When you find them, bring them to me straightaway, and I'll see they're warmed up proper."

Beyond the door, rain still spattered loudly. Quin gave a tight nod and ducked back out into the weather. Vaguely, he wondered what was wrong with Lucy Watson. There was something there in what she had said—something important that was escaping him. But just now he could think only of Cerelia and Viviana, of the urgent need to find them.

As darkness crept nearer, the rain finally eased, and he found himself at the foot of the old forest road. This was the way into the pines which Herndon would have taken. It was here, Lottie had said, that Cerelia slipped off the wagon and ran back into the trees. It was a long shot, surely. The road was clearly marked, such that even a confused child could have found her way back out again. But something, instinct perhaps, impelled him forward.

He remounted, and allowed the horse to pick his way up the rough, needle-slick path, for it was hardly what one would call a road. At last the rain slackened. He caught the scent of damp ashes well before he saw them. There was an old fire pit near the turnaround, he recalled. Someone had recently used it. Just Herndon, most likely. Still, hope drove him hard up the hill, bellowing Cerelia's name into the gloom.

In the clearing, something which looked like a bundle of old rags lay near the steaming, sodden fire pit. He leapt from his horse, unstrapped the blanket, and rushed the rest of the way up he hill. "Cerelia?"

The bundle moved, and lifted up. A mop of bronze hair popped out beneath it, and two bereft blue eyes looked up at him. Quin fell to his knees, and dragged the child hard against him. "Cerelia, thank God!" he whispered. "Oh, child! Where have you been?"

At that, Cerelia burst into tears. Not knowing what else to do, Quin just held her tighter. Her entire body seemed to shudder against his. Quin pressed his lips to her hair and surveyed the scene.

The child had been huddled beneath some sort of old rug or horse blanket, it appeared. The fire was made of thick, heavy logs which had been barely burnt, then kicked hither and yon. Herndon's work, he assumed. But it looked as though Cerelia had been industrious enough to prod it back to life for a while. A little heat yet radiated from the ground, and the scent of smoke was thick in the air.

"You were very smart, Cerelia, to rekindle the fire," he said, patting her gently between her narrow shoulder blades. "Are you all right, my dear?"

Her sobs were like little gulps now. She felt like a fragile, almost ephemeral creature in his arms. Like something precious that might slip from his grasp at any moment. There was an awful knot in his throat, and his every instinct wished to protect her. At last, she lifted her head from his coat front.

"I—I thought someone w-would come back for me!" she sobbed.

He set his lips to her forehead. "And so they have, mouse," he answered. "I'm sorry we were so slow."

"I tried to c-catch up with the others," she said between sniffles. "But when I got to the road, I—I couldn't remember whether I was to go left, or go right. I got so scared. I did not know what to do."

Quin bent his head to look at her. "And so you came back here, and stayed put, hmm?" he said. "Very wise. Now, let's get you wrapped in a blanket and find a good, roaring fire."

Cerelia snuffled loudly, and pulled away. It was then that he noticed her curled fist. "Am I g-going to be in t-trouble now?" she asked, staring at it.

Quin tipped her chin up with his finger. "Accidents happen, mouse," he said. "Why would you be in trouble?"

Slowly, the child uncurled her fist. In the fading daylight, he could see something metallic pooled in her hand. She had been clutching it so hard, the big, square stone had left an almost brutal impression in her palm. Quin lifted it up, and studied it. The jewel looked lifeless in the gloom, but he recognized at once the strange fob Cerelia wore about her neck.

"Is this the thing you lost, Cerelia?" he asked quietly. "The thing you went back to search for?"

Mutely, the child nodded.

"Are you not supposed to have it?"

She shook her head.

"Then it is not yours?"

"No, it . . . it *is* mine," she said. "Mamma gave it to me. A long time ago. It's my magic ring. It has special powers. But she does not like me to wear it."

Her mother gave it to her?

Why had Viviana lied? Cerelia had not simply "found" it. Nor was it paste and pinchbeck, he'd wager. A strange, surreal feeling was coming over Quin as he studied it. A kind of numbness—and yet not numbness at all. It was rather as if one's leg had gone to sleep, and now all the feeling was flooding back, nerve by nerve, and hurting all the worse for it. Except that it was not his leg, but his entire body. His brain. His heart. A rush of emotion and suspicion which left him breathless. And then an agonizing certainty. He felt frozen to the ground, rooted to the forest floor with Cerelia still in his arms.

Just something Cerelia found. He could hear Viviana's emotionless words echoing in his head. Lies. All lies.

He held the large ruby to what was left of the light. He could feel his heart thudding in his chest. "What happened to it, Cerelia?" he choked. "How . . . how was it damaged?"

A look which could only be described as fear sketched over her face. "My—my *papà*—Gianpiero—he got very angry," she whispered.

"What did he do?" Quin's voice was a raw whisper.

Her wide, innocent eyes looked up at him plaintively. "I do not think I am supposed to tell."

Somehow, he smiled. "It is all right, Cerelia," he answered. "You need to tell me."

The child licked her lips uncertainly. "I think he—he did not wish Mamma to wear it," she confessed. "He—he took it off her finger. And then he smashed it with a—a *martello*. A thing to hit with."

Quin tried to think. "A—a hammer?"

"A hammer," she agreed. "A big one, for the garden. For the working of stone."

Good God! A sledgehammer?

Cerelia's eyes were glazed over with terror, as if she saw not the present, but the past. "He smashed it," the child whispered. "And said very bad words. He said he did not love me. And that Mamma was a—a—oh, I don't know the word. Something ugly. She cried, and begged him for the ring, so that I might have it instead. But that made him angrier still, and so he . . . he—"

"He what, Cerelia?"

The child dropped her gaze. "I—I cannot remember," she whispered.

Quin looked at the girl's bereft face. He did not for one moment believe she did not remember. She had the look of one who remembered all too well. But what? Dear God, what had this child suffered? For an instant, he feared he might be ill. He felt himself literally trembling inside, shaking with rage and fear and the almost overwhelming urge to pull Cerelia to him and never let her go. He put his arms around her, and she all but threw herself against him.

"You do not need to remember, Cerelia," he whispered into her hair. "And I shan't ask you about it. Do not think of it ever again. All right?"

"All right." The words, tinged with relief, were muffled against his chest.

Cerelia. Poor, precious child! *His* child—left at the mercy of a raving bedlamite! God damn Viviana Alessandri to hell for this. And God damn *him,* too.

Just then, the wind kicked up, bringing him back to the present. He must control himself. He must get Cerelia out of this chill. It was his duty, in every sense of the word now. A duty long overdue. Gently, he tucked the fob and chain deep in his coat pocket. From here, there was a shortcut up through the forest which should take them straight to Hill Court. He only prayed he could remember the way.

"Come along, mouse," he said, unfurling the dry blanket he'd carried up the hill. "Let's get you safely home."

The wide-eyed uncertainty returned. "I w-want my Mamma," she whimpered. "I j-just don't want her to be angry with me."

Quin came to his feet with Cerelia in his arms, though he still trembled with rage. "Don't fret, sweet," he answered making his way back to his horse. "She will not be angry with you."

She wriggled herself deeper into the blanket. "Are— are you quite sure, my lord?"

Somehow, Quin managed another smile. "I promise you, Cerelia," he answered, giving her a quick peck on the nose. "And I always keep my promises. Trust me, that lost ring will soon be the least of your Mamma's concerns."

Viviana was in tears by the time her father and Lord Chesley returned home. She had been quarreling with Signora Rossi for the last half hour, to no avail. Basham had sent every footman and groom out into the night with lanterns, but it had done nothing to calm Viviana. She demanded to be taken out in a cart to search for Cerelia, but Basham and Signora Rossi had conspired to keep her at home. She would be a fool, the old nurse kept insisting, to leave the house when Cerelia might be carried in at any moment, terrified and crying for her mother.

Viviana was certainly terrified. The gentlemen found her flung across the divan in the parlor, a damp handkerchief crumpled in her fist. Her father paled when he saw the cane beside her. "Viviana, *bella, che cosa è quello?*"

"Gad, Vivie, a cane?" boomed Chesley, coming in with Lord Digleby. "And Basham looks like his mother just died."

Somehow Viviana dragged herself up off the divan. She had given up trying to be strong; trying to be in control of the situation, when she so obviously was not. "Oh, *Papà!* Oh, Chesley! *Non ci credo!* Such terrible news!" With her father clutching her hand, Viviana tearfully relayed the day's events, ending with her impetuous ride, and the humiliating fall from Champion which ended it.

"And now they won't drive me back out!" she cried. "Chesley! Chesley, *affrettarsi, per favore!* You will take me in your barouche, *si?*"

"Poor little Cerelia!" murmured Chesley. "And poor you, Vivie. But never fear, my girl. Quin will fetch our Cerelia home, of that I've no doubt. Far better that you should stay put."

Viviana began to vehemently protest in a firestorm of bad English and overwrought Italian, but Chesley was saved from the worst of it when hoofbeats rang out in the carriage drive. Viviana snatched her cane and limped to the window. A lone rider in a sodden, broad-brimmed hat appeared in the pool of lamplight beyond the front steps, carrying someone or something before him. "Oh!" Her hand went to her heart. "Oh, can it be?"

"See, Vivie!" said Chesley. "All's well. Quin has seen to it."

But Vivie had already headed for the entrance hall. The door stood open, the sharp air blessedly cool on her feverish, tear-stained face. Basham had gone out to assist, but Quin had already dismounted. He shouldered his way through the door and into the passageway, carrying Cerelia wrapped in a thick wool blanket.

"Oh, *mia cara bambina!*" Viviana's hands clasped her face, which was cold as death. "Oh, *grazie a Dio!*"

"Mamma," she said quietly. "I . . . I got lost."

"But you are home now," said Viviana, choking back a sob. "Home, and safe, my precious. Oh, *grazie,* Quin. Thank you. Thank you so very much. Where was she? Is she hurt?"

Behind her, Chesley and her father had begun to ask questions, too. Digleby joined in the agitation. But Quin was having none of it. "Cerelia was still by the fire," he said curtly. "And now, if you will pardon me, I must take her upstairs at once."

"She is shaking terribly," murmured Viviana. "Oh, *Dio mio!* Is she ill?"

"I pray not," Quin answered. "Basham, send someone for Dr. Gould, and tell them to be quick about it." He cut a glance down at Viviana's cane. "What happened to you? You look as if you need a doctor, too."

Later, she was to realize how cool and brusque his tone was. But in that moment, her fear was too newly assuaged, her gratitude too great. "I took a tumble off my horse," she answered. "But never mind that. Let us get her warm at once."

"Yes, yes," said Chesley. "Just the thing! Go up at once. I shall wait for Dr. Gould."

Viviana scarcely heard him. Her sole concern was for Cerelia. Her hands were blue, her eyes half-closed. "To my room," she said, hobbling toward the stairs. "There's a roaring fire, and Mrs. Douglass has set up a trundle bed."

"Lead on," he commanded.

At the landing, Viviana looked back anxiously. "How long has she been shaking like this?"

"Since I took her up onto my horse," he answered tightly. Then he told her of how Cerelia had rekindled the fire for a time and covered herself with the rug for warmth. Viviana sent up a grateful prayer for their forgetfulness in having left it.

"At first, she seemed fine," Quin continued as they turned into the shadows of the corridor. "But as soon as she began to warm, she grew silent and began to shake. I fear she is taking a chill."

"Dear God!" Urgently, Viviana pushed open her door. Inside, two of the housemaids were drawing a slipper bath up to the fire. "I've rung for the hot water, ma'am, as

Mrs. Douglass ordered," said the first, straightening up from the tub. "She says a very warm Epsom bath will take the chill from her most quickly. Then Nurse says she's to have a cup of chicken broth."

Quin was unwrapping the big blanket from Cerelia. "Where is Nurse?" asked Viviana.

Just then, Signora Rossi came in. The old woman had been with the Bergonzi family for some forty-five years, though her duties consisted of little nowadays. Tonight, however, her special touch would be greatly needed.

Ignoring Quin and Viviana, she went straight to Cerelia, who had become fretful. Gently, the nurse began unfastening her clothing as she cooed at her in mix of Italian, Venetian, and English. The words did seem to soothe the child. Quin made a curt bow in Viviana's direction.

"I will excuse myself," he said. "Is there somewhere I might wait until Cerelia is safely in bed? I wish to speak to you."

Viviana looked at him uncertainly. *"Si, certamente,"* she answered. "The family sitting room? It is two doors down."

He bowed again and left.

Viviana waited until Cerelia had been dressed in her warmest nightdress and tucked into the little trundle bed. Signora Rossi rang for the broth to be brought up, and Viviana spooned it into her. Cerelia had stopped the dreadful shaking and seemed perhaps a little more herself.

Another two minutes, and the child fell into a deep sleep. There was nothing more to do save pray for Cerelia's health. Already, Signora Rossi had taken out her rosary. In all fairness, Viviana could keep Quin waiting no longer. With a sense of unease, Viviana kissed Cerelia's cheek and left Signora Rossi to sit by the bed. Her blind fear over Cerelia was subsiding, leaving room for a far more logical sort of trepidation.

She found Quin in the family parlor. A fire had been newly kindled in the grate; Quin's work, she was sure. He was remarkably self-sufficient. He was not seated, but instead was pacing the floor, still in his wet clothes. If he were cold or uncomfortable, he gave no indication. Indeed, so absorbed in thought was he, it seemed he did not hear her enter.

As he turned away and paced the length of the room again, Viviana took in his solid, impossibly wide shoulders, and his long, strong legs, still encased in what must have been miserably wet riding boots. No, not a boy any longer. She wondered if he ever had been. But boy or man, he had always been honorable. And suddenly, despite all her trepidation, an almost choking sense of gratitude sweep over her.

Quin had brought Cerelia safely home. *He had not failed her.*

She cleared her throat, and he spun around to face her. He did not seem surprised to see her. "What does Gould say?" he demanded. "How is she?"

Viviana shook her head. "Cerelia is sleeping soundly," she said. "Dr. Gould was from home with an emergency, but is on his way now. What did you wish to see me about?"

Quin did not hesitate, but came at once to his point. "You spoke sometime back, Viviana, of returning to Venice." His voice was cool. Emotionless. "I am afraid I must ask you to reconsider."

Viviana blinked uncertainly. "Reconsider going home?" she answered. "But I cannot."

His gaze swept over her appraisingly, but there was no hint of desire, or even admiration, in it. "So you are resolved, then," he said. "Have you any better idea of when you will leave?"

"I—I am not sure," she confessed. "By early spring, at the very latest, I should think."

His eyes were hard and dark. "If you insist, Viviana, on going, I must warn you that Cerelia will not be accompanying you," he said. "I wish you to gently accustom her to that fact. Beginning tomorrow."

"Scusa?" She looked at him blankly, her heart almost thudding to a halt. "I—I do not perfectly comprehend you."

He tilted his head to one side and studied her. "I think you comprehend me quite well, madam," he returned, his tone so flat they might have been strangers discussing the weather. "You were never going to tell her the truth, were you? Certainly you were never going to tell *me.* You have built that poor girl's life on a lie, Viviana, without one ounce of compunction. Not one whit of remorse or regret. Did you think me such a fool I would never guess the truth?"

The room fell suddenly and deathly still. The reality of what was happening—the horror of her worst fear come true—sank in on her. Viviana grappled for another convincing lie, but instead, her knees nearly buckled. A pair of fragile French armchairs sat nearby. She seized one as though it were a lifeline, her nails digging into the upholstery.

Quin was undeterred. "Sit down, Viviana," he said roughly. "Sit down, for God's sake, before you swoon."

She did so, making her way gingerly around the chair. She had no choice. She was but vaguely aware of his closing the distance between them and standing before her, his boots set stubbornly apart. He shoved a hand into his pocket, and in an instant, the ruby ring dangled before her face, sparkling bloodred as it slowly rotated in the lamplight.

Viviana closed her eyes and looked away.

She felt his hand slide beneath her chin, and force her face back to his. Her eyes flew open of their own accord, and fear made her stomach bottom out. Oh, *Dio!*

"Do not close your eyes, Viviana," he growled. "Do not in any way try to evade my questions. The deceit is done and over with, do you hear? Disregard what I say now at your peril."

Viviana jerked her face from his hand, but did not avert her eyes. "I—I am not disregarding you," she answered. "I do not know what you want of me. What you are asking. You make no sense to me, Quin. *Per favore,* I . . . I wish to return to my daughter now."

He leaned down and sneered into her face. "As I wish to return to *mine,*" he growled, his every word growing louder. "But there is an annoying little problem standing in my way, is there not? Someone forgot to tell that poor child who her father is!"

"Quin, stop!" Viviana held out her palm, as if she might avert him. "You do not know what you speak of!"

His face twisted with rage. In a flash of motion, his boot lashed out, kicking the other chair against the wall with almost superhuman strength. "God damn you, don't you lie to me!" he roared as the chair clattered to the floor, splintering one leg apart. "Let another lie pass your lips, Viviana, and I swear I will take her back to Arlington this very night."

Viviana fought down her fear. "Don't be a fool, Quinten," she answered. "Calm yourself, for God's sake, before every servant in the house has an ear pressed to the door."

"I don't think you grasp the gravity of your situation, Viviana," he snapped. "I don't give a good goddamn if the whole village hears! I am not ashamed of her. And what have I to lose, anyway? What? You have my child. *You took her from me.* And now I want her back."

Nervously, Viviana licked her lips. He looked and spoke like a madman. Could he do such a thing? Could he just declare Cerelia his, and—and just *take her?*

"I see your devious brain at work, madam," he said with a sneer. "You are wondering if I can get away with it. Well, this is England, Viviana. Peers of the realm have rights here—indeed, we make the very laws we all live by—and foreigners have next to *none.* The child is mine. And for eight years—or is it nearer to nine?—you have enjoyed her company exclusively. You have told her lies and taught her what you pleased, ignoring her rights. Ignoring that she was half-English. That is all at an end now."

"You . . . you cannot take my child." Viviana's hands were starting to shake uncontrollably. "You cannot. I am . . . I am her mother, Quinten."

"And I am her father." He lifted the ruined ring again and let it twirl in the light, tiny, bloodred sparks flickering at every turn, as if it did indeed hold magical powers. "Deny it, Viviana, if you dare. Deny it before God. No? No, I did not think you could."

To her undying shame, Viviana burst into tears. "Cerelia is *my child,*" she sobbed. "You . . . you cannot take her from me."

"I think I can," he gritted. "And I'll bloody well try if you push me to it. I demand the right to be a parent to my child. I demand what is right for Cerelia. I have no intention of permanently ripping a child from her mother's bosom—I am not a monster, Viviana—but if you must return to Venice, that is your problem. You shan't take her from England ever again."

"You are insane," she whispered. "Cerelia belongs with *me*."

"Cerelia belongs with you?" he echoed incredulously. "With the woman who has cheated her of her birthright? With the woman who has cheated her father of his child? With the woman who tricked her husband into marriage? Oh, no, Viviana. I am being generous. I am being far more generous to you than you ever were to me."

But Viviana's anger was fast overcoming her fear. "I never lied to my husband," she said, her voice tremulous with rage. "What was between Gianpiero and me is none of your business. Go ahead, Quinten! Try to claim her. I will deny it all. Everything. And you cannot prove otherwise."

"Another lie on top of a lifetime of lies," he returned. "That is your solution to everything, is it not?"

"I did what I had to do," she hissed. "Cerelia is my daughter, and I have dealt with it as best I could. I had to. You will recall, Quinten, that you left me no choice."

His every facial bone seemed to harden. His eyes flashed with fire. "Why, you heartless bitch," he whispered, stepping closer. "How dare you fling that half-hearted marriage proposal in my face again? Had you told me the truth, Viviana, I would have done the right thing."

"Oh, *si,* you would have married me?" Her words were bitterly sarcastic. "Your foreign, bourgeois opera-singing mistress? Now, why is it, Quinten, that I doubt you?"

The lines about his mouth went taut, and he fell silent for a long, expectant moment. "I want Cerelia to know the truth, Viviana," he finally said. "I do not want her to think that—that some *monster* was her father."

"Some define 'monster' in more than one way," she retorted. "Me, I have known many kinds."

"Just shut up, Viviana," he snapped. "Cerelia hated Bergonzi. She was terrified of him. And anyone who spends more than five minutes asking her about it can see that. All I am asking—no, ordering—is that you tell her the truth."

"She knows the truth." Viviana's voice sounded weary now, even to her own ears. "Trust me, Quinten. She knows the truth."

"What?" he demanded. "What does she know?"

Viviana faltered, and looked away. "Cerelia knows that Gianpiero was not her father," she said quietly. "He ... he told her so himself and took great satisfaction in doing it. So you have nothing to worry about on that score."

"He told her himself?" Quin echoed. "And you—what did you tell her?"

The overwhelming grief swept in on her again like a rushing tide, dragging at her body, making her shoulders sag and her heart sink. "I told her that her father was an Englishman," she quietly confessed. *And that I loved him with all my heart, as he loved me in return.*

"Go on," he prodded.

She drew a deep, shuddering breath. "And I told her

that he was very handsome and very rich, but that his parents would not let us marry, and so I had to return to Italy."

He gaped at her incredulously. "But—But Viviana, that is just not true!"

"It is exactly true," she returned, her voice soft. "You said they would disapprove, perhaps even cut you off. You said they wished to arrange a marriage for you to a suitable English girl. Quin, *per amor di Dio,* do not let us fight about it now—but did I somehow misunderstand you all those years ago?"

For an instant, he hesitated. "I—I don't know what my parents would have done," he admitted.

But Viviana could not let him off the hook that easily. "Did I somehow misunderstand you, Quinten?" she repeated.

At last, his eyes fell. "No, not entirely," he answered. "It would have been difficult. But perhaps we could have seen it through, Vivie."

"Perhaps," she softly echoed. "Alas, Quinten, one cannot raise children on 'perhaps.' They must have certainty. They must have security. And, if at all possible, they must have a family. Cerelia had those things, Quinten. And I sacrificed in ways I should sooner die than talk about in order to give them to her. So do not speak to me, *caro,* of 'perhaps.' That word cannot be permitted to exist in Cerelia's life."

"Very well, then." The words were still curt, but some of the fight, if not the inner rage, had left him, she thought. He opened his hand and let the chain slither through his fingers to pool in her lap. "But I am not speaking of *perhaps* now," he continued. "I am speaking of a certainty. I mean to play a role in my child's life. I mean to be her father. I shall give you time, Viviana, to accustom yourself to that notion, too."

She lifted one arching black brow. "How very kind of you."

He nodded curtly. "I shall bid you farewell for the time being," he said. "Send word to me tomorrow when Cerelia is awake. I will wish to visit her."

Reluctantly, Viviana returned his nod. He meant to leave her no choice, it seemed. "I shall send someone, *si,*"

And before she could utter another word, Quin Hewitt had slammed the parlor door and was gone.

Fifteen

Lady Alice and the Gypsy Curse.

Quin returned to Arlington Park in a turbulent frame of mind. He did not notice that the rain had vanished, and the wind had quieted. He did not feel the deep chill which had set in in earnest, or smell the promise of snow, which now clung fast to the air. He did not appreciate the pure and unexpected stillness of a holy night as it enveloped the land all about him.

Instead, he could think only of Viviana, of what he perceived as her betrayal, not just of him, but of Cerelia, too. They cut to the bone, both the anger and the aching sense of loss. And yet he was wise enough to comprehend that he walked a sharp, perilous edge between his outrage on behalf of Cerelia and his hatred of Viviana.

He hated her because she had not loved him. After nine long years of misery, did it still come down to something so simple, and so petty? A better man would have admitted it, perhaps, and walked away. He was not a better man. He was filled with a burning desire for revenge.

What he felt for Viviana would never die. Instead it would turn caustic again, and devour his heart from the inside out. The thought tortured him, even as he gave his horse over to his groom, and walked silently up the steps into his house. His very big, and relatively empty, house.

Alice found him long hours later, drinking brandy by the fire in his private sitting room. She pecked lightly on his door and came in without permission. He turned at once to scowl at her. Alice already wore her nightdress and wrapper. Her hair was down, her long bronze tresses so silken they reflected the lamplight, reminding him of Cerelia. How in God's name had he missed all the signs?

"Is it now the fashion, Alice, to walk in on gentlemen in the privacy of their bedchambers?" he asked.

Alice slid into the chair opposite him without invitation. "This is not your bedchamber," she returned, tucking one foot underneath her, as had been her childhood habit. "You did not come down to dinner. Mamma was worried."

Somehow, he smiled. "And you were not?"

Alice shook her head. "Very little," she admitted. "You are far more stalwart than Mamma has ever given you credit for—to her great dismay of late."

Quin gave a muted smile. She was speaking, of course, of his having backed their mother down on the issue of Henry Herndon. Pensively, he swirled the last of the brandy in his glass and wondered if perhaps he should have taken a stand sooner. Perhaps he should have stood up for Alice years ago, when his parents had arranged her marriage to John, announcing it as a fait accompli, and ignoring Alice's tears.

But he had not dared interfere, just as he had not dared

tell them about Viviana. And look what his cowardice had cost all of them. Alice had spent a decade of her existence married to a man she could not love, consigned to a life of longing for the one she adored. Viviana had been compelled to wed one whom she not only did not love, but affirmatively loathed—at least that was the conclusion Quin was fast coming to. And Cerelia . . . ah, Cerelia. She had paid perhaps the greatest price of all.

"Quin?" His sister's voice came as if from a distance. "Quin, are you all right?"

"Well enough." He snatched up his glass and polished it off. "Just tired."

She looked at him appraisingly. "I do not believe you," she said. "What happened tonight after you brought Cerelia home? You do not seem yourself. Is it . . . is it something to do with Viviana?"

Quin could not bear to look at her. "Blister it, Alice, do not meddle in my business."

But for an instant, he considered telling her. The truth was, he thought, fixing his gaze on the fire, Alice's sympathy would almost make it worse. He felt pathetically like a child again, as if he'd fallen, and was waiting for his elder sister to pick him up and dust him off once more. But Alice could not help him now. No one could. His rage toward Viviana Alessandri was eclipsed only by his own self-loathing.

Alice sensed his unease, and turned the topic. "Did you have a hot bath, then?" she asked lightly. "Did you get something to eat? You should, you know. Even dashing heroes, Quin, must take care of themselves."

"Mrs. Prater sent up a tureen of soup." Quin tore his gaze from the fire and looked at Alice. "I've been abusing my body all my life, my dear—hardened it in hellfire, you might say—so it will take a little more than a long, wet ride in a rainstorm to do me any harm. But there is nothing heroic about it."

Alice propped her chin in her hand, watching as he yanked the stopper from his decanter. He could sense her disapprobation as he poured another measure of brandy. "Celebrating early, are we?" she asked.

He lifted one brow and kept pouring. "Good Lord, Alice," he muttered. "What have we to celebrate?"

Alice looked a little hurt. "Oh, only my wedding day!" she chided. "I hope you shan't have a sore head tomorrow morning when you give me away to Henry. If you do, Quin, keep it to yourself. Do not you dare ruin my ceremony, do you hear?"

Holy God. Quin set the decanter down with an awkward *thunk*. Alice was to be married tomorrow?

Alice was looking mildly irritated now. "Quin, this *is* Christmas Eve," she complained. "I vow, you seem not to attend anything anyone does or says nowadays." She shoved her hand into the pocket of her wrapper, and extracted a small package. "Here, I got you a Christmas gift. I asked Henry to bring it back from London—though perhaps I oughtn't have bothered."

"No, you oughtn't have bothered," he agreed, taking the package from her outstretched hand. "But I thank you, Allie. I'm very sorry to have forgotten about tomorrow."

Alice looked somewhat placated. "Well, open it."

He lifted the lid of the small box. Nestled inside was an ornate silver vesta case, engraved with their family crest. Gingerly, he thumbed it open. It was filled with matches.

"Those are the new, less odorous kind," said Alice

proudly. "One can find them only in London and Paris, you know. Viviana told me about them. As to your old case, well, it is not very attractive, is it?"

Quin managed to grin. "It has had a hard life," he admitted. "Much like its owner. I shall enjoy this new one greatly, Alice. I thank you."

She relaxed back into her chair, looking pleased with herself.

"I have something for you, Allie," he said, rising from his chair and going to his desk. He returned with a thin box made of inlaid rosewood. "This is as much a wedding gift as a Christmas gift, I daresay," he explained. "I just saw it, and . . . well, I wished you to have something special for your wedding day."

Eyes alight, Alice opened it, and gasped. On a bed of black velvet lay a triple strand of pearls, big ones, each strand a little longer than the one above it. The heavy gold clasp was in the shape of two clasped hands, with a diamond mounted on each side. "Dear me!" whispered Alice. "This is . . . well, this is quite something, Quin. And that clasp! How lovely! One hardly knows whether to wear it in front, or in the back."

"I thought the diamonds would show to good effect when your hair is up," he explained. "I am sorry, Allie. So very sorry you have had to wait so long for a life with Henry. Perhaps—perhaps I ought to have done something sooner."

"Such as what?" Alice looked bemused. "Shoot John? He was pompous, Quin, but even he did not deserve to die."

Quin smiled, but it did not last. "I meant I should have stopped your marrying him altogether," he explained. "I should have stood up for you, Allie. I should have done . . . something."

"Oh, Quin." Her voice was so soft. "Oh, my dear, you must not torture yourself over that, of all things. John's father was Papa's best friend. They meant us to marry from the cradle, and there was no stopping them. Quin, you must know that. Tell me you do."

His smile soured. "I don't know that," he said quietly. "Because I never tried. And as soon as I was able to escape Papa's thumb, I just . . . went away, and lived my own life in London. And a rather meaningless life it has turned out to be."

Alice closed the rosewood box and folded her hands atop it. "I have no notion, Quin, what you can be thinking," she answered. "But you seem mired in some sort of odd self-loathing tonight. Something which I have never seen in you before. I—I cannot like it. Pray stop flogging yourself, and remember how things really were."

Quin grew silent for a moment, and drank down half his brandy. He had had more than was wise, perhaps, given his strange, melancholy mood tonight. For an instant, he hesitated. "Alice, I wish to tell you something." The words sounded abrupt, even to him. "Something in the greatest of confidence. Something I need to entrust to you."

Alice looked surprised. "By all means."

Fleetingly, he closed his eyes. "It is about Viviana," he began. "She . . . she and I—"

Alice held up one hand. "You need say no more, Quin," she interjected softly. "I have already guessed. Anyone with eyes can see that you are in love with her. Even Mamma has begun to suspect."

He laughed, but it was a harsh, derisive sound. "That transparent, am I?" he said. "But no, that is not it. What little there was between Viviana and me has ended, and rather bitterly. Mamma need have no fear of being saddled with yet another unwelcome in-law."

Suddenly, Alice's hand reached for his and clasped it tightly. "Perhaps you misjudge Mamma, Quin," she said gently. "She . . . well, she is changing toward Henry. And whilst she is wary of Viviana, she does not dislike her. Indeed, she has made one or two very pretty remarks about her of late, and was very taken with Signor Alessandri at Uncle Ches's party."

"It does not matter," he said, withdrawing his hand, and returning it to his brandy. "It is only the child which concerns me now. Cerelia, I mean. She is . . . well, she is mine, Alice."

"Good God!" said Alice. She set her pearls aside and leaned nearer. "How in heaven's name did that happen?"

Quin managed a sour smile. "The usual way."

"Oh, Quin!" whispered Alice. "Oh, Quin, surely . . . surely you did not—"

"Abandon her?" he interjected. "Bloody hell, Alice. I hope you know me better than that. Viviana left me and returned to Venice. I expected us to be together forever—at least, that was the assumption I made in my young, not-very-experienced brain. But Viviana wished to marry. I refused her. So she left me, never telling me . . . never telling me the truth. About anything."

Alice blanched, and set a hand atop her stomach. "Well, you won't wish to hear this, Quin," his sister said quietly. "But I know just how she felt. Even knowing that Henry loved me, I was afraid to tell him the truth. Even now, Quin, I wish we were marrying only because we choose to, not because we must. But until this child was conceived, he refused me. So there will always be a little part of me . . . that will wonder. Can you not understand?"

"At least Henry was given a choice, Alice." Quin's voice was raw with suppressed emotion. "At least you had the courtesy to tell him and give him the option of raising his own child. Viviana simply married elsewhere and passed the child off as belonging to another."

Alice looked askance at him. "That was an arranged marriage, Quin," she answered. "Viviana told me her father arranged everything. And I cannot think that Viviana would deceive someone so. I am sure her husband knew, Quin, what he was getting into."

"He must have wanted her very desperately, then," Quin replied. "But he was no father to Cerelia. The child is badly wounded, Alice. I think . . . I think he was cruel to her. Her eyes, when she mentions his name—oh, God. It is almost more than I can bear."

Alice's color had not returned. Despite his turbulent emotions, Quin almost wished he had not burdened her. "What—what is it that you wish of me, Quinten?" she asked. "I am relatively certain we are not having idle chitchat."

He shook his head. "I hardly know, Alice," he answered. "I just thought . . . well, I just thought that someone else in this family should know. Cerelia is a part of us, Alice. I have a duty to her now. God forbid something should happen to me, I . . . I just wanted someone else to know the truth."

Alice touched him lightly on the shoulder. "Perhaps, my dear, we ought to leave well enough alone."

Her words, and their implication, were clear. "Oh, it is far too late for that," he said grimly. "Bergonzi disowned the child to her face. But I do not know if he disinherited her. I do not know if there is money set aside for her education, or—or for her dowry. For anything. I just do not know. And it worries me, Alice."

"I collect that Viviana is a wealthy widow, Quin," said Alice. *"Exceedingly* wealthy, though she is hardly vulgar enough to speak of such a thing. Bergonzi doubtless agreed to generous marriage settlements. Or perhaps their laws are different from ours? Perhaps a widow inherits all. Or singing is more lucrative than one might guess. In any case, you need not worry about Cerelia in that way, at least. If Bergonzi disinherited the child, Viviana will manage very nicely for her."

Quin dragged a hand through his hair. "Yes, of course," he said. "Of course you are right. I just feel this need to do right by the child since it seems so much wrong has been done her already."

"A notion which I greatly respect," said his sister. "And you may trust that should all else fail, Henry and I will see to Cerelia's welfare. You know that we will, do you not?"

Solemnly, he nodded. "I know that you will, Allie," he said quietly. "I trust you to do the right thing."

Alice gave a weak laugh and set her palm to her forehead. "Dear God, Quin," she said. "How does life get so convoluted? How is it when we are so perfectly certain of our paths, God snatches up the pieces of our lives and throws everything askew?"

Somehow Quin, too, managed to laugh. "It is all like a bad game of hazard gone horribly wrong, is it not?" Then, even though he knew he should not, he refreshed his brandy yet again. "Do you remember, Allie, that silly story Merrick told at Mamma's dinner party last month?"

Alice lifted one brow. "At your betrothal dinner, do you mean?" she murmured. "I recall that something Merrick said had poor Uncle Ches in stitches, but I did not quite get the gist of it."

"Indeed, Chesley could not stop laughing," he agreed. "You see, a Gypsy put a curse on us."

"I beg your pardon?"

"Alasdair, Merrick, and me," Quin clarified. "September last. We three were off on a lark, an illegal boxing match out in Surrey."

"Merrick attended a boxing match?" she said incredulously. "You two scoundrels, I can easily see. But Merrick? Never."

"Well, he shan't do so ever again, I'm sure," said Quin. "Not with his brother. Alasdair got caught playing tickle-tail with the blacksmith's wife, and the chap decided to kill us all with a pair of old blunderbusses."

Alice grinned. "How frightfully exciting! I must remember to tell Mamma."

Quin shot her a dark look. "I cannot think you serious," he said. "In any case, this Gypsy allowed us to hide in her tent."

At that, Alice burst into giggles. "You had to *hide*—?"

"Yes, but in return, she made us show her our palms and pay to have our fortunes read." He paused to smile acerbically. "At the time, it seemed quite comical."

"Oh, even now it seems quite comical," said his sister. "So? What did she tell you?"

Quin grew quiet for a moment, and when he spoke again, his tone was grave. "She said that in the past I had often acted rashly," he admitted. "And spoken too quickly. She said that I would pay for it, and dearly. Then she said that my chick was coming home to roost."

"But she meant 'your chickens,' did she not?"

He shrugged. "I asked her that, and she made me no answer," he replied. "Then she said that the three of us had cursed ourselves with our dissolute ways, and that our pasts would come back to haunt us. Something to that effect. She said, too, that we would now be required to 'make things right,' whatever that meant."

"Dear me," murmured his sister. "You shall be very busy indeed if you're to atone for your sins this side of the grave."

Quin flashed her a chagrinned smile. "Yes, it is silly, isn't it?" he said. "Still, it does make one think."

"You, Quinten, are thinking too much," said Alice tartly. "You must stop it at once, and go to bed, as I mean to do. And yes, I am only jesting about Mamma."

Just then, somewhere deep in the bowels of the house, a clock stuck midnight, each bell a slow, almost mournful sound.

Alice rose from her chair, picked up her new pearls, and smiled. "Well!" she said with an enthusiasm which was only faintly spurious. "My long-awaited wedding day has arrived. Wish me happy?"

A smile twisted at his mouth. "More than you will ever know, Allie," he whispered. "May you have a long and happy life with your Henry."

"Thank you, I believe I shall." She bent and kissed her brother on the cheek. "Merry Christmas, Quin."

Sixteen

The Long Vigil

Alice's wedding day dawned in an almost magical burst of brilliant blue sky above a sparkling, snow-covered landscape. The snow was neither deep nor destined to last. Instead, it was just enough to dust over the winter's stiff, ugly grass, and disguise the muddy, rutted roads, like some a fairy-tale carpet of white.

The vicar arrived just after breakfast. Alice and Henry said their vows in Arlington's withdrawing room in a small, private ceremony, just as his mother had wished. The service was attended only by Quin, his mother, the children, and three of Arlington's most senior servants. Alice was a beautiful bride in dark blue silk, and her brand-new pearls. Henry looked every inch a gentleman in clothes as fine and well fitted as any Quin had ever seen. Another benefit, no doubt, of their trip to London.

Afterward, Mrs. Prater cried, and kissed the bride and groom. Quin's mother, too, dabbed discreetly at the corners of her eyes when she thought no one was looking. Quin shook Henry's hand and kissed his sister's cheek. The vicar beamed as if it were all his idea. And then the excitement was over, and it was time to go to the more public venue of St. Anne's. It was Christmas Day.

Quin sat beside his mother in the tiny village church and tried to absorb the significance of the sermon, but his thoughts were admittedly elsewhere. He hoped a bolt from heaven did not strike him dead, but he could think only of Cerelia. Cerelia his daughter, cold and wan and trembling. Though paternal concern was an altogether new experience for Quin, the worry fit him like a well-worn shoe. He slid into it with ease.

When the service was over, the congregation flooded forth into the crystalline sunshine, the adults to quietly chat, and the children to expend their nervous energy in attempting to make snowballs out of what was fast becoming slush. Word of the morning's marriage had spread through the crowd, and Alice and Henry were soon surrounded by well-wishers. So much for Alice's wish for total privacy, thought Quin. Arlington Green was too small a village for that. He joined his mother in flanking the happy couple and tried to look pleased—which he most assuredly was. But the worry over Cerelia kept pressing in on him.

Soon, and much to his relief, the crowd about Henry and Alice began to disperse. Quin looked about, realizing that no one from Hill Court had attended the morning service, not even the servants. How very odd. Just then, he saw Lucy Watson winding her way through the crowd, two of her red-haired rapscallions in tow. She came straight at him with obvious purpose.

"Happy Christmas, Lucy," he said.

"Your lordship." She greeted him with a perfunctory curtsy. "I was thinking you might have took notice no one's come down from Chesley's."

He looked at her curiously. "I did wonder at it, yes."

"Well, happen I went by early to give Aunt Effie her Christmas present." Lucy's eyes held his, as if she were judging what she might comfortably say. "Things are in a bit of a state up there. Lady Cerelia took bad in the night."

Panic shot through him. "Bad?" he rasped. "Dear God! How bad?"

Lucy looked solemn. "She's turned febrile," she answered. "It came on quick-like. They've sent for Dr. Gould, and that's all I know. But a body might wish to get up there straightaways if—well, if they wished to, my lord. That's all I'm saying."

Before Quin could make her any response, Lucy bobbed again quickly and vanished.

It took him but a moment to speak a quiet word in Alice's ear, shake Henry's hand, and make his way from the churchyard. He had been anxiously awaiting word from Viviana all morning. Only his concern for Cerelia outweighed his anger that she had not kept her promise.

When he arrived at Hill Court, Basham let him in without surprise. "I'm given to understand that the child became feverish around midnight, my lord," he said. "Dr. Gould is with her now."

Without explanation, Quin rushed up the two flights of stairs to Viviana's bedchamber. He did not knock, but went straight in. The room seemed full of women. The governess—Miss Hevner, he thought—stood alone in one corner, her expression one of grave concern. Cerelia had been moved to her mother's bed. Viviana was leaned over one side, the old Italian nurse at her elbow.

Bent low over the opposite side, Dr. Gould looked up and, seeing Quin, raised one eyebrow. Then he returned his attention to the wooden tube which he had pressed to Cerelia's chest and set one ear to it, whilst sticking one finger in his opposite ear. Periodically, he moved the tube around, always keeping his ear against it. At last, he straightened up, placed an elaborate piece of ivory over the end of the tube, and restored it to his leather satchel.

"The heart is strong, but the lungs are growing congested," he pronounced. "Her pulse is far too fast."

Cerelia thrashed restlessly in the bed, but her eyes did not open. "What can be done for her?" Viviana whispered, her expression stricken.

Dr. Gould set one hand on Cerelia's forehead. "Give the willow bark tonic more often," he said. "Every hour. Spoon it in if you must. When she wakes, give her water or broth, as much as she will take. Should she worsen, send for me. If the fever does not break by tomorrow, we will need to bleed her."

Solemnly, Viviana nodded. Gould spoke a few quiet, encouraging words to her, then took his leave. If he wondered at Quin's presence, he gave no sign.

Slowly, the room returned to "normal," whatever normal was under such dreadful circumstances. The housemaids, who had apparently come to change out the bed linen, finished with the little trundle bed and left. Miss Hevner excused herself, mumbling something about attending to the other children. Signora Rossi, the old nurse, busied herself by uncorking the brown bottles which sat on a tray by the bed and mixing their contents into a mug of water.

Viviana eased herself down into a chair by the bed and did not glance at him. Today, to his shock, she looked every one of her thirty-three years. Though Viviana was a tall, voluptuous woman, just now she gave the impression of being terribly fragile. Her eyes appeared sunken, and rimmed with dark circles. Her hand, clutching the chair's arm, looked almost birdlike. Her hair was caught back in a bland, very ordinary arrangement, and for the first time he could see the slightest hint of silver glinting against the jet-black of her temples. He wondered if it had appeared overnight. One heard of such things occurring.

Perhaps it was Viviana's gaunt appearance which tempered his ire, or perhaps it was the sight of Cerelia, so small and still in the massive bed. Whatever the cause, his anger seemed to dissipate, pouring out of him like some terrible, tangible thing and leaving him to feel enervated by grief. Whatever she had done to him, Viviana did not deserve this.

He looked about for a chair and pulled it beside hers. Viviana's hand still lay on the chair arm, and impulsively, he covered it with his own. "How long has she been like this?"

"She began wheezing just before Dr. Gould arrived last night," Viviana answered hollowly. "Then the fever came on, and she grew fretful. Around daybreak, there was something . . . something like *una convulsione?*"

"Like a fit?"

Viviana nodded, but her gaze never left Cerelia. *"Si,* like a fit," she said quietly. "Nicolo had one as a baby. It was the same."

Quin tried to sound calm, though he was anything but. "She seems so still now. Has she not awakened?"

"A little," Viviana admitted. "But she talks nonsense and thrashes wildly if we try to hold her or restrain her."

Just then, Signora Rossi held up a second brown bottle, and said something to Viviana in rapid Italian. *"Si, grazie,"* Viviana replied, rising. The old woman left the room, taking the bedside tray with her.

Quin followed Viviana as she limped to the opposite side of the bed. She picked up the mug which the nurse had dosed from the brown bottles, and stirred the contents with a spoon.

"What are you doing?" he asked.

"Signora Rossi has mixed the tonic," she said, dragging the back of her wrist across her forehead. "We must spoon it in, *un po' per volta*—in drips, *si?*—so that it does not choke her."

He watched her finish stirring. Her hand was shaking noticeably, and the opposite wrist was bandaged, from her fall the previous evening, most likely. "Viviana, have you had any sleep?"

"Non molto," she muttered. "Enough."

Quin frowned. "No sleep, and you can scarcely bear weight on that leg." Gently, he took the mug from her hand. "Show me how to do this," he ordered. "Then sit back down and rest."

She looked up at him in some surprise, her eyes wide and questioning.

"I have a right, Viviana, to help her," Quin said softly. "Do not refuse me a chance."

Viviana swallowed hard and nodded. "Just put a little in the spoon," she said. *"Si,* like that. And press down on her bottom lip. Sometimes, she will take it. If not, give drips only."

It was a painstaking process indeed, though Quin did not complain. Viviana watched quietly, saying little. At first, he dribbled it down her chin, and had to hastily wipe it up again. Sometimes he could only press the lip of the spoon against Cerelia's teeth, and hope for the best. In between the spoons of tonic, he would set the backs of his fingers against her feverish forehead. It was then that one truely realized the grip the illness held on her. Quin began to pray the fever would soon break.

Toward the end, Cerelia began to speak in muttered bursts of Italian, and thrash wildly.

Viviana scooted forward on the edge of her chair, her fingers clutching at the bedcovers. "She has been like this since the spell at dawn," she said anxiously. "Signora Rossi says it is to be expected, but it . . . *Dio,* it frightens me."

"It frightens me, too," he admitted, looking pointedly at her. "But Signora Rossi knows best, does she not? You trust her?"

Viviana nodded, and slumped back into her chair. "She is wise," she agreed. "But she is too old for this. She is . . . she is *stanchissima*. Very weary."

Quin tried to smile. "As are you," he remarked. "But I am neither, despite any appearance to the contrary."

At that, she gave him a faint smile and sank back into the chair, her arms crossed over her chest. He was not sure if he should take the gesture as a sign of recalcitrance or just pure fatigue.

Quin returned to his work. Near the end, his back went a bit stiff from being crooked awkwardly over the bed, but at last all the tonic—well, most of it—was down.

"Bene," said Viviana with relief, when he set the mug down. *"Molto bene."*

Across the bed, he looked at her. The morning sun was flooding in through the windows, bathing her in cool, wintry light. Even in her agony, Viviana was beautiful. But the halo of madonna-like serenity no longer surrounded her; she had become the tormented mother, fearing the worst for her child.

Good God, how he hated to see her this way. Never had he wished to see her suffer. Suddenly, he wanted to snatch back every spiteful thought he'd ever harbored toward her. He was still angry, still felt he'd been wronged. But seeing Cerelia so diminished, he could understand a little better, perhaps, what drove Viviana.

He put away the mug and spoon, and returned to sit beside her. "Viviana, it is Christmas Day," he said quietly. "Why do you not go spend just a little of it with Felise and Nicolo? I will stay here. I will call you if there is even the slightest change."

"We have postponed Christmas," she answered. "We have put it off until . . . until Cerelia is well again. It was Felise's idea."

Quin understood. "I brought some things back from London for the children," he said. "I—I forgot them. I came straight from church. Shall I ask Basham to send someone to fetch them, just in case?"

She lifted her shoulders. *"Si,* as you wish."

But Quin did not rise to go out, or to ring the bell, or to do anything. He was reluctant to leave Cerelia's beside, even for a moment. Perhaps he was beginning to understand how Viviana felt in that respect, too. There was a sense of the ephemeral in the room; an illogical belief that so long as one remained vigilant, so long as one observed the rise and fall of Cerelia's chest, and listened to the faint rasp of her breath, the life force would go on. But if one dared turn one's back . . .

Viviana ran a hand through her hair and dropped her voice to a whisper. "I am so sorry, Quinten," she said, staring down at the opulent Oriental carpet. "This is all my fault. I should have been watching her more carefully."

"Viviana, do not be too harsh with yourself," he cautioned. "How many children were there? Fifteen? Sixteen?"

Her eyes flashed with frustration. "*Si,* but only three of them were mine," she responded. "And to them I owed my undivided attention. Instead, I was—" She jerked to a halt, and shook her head, her lips set in a tight line.

"You were what, Vivie?" he prodded.

A look of disgust flitted across her face. "Gossiping," she said. "Chattering away with your mother like some foolish—foolish—oh, *what* is that silly thing, the bird name?"

Quin lifted one brow. "A magpie?"

"*Si,* like a magpie," she hissed. "Not paying attention, but thinking only of how to . . ." Her words fell away, and tears sprang to her eyes.

"How to what, Vivie?" He reverted to her nickname unthinkingly.

Viviana pressed her lips together and shook her head again. "How to impress her," she whispered. "How to—to make her think that I was a person worthy of . . . of her good regard."

"Oh, Vivie!" he said. "Vivie, you do not need the approval of my mother. Not for any reason. And yet, I believe you already have it. I believe you have even managed to cow her a little, which is no bad thing."

Viviana sniffed a little pitifully. "Is it not?" she asked. "It sounds very bad indeed. I certainly do not think she is a cow."

At that, he smiled. "Never mind, Viviana," he said. Then wordlessly, he rose and touched Cerelia's brow. "What about bathing her in cool water?" he suggested. "Mightn't that make her feel better?"

Viviana nodded. "Perhaps."

Quin went to the washstand, and returned with a face flannel and basin of cool water. He bathed her face, her throat, and even her arms. It did indeed seem to make her less restless. At one point, Cerelia's eyes fluttered open, and she looked at him unseeingly. "Mamma—?" she rasped.

Viviana flew to her side and cradled the child's face in her hand. "I am here, *mia cara bambina,*" she whispered. "Mamma is here. Mamma will never leave you."

Mama will never leave you.

Quin thought again of the threats he had made. He meant them, did he not? But as he looked at Viviana's elegant, long-fingered hand cradling Cerelia's feverish cheek, and at the agony in her eyes, he was suddenly not so sure. *Would* he make Viviana choose between the two? Her home or her child?

Quin shook his head and set the water away. He could not bear to think of it just now. He had been a father for less than one day, and the emotions which that knowledge engendered were overwhelming. All that mattered now, all that could be dealt with, really, was Cerelia's recovery. Anything beyond that must be set aside. His needs, his wishes, even his vendetta, if he still had one, must be made secondary.

Cerelia fell into a more peaceful slumber, though the bright red flush on her face did not abate. Viviana returned to her chair, and slowly, the minutes ticked by. Eventually, Signor Alessandri came in. As he held and patted Cerelia's hand, he whispered urgent questions to Viviana in Italian. He seemed too distraught to wonder what Quin was doing there.

Soon, Chesley popped in to *tut-tut* at Viviana and pat the child's knee fondly. Signora Rossi returned with a more water, some warm broth, and the ubiquitous brown bottles. Together, with Viviana cradling the child, they managed to persuade her to sip a little of the broth. Cerelia's eyes, however, were still distant and glassy. She was not really awake.

When that was done, Viviana spoke to the nurse her in firm, rapid Italian. She was sending the woman away, as best Quin could make out. Signora Rossi gave her a dark look and went out.

"She sleeps now," said Viviana. "For an hour or two, at least."

Quin motioned at the empty trundle bed. "As you should do," he advised. "If Cerelia needs you, I promise to wake you at once."

Viviana shook her head. "It is time again for the tonic."

Quin attempted to take the medicine bottles from her. A minor squabble ensued, which resulted in Viviana's agreeing to sit on the bed to take the weight from her bruised leg. They were both on edge, both frightened. And so the afternoon approached. As if by agreement, they took turns bathing and dosing Cerelia. Her restless thrashing would abate, then return. At its worst, Cerelia cried out for her mother and clawed wildly at the air.

When at last it stopped, Viviana sat back down and rested her forehead on the bed. "Oh, *Dio,* my poor baby!" she said. "Why did I not watch her? What was she thinking, to go back to that place alone?"

"She had lost her ring," he said quietly. "She must have wanted it desperately."

"She was not supposed to wear it!" said Viviana. "Why was I not more strict? Why in God's name did I ever give it to her? Had I not done so, none of this would have happened."

Again, he covered her hand with his. "Her magic ring, she called it," he said. "I think, Viviana, that it comforted her."

"*Si,* it comforted her," said Viviana bitterly. "But life is not all comfort, is it? I told her a fairy tale, and I let her believe it. Better I should have told her the truth."

Quin sat back down and turned in his chair to face her. "Why did you give her the ring, Viviana?" he asked. "May I not be allowed to know?"

She shook her head. "It is so very hard to explain, Quinten," she answered. "You feel that I have wronged you, and perhaps I have done so. I . . . I do not know. But if I have done so, then know, *caro,* that God has already punished me for it. You need not trouble yourself."

"Vivie, you are talking nonsense," he said. "This is not about punishment."

But Viviana was not listening. Her gaze had turned inward. "Perhaps Cerelia's sickness means that he still punishes me," she whispered. "I thought it was over, but I look at her, so frail and small, and I cannot but wonder."

He set his hands on her shoulders, and gave her a little shake. "Vivie, what on earth are you talking about? God is not punishing you. And what has any of this to do with the ring?"

Her gaze returned to him, sharp and piercing. "You once asked me, Quinten, if *Papà* quarreled with Gianpiero over me," she whispered.

"And I should still like to know," he admitted.

She swallowed hard, and nodded. "Many years ago, Gianpiero wished to take me as his mistress." Her voice was so quiet he had to strain to hear her. "*Papà* and I lived on his estate, and I could not escape his attentions. He was . . . relentless. My life became a misery. Wherever I traveled on the Continent, wherever I sang, there he would be. Smiling so charmingly. *Papà* became worried, and finally, he sent me away."

"To Uncle Ches, you mean?"

She nodded again. "*Si,* to England," she answered. "To the one place Gianpiero had little influence."

He waited for her to speak, and when she did not, he said, "Go on, Viviana. Please."

She gave a sharp sigh. "Gianpiero was enraged when he found me gone," she said. "He cut *Papà* off—not just financially, but artistically. But *Papà* would not relent. Many months passed. Then a year. As time went on, and none of his tricks availed him of what he wished, Gianpiero became charming again. He proposed marriage. He begged *Papà*'s forgiveness. And so I went home, and I told him the truth. That I did not love him, and never would, and that I carried a child. But I pledged to be a good and faithful wife if he would give my child his name. The rest, *caro,* you know."

Quin felt faintly ill, as if the room were spinning round him. "Good God, Viviana," he whispered. "Why did you not come to me and tell me?"

"You did not want me," she said simply. There was no anger in her words.

He gripped her shoulders tighter. "Viviana, you know that is not so."

"You did not wish to marry me," she corrected. "Do not lie and say you did, Quinten."

He looked at her grimly, but said nothing.

Viviana continued speaking. "You did not want to wed me—but would you have taken care of me?" she mused, her voice distant now. "*Si, caro,* probably. But how could I dishonor my father with a bastard child, after all he had sacrificed? He had given up his security, his career—all this, so that I might keep my precious honor. So that I could be more than just a rich man's mistress. Oh, Quinten, how could I let him see that I had squandered his gift?"

The agony in her voice cut into his heart. "I . . . I do not know, Viviana," he said. "I am sorry."

Beneath his hands, he felt her shoulders sag. "In the end, perhaps it was not a wise choice which I made," she went on, pressing the heel of her hand to her forehead. "Better I should have borne my child alone, perhaps, than make my devil's bargain with Gianpiero. Fallen women are not necessarily shunned—not in opera. *Papà* would have survived. We would not have been well received in society, but we would not, I think, have starved."

We would not have starved? Good Lord, how had it even come close to that? He hated to hear her speak of it, hated to think of the choices his blind stupidity had forced her to make, even if she had chosen unwisely.

God in heaven, how he wished he had never made love to her. Never touched her. No, not even once. He should rather have given up his sweetest memories, and even Cerelia, than to know what Viviana had been faced with. Men fathered children, and walked away—if that was their wish. Women bore their children and were bound by duty for the rest of their lives. Those were the horrible, ugly truths.

Restless and on edge, he got up and began to pace the room. Viviana sat stoically at her place by the bed. Once, Cerelia made a sound, and he went to her before Viviana could spring to her feet. The bedcovers were tangled around the child's foot. Mechanically, he straightened them, then wiped her brow and throat with cool water again. Something in his heart clenched each time he looked at her. She was so small and so pretty.

He let his eyes drift over her, and wondered again how he had missed all the signs. Her face was Viviana's, yes, but her dark blue eyes—oh, they were his. And her hair? Unmistakably Alice's; not just the color, but the luster, texture, and thickness. She had Alice's slender shoulders and long legs, too. Her lovely coltishness would remain into womanhood, he was sure, as his sister's had done. Cerelia would never have Vivie's lush, exotic sumptuousness, but she would be a beauty. And a tone-deaf beauty, too, for she had no musical skill whatsoever—and he knew too well whence that deficiency had come.

Dear God. Such thoughts put into stark perspective a part of fatherhood which he had never stopped to consider. *He had given parts of himself to her.* Lord, he hoped it was mostly the good parts. He hoped Cerelia had not inherited his amazingly poor judgment. He hoped she had not his mother's sweet tooth, or his father's bad heart. He hoped she would be lively and curious to a great old age, like his aunt Charlotte. He hoped she would take from Uncle Ches the fine qualities of consideration and kindness. He prayed to God she would never wake up as Quin had done, caught in a life of emptiness and bitterness, before he'd yet turned thirty.

With slow, deliberate motions, he folded the face flannel and draped it over the basin of cool water. A housemaid slipped in after a faint knock and set down a tray of sandwiches and fruit. Viviana thanked her, and she went out again. Neither of them paid the food any heed.

"You were telling me, Viviana, about the ring," he said quietly. "Cerelia told me Bergonzi damaged it. May I ask why?"

Absently, Viviana began to fidget with the ring she wore; a wide band of gold set with small diamonds.

"Vivie?" he said again.

Her head jerked up, her eyes shining with tears. "Gianpiero always knew where the ring had come from," she whispered. "I did not tell him, Quin. And he did not ask. But he knew. I kept it, you see, just as you asked."

"Did . . . did you ever wear it, Vivie?" It was not the question he wished to ask—had she ever missed him?—but it would do.

She shook her head, and began to twist the diamond band round and round on her finger. "Not at first," she said. "I put it away, for in the beginning, I tried to love my husband. I tried very hard. But the years came and went, and I could not love him in the way he wished. He grew bitter, and his bitterness deepened until it maddened him. Toward the end, he took lovers, kept mistresses. I—I did not care. And that made him all the angrier."

He returned to her side. "Oh, Viviana," he said. "I am so sorry."

She shrugged. "It did not kill me," she said. "In any case, after Nicolo, we began to live apart, more or less. Cerelia and I were happier, I think, though Felise was less so. I lived my own life. And one day, I just . . . I just put the ring back on. I cannot say why. I just wanted to wear something bright and pretty. I wore it off and on for months. I did not think Gianpiero would notice or care. Certainly he said nothing."

"But he did care?" said Quin quietly.

Weakly, she nodded. "One Sunday afternoon, I was reading with Cerelia on a bench in the garden. Gianpiero came out to say that he was going away again. He was to spend a fortnight at our villa on Lake Como with his mistress. His tone was cold, very ugly. For some reason, Cerelia took it into her head that this time he was not coming back. Felise always felt his absences most keenly, but he never paid any attention to Cerelia. And yet she was the one who began to cry and to beg him not to go away. I think . . . I think she did it for Felise."

"What happened, Vivie?"

"Gianpiero went wild with fury." Viviana held up her hands as if uttering a plea to heaven. "Like an animal. Never have I seen the like. He spit, and called Cerelia a little *monella—si,* a greedy little brat—and worse. The harder she cried, the uglier his insults became."

"Bastard!"

"Finally, he jerked me off the bench by my arm and said, 'Oh, poor little brat! She is crying for her *papà!*' Then he tore the ring from my finger and hurled it at her. 'There, Cerelia,' he said. 'There is your *papà*. I am not he. Take this precious ring, *cara mia,* to England and see if you can find him, eh?'"

"Dear God."

"At first, Cerelia did not understand," Viviana whispered. "She got down in the grass and found the ring, and tried to put it back on my hand. Gianpiero turned around. His face—*Dio mio,* his face! It was like a mask of rage. He came back and snatched the ring from her grasp. There had been stonemasons in the garden, repairing a wall. They left a—a big hammer. He took it and he smashed the ring on the stones.

"Again and again, he smashed it, and with such strength as you have never seen. He kept screaming at Cerelia, saying that he was not her *papà*. And that I was a faithless bitch. That he hated us all."

Her words fell away on a note of uncertainty. She would not look directly at him. Quin dipped his head, trying to catch her eyes. "What happened after that, Vivie?"

Viviana said nothing. She looked at the floor and blinked her eyes rapidly.

Quin took her hand in his. "If you wish to say no more, I will understand."

Her chin came up, and her gaze snapped to his, sorrowful, yet angry. "I asked him to give me back the ring, so that Cerelia might have it," she whispered. "And he struck me."

At first, he thought he'd misunderstood. "What do you mean, *struck* you?"

Viviana looked at him unflinchingly. "He hit me," she answered. "But this time, it was not the palm of his hand, or a leather strap, as was his habit. This time, it was his fist. And this time, it left bruises I could no longer hide."

"Dear God!" Quin felt a surge of hatred, and a sense of dawning horror, too.

Viviana's words were still soft, but unwavering. It was as if she told a tale she'd reiterated a thousand times. Dispassionately, as if she were far removed from that life, that time, and that place. "I awoke on the garden path in my own blood," she continued. "Cerelia was on her knees, crying. She was only six. She did not know what to do."

"Dear God!" he said again, squeezing her hand. "What did you do?"

"What else was there to do?" she asked calmly. "I got up and took her into the house. I asked the housekeeper to fetch a doctor. I told her that Gianpiero had hit me and that I believed my nose was broken. It was. And there was nothing to be done, the doctor said. So I threw away my bloodstained clothes, took a warm bath, then I went back to Cerelia."

"She must have been terrified."

Viviana hesitated. "She was," she admitted. "And she asked me if what Gianpiero said was true, that he was not her father. So I—I told her that it was. What else could I say? She was so sad. She barely understood then, I think. She asked if Gianpiero meant to send her away, and I told her that it did not matter. That whatever happened, we would never be parted. And then I gave her the ring. I told her that Gianpiero smashed the ring because there was magic in it."

"Magic?" he echoed.

"The magic of love," said Viviana quietly. "I told her that her *papà,* her—her blood father—gave it to me for her, and that it was an eternal circle of his love for her. I told her that as long as she had the ring, she had the love of her *papà*. It . . . it sounds so foolish now. But in that moment, she needed something. Something I could not give her. And so . . . and so I lied."

"No, you did not lie, Viviana," he whispered. "You did just the right thing."

"I tried to do the right thing," said Viviana sorrowfully. "But like my marriage to Gianpiero, it has turned out all wrong somehow. She . . . she has developed an unnatural affection for the ring. Can you see why she would wish always to wear it? Why she would do such a foolish thing as go back into the forest after it?"

"I certainly can," he said grimly.

And it was all the more reason, he feared, why it would be wiser to tell the child the whole truth. Then she would have at least a little something more than a ring to pin her hopes and dreams on. Perhaps he wasn't much better than an inanimate lump of metal—clearly, that was Viviana's impression—but at least he could make Cerelia feel loved in the truest sense of the word.

Viviana sighed again, and stood. Moving carefully on her sore leg, she went to the window, then to the desk, her movements restless despite her hampered pace. Back at the window, she set her fingertips to the glass and looked out as if doing so might transport her to a happier time, or a better place.

"And so you know, Quinten, what I have done," she said quietly. "And you should know the price God has extracted. My nose—it is not just ugly. It is ruined."

"I think it is still a lovely nose," he protested, and he meant it.

She turned from the window to face him. "But it is ruined," she said again. "The—the *cavità*. In my head— the spaces where the air resonates. It is . . . not right. Something is gone. Changed."

"Changed?" Quin felt his brow furrow. "What are you saying, Viviana? Is it difficult to breathe?"

She shook her head slowly. "No, no, not that," she said. "It is difficult to *sing*. My voice, *caro,* it is gone."

Gone? His heart skipped a beat. "Vivie, how can this be? You—you sound fine to me."

She came toward him slowly, her hands outstretched, as if pleading for him to understand. "Talking, *caro,* it is not the same," she whispered. "I cannot sing. I cannot hold the notes so strongly as before. My vibrato, it does not come as it should, the volume, the resonance, it is . . . well, not gone, perhaps. But it is mediocre, at best."

"But what does Uncle Ches say?" he asked. "And your father?"

She shook her head. "They have not yet noticed," she answered quietly. "But I notice—and they will, too, eventually. In the right room, with the right piece of music."

"Oh, Vivie," he said sorrowfully. "Oh, Vivie. Are you sure?"

"É certo," she whispered.

And there could be no worse punishment for her, he knew, save to lose her father or one of her children. Yes, he could understand how she might feel God was punishing her. To Viviana, her voice had been her joy. Her greatest pain and pleasure. She had truly lived to sing, and the world had worshiped her for it.

"Vivie," he whispered. "Could you teach? Could you . . . could you compose?"

She shook her head again. "I am not ready to think of such things," she answered. "Let me mourn my loss, Quinten."

Her use of the word "mourn" was entirely correct. Viviana looked as if she had suffered a death.

Were he to think on it for a thousand years, he would not be able to comprehend what this woman had been through during her marriage. One could not, he was sure, unless one had lived the terror. Even now, there was an ice-cold horror in the pit of his stomach and a righteous anger burning in his heart. But if Viviana felt any of that, one could not discern it. Her proud, stoic silence amazed him; her unequivocal acceptance of what fate had dealt her went beyond brave.

Viviana was watching him quietly, as if assessing his mood. "I have no wish for your sympathy, Quinten," she said. "I just tell you this so you will know that none of this has been easy for me. I have learnt that there are no right answers. And if I have chosen wrongly, I have paid for it."

There seemed to be nothing more to say. Clearly, Viviana believed in an exacting and punitive God. Perhaps that had been her way of coping.

Ah, well. No matter how much he might wish otherwise, he had not the power to change the past. If he had, Gianpiero Bergonzi would have never even existed. Here in the real world, the world of the present and the difficult, it was time to give Cerelia her medicine. They were also out of cold water. And Viviana clearly had no wish to be comforted, not by him, at any rate.

Unthinkingly, he rang for a servant. When the housemaid arrived, Viviana ordered more broth as well as fresh water. She prepared the tonic from the two brown bottles. Quin straightened Cerelia's bedcovers, and found her a fresh, cool pillow. They worked together instinctively, as if they had been doing it for years instead of just hours.

Signora Rossi came in with another heavy tray. Together, she and Viviana managed to get both broth and tonic down Cerelia. The child looked perhaps a little more aware, but quickly fell into a deep sleep.

The old nurse surveyed her from the foot of the bed. *"Addormentato,"* she said, hands on her hips. "Now, Contessa, you sleep, too. I get you warm milk."

Viviana shook her head. *"Grazie,* Signora Rossi," she said. "But I cannot sleep."

Quin extracted his watch and glanced at it. Half past three. It would be dark soon. He wondered how many hours Viviana had been awake. Signora Rossi left the room, only to return ten minutes later with a steaming mug. "You drink it," she said, passing it to Viviana. *"Subito."*

As if to placate the old woman, Viviana took the mug from the tray and slowly sipped it. Quin already knew a cup of warm milk would have no chance at overcoming Viviana's powerful maternal instincts. She would not sleep until she utterly broke down, of that he was certain.

The old nurse puttered about the room, checking the brown bottles, tucking in the bedcovers, and in general, folding and neatening anything that could be folded or neatened. All the while, however, she kept one eye on Viviana. Perhaps it was the quiet of the room, or perhaps just his overset nerves, but Quin somehow found it soothing to watch the old woman work.

A strange little sound by his elbow soon distracted him.

He looked over in some surprise to see that Viviana had indeed drifted off. Her head had fallen to one side, causing her to make a faint, and very sweet, snoring sound on each exhalation.

The old nurse crossed the room and looked her over assessingly. *"Buono,"* she said in satisfaction. "She sleep now."

"Good Lord," said Quin.

The old nurse looked at him, then pulled yet a third brown bottle from the pocket of her apron. "She sleeps long, *signore,"* she repeated, wiggling the bottle. "You take her to the small bed now, *per favore."*

It was not a request. Obediently, Quin jumped to his feet and scooped Viviana up, mindful of her bruises. Gingerly, he carried her to the trundle bed. She did not so much as twitch when he laid her down again. Quin wondered what the old woman had given her. Nothing she had not needed, most likely.

The nurse looked at him guardedly. "You, go home now," she said.

Quin smiled wanly and shook his head. The nurse shook hers, too, as if thinking him a fool, then they sat back down together. And so they kept their vigil together, he and the old woman, until well into the evening. Signora Rossi was not much of a conversationalist, he soon discovered, but she could darn stockings like a house afire. He watched in amazement as she whip-stitched her way through one basketful and started in on another.

Eventually, the moon rose, and Quin began to light the lamps and build up the fire. Viviana still did not stir. Cerelia, however, seemed more restless, and yet some of the brilliance seemed to have left her cheeks. At one point, he rose and pressed the backs of his fingers to her forehead. Was it cooler? Or was it his imagination?

"*Si,*" said Signora Rossi, looking up from her darning. "She heals."

She heals. Lord God, he prayed the old woman was right.

At eight, there was a soft knock at the door, and Miss Hevner came in. Niccolo was balanced on her hip, and Felise was beside her. Both children were dressed for bed. "Oh, I beg your pardon, your lordship," said the governess when she saw him. "The children wished to say good night to Cerelia and their mother."

Signora Rossi tilted her head toward the trundle bed. "*Stare tranquillo,*" cautioned the old woman. "Your Mamma, she needs sleep."

Dutifully, the children tiptoed across the room and knelt to kiss their mother's cheek. When that was done, Felise went to the bigger bed, crawled in beside Cerelia, and began to play with a strand of her sister's hair.

The old nurse glanced up from her sewing. "Careful, *carissima.*"

The child looked at her earnestly. "Is she getting better, *Tata?*"

"Oh, *si,*" said Signora Rossi. "She gets better. By Monday, you will have your Christmas. And by Thursday, she will chase you round the house and pull *your* hair."

Felise laughed softly. Nicolo had crawled onto the big bed, too. He curled himself into a ball near Cerelia's knees and stuck his thumb in his mouth.

"Come, children," said Miss Hevner quietly. "We should return to our own rooms now."

Felise looked reluctant. "What if Cerelia has bad

dreams?" she asked. "We always sleep together if we have bad dreams."

Signora Rossi jerked her head toward the door. "Go, *carissima,*" she ordered. "I sleep with you if bad dreams come."

The little girl bubbled with laugher. "*Tata,* you cannot fit into my bed!"

The old woman shrugged. "Then I break it down," she answered. "*Boom!* We sleep on the floor."

Both children erupted into giggles, but quickly slapped their hands over their mouths. Miss Hevner opened the door and crooked a finger. Nicolo crawled on all fours so that he might kiss his sister's cheek. Then, with obvious reluctance, they slid from the bed and padded across the room, bottom lips protruding.

They were a family, he realized. Felise and Nicolo possessed an abiding and guileless love for their elder sister. He doubted very much whether they cared how Cerelia had been conceived or who her father was. They were a family, and they loved one another. They were there for one another.

His own childhood would have been a miserable existence indeed without his elder sister. They had been close in age and the best of friends. Perhaps this was what Viviana meant when she said that Cerelia needed a family?

So he was left to ask himself if these were the people from whom he would willing take Cerelia. Even if the law would permit it—which, despite his bold words, he was not at all sure of—it was such a foolish, foolish notion. Family came first. Family was everything.

Quin might have been blood kin, but he was not a part of their family. He was just an outsider looking in, and no matter how hard he tried, no matter what manner of threats he leveled at Viviana, he could not replace this, could he? He could not replace what Cerelia would lose. He would have to be a selfish bastard even to try, and his selfishness had already done harm enough.

He realized in some surprise that he had drifted back to the bed and was stroking Cerelia's hair. Signora Rossi gave him another chary look. "You go home now, *signore,*" she said again, her tone more kindly this time. "Come again *domattina.* Tomorrow morning, *si?*"

Just then, Viviana made a soft, groaning sound from behind him. He turned to see her languidly stretch one arm. She would be awake soon. Nurse Rossi was clearly here to stay. There really was no need for him to remain.

He wondered again what the old woman thought of his presence in the room. He really did not care. He bent down, and kissed Cerelia lightly on the forehead. His lips came away feeling . . . not cool. But not hot, either.

"Domattina," said the old woman again. "She will be awake then."

Quin looked at her uncertainly. "You . . . you are quite certain?"

The old woman nodded. *"Di sicuro,"* she answered. "Weak, *signore,* like a kitten, eh? But awake to the world."

Quin prayed to God she was right. He went to the door, stopping long enough to bow to her. *"Grazie,* then, Signora Rossi," he said. "I shall bid you *buona notte.*"

Seventeen

*In which Wynwood gives the Contessa
yet another Gift.*

Quin rose at dawn the following morning and rang at once for Blevins. He wished to dress in some haste, so that he might return to Hill Court as soon as possible. He had slept very little, and the little sleep he had got was roiled by disquieting dreams of Cerelia and Viviana. He prayed the child was at least a little bit improved. He was afraid to believe Signora Rossi's prediction of a recovery until he'd seen Cerelia for himself.

As soon as Blevins finished his handiwork, Quin started for the door. At the last instant, however, he remembered the small package he'd carried home from London some four days previous and returned to his desk for it. There was also the satchel of books for the children. Best to call for his gig, then.

Downstairs he informed a footman of his wishes, then hastened into the breakfast parlor in hope of catching Henry. To his surprise, he found instead his mother and his sister. He forced himself to smile.

"Good morning, Mamma," he said, kissing her swiftly

on the cheek. "Alice, you are up awfully early for a bride. Where is Henry?"

She made a small pout with her lips. "Off to Squire Lawton's already," she complained. "Your water or your runoff or some such thing is still draining into Lawton's lower meadow, I collect, and leaving it boggy."

Quin was pouring coffee. "Henry mentioned it," he murmured vaguely. "We cleared a hillside of timber, and now a wet autumn has conspired against us. We'll put in some ditch work, I daresay."

"Well, I cannot think why it couldn't have waited another day or two," said Alice irritably. "We just got married yesterday."

Lady Wynwood put down her teacup with a clatter. "Your husband is *employed,* Alice," she tartly reminded her. "Marrying him was your choice."

Alice rolled her eyes. "Well, he shan't be employed much longer, Mamma, shall he?" she asked. "We must go home in another few weeks. Henry will manage Melville Manor until Chris is of age. Lord knows I've made a shambles of it."

Quin pushed away his plate, which held only a slice of dry toast. "Actually, Alice, I have been meaning to talk to you about that," he said. "I might need you and Henry to stay here for a few months. Could you, were it necessary?"

Alice looked pleasantly surprised. "I daresay," she answered. "Why?"

Quin shrugged, and got up from the table. "I may have to go away for a while," he said.

"But must you do so at this very moment, Quinten?" asked his mother tartly. "Surely there is time enough for that little sliver of toast?"

He turned around and looked at it, scarcely remembering he'd carried it to the table. "No, thank you, Mamma," he said. "I must go."

But Alice was still looking at him strangely. "Away?" she interjected. "What do you mean, *away?*"

Quin hesitated for a moment. "I have been thinking of going to Venice for a few months."

"Venice!" cried his mother. "Oh, good heavens, Quinten! You cannot. You have duties. Responsibilities. Why, you have Arlington Court!"

He shook his head. "Henry can see to Arlington Court, or he can hire someone to do so."

His mother looked irritated. "This has something to do with the Contessa, does it not?"

Quin nodded tightly. "In part, yes," he admitted. "I am going over to Hill Court, Mamma, to see about Cerelia and to ask Viviana to marry me."

Lady Wynwood half rose from her chair, then sat back down again. "Well!" she said with asperity. "Well! And there is nothing I can say, I am sure, to convince you otherwise."

"Oh, I rather doubt, Mamma, that you'll have worry about it," he said grimly. "I don't think Viviana will be fool enough to have me. But regardless of her answer, I shall likely be going abroad."

"Well!" said his mother again

"Well!" echoed Alice teasingly. "Nothing ventured, nothing gained, old thing. Perhaps you will wear her down. For my part, I wish you luck."

"Thank you," he said. "And what of you, Mamma? Do you wish me luck?"

Lady Wynwood had wadded her napkin into a tight

little ball. For an instant, she just sat there and quietly quivered. Then a little squeak, as if she were restraining some sort of outburst, escaped her lips.

"Mamma!" said Alice warningly.

Lady Wynwood turned pink. "Oh, very well!" she said at last. "Do as you please. Yes, yes, I wish you luck. I hope that you have found something which will at last make you happy."

He looked at her very solemnly. "It will make me quite giddy with delight, ma'am," he informed her. "If Viviana will but say *yes.*"

Alice looked at him drolly. "Giddy with delight, hmm?" she said. "Now, that, Quentin, I would very much like to see."

Viviana was at the window with her coffee, watching as the morning sun peeked from behind a bank of reddish pink clouds when she saw the Earl of Wynwood's gig come tearing up the carriage drive. He was unmistakable, even at a distance. Her heart gave a little lurch of some confused emotion. Hope, perhaps. Or perhaps something sillier still.

She had no time in which to consider it, however. In the next instant, she heard the faint stirring of bedcovers behind her.

"Mamma?" came the faint little croak.

On a sharp cry, Viviana turned at once and hastened toward the bed. "Cerelia—!" she exclaimed. *"Oh, mia cara bambina!* Oh, Cerelia!"

At the commotion, Signora Rossi jerked awake in her chair. *"Che cosa? Che cosa?"* She sat up so awkwardly, her spectacles tumbled off the tip of her nose.

"Mamma . . ." The child's voice was a raspy whisper. "I am so thirsty."

Viviana slicked a hand over Cerelia's disheveled locks. "Poor angel!" she said, staring into her eyes. *"Tata* will send for something. What would you like?"

The girl looked up at her dolefully. "Lemonade?" she whispered. "Have we any?"

The old nurse was on her feet, feeling the child's forehead. *"Sia Gloria a Dio!"* she proclaimed. "The fever, it breaks!"

"She feels quite normal," said Viviana almost tearfully. "She is awake. She wishes lemonade. That is a good sign, is it not?"

The old nurse was smiling. *"Si,* I fetch it myself!" she declared, giving Cerelia's cheek a little pinch. "Come now, show *Tata* your throat. Open!"

Dutifully, the child stuck out her tongue. "It is red," said the nurse. "Not so bad, I think. But you are for the bed today, *cara,* and many days after, that is certain."

"Can you eat something, Cerelia?" asked Viviana. "Are you hungry?"

But Signora Rossi was already shaking her head.

"No," said the child. "Just a drink, *per favore?"*

Viviana had settled onto the mattress beside the child. "Oh, Cerelia, *carissima,* what a fright you have given us!" she said, scooping the child against her. "How do you feel?"

"Tired," came the pitiful rasp. "Mamma, did I miss Christmas?"

Viviana shook her head. "No, we have saved Christmas, *cara,"* she said. "We will celebrate it when you are well."

"I think I feel well enough to open presents," said the girl hopefully.

Just then, Signora Rossi opened the door to carry out the tray. She jerked at once to a halt. *"Buon giorno, signore."*

Viviana looked up to see Quin. His height and broad shoulders filled the door. On the threshold, however, he hesitated almost boyishly. "Good morning, Signora Rossi," he said. "How is our patient?"

The old woman beamed, and stepped aside so that he might see for himself. "You return, *signore,* and all is well, as I tell you."

Viviana felt suddenly awkward. She stood, and smoothed her hands down her skirt. She wondered, fleetingly, what she must look like. A fright, no doubt. "Cerelia is much better, my lord," she said. "Come, see her for yourself."

He came into the room, and set down a leather satchel at the foot of the bed. "Well, mouse, you have given us quite a turn," he said. "How are you?"

"Buon giorno, Lord Wynwood," she whispered. "I am tired." Then she paused to cut a quick look in her mother's direction. "But not, I think, so very tired."

Quin sat down on the edge of the bed and took her hand in his. "Everyone has been worried about you, my dear," he said. His relief looked intense, and quite genuine. "Your Mamma and Signora Rossi have been poking you full of vile potions. Do you remember none of it?"

She shook her head, her bronze-colored locks rubbing on the pillow. "No, my lord," she said softly. "I . . . I do not think so." Cerelia's voice was already losing some of its scratchy edge.

Quin brushed the back of his hand over Cerelia's

cheek, an exquisitely tender gesture. Viviana had never seen his eyes look so gentle. "That is good that you do not remember, is it not?" he said quietly. "One should never have to remember unpleasant things."

Just then, Viviana's father appeared in the doorway. He went to Cerelia with a cry of joy. Soon, Lord Chesley followed. Then the servants began to drift by, peeking into the room with a smile as they passed. Viviana watched from one corner of her eye as Quin withdrew. He took up a position near the front windows and remained there, silently observing the goings-on about Cerelia's sickbed. He gave one the impression of standing sentry, as if he might leap forward at any moment and order everyone from the room. He just might do it, too, she inwardly considered. He had a way of stepping in and taking charge.

Signora Rossi returned with fresh nightclothes and bed linens. She was followed by a dutiful kitchen maid, bearing a tray of lemonade and several mugs. The gentlemen bowed themselves out of the room, and Miss Hevner appeared with Nicolo and Felise, who slipped from her governess's grasp and bounded onto her sister's bed with unbridled enthusiasm.

"She is awake!" said Felise. "Look, Mamma! Cerelia, you slept for a whole day! Now we can have Christmas. We can open our presents and play and eat *panettone!*"

"I am not sure that is wise," said Viviana as she bent over to pick up Nicolo. The child was tugging impatiently at her skirts. "Your sister is still quite unwell, Felise. We must let her rest."

"I do not think, Mamma, that I am that tired," said Cerelia.

"Bah!" said Signora Rossi, who was rearranging her

pillows so that Cerelia might sit up in bed. "Here, *carissima,* is your lemonade. If the eyes will still open after that, then . . . ?" She gave one of her mysterious shrugs.

The girls had curled up in bed almost conspiratorially. Cerelia was strong enough, Viviana noticed, to hold on to her mug, which was half-full. Felise had extracted a handful of dominoes from her pocket and was laying them out across the counterpane in some little game known only to the two of them. But within moments, Cerelia's eyelids were growing heavy.

Viviana felt Quin brush against her elbow. "She is fading fast," he murmured.

Viviana hated to admit that he was right. "I think Nicolo and Felise must go back to the nursery," she said reluctantly. "I do not think there can be any question of a Christmas celebration."

"Perhaps I might offer a compromise?" he murmured.

She lifted her brows and turned to him. *"Si?* Of what sort?"

Quin was scrubbing his chin thoughtfully. His eyes looked tired, too. Her heart went out to him, then clenched in her chest. How could she have such confused emotions? How could she forget his ugly demands of two days past?

The answer was that she had not forgotten. She could only pray that he had.

Quin picked up the satchel he'd left at the foot of the bed. "I have three books which I brought back from London," he answered. "Books are quiet entertainments, are they not? Each child will have a little something by way of distraction. Then Cerelia will wish to sleep, I am quite sure."

"You are very kind," she said stiffly.

Nicolo was squirming, and saying something in Italian to his mother. She put him down, and he went at once to his sisters on the bed.

Viviana approached the bed, and kissed Felise on the cheek. *"Cara,* we cannot have Christmas just yet," she said. "But soon, I promise you. In the meantime, I think Lord Wynwood has a little something which might tide you over."

"What is *tide?"* asked Felise. But her eyes were on Quin, who was reaching into his bag.

Quin handed her a book which was mostly pictures, with a few words. "This is a book about mythical creatures, Felise," he said to her. "Sea serpents and unicorns and all manner of amazing things. I found it in London, and I thought you might like it. We shall call it an early-late—or is it a late-early?—Christmas gift."

Felise's eyes brightened as she opened the book's exquisitely drawn pages. *"Grazie,* signore," she said politely. "It is beautiful."

"Io voglio!" said Nicolo, trying to wrestle the book from her.

"Nicolo, no!" said his mother, peeling away his hand.

Quickly Quin handed him a book just as large, and more colorful. *"Buon Natale,* Nicolo," he said. "Will you tell him, Vivie, that this is a book about a dog? I believe he has delightful adventures. It is primarily a picture book. Unfortunately, the few words are only in English."

But Nicolo did not seem to object. He snatched the book quite greedily and opened it to one of the middle pages.

Quin turned his attention to Cerelia, who was very still

and quiet now. He handed her a book from the bottom of the satchel. It was quite thick, and tooled in find Morocco leather. Viviana crooked her head, and attempted to make out the title. *Kinder-und Hausmärchen der Gebrüder Grimm.* How very odd!

"This is a book by Jacob and Wilhelm Grimm," Quin explained. "Do you know who they are?"

Cerelia shook her head.

"They are professors at the university in Göttingen," he explained. "And there is a third brother, Louis, who did the amazing sketches which you see there. The book is a collection of fairy tales which, I am reliably informed, is destined to be a classic. I thought you might like to have it."

Cerelia was turning the pages and studying the finely detailed drawings. "It looks splendid," she rasped. "And a little scary, too."

"Well, only a little, I hope," said Quin. "And it is, of course, written in German. So I am afraid, my dear, that you will have your work cut out for you."

Viviana was looking over Cerelia's shoulder at the lovely, fanciful book. "Why, Cerelia is to begin German lessons when we return home in the spring," she said in mild surprise. Then, realizing what she had said, she flicked a quick, uncertain glance at Quin.

"Yes, I remembered her saying so," said Quin quietly. "I am sure she will learn quickly, too." But he did not really look at her, as he was engaged in helping Nicolo with a couple of his pages, which were not cleanly cut. "There," he said when the pages were free. "Now you may open them."

"Mamma, look, a dragon!" said Felise, holding up her book. "His mouth is on fire!"

"Heavens, what a fearsome creature," said Viviana.

She glanced at Cerelia to see that the child had closed the book of fairy tales, but still held it tight to her chest with both arms crossed over it. It was obvious that she was pleased to receive such a fine gift, and just as obvious that she was exhausted by the excitement.

"*Va bene,* children," said Viviana, shooing them from the bed. "Both of you out. Miss Hevner will take you back to the nursery now, so that Cerelia can get some sleep."

"But she's been sleeping for days and *days,*" complained Felise.

"Not that long, *bella mia.*" Viviana bent to kiss Felise on the forehead.

"I wonder, Viviana, if I might have a moment alone with Cerelia?" Quin quietly interjected.

Viviana hesitated, the refusal on the tip of her tongue. Cerelia was tired. And this, she knew instinctively, was a moment of no return. But the decision was no longer hers alone. At last, she gave a terse nod. "Of course," she answered. "Signora Rossi and I will go and admire the new books."

Quin watched as they urged the children from the room. Signora Rossi did not look at all inclined to go, but Viviana caught her quite determinedly by the arm and propelled her out the door.

Cerelia yawned, and stretched. Quin sat down on the edge of her bed and covered one of her hands with his. "I want to talk to you, mouse, before you drift off again."

She raised her expectant gaze to meet his. "About the book?"

He smiled and shook his head. "About your magic ring."

Her face fell. "Is Mamma very angry?"

"No, but she was very worried about you," he said. "She wants you to have the magic ring, my dear. She gave it to you because . . . well, because it was from your father. She told you that, did she not?"

Cerelia's eyes widened, as if she were surprised he knew the truth. "Did Mamma tell you that?"

He shook his head again and squeezed her hand. "No, my dear, she did not need to tell me," he said quietly. "That is what I wished to speak to you about. You see, well, I *am* your papa, Cerelia. I gave your mamma the ring a long time ago. I . . . I just wanted you to know that."

"Are you really my *papà?*" There was a hitch in her breath. "Really, truly?"

"Really, truly," he said. "And very glad to be so."

Eyes alight, Cerelia rolled up on one elbow. "I wondered if you mightn't be," she responded. "You said you were her friend long ago. I have been wondering who he was ever since we came to England. I thought that if I looked really hard, I might see him."

"You wished to see him, did you?" He slid one finger beneath her chin. "Well, here he is, Cerelia. In the flesh, and, I hope, better late than never."

Earnestly, she nodded. "Oh, it *is* better."

Quin felt something catch a little oddly in his throat. There was so much he wished to say, but for the moment, this would have to suffice. Cerelia was still very ill, and still just a child. So he bent and lightly kissed her cheek. "I have not been much of a father to you, Cerelia," he said. "Circumstances conspired against your mother and me. But in the future, I will try very hard to do a better job of it."

"I think you must be a very good father," she said
solemnly. "I am sorry circumstances con . . . conspired,
whatever that means."

It meant that he and her mother had been fools. The very
worst sort of fools: the prideful and stubborn kind. But it
would not do to say that just now. And so he said only
what was in his heart, after clearing away the little frog in
his throat. "I love you, Cerelia," he whispered. "Whatever
else happens, never, ever again imagine that your father
does not love you. You are eight years old now, so—"

"Almost nine," she interjected.

"Yes, I daresay you would be," he murmured. "So you
are growing up fast. And so you know that there are
things we cannot speak of outside our family, do you
not?"

Solemnly, she nodded. "I know," she confessed. "Mama
told me some things are for family only."

"But it no longer need be a secret between us," he clarified. "And who knows what the future will hold, mouse?
But no matter what life brings you, I will be a certainty in
it. You will be seeing a good bit of me from here on out. I
will visit you in Venice at the very least. And perhaps you
will return here, and visit me, from time to time?"

With surprising energy, she threw her arms around
his neck. "Oh, I should like that above *anything,*" she
admitted.

"I should like it above anything, too, child." He held
her close for a long moment, then gently set her away so
that he might look into her eyes.

Almost shyly, her face broke into a smile. "I . . . I am
very glad, *signore,* that you are the one."

"Are you?" he said in surprise.

She nodded. "My Mamma, she likes you very much," she said on another huge yawn. "And you are very handsome. The handsomest father ever, I think."

He gave her a bemused smile. "Well, enough of that, mouse," he said. "You are still very ill. When you are better, you will have a great many questions, and your mother and I shall endeavor to answer them all as best we can. But I could not bear another day to pass without your knowing the truth. And without your knowing how very much I care for you."

Cerelia yawned again and smiled drowsily.

Quin tucked her back into her bed and pulled the covers up to her chin. But before he could stand up again, Cerelia's eyes had dropped shut.

He did not know how long he remained there, seated on the edge of the bed, simply gazing at his sleeping child and wondering what their future together might bring. He did not even hear the door open when Viviana and the old nurse returned. Signora Rossi stirred him from his reverie by going to the dressing table and shaking the wrinkles from a fresh nightdress for Cerelia.

Viviana did not miss the look of tenderness on Quin's face when she returned to Cerelia's bedside. She went to the opposite side of the mattress and quietly watched them. Father and daughter. Together. *Dio,* how life had changed. For the good, she hoped. At least for Cerelia.

"It is too late," she whispered when Signora Rossi brought the fresh nightdress. "She is asleep."

With another of her shrugs, the nurse laid the gown aside, then came back to press her hand to the child's forehead. "It is a good sleep, Contessa," she said to Viviana. "Not hot."

Viviana swallowed hard and nodded. Cerelia did indeed seem to be resting comfortably. "Will you be so good as to sit with her awhile, *Tata?*" she asked, reverting to the children's nickname for her. "I have something which I must do."

The old woman waved her away. "Go, go," she said. "You rest. You sleep."

But Viviana had scarcely slept in two days, and she certainly had no intention of doing so yet. Instead, she stiffened her spine, sucked up her courage, and turned to Quin. "My lord, may I speak with you?"

He did not look surprised. "But of course."

"You have told her?" she whispered as she pulled the door shut.

"I did," he said. "But I said only what could not wait."

Viviana cut a strange glance at him. "How did she take it?"

Inwardly, he smiled. "I think she was pleased," he said. "But I am not deceived. There will be hard questions later. For both of us."

Viviana was very much afraid there were hard questions to be answered rather sooner than that. Indeed, she had a few of her own. She led the way to the family parlor and pushed open the door. No fire had been lit today, but the splintered chair, she saw, had been taken away. It seemed a lifetime ago since last they were here. A lifetime since she had endured Quin's rage and faced up to her near decade of deceit. She drifted deeper into the room, trying to gather her thoughts.

"Viviana, I . . ." Quin spoke from behind her, but his words fell away.

She went on the offensive and turned to face him. "I

thank you, Quin, for your kindness yesterday," she said. "And again today."

"It was nothing."

She set her head to one side. "It was not *nothing,*" she countered. "And I am glad—I think—that you have spoken with Cerelia. But I wish to say, too, Quinten, that I have thought a great deal about . . . about your demands of two days ago."

"As have I, Vivie," he said quietly.

Viviana held up a hand to forestall him. "And I must tell you here and now, Quin, that I cannot do it," she said. "Indeed, I won't do it. But you knew that already, did you not? You knew that I would fight you to the death. Indeed, I daresay you are looking forward to the battle."

He gave a rueful smile. "At first, Vivie, I was thinking only of Cerelia," he said. "Or at least that is what I told myself."

Out of sheer emotional and physical exhaustion, Viviana fell onto the sofa. "I—I cannot leave my daughter, Quin," she said, dragging her hands through her hair, which had more or less fallen completely from its haphazard arrangement. "I cannot leave Cerelia . . . but I do not think that there is any way I can bring myself to stay here. The pain of what we once had—or almost had—it is too raw. But never have I denied Cerelia her English heritage, Quinten. I have given her the best English governesses, taught her the language, and done all that I could within the confines surrounding me. But I am sorry. I can do no more."

Quin joined her on the sofa. "I am sorry, too," he said. "And I am sorry, Viviana, that you could not trust me to do the right thing all those years ago. I am sorry I caused you pain."

She started to protest, but he laid a finger to her lips. "I wish, Vivie, that I could convince you that I would have done what was proper for the child you carried," he said. "But you had doubts, and I understand why. But know this, Vivie. I have always loved you. And I came within an inch of telling you so that awful day. Within an inch, Vivie, of asking *you* to marry *me.*"

She shook her head. "Oh, Quin. Please do not."

His hands were fisted now, as if he grappled for control. "No, it is time I spoke the truth." His voice was rough with emotion. "I have always loved you, Viviana, and that has never changed. But all those years ago, I could not believe that you loved me. Certainly you never said so. And when I finally dredged up the courage to ask, you admitted that you did not, and God help me, it . . . it just crushed me. And that did not take much doing, to be honest. I had no real confidence—or nothing beyond the cocky façade of a young man's swagger."

"You did have a very fine swagger," she whispered, with a watery smile. "And an exceedingly cocky façade."

His dark blue eyes went soft with pain. "It was my downfall."

Unable to bear it, Viviana leaned into him and set one hand on his shoulder. "And I did love you, Quin," she whispered. "I did. But my pride would not let me admit it."

"But why, Vivie?" he said. "Why not?"

She tore her gaze away. "I felt, Quinten, as though I had been bought and paid for," she whispered. "And I knew, even then, that English gentlemen do not marry their mistresses. Instead, they tire of them, and they move on. So all one can hope to do is to hold on to one's pride and stand stalwart when the end comes."

"I would never have tired of you, Viviana," he answered. "There would have been no end."

She shook her head slowly. "I do not believe that," she said.

"And you do not believe that I love you, either," he said. "So I will prove it. I will make you the greatest gift of all. I will—"

"I do not want a gift," she interjected.

He set the finger to her lips again. "I will give you our child, Vivie," he said quietly. "And the right to go on as you have in the past, the right to raise her as you see fit."

Viviana looked at him plaintively. "Oh, Quin . . ."

He surprised her then by picking up her hand, and carrying it to his lips. "But please, Vivie," he went on. "Let me see her without our fighting. She needs her father—her *real* father. A father who loves her and wants to be with her. Someday, Vivie, Cerelia will wish to marry and have a family of her own. It will help her to remember that she was the child of two people who loved one another very much. I would like . . . Viviana, I would like my daughter to have faith in love."

Viviana felt as if the room had just shifted unsteadily about her. She had come here prepared to fight for her child. And now, just like that, the fight was over. Yet the rage and fatigue and worry still churned in her heart and in her stomach. "You . . . you give me leave to do as I wish?"

He still held her hand in his. "I give you leave, Vivie, to what you think best," he answered. "Just as I have faith in love, I have faith also in your good judgment."

She gave a bark of bitter laughter. *"Dio mio!"* she said. "I cannot think why! It was my good judgment which saddled Cerelia with Gianpiero."

He gave her hand a reassuring squeeze. "You did what you thought was best," he said. "And in your own way, Vivie, you were as naive and inexperienced as I was. You just hid it better, I have belatedly learnt."

She rolled her eyes. "Oh, I knew nothing!" she agreed. "I played with fire, Quin, when I became your lover, and I did not even know it."

His face fell a little. "Ah, I am sorry for that, too," he said. "Sorry for thinking you were experienced when you were not. And sorry for pushing you into something which you did not want."

Her hand flew to his face, caressing his cheek instinctively. "I was not that I did not want *you,* Quin," she whispered. "And it was not because I did not love you that I left you, *caro.* Never think that."

"When you left me, I did not know what to think," he confessed. "As a young man, I tortured myself over you. Wooing you, winning you; Vivie, it was like an obsession with me. I actually believed I knew how the world worked and what sophisticated women like you expected. It has taken me all these years to realize that I had understood nothing at all."

"Ah, *caro!*" she whispered. "Too young. We were too young."

Slowly, he shook his head. "I believed you experienced and worldly, Viviana, because I was not," he admitted. "I spent all our months together half in fear, half-believing that at any moment, you might leave me for someone older, or richer, or better placed in society. And worst of all, I believed you were embarrassed to be my mistress—which, as it turns out, was perfectly true. But not for the reasons I had imagined."

Fleetingly, Viviana closed her eyes. "How we have hurt one another," she answered. "So foolishly, we have hurt one another—and I, well, I have done worse, perhaps. I have hurt Cerelia. And now I would do anything—anything, Quinten—to give her a happy life."

He turned his face into her palm and kissed it in that old, familiar way. "Then I have two other questions, Vivie," he said softly. "The first is a favor I mean to ask of you."

She nodded her head, and blinked back a tear. *"Certamente,"* she managed. "I will do what is in my power."

"I wish to return to Venice with you, if you must go," he said.

She could not believe him serious. "To—to Venice?" she whispered. "Oh, *caro*. That is—oh, that is so very . . . *lontanissimi*. So very far from England."

His eyes danced with good humor. "I remember at least a little of my schoolroom geography, Vivie," he said. "I think I know where Venice is."

She felt her face flush with heat. "Forgive me," she said. "Of course you do."

He leaned back against the arm of the sofa and studied her. "And there I will take a house—a villa? But not a mansion. Just something small. What do you call that?"

She laughed nervously. "A *casa,"* she said. "Or an *appartamento.*"

"A *casa* it is, then," he said, smiling. "And then I would like to spend a little time getting to know Cerelia. Felise and Nicolo, too. Let them view me as a fond uncle or a godparent, or—well, choose any polite euphemism you like—I wish only to spend time with them. But I do not wish to interfere in your life, Vivie, if you do not wish me in it."

Her blush deepened. "I did not say that, Quinten," she whispered. "I did not say you were not wanted."

Quin smiled again, and this time, the smile reached his dark blue eyes. "Then I have something for you, Vivie." He released her hand, dug into his coat pocket, and handed her a jeweler's box.

Viviana pushed it away. *"Grazie,"* she said. "But no present. And *per amore di Dio,* no more jewelry. Ever."

"It isn't jewelry," he said, giving it a little shake. "Though you may like it even less well."

Viviana drew back skeptically and studied it. Then feminine curiosity got the better of her. She took it from him, and lifted the lid. The box held nothing but a folded sheet of foolscap, tucked into the velvet where a bracelet or necklace should have lain. She looked at him and saw his blue eyes dance. "Quinten, I do not understand."

"Read it," he said.

She unfolded it, and did so. "I . . . Quinten, I still do not . . ." But a feeling of hope was coming over Viviana, an emotion so swift and so intense, her hand began to shake. "It has my name on it," she whispered. "Yours, too."

He smiled almost wistfully. "That is the reason Herndon and I were a day late back from London," he explained.

"What . . . what are you saying, Quinten?" she asked unsteadily. "What does this—this *documento* mean?"

"Herndon needed a special license to marry Alice," said Quin. "And one has to do quite a bit of work to obtain such a thing. But we succeeded. And then—well, I cannot explain it, Viviana. You had given me no hope. Indeed, you still have not. But I could not leave London without my own little piece of paper. Just in case, you see. Just because I have been in love with you for a full third of my life, and I know now that that will never change. So I went back the next day to get one for myself. For *us,* Vivie."

Viviana set her fingertips to her forehead in some vain attempt to clear her dizzying thoughts. "Quinten, I am confused."

"I am not," he said. "For the first time in my life, Vivie, I am thinking with perfect clarity."

"But—but Quin, I have done a terrible thing to you, and to Cerelia," she protested. "And I am too old for you. And too Catholic. And a mother of three very lively children. And then there is *Papà,* who needs—"

He cut her off with a kiss that was swift and firm. "Enough," he said. "None of that matters. So far as I am concerned, those are not obstacles. They are just details, and details can always be sorted out, *if* it is what we both wish. This license gives us six months, Vivie, to do just that. To sort it out. But *you,* Vivie—will you give us six months? Can you ever learn to love me again?"

She lowered her gaze to the floor. "I have never stopped," she finally said. "You must know, Quin, that I never have."

He shocked her then by taking her empty hand in his, and going down on one knee before her. "So, Viviana Alessandri, love of my life, woman whom I utterly do *not* deserve, will you have me anyway? Will you marry me, and make a family with me? And be warned, my love, that whilst this little piece of paper will eventually expire, my persistence will not. I will just wait a year or a month or a fortnight—or perhaps even another decade—and ask again."

Viviana laid the paper aside. "Do you forgive me, then, Quinten?" she whispered. "For what I have done to Cerelia? For what I have done to us?"

He shook his head. "We must both forgive ourselves, Vivie," he whispered. "We must think only of the future, and of the children—and even, perhaps, of the children to come. And we must tell Cerelia that we love her, that she is wanted, and that from this day forward, we will care for her. Either together. Or apart. I will take what I can get. Which, Vivie, would you rather it be?"

"Together," she softly whispered. She dived into his arms, and somehow ended up on her knees on the floor with him. "Yes, yes, Quinten, my beautiful English boy, I will marry you. *Caro,* I will marry you a thousand times over."

Quinten's face lit with a happiness which at last seemed true. "Just once, Vivie," he said. "If I can get you to the altar just once, it will be enough for a thousand lifetimes."

Epilogue

A Dress Rehearsal.

The night was warm and heavy with rain when Lord Wynwood left his Curzon Street town house and set out at a brisk clip for the Haymarket. It was a short walk, but not a quiet one. Beyond the elegant seclusion of Mayfair, the pavements and streets were choked with traffic as the city's working class flooded forth to make last-minute purchases from the markets or enjoy the first of what might be many libations in the local coffeehouses and pubs.

At the opera house, his destination, he pushed through the crowds and made his way along to the stage door just as it burst open, disgorging perhaps a dozen gay and laughing people into the muted gaslight. At first, they paid him no heed. But upon seeing him in the shadows, someone in the crowd whispered, "Hush, hush, it is *him.*"

Quin stood to one side and lifted his hat, allowing the crowd to pass. "Good evening," he said. "Is rehearsal over?"

"At last, my lord," answered one the tenors deferentially. "Shall we see you at opening night?"

"I would not miss it," he said. Nor did he miss the smiles and awkward, sidelong glances which came his way, particularly from some of the females in the crowd.

"Ah, Wynwood, that you there?" Lord Digleby Beresford was straggling in the rear of the crowd, his nose half-buried in a sheet of music one of the others had just passed him.

"I wouldn't read that whilst strolling in the Haymarket, old man," Quin advised. "One of those brewer's drays will likely plow you down with a load of porter and deprive the world of your genius."

Lord Digleby grunted. "Yes, well, we shall see what the world thinks of my genius come tomorrow night, will we not?" he answered. "I collect you are looking for your wife?"

"I am indeed."

"She kept Signorina Fabiano after rehearsal," he said. "The orchestra's still in. Make yourself at home."

Quin made his way through the stage door and along the narrow corridor. A violinist approached, his expression dark, a broken string sprouting from his violin scroll like a strand of hair gone wild. "Lady Wynwood?" he enquired, lifting his hat as they passed.

"Fabiano's dressing room," grumbled the musician, jerking his head toward another corridor.

The direction was not necessary. Above the choppy, discordant notes of the orchestra's retuning, he could already hear the strains of *Nel Pomeriggio*'s most challenging aria, its high notes punctuating the air like staccato bursts of gunfire.

Upon reaching the door, he peeked inside. Viviana paced back and forth before Signorina Fabiano, her eyes almost shut, her brows in a knot. Quin watched as the piece drew to a close. The young lady hit her last notes perfectly—at least so far as he could tell.

Silence fell across the shabby little room. Viviana's furrowed brow melted. "Brava! Brava!" she said, her eyes flying open. *"Grazie,* Maria. That was excellent!"

The younger woman blushed and dropped her chin. Just then, Viviana saw Quin standing in the doorway. "Quinten, *caro mio!"* she cried, coming toward him, arms outstretched in greeting.

"I hope I am not interrupting, my love?"

"No, not at all."

Signorina Fabiano curtsied. "We have just finished, my lord," she said, snatching up her music. "I bid you both good night."

"Buona notte, Maria," said Viviana. "I shall see you tomorrow."

Quin critically observed the young woman's departure. "Has she really got hold of it, do you think?"

Viviana nodded. "Oh, Maria is ready," she answered confidently. "She will never be the world's greatest soprano, perhaps. But she is very good."

"In other words, Vivie, she will never be you," he remarked.

"I did not say that," averred his wife.

Quin smiled down at her. "You did not need to," he answered. "Your father said it for you. As did Lord Digleby and Uncle Ches. Their noses are still out of joint over your refusal to sing the lead. After all, they cast this opera in London just to suit you."

"Just to suit me?" she exclaimed. "I never suggested they should do so!"

"One can scarcely blame them for hoping," he said, kissing her lightly on the nose.

She shook her head. "My voice is not good enough," she said. "Moreover, I have other duties now." The last was followed by a sly smile.

"Other duties, eh?" Quin drew his wife close. "Of what sort?"

"Of the very pleasant sort," she said on a laugh. "Ah, Quinten! I am glad to see you. It has been a long afternoon. What have the children been up to?"

He tucked her head beneath his chin. "Oh, Cerelia put poor Mr. Schmitt through his paces this afternoon," he said. "Already she is beginning to conjugate German verbs. And Nicolo broke a jar of Felise's favorite paint, and spilt it all over the schoolroom. And—well, I shan't tell you yet about the frogs."

"The *frogs*—?" She pressed her lips together and shook her head. "No, pray do *not* tell me. I am quite sure the tale will involve Nicolo and a good deal of mud."

Quin threw back his head and laughed. "The voice of maternal experience!" Then his expression sobered, and he kissed her soundly.

"But back to that pathetic excuse of yours," he went on, when he'd lifted his mouth from hers. "Uncle Ches does insist that you, on your worst day, are still better than everyone else on their best. He claims you have made too much fuss about this nose business and that he can barely tell the difference."

"Ah, *barely!*" she echoed. "What a telling word that is, *amore mio*. Opera requires—no, it *demands*—total perfection. But more importantly, Quinten, I find I much prefer to teach. All my grumbles and complains aside, I have enjoyed these last few months so very much. Teaching does not require one's utter devotion and all of one's time."

Quin sat down on the tattered divan, the old leather crackling beneath his weight. Playfully, he pulled his wife between his legs and set his lips to her belly. "And then there is that other little problem," he murmured against the silk of her gown. "That troubling little matter of squeezing oneself into all that costuming, night after night—and month after month."

Viviana drew back a few inches and laughed. "Wretch! Do be quiet!"

"But indeed, I think you've gained at least a stone," he said, eyeing her bodice. "Those stitches are pulled quite positively tight."

His wife drove her fingers into his hair and pulled his cheek against the silk of her gown. "That is still our little secret, *caro mio,*" she reminded him. "It is too soon."

He pulled her closer still. "It *is* too soon," he admitted, his voice going thick with emotion. "I don't wish to share it with anyone just yet, Vivie. Only you. I am awestruck still. I feel the most fortunate of men."

Viviana turned and settled herself on his knee with a gentle smile. "And I, Quinten, the most fortunate of women," she answered.

He held her there for a time, cradling her in his arms, his face buried in her hair. He could hear the orchestra leaving now, the unmistakable sound of chair legs scraping and instrument cases closing. Little by little, silence fell across the old theater, and still he did not move. He was afraid to break the spell. The spell of complete and utter happiness. And yet there had been a hundred such instances these last few months. It all seemed too perfect. And more than a little fragile.

Ah, but there was not time for his maudlin notions. It was time to see his wife safely home, where they would spend an hour or so with the children, then have dinner with Signor Alessandri. After that, he would have to urge Viviana and his father-in-law into bed early, for they had a very big day tomorrow.

He shifted his weight as if to move, making the old divan crackle again. A sudden, and slightly humorous, thought struck him. "Vivie?"

"Yes, *amore mio?*"

"Is this—" He looked about him and blinked. "Is this your old dressing room?"

Lightly, she laughed. "It is," she admitted. "Does it bring back memories?"

Quin looked down at the cracked and peeling leather surface. "And this old piece of rubbish—is it that same divan? The one we—well, never mind that. But *is* it?"

Viviana looked down. "Why, I daresay it might be," she mused. "It certainly looks old enough and tatty enough, does it not?"

He set his mouth to the soft spot beneath her ear and kissed her again, a long, lingering kiss that slid slowly down to the turn of her throat. In his arms, she shivered ever so slightly. "Vivie," he murmured, "are you thinking what I'm thinking?"

"I—I do not know." The words were thick, and a little husky. "What are you thinking, *caro?*"

"I am thinking that the orchestra is gone," he said suggestively. "And that perhaps this old divan has not seen its last hurrah."

His wife actually *giggled*. "Why, whatever can you be suggesting?"

He smiled. "I am suggesting that, where this room and this particular piece of furniture are concerned, perhaps I should leave you with a good memory? One that will once and forever wipe away your recollection of the bad."

"A nefarious plan indeed." But her slender, clever hands had already gone to his waistcoat buttons.

Quin shrugged. "Well, you must admit, my love, that the technique worked very well indeed the last time we tried it."

Viviana slipped the next button free and kissed him again. But not for the last time that evening.

POCKET STAR BOOKS
PROUDLY PRESENTS

Three Little Secrets

Liz Carlyle

Coming soon
from Pocket Star Books

Turn the page for a preview of
Three Little Secrets. . . .

The walk along the river was not a long one, and the breeze blowing in off the Thames helped clear Merrick's head. The sun was unusually warm for May, and both he and Lord Wynwood were compelled to loosen their neckcloths. Soon they reached an area of excavation where six sweat-stained men were assiduously digging out a cellar. Adjacent, three masons were mortaring the stone foundation of a second house, and beyond that, carpenters were framing up the skeleton of yet a third. Running up the street beyond them were another ten terraced houses, the next nearer completion than the one before it.

"Good Lord," said Wynwood, surveying the scene. "This is like a mill without walls—except that you are churning out houses instead of stockings."

"Just so," said Merrick. "And therein lies a part of the cost savings—or perhaps I should say profit. Now, do you wish a corner house?"

"I should prefer it, yes."

"Well, the topmost house has been spoken for," said Merrick. "Rosenberg sent the papers last week. You will have to wait on these two at the bottom of the hill."

Wynwood's face fell. "Blast!" he said. "That house above is perfect."

"But it will take the wind coming off the river," said Merrick with a shrug. "So will be more expensive to heat. Besides, a widow from Yorkshire has already contracted for it."

Wynwood winked. "Contracted—but not yet taken title, eh?" he said. "Come, Merrick, we are old friends. The heating means nothing to me. And you do not even know this woman. What if I paid the costs associated with breaking the contract?"

"My word is my bond," said Merrick coldly. "Choose another, my friend. Or go back to Belgravia and buy one of those white monstrosities from Tom Cubitt. It is neither here nor there to me."

"Yes, yes, you are right, of course," Wynwood had the grace to look embarrassed. "I am just desperate to please my wife. These lower houses are lovely. But they are not even. One will sit a little higher up the hill, will it not?"

"Yes, and I shall use it to good advantage," said Merrick. "If they are connected by short flights of stairs in the public rooms, it will have the feel of two houses, but there will be a measure of privacy on the upper floors. I can design it such that musical rooms and Bergonzi's parlor are on one side, and the school room and nursery needs are confined to the other. Two dining rooms, even, if you wish."

"That sounds perfect." Wynwood scrubbed a hand thoughtfully along his jaw. "Now, what will the interior look like generally? That's the part females concern themselves with. I must give Vivie a full report."

"I can show you the house at the top of the hill." Merrick extracted a key from his coat pocket. "The millwork, the joinery, the floors and ceilings, all that will be similar unless you wish otherwise."

There were no workmen near the top of the hill, and the din of construction faded into the distance as they walked. Still, Merrick could hear a muffled banging noise from within the topmost house as they went up the steps. How very odd.

Wynwood turned to Merrick with a quizzical look. "Someone is inside."

"They damned well oughtn't be," said Merrick. "The first coat of paint went on yesterday and has scarce had time to dry."

The banging did not relent. Merrick twisted the key and went in. Sun glared through the large, undraped windows, leaving the air stifling hot, and rendering the smell of paint almost intolerable. At once, he and Wynwood started toward the racket—a side parlor which opened halfway along the central corridor. A tall, slender woman with cornsilk-colored hair stood with her back to them, banging at one of the window frames with the heels of her hands.

Merrick looked at Wynwood. "Excuse me," he said tightly. "The buyer, I presume."

"I shall just wander upstairs," said Wynwood, starting up the staircase. "I wish to size up the bedchambers."

"Oh, bloody damned hell!" said the woman in the parlor.

Merrick strode into the room. "Good God, stop banging on the windows!"

The woman shrieked and spun halfway around. "Oh!" She pressed both hands to her chest. "Oh, God! You nearly gave me heart failure!"

"It would be a less painful end than bleeding to death, I daresay."

"I beg your pardon?" She turned to face him and, inexplicably, his breath hitched. Her cool blue eyes searched his face.

"The paint sticks the windows shut," he managed to explain. "They must be razored open, ma'am. And if you persist in pounding at the sash, you're apt to get a gashed wrist for your trouble."

"Indeed?" Her eyebrows went up a little haughtily as she studied him. For a moment, he could not get his lungs to work. Dear God in heaven.

No. No, it could not be.

Merrick's thoughts went skittering like marbles. There must be some mistake. That damned wedding yesterday—that trip to the church—it had disordered his mind.

"Well, I shall keep your brilliant advice in mind," she finally went on. "Now, this room was to be hung with yellow silk, not painted. Dare I hope that you are someone who can get that fixed?"

"Perhaps." Merrick stepped fully into the room to better see her. "I am the owner of this house."

The brows inched higher. "Oh, I think not," she said, her voice low and certain. "I contracted for its purchase on Wednesday last."

"Yes, from my solicitors, perhaps," said Merrick. *Good God, surely . . . surely he was wrong.* For the first time in a decade, he felt truly unnerved. "I—er, I employ Mr. Rosenberg's firm to handle such transactions," he managed to continue. "Pray look closely at your contract. You will see that the seller is MacGregor & Company."

But her look of haughty disdain had melted into one of grave misgiving. "And—and you would be Mr. MacGregor, then?" There was more than a question in her words. There was a pleading; a wish to avoid the unavoidable. Her dark green eyes slid down the scar which curved the length of his face. *She was not sure.* But he was. Dear God, he was.

"You look somewhat familiar," she went on. "I am . . . I am Lady Bessett. Tell me, have—have we met?"

Dear God! Had they met? A sort of nausea was roiling in his stomach now. He could feel the perspiration breaking on his brow. He opened his mouth with no notion of what he was to say. Just then, Wynwood came thundering down the stairs.

"Eight bedchambers, old chap!" The earl's shouting echoed through the empty house. "So a double would have sixteen, am I right?" He strode into the room, then stopped abruptly. "Oh, I do beg your pardon," he said, his eyes running over the woman. "My new neighbor, I collect? Pray introduce me."

Merrick felt as if all his limbs had gone numb. "Yes. Yes, of course." He lifted one hand by way of introduction. "May I present to you, ma'am, the Earl of Wynwood. Wynwood, this is . . . this is . . ." The hand fell in resignation. "This is Madeleine, Quin. This is . . . my wife."

The woman's face had drained of all color. She made a strange little choking sound, and in a blind, desperate gesture, her hand lashed out as if to steady herself. She grasped at nothing but air. Then her knees gave, and she crumpled to the floor in a pool of dark green silk.

"Christ Jesus!" said Wynwood. He knelt and began to pat at her cheek. "Ma'am, are you all right? Ma'am?"

"No, she is not all right," said Merrick tightly. "She can't get her breath. This air—the paint—it must be stifling her. Quick, get back. We must get her air."

As if she were weightless, Merrick slid an arm under Madeleine's knees, then scooped her into his arms. A few short strides, and they were outside in the dazzling daylight.

"Put her in the grass," Wynwood advised. "Good God, Merrick! Your *wife*? I thought—thought she was dead! Or—or gone off to India! Or some damned thing!"

"Athens, I believe," said Merrick. "Apparently, she has come back."

Gently, he settled Madeleine in the small patch of newly sprouted grass. She was coming around now. His heart was in his throat, his mind racing with questions. Wynwood held one of her hands and was patting at it vigorously. On his knees in the grass, Merrick set one hand on his thigh and dropped his head as if to pray.

But there was little to pray for now.

He had prayed never to see Madeleine again. God had obviously denied him that one small mercy. He pinched his nose between two fingers, as if the pain might force away the memories.

Madeleine had managed to struggle up onto her elbows.

"I say, ma'am." Wynwood was babbling now. "So sorry. Didn't mean to frighten you. Are you perfectly all right? Haven't seen old Merrick in a while, I collect? A shock, I'm sure. Yes, yes, a shock."

"Shut up, Quin," said Merrick.

"Yes, yes, of course," he agreed. "I shan't say a word. Daresay you two have lots to catch up on. I—I should go, perhaps? Or stay? Or—no, I have it! Perhaps Mrs. MacLachlan would like me to fetch some brandy?"

On this, the lady gave a withering cry and pressed the back of her hand to her forehead.

"Do *shut up,* Quin," said Merrick again.

His eyes widened. "Yes, yes, I meant to do."

Madeleine was struggling to her feet now. Her heavy blond hair was tumbling from its arrangement. "Let me up," she insisted. "Stand aside, for God's sake!"

"Oh, I shouldn't get up," Wynwood warned. "Your head is apt to be swimming still."

But Madeleine had eyes only for Merrick—and they were blazing with hot green rage. "I do not know," she hissed, "what manner of ill-thought joke this is, sir. But you—you are not my husband."

"Now is hardly the time to discuss it, Madeleine," Merrick growled. "Let me summon my carriage and see you safely to your lodgings."

But Madeleine was already backing away, her face a mask of horror. "No," she choked. "Absolutely not. You—you are quite mad. And cruel, too. Very cruel. You always were. I came to see it, you know. I *did*. Now stay away from me! Stay away! Do you hear?"

It was the closest she came to acknowledging she even knew him. And then she turned and hastened up the hill on legs which were obviously unsteady.

A gentleman would have followed her at a distance, just to be sure she really was capable of walking. Merrick no longer felt like a gentleman. He felt . . . eviscerated. Gutted like a fish and left to rot in the heat of his wife's hatred.

Lord Wynwood watched her go, his hand shielding his eyes as they squinted into the sun. "You know, I don't think she much cares for you, old chap," he said when Madeleine's skirts had swished around the corner and out of sight.

"Aye, that would explain her thirteen-year absence, would it not?" said Merrick sourly.

"More or less," his friend agreed. "I hope you were not looking forward to a reconciliation?"

"Just shut up, Quin," said Merrick again.

Wynwood seemed to take no offense, nor did he listen. "Tell me, Merrick," he said. "Have you any of that fine Finlaggan whisky in your desk?"

"Bloody well right I do. A full bottle."

Wynwood let his hand fall. "Well, it's a start," he said, turning and heading down the hill.